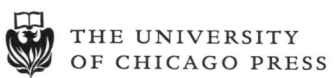
THE UNIVERSITY
OF CHICAGO PRESS

VAS: AN OPERA IN FLATLAND

A NOVEL

BY STEVE TOMASULA
ART+DESIGN BY STEPHEN FARRELL

THE UNIVERSITY OF CHICAGO PRESS, CHICAGO, 60637

First published in 2002 by Barrytown/Station Hill Press

University of Chicago Press paperback edition 2004

This edition was made possible in part by support from the Institute for Scholarship in the Liberal Arts, College of Arts and Letters, University of Notre Dame, and from the School of the Art Institute of Chicago.

This fourth impression is made possible in part by additional support from the Institute for Scholarship in the Liberal Arts, College of Arts and Letters, University of Notre Dame.

Portions of this novel were published in their original concrete form in *The Berkely Fiction Review* and *Hard_Code*, Boulder: Alt-X Press, 2001.

The lyrics to Act I of the opera "The Strange Voyage of Imagining Chatter" are from Lord Byron's poem "She Walks in Beauty."

Printed in China

25 24 23 22 21 20 19 18 17 16   4 5 6 7 8

ISBN-13: 978-0-226-80740-9 (paper)
ISBN-10: 0-226-80740-1 (paper)

LIBRARY OF CONGRESS CATALOGING-IN-PUBLICATION DATA

Tomasula, Steve.

    VAS : an opera in Flatland : a novel / by Steve Tomasula : art and design by Stephen Farrell.

       p. cm.

    ISBN 0-226-80740-1 (pbk. : alk. paper)

    I. Genetic engineering—Fiction. 2. Biotechnology—Fiction. I. Title.

    PS3620.O53V37   2004

    813'6-dc22   2004047876

♾ This paper meets the requirements of ANSI/NISO Z39.48-1992 (Permanence of Paper).

FOR JIWON.

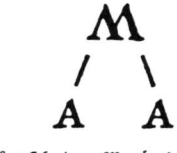

for Maria, Alba & Ava

Men are to be viewed as
the organs of their century, which operate mainly unconsciously.

JOHANN WOLFGANG VON GOETHE

FIRST PAIN.

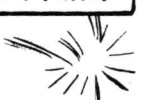

Then knowledge: a paper cut.
He kissed his finger, a gesture of
"shhhh" making him both Judas and
first-and-truest lover to his body?—a kiss,
like hers—for hers—comforting as he lay
down with the scalpel?

bright and shining

On the page in his lap, the
truth world he'd been writing into existence was
slicing membranes
dead-skin white—paper sans corpuscles—
nothing more—the bubble of presence its
people and dramas had occupied pricked
by less than a sting and he buried them
beneath the hospital form he had cut
himself on.

so effortlessly
that it would be bloodless

His daughter's science experiment took
technique's first baby steps on the coffee
table before him: a white carnation in
water dyed a lurid TV-red no flower could
be. Except this one, already turning color,
capillary action manipulated by the
insertion of a dye doing the trick.

He had already written his name where it said:

PATIENT

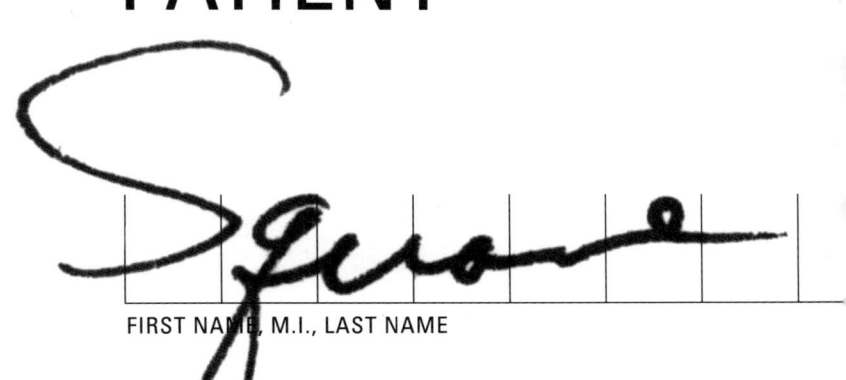

FIRST NAME, M.I., LAST NAME

On the Nature of Flatland

*Imagine a vast sheet of paper on which straight Lines, Triangles,
Squares, Pentagons, Hexagons, and other figures move freely about,
but without the power to rise above or sink below it, and you
will then have a pretty correct notion of my country and countrymen.*

EDWIN A. ABBOTT
FLATLAND: A ROMANCE OF MANY DIMENSIONS, 1884

Square heard his wife coming and
reshuffled the consent form behind the
story he'd been trying to write.

A basic story

She sat down in an easy chair and crossed
her smooth legs. *Intimate Apparel*, said
the catalog she held, cover model sporting
lacy bra, silky smile. "Figure out how
your story's going to end?" she asked,
endorphin flattening canals to dampen
an up-rush of breath through her body into
a note of sadness, an octave lower than a
bassoon—because she hadn't found
him filling out the consent form, he knew.

His own electrochemistry opened the
circle of his mouth to make a soft "No."

Barely perceptible changes in facial muscles
"clouded her features."

as they say in
literature.

And he added, "But I will."

She only continued a display of
"nonchalance" by flipping print; so he
followed her lead—a two-step—she with
her catalog, he with his draft.

She knew what he was thinking, of course.
And the contraction of corrugator muscles
that furrowed her brow said what she was
thinking: that it was "His turn." She didn't
need to write a story for him to know she
had taken hers—it was written in wrinkles
from worry over counseling sessions when
she couldn't get pregnant. It was written
in a tiredness from lack of sleep, from
monitoring ovulation, monitoring basal
temperature. It was written in microscopic
fonts—the shadows of X-rays on fallopian
tubes—Did the pill cause cancer?—Prenatal
exams—big bold letters, a pregnancy leaving
stretch marks that made her belly shimmer
like an illuminated manuscript.
Then a miscarriage. With a back flip to
Do It Again. A champagne pop this time,
for a birth, a c-section opening her up to let
out a daughter, purple as Vishnu and too
big to come into the world in the normal
way—this epic recorded by a white-hot scar.
Then a fever from infection. Then to do it
all yet once again, only this time the cycle
interrupted because of her age by

amniocentesis · a "precaution" in the seventeenth week,
a ten-inch needle inserted through her
belly to extract "just a teaspoon" of the
amniotic fluid that revealed a 75% chance
of "unlucky alleles," and ended in an

D&C · abortion, "the procedure," as the nurse
technicians called it, fitting her feet into
stainless steel stirrups. And Circle had had

terminology · enough. So now it was "His Turn."

A simple thing to ask, considering.
Just "a little snip," as she put it—as
if that was supposed to give him courage.
And she was right. It was just a snip
compared to what she had gone through.
And she'd come out okay. Handsome even,
though her beauty was best described as
"rugged." The way the earth was made
operatic by the ages. Gray outcroppings in
her hair gave her a seriousness befitting
the judge she one day hoped to be, but a
seriousness that was sensual, her body,
like those of the catalog models, young
enough to look better without robes, though
unlike the models, old enough to have had
all trace of frivolity weathered away, the
combination of a mature face on a toned
body speaking of sensual depth beyond the
young, informed as it was by requiem.

Just as a naturalist understands an organ by tracing it back to its embroyonic development, so the habit of contracting the brows that is as common in us as in Hindoos, Malays, and Kafirs of South Africa can be traced through its use in infants. There, in these infants, the habit of contracting the brows has been practiced by innumerable generations as the commencement of every crying fit. Thus we can conclude that the contraction of the corrugator muscles which lower the eyebrows and brings them together producing furrows in the forehead—that is, a frown—are a mingling of mind and body to convey disappointment, a desire that something not right should be made right. This same expression has been observed in tribes of chimpanzees, suggesting to us the roots of culture.

CHARLES DARWIN
The Expression of the Emotions in Man and Animals

Now, stealing glances at her stealing glances
back at him, he could tell she wanted to say
'So, have you made the appointment yet?' And
he braced himself for the cross examination
that would follow his, 'No, not yet.'

When she did speak, though, it was to try
another tactic. "Do you like this?" She
held up the catalog, smiling a smile of
reconcilition, of promise. Bauhaus dimensions
always made her face seem modern to Square,
symmetrical with her angular body—unlike
Rubens's puffy women. Likewise, Circle's
wide smile, full lips were nothing like
the pinched mouths of Victorians, a
heritage of genes giving her face and body
proportions that happened to be in vogue
at their moment in history. A gift.

With strings attached. Snip, snip. Dark nipples
showed through the nightgown worn by a
catalog model running her hands through
jet-black hair (an ancient cliché), lips parted as
in a moan of desire longing to be fulfilled
(still pushing the right buttons).

He nodded, sure she was right, sure that
having the "procedure," as Dr. Silverstein
called it, was the thing to do. Sex severed from
complication—what could be more exciting?
More exciting, even, than that first teenage time.

The reddening flower sat in its water on
the coffee table between them.

The Greek for color is *chroma*;
the Greek for body is *soma*.
Thus *Chromosome*.

snip, snip

The average ejaculation contains 5 cc,
not even a teaspoon.

While primates such as the Tibetan macaque ejaculate voluminously.

How odd it was to go into a library and find
the crumbling volumes of *The Eugenics Review*
and other learned sciences now so completely
dismissed that coming upon their artifacts
was as startling and enigmatic as coming upon
pyramids and great stone heads.

Mute.

Overgrown by vines.

Letters and words take the shape of great mountains

ANONYMOUS KABBALIST *13TH C.*

How innocent he'd been when it hadn't
yet been his turn.

A common story

nouns become rocks

*So common that many people
wouldn't even consider it a story.*

verbs rivers

Last Christmas, Circle's Mother gave their
daughter Oval a gift: *The Big Book of Opera*.
Their Xmas gift to Mother had been a trip to
La Scala and she had returned with opera gifts
for all. "Oh look here," she said, trying to
interest Oval in glossy photos of Rhine maidens.

Oval's eyes rolled forlornly upward, then
imploringly toward her parents, then longingly
toward the other sparkling boxes (a semiotics of
paper) under the tree. Because Circle's Mother
had been gone, they had put off opening those
gifts until her return and the boxes had gotten
bumped about and shaken so much in the meantime
that they crowded out the Nativity scene.
Oval's pet cat stepped gingerly around the fallen
shepherds and wise men, then looked up to her,
its tail a question mark (a semiotics of vertebrae).

Opening Christmas gifts in January gave Square
the disorientation he'd felt when VCRs first came
out and he found himself watching Wednesday's
Late Night News at noon on Friday. The tree
looked as fresh as it had been a month ago when
they put it up, an altered gene keeping it green
even though it was dead—the way Xmas trees
used to be dyed green back in the old days.
For atmosphere, he had put on their videotape of
a burning Yule Log, its flames crackling in
stereo along with a medley of Christmas carols.

A pedestrian story.

rocks become paths

paths roads   *common as paper cuts*

So common that its commonness was the story.

Circle smoothed a La Scala scarf that would be donated to Goodwill the moment Mother left. She nudged their daughter to feign interest.

"What's this one about, mom?" Circle asked, holding Oval in a hug that said 'Stop squirming.' *La Traviata*. The cat shut its eyes, tail curled around its paws, slipping into one of the twelve hours a day that all cats slept. Even tigers.

Roads become city streets, streets highways

"It's so beautiful because it's so sad," Mother answered, moving the *Big Book* so all could see. **The Romance of Opera.** An engraving showed a woman in a ball gown swooning into the arms of her lady friends, a hand raised theatrically to forehead. Circle's smile remained as unchanging as the Christmas tree while her mother told them the whole story, act by act:

ACT I.
A long time ago at a gay party in Paris, Alfredo falls in love with Violetta, a fallen woman, and mistress of a baron (isn't it interesting how both acts are described as "falling"?). But she only laughs at his youth and seriousness (aria: *Un dì felice, eterea*) and dances the night away. Still, as dawn approaches, she gives Alfredo a carnation and asks if he'll visit her when it has wilted.

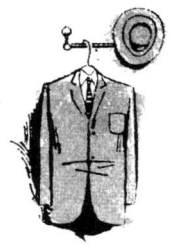

For pair bonding and therefore civilization to develop, the naked ape had to acquire a capacity to become sexually imprinted on a single partner. It did so by linking sex to identity through evolutionary changes that favored face-to-face copulation....Copulation is most commonly performed with the naked male over the naked female, with the female's legs apart.

DESMOND MORRIS
The Naked Ape, 1967

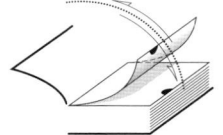
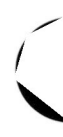

Clothing is partially or fully removed.

Skin−to−skin tactile stimulation increases over as wi

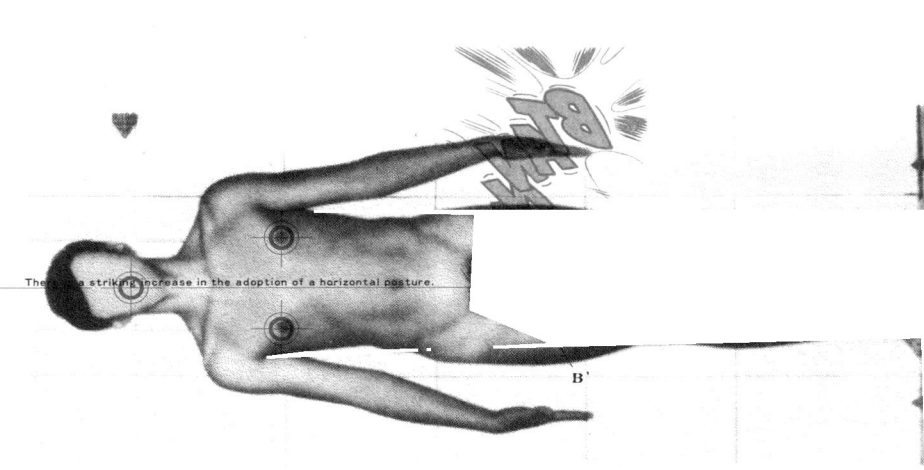

The is a striking increase in the adoption of a horizontal posture.

B'

In the pre−copulatory phase, privacy is sought

Profile from B to B'

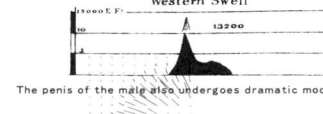

The penis of the male also undergoes dramatic modification.

area as possible. ➤

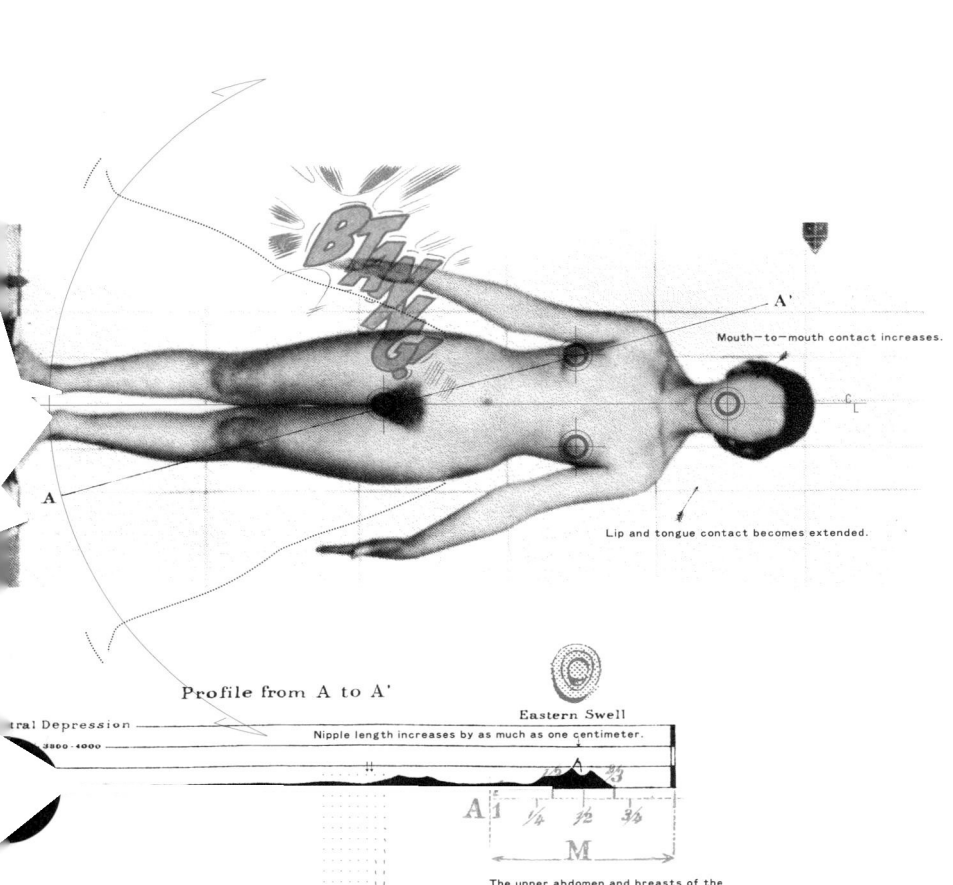

Mouth—to—mouth contact increases.

Lip and tongue contact becomes extended.

Profile from A to A'

Eastern Swell

tral Depression

3800-4000

Nipple length increases by as much as one centimeter.

A 1 ¼ ½ ⅔

M

The upper abdomen and breasts of the female redden as a visual signal.

The partner's genitals may also become the target for repeated actions.

Often rhythmically.
Often rhythmically.
Often rhythmically.
Often rhythmically.
Often rhythmically.
Often rhythmically.
Often rhythmically.
Often rhythmically.
Often rhythmically.
Often rhythmically.
Often rhythmically.
Often rhythmically.
Often rhythmically.
Often rhythmically.
Often rhythmically.
Often rhythmically.
Often rhythmically.
Often rhythmically.

ACT II

opens with the couple living together (privately) in the country and rhapsodizing about their love and happiness (*De' miei bollenti spiriti*). While Alfredo is out, though, his father arrives; Alfredo Sr. pleads with Violetta to leave his son—the scandal they've created is ruining a younger sister's chances for marriage. Reluctantly, Violetta agrees to make this sacrifice. For Love. And she departs before Alfredo returns. Unaware of the supreme sacrifice Violetta has made, Alfredo tracks her down, finally finding her at another of the Baron's balls. Despite her pleas, he is convinced that she left him to return to the Baron's bed and money and storms out, but not before throwing his gambling winnings in her face. Violetta weeps that she does not deserve Alfredo's contempt, then faints.

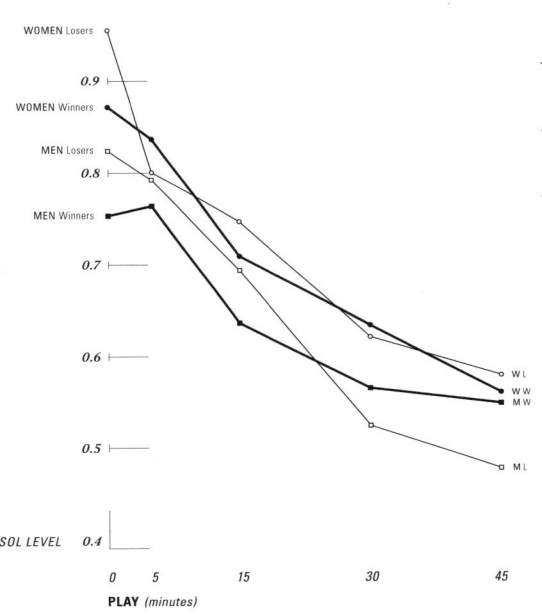

SEX DIFFERENCE IN TESTOSTERONE RESPONSE TO A VIDEO GAME CONTEST

WOMEN Losers
WOMEN Winners
MEN Losers
MEN Winners

ORTISOL LEVEL

PLAY (minutes)

W L
W W
M W
M L

Table 2.
JEALOUSY EVOCATION, PARTNER REASSURAN

Response	Combined	Partner initiated
+ POSITIVE REACTIONS	16 %	14 %
Something special	3 [a]	1 [ab]
More attention	13 [b]	13 [b]
○ NEUTRAL REACTIONS	60 %	44 %
No change	43 [c]	20 [c]
Keep tabs	17 [b]	16 [b]
− NEGATIVE REACTIONS	24 %	32 %
Fight with partner	22 [d]	30 [d]
Break up	2 [a]	4 [a]

Table 3.
EVOLUTIONARY PSYCHOLOGY: EXTRA-PAIR SE

MEN

Predictor variable	Beta	t(164)
FA	-.17	-2.27
Age	.01	.09
SES	.07	.87
Expected income	.02	.24
Facial attractiveness	-.02	-.22
Anxious attachment	.09	1.11
Avoidant attachment	.13	1.71

WOMEN

Predictor variable	Beta	t(164)
FA	-.04	-.58
Age	.13	1.73
SES	-.06	-.71
Expected income	-.05	-.64
Facial attractiveness	-.07	-.87
Anxious attachment	.20	2.60
Avoidant attachment	-.21	-2.69

ACT III.

Months later, abandoned by both the Baron and Alfredo, Violetta lies dying of consumption. Suddenly, Alfredo, who has learned the truth, bursts in. The lovers dream of a new life together (duet: *Parigi, o cara*) and "Violetta, feeling her pain stop," Mother said, rising from the couch, "rises as if lifted by love. But from this pinnacle of happiness, she collapses—a bride only to death—*Morto!*"

Square saw that Mother's dramatic performance had made Circle bite her lip to keep from laughing. But Square couldn't laugh, seeing that the opera was meaningful to Mother because of her own "tired blood": what she called the cause of symptoms she could never specifically describe, doctors with their continual testing couldn't find, and Circle, worry spent, could no longer marshal empathy to do more than humor.

"*Now*, can I open my other presents?" Oval asked. "Oh go ahead, monkey," Circle said, obviously relieved for a chance to speak before she burst into snorts of laughter, "before you make us all crazy."

Oval threw the opera book off of her lap and tore into the biggest package: the *Science is Cool* kit of home experiments that she had wanted. "Science rocks!" she squealed, repeating the catch phrase for the portion of the show where gravity or osmosis or static electricity was demonstrated by kids using sponges, or straws, or other stuff any kid could find around the house. On the box, a collage mixed grade-school and commercial/government experiments. Fruit flies and rock bands. The lips of a monkey wearing a space suit were stretched back by the force of Gs into a monstrously exaggerated grin. *Going Where No Man Has Yet Gone!*

"It's certainly a different world," Mother sighed, watching her granddaughter unpack beakers. "The other day I saw a Barbie doll that was pregnant. You just unsnap her belly and out *simple as...* pops the baby." Ears cocked, the cat cautiously approached the wrapping paper, smelling it with the 19 million nerves of its nose while Square's mind filled with the anatomical models that doctors used to explain "procedures." The day he and Circle waited in an office to hear her amniocentesis results, he had been nervously toying with a snap-apart model of the womb when the counselor entered and it suddenly sprang apart in his hands.

All the king's horses and all the kings men....

"She gives birth and doesn't even flinch."

Oval tore open a packet of baking-soda tablets that looked like sperm to Square, though he didn't know why they should; even as they were doing so, he realized that they didn't look anything like sperm. She dropped them into a test tube. Then she squat over it to watch, elbows on boney knees forming a pretzel of limbs—exactly like a cave boy from Square's own youth, blowing on an ember in a diorama that Square's parents made a point to visit during every pilgrimage to that neo-classical book visitors could wander within: the Museum of Natural History.

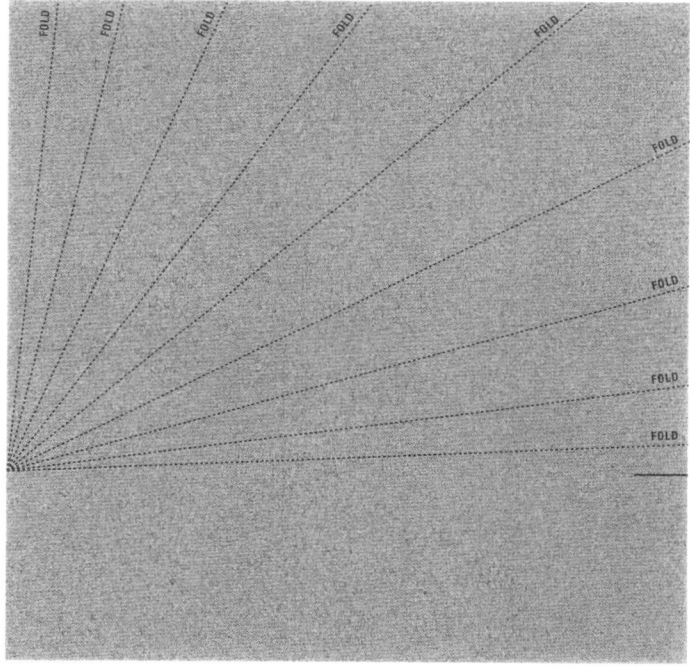

A LINEAR PLOT...

Entering its stone veracity, dim as the past,
they would saunter through centuries. Each
time, American Natives eating out of a communal
bowl became again Asians on the far side of the
Bering Straits; then cave painters, then—

At the end of the hallway, near a janitor's
closet, was The Origin. They had been the
same age, he and that feral double, twins if
one weren't naked in the Hall of Man.

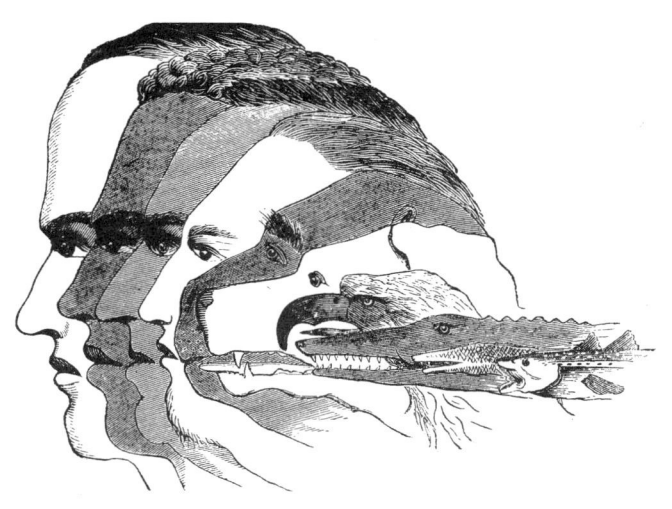

The boy's hairy father brandished the state of
their technology, a sharpened stone, while
Square's father froze in place, sharpening the
focus of his, a 35mm Leica camera, snapping a
copy of a copy of an original that never was?—a
savanna scene, with father's simian pecker a pink
bud nearly lost in the fur of his groin, a dirty-
faced mother with deflated monkey teats, staring
stoically and eternally from the acrylic sunset of
their sapiens dawn: a seamless story where gaps
were bridged by model-making and a timeline as
straight as the baseboards, sons and three-point
perspective supplying the continuity of nuclear
family/hearth/God, each a faded world without
end where only the products changed. Daughters
didn't yet exist. Grandmother was absent,
presumably eaten by wild animals, unlike Mother,
modern medicine and a lack of natural predators
placing her in this living room, their diorama,
Square's own *National Geographic* costume a
blend of polyester and rayon (tumble dry), martini
in hand (Government Warning to Pregnant Women), the
largest of all primate penises (6 inches vs. 2 for gorillas),
in underwear (BVDs) with an elastic band as
the Yule Log played, his body not so hairy as
those Dead Fathers' yet not so hairless as
Circle's waxed lines. If some anthropologist
witchdoctored them into resin—Oval, Circle,
Square and Mother—they'd complete a Period
Room of Flatland, with their VCR (VHS) and
colonial-style computer desk, the 'herd mentality
among primitive races that so often erupts
into the mutual excitation of collective dance'
expressed here through a depressingly
narrow semiotics of product.

"Well, you sure wouldn't have bought anything like that for me," Circle was saying, the smart cut of her lawyer's jacket speaking modern yam gathering, not housewifery, though the vee of bare chest where a man would wear a tie still intimated things French. "Remember when I was her age, Mom, and you wouldn't let me have that doll that peed? You said it was too real. Nobody even made toys like this science set back then."

"No, that wasn't why," Mother said. She suppressed a burp, Flatland etiquette differing from that of the 'Mohamedan who expresses gratitude at his entertainment by eruption after the meal.' "It wasn't real enough. I didn't want you growing up thinking that babies were nothing but eating and peeing machines."

Square quit his stereo-optic viewer. "Science sets were around," he said, laying it on the day's newspaper: **TITANIC RESURRECTED!**
"Girls just didn't play with them."

"You should take Oval to the opera when she gets older," Mother said, watching her fit a balloon over a test tube. She moved to help but then stopped, seeing that Oval handled her equipment as expertly as savage Papua children hunt lizards with miniature versions of adult blowpipes. Mother smoothed the banana leaves she had plaited into a skirt that recorded the ancient wisdom of her people. "It would be good for her."

As if she hadn't heard, Circle continued, "Yeah, most of my friends' brothers had chemistry sets. Or microscopes. We girls just missed out on it all."

"Wow!" Oval yelled, a sudden gush from the test tube inflating the balloon to the size of her stomach.

The cat hissed, eyes wide, ears twitching defensively toward every sound.

"You didn't miss anything," Mother said.

Imagine a penny on a table, Square remembered thinking the first time he set eyes on Flatland.

If you look down at it from above it appears as a circle.

The plane they had been on continued its slow descent.

But if you gradually bring your eye down to the level of the table top,
it becomes a line and this is how I and the other inhabitants of Flatland
appear to each other.

Standing on the tarmac, he realized
that circumstance had given him
a glimpse of the world as it must
have appeared to Columbus—or
a fruit fly—the world a tabletop that
extended as far as the eye could see.
Now after living here for three years—
it only took three years!—it was
hard to imagine the world
any other way.

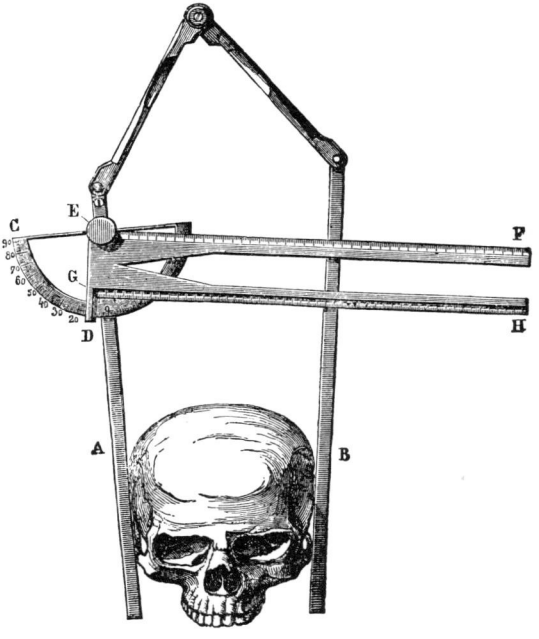

Type ....

Left orbital index.....................
External palatal.......................

Cranial capacity......................
Skull module..........................
Vault module..........................

Stature...............................
Asymmetry or Deformation.............
Kind..................................
Degree................................
Cause.................................

Vault.................................
  Ill-filled...........................
  Medium.............................
  Well-filled.........................
Norma verticalis
  Spheroid...........................
  Ellipsoid...........................
  Ovoid ....
  Byrsoid ....
  Sphenoid...........................
  Square.............................
  Rhomboid ....
  Pentagonoid ....
Norma Lateralis
  Ellipsoid...........................
  Ovoid ....
  Pentagonoid........................
  Round..............................
  Square.............................
  Sphenoid...........................
Norma occipitalis
  Spheroid...........................
  Rounded...........................
  Gabled.............................
  Hausform ....
  Hayrick............................
  Barrel-vault........................
  Ellipsoid ....
Norma facialis
  Rounded...........................
  Heart..............................
  Pentagonoid ....
  Squat hexagon......................
  Long hexagon.......................
  Square ....
  Rectangular ....
  Trapezoid ....
  Triangular..........................

Proper Marks	Improper Marks
●●●●	⊘⊘⊙⊘

1. Ⓐ Ⓒ Ⓓ Ⓣ
2. Ⓐ Ⓒ Ⓓ Ⓣ
3. Ⓐ Ⓑ Ⓓ Ⓣ
4. Ⓐ Ⓑ Ⓓ Ⓣ
5. Ⓐ Ⓑ Ⓓ Ⓣ
6. Ⓐ Ⓑ Ⓓ Ⓣ
7. Ⓐ Ⓑ Ⓓ Ⓣ
8. Ⓐ Ⓒ Ⓓ Ⓣ
9. Ⓐ Ⓑ Ⓓ Ⓣ
10. Ⓐ Ⓒ Ⓓ Ⓣ
11. Ⓐ Ⓒ Ⓓ Ⓣ
12. Ⓐ Ⓒ Ⓓ Ⓣ
13. Ⓐ Ⓒ Ⓓ Ⓣ
14. Ⓐ Ⓒ Ⓑ Ⓣ
15. Ⓐ Ⓑ Ⓓ Ⓣ
16. Ⓐ Ⓒ Ⓓ Ⓣ
17. Ⓐ Ⓒ Ⓓ Ⓣ
18. Ⓐ Ⓒ Ⓓ Ⓣ
19. Ⓐ Ⓒ Ⓓ Ⓣ
20. Ⓐ Ⓒ Ⓑ Ⓣ
21. Ⓐ Ⓒ Ⓑ Ⓣ
22. Ⓐ Ⓒ Ⓑ Ⓣ
23. Ⓐ Ⓒ Ⓓ Ⓣ
24. Ⓐ Ⓒ Ⓑ Ⓣ
25. Ⓐ Ⓒ Ⓑ Ⓣ
26. Ⓐ Ⓒ Ⓑ Ⓣ
27. Ⓐ Ⓒ Ⓓ Ⓣ
28. Ⓐ Ⓒ Ⓑ Ⓣ
29. Ⓐ Ⓒ Ⓔ Ⓣ
30. Ⓐ Ⓒ Ⓑ Ⓣ
31. Ⓐ Ⓒ Ⓑ Ⓣ
32. Ⓐ Ⓒ Ⓑ Ⓣ
33. Ⓐ Ⓒ Ⓑ Ⓣ
34. Ⓐ Ⓒ Ⓑ Ⓣ
35. Ⓐ Ⓒ Ⓑ Ⓣ
36. Ⓐ Ⓒ Ⓑ Ⓣ
37. Ⓐ Ⓒ Ⓓ Ⓣ
38. Ⓐ Ⓒ Ⓑ Ⓣ
39. Ⓐ Ⓒ Ⓑ Ⓣ

Continue on next page

A lot of people who were smarter than him and had figured it out.

A simple story
With a plot as conventional as a museum's base boards

The contention that differences in IQ depend on the individual's genetic constitution appears incontestable.

CYRIL BURT *1972*
"The Inheritance of General Intelligence."
American Psychology 27: 175-190.

Still, the odd thing about that Hall of Man
diorama was that its mannequins were posed
exactly like the stuffed apes in the Hall
of Primates: mother, child and father ape,
with father frozen in mid-snarl as he beat his
chest at tourists. Provider and provided for.

A nuclear family.   **Synthetic dirt**
A molecule of three atoms

survival of?—

projection?

Reflection?

polymers?

Square had to work to get the child-proof cap off of a bottle of Bio-Clean. On the label was a before-and-after cartoon of a drain pipe, first clogged, then free flowing. As he measured out a cup of blue liquid (a rhetoric of color), he remembered reading years ago about the microbes that were its active ingredient. It had been big news at the time. *First Patented Life Form: Using genetic engineering, scientists have developed a microbe that eats petroleum-based substances. Practical applications include the release of this new product into oceans to help clean oil slicks....* Back then, the thought of chemical companies releasing new life forms into the ocean had scared people. Fish with human hands for flippers or worse (and more realistically?) global plague.... Doomsday movies had been based on such scenarios. Then somehow he, and apparently everyone else, had moved on or had otherwise forgotten about it and here it was, U.S. Patent No.5577098, going down his kitchen drain to devour sludge that had been building up like cholesterol in the pipes since before he was born. The label also depicted a happy housewife (translation: so safe and easy that even a woman...) and he could imagine cupfuls of the stuff going down drains all over the world, rivulets of blue Bio-Clean coursing like spring run-off into oceans just as everyone in their individual automobiles supposedly had far more effect on the air than the blackest of industrial smoke stacks.

When he was finished, he put the bottle up on the high shelf with other household cleaners and things they didn't want Oval to swallow. Then he washed his hands and took three iced teas out to the pool.

The cat was stalking something in the bushes, its entire being focused with an intensity attainable only by primitive brains. Oval was splashing in the water while Circle sat pool-side with Mother, Mother's puffy white arms and legs striated by the elastic of her one-piece bathing suit. Approaching their table, he could tell something was wrong.

"Don't you think Oval would like a playmate," Mother asked Square too eagerly.

Circle sat motionless behind large sunglasses. Her own one-piece bathing suits always reminded him of the bikinis she used to wear before Oval's birth marked her stomach with a large white scar. The taut line that was her mouth said that she and Mother had been at each other again.

He readjusted the umbrella fixed to the table, then sat down and passed around packets of an artificial sweetener. "Oh I don't know," he tried to answer neutrally. But the lack of conviction in his voice was seized on by both women. Circle's face hardened as if to say 'Don't you dare think of using my body to avoid your turn,' while Mother saw it as confirmation of what she believed: that Circle really did want to have more children but that she was scared because the last pregnancy, like the first, had ended in a miscarriage.

They had told her that lie—that the last pregnancy had ended in a miscarriage instead of the "procedure" they had actually "elected"—partly because Mother's view of the world was so antique and partly because it would have been so hard to explain theirs. Now they were living with the consequences: a Mother's conviction to help her daughter overcome her "fear" of conceiving—for her own good.

"Look at her," Mother said, nodding toward Oval in the pool, trying to play a game of volleyball by herself. She hit the ball high into the air, her young body simultaneously jackknifing like an otter under the net, emerging only a split moment too late to hit the ball back to herself. The water looked a little foggier than it should and Square wondered if the oil-eating microbes he used in the kitchen could be used to clean the pool.

"She needs a playmate."

Or would the chlorine kill the microbes?

"She's got me and Square," Circle said.

Or would the microbes eat the chlorine?...

"And a lot of friends at school."

...and in the end make the water dirtier than ever? How could anyone predict these things? Still, people a lot smarter than him said they had figured it out.

"You know what I mean. And Square does too,"
Mother said, drawing him back in. Her ally.
But their bodies were arguments enough, if only
they'd look: during the summer, Oval seemed
only to live in the water as flashes of young limbs
and sunlight; Mother never put her parchment
in the pool anymore, except to dangle swollen
feet in the shallow end, while Circle increasingly
only went in to swim against the force of their
artificial wave machine. Witnessing her goose flesh
just before she plunged in on cold mornings,
then seeing the shock of the water melt into a
meditative look as she settled into her exercise
rhythm, Square couldn't help but be reminded
of medieval flagellants. What one believed, they
professed, was indistinguishable from what one
did with his or her body. And what Circle's body
said she believed was that each stroke, each
kick of her legs, staved off a while longer the
undertow of the shallow end.

But, of course, they wouldn't look at each other
that way. So Square tried to stay out of the
argument by making a joke about his own body:
"Raising children is like bullfighting: a young
man's sport."

No one laughed. "Wouldn't you like to have
another little Oval running around?" Mother said.
"Or a little Octagon? Children are so precious!"
She clapped her hands, sending a tremor through
the aging flabbiness of her arms.

"Grandma! Grandma! Look at me! I did it!"
Oval yelled from the water, her youth taut
as a syllogism.

"I saw you darling!" Mother waved. Then she sat
back and smiled, nature on her side after all.

"Well sure," Square began—
He heard the suck of Circle's chest cavity, speech
lobes echoing the startle of her brain's emotive
region to vibrate vocal chords so that the up-rush
of breath through her body would come out as,

"What?!"

She pushed her sunglasses up onto her head
to reveal that her eyes had widened to the size
of an animal's before it pounces. And in response,
an electro-chemical jolt contracted his muscles
to quickly voice "But it's more complicated than
that" *(accelerando)* as he tried to recover.

Tried and failed, he saw, realizing that Mother
would take his words as confirmation of Circle's
phobia of conceiving. Circle's eyes remained
trained on him."Sometimes more kids just
aren't in the cards," he tried.

"What he means," Circle said, emotion beginning to
raise veins, "is that we've decided to limit our family."

"Limit your?—"

"It's not like when you and dad were raising
a family. Kids cost a lot. The public schools are
worthless so you can't even think about sending
them there. And anyway, who's going to watch a
baby while I'm at work? Square doesn't have time.
He can't even figure out the ending to his dumb…"

Dumb?

"…story, watching Oval after school like he does
and I don't have time to be around them.
Not like you were with us."

a common story

"Well, things have certainly changed," Mother
sighed in that exhausted victim tone she adopted
whenever she was about to play her "tired blood"
card. "In my day, children just came or they
didn't. We were just the organ they did it through."

of a common man

"Geez, that's what you want me to go back to?"
Circle laughed, her smile an incipient "fear
grin" primates often exhibited just before
tension broke into fight or flight. "A crap
shoot?" This last was meant for him. He decided
to let pass the crack about his "dumb" story.

Homo being common to all men

"I only meant—"

and women (obviously)

"Mother, I can't not know what I know!" Her
exasperated tone left a pregnant silence at the table.
"Excuse me," she said, "I need a refill on my ice."
She stood up and there was the shock of her body:
a flat athletic torso, muscular shoulders and arms
in a cheetah-print swimsuit (a legacy of African,
i.e. savage sexuality) that made him want her.
"Anybody else want anything?"

She headed off toward the kitchen, stooping to
swat Oval's ball back into the pool with one easy
motion, muscles flexing beneath the skin of her
Speedo. Square wanted to follow her. She'd been
angry and had said things she didn't mean and
they'd make up, violently, right there in the kitchen—
But Mother was here, and even if she wasn't, there
was the matter of the diaphragm, sexual preparation,
not cheetah spontaneity, and he realized that Circle's
"dumb story" remark could also be exactly what she
meant but would have never said until... Snip, snip.
The thought of trying to explain it to her again
wearied him....

Oval climbed out of the pool to retrieve her
ball again (a Little Mermaid® bathing suit a legacy of
marketing savagery). She plunged back in.

The arrangement of claws, powerful hind legs
and flexible spine known as "cat" sprang away,
an abhorrence of splash as inherent as pounce.
Clamped in its jaws was the broken body
of a sparrow (feathers spelling a different destiny).

Mother was saying something. "I said,"
she repeated, "I wouldn't worry about what
Circle said." Misreading what must have been a
still-born desire on his face, she continued slyly,
"Accidents happen. And once another baby's born,
she'll thank you."

Square nodded, though that ending seemed
so antique he could only imagine it as a silent
movie—even though he was old enough to have
known guys—older brothers of friends—who had
married their pregnant girlfriends because
'There wasn't any other choice.'

By the time he'd begun dating, though, there was Alaska where the "procedure" was legal. Then there was Hawaii. Then New York, then you didn't have to travel anywhere, not even to the anonymity of a drug store in the next town and though he hadn't realized it at the time, stories about shotgun weddings (how our language dates us!) began to take on the urgency of his father's stories about radio back before there was television. He couldn't remember a time without television. But he could remember when there were no VCRs. Still, after he got married, getting pregnant simply wasn't a thing people worried about anymore. Judging from the music channels, it no longer even rated a song.

"I didn't want to say anything in front of Circle," Mother said, "but my platelet count was only nineteen last week." Square waited for it, and here it came: "I don't know how much longer I'll be around—"

"Oh, Mom, it's not like that."

"And I know Circle doesn't think I'm in danger—"

"Your doctors don't think you're in danger. And Circle is just—" He almost said that Circle was just tired of her complaining, tired of her using her tired blood to get sympathy. And doing it so often that even if there was something to her complaints, they had become as worn as the plot of a folk tale (wolf included).

Mother put her hand on his arm and said tenderly, "When's the last time you and Circle went to the opera?"

She was referring to another history of
hers that would be impossible to correct:
that he and Circle had gone to the opera for
a second honeymoon. To see *L'Elisir d'Amore*.
Mother had given them the tickets and took
Oval for the weekend but Circle hated opera
so they gave away the tickets and rented an old
movie instead. Afterwards, trying to be a good
son-in-law, Square had gushed about the opera
and Mother took that to mean that it had in part
been responsible for Circle's pregnancy,
the one that had been conceived on that
"honeymoon," but then ended in "miscarriage."

Square suddenly remembered that they had
rented one of those movies about genetically
engineered plagues that he'd been thinking
about earlier and for a moment he wondered
if there was some connection after all.

That had been five years ago.
"It's been forever," he said truthfully, lying.
"The firm keeps her awful busy."

"That's what I mean. You can't neglect
romance. Otherwise, you turn into some
kind of bureaucrat that balances a family
like it's a ledger. You take her to the Opera,"
she said, patting his arm. "It worked once,
it'll work again."

In the shower, Square examined his scrotum—wrinkled—another kind of body shock—compared to what it had been when he was a teenager, the last time he'd looked this intently. The hair had been so light then that it was almost invisible. Now, trying to find the spot where the incisions would be made, wiry tufts got in the way. Even some gray. For the first time he noticed a similar aged slackness in the face that stared back at him from the mirror he used for shaving— even though he looked at it every day— and an odd sense of déjà vu placed him back in the hospital he'd been rushed to the night of his heart attack scare two years ago. Several years before that, when his own aged parents had been dying, he'd been in the hospital a lot so the nurses and doctors and all their equipment were familiar. Yet that night it all looked so surreal somehow that he had thought he was buzzing from the oxygen being fed into his nostrils. But as he lay there puzzling over what the difference could be, fluorescent lights shining down into his eyes, it hit him—he was seeing it all for the first time from flat on his back, from the perspective of a patient not a visitor who stood upright, and it was all radically different. Not even the same world.

science Rocks.

EXPERIMENT No.23 **PERCEPTION**

Arrange 10 toothpicks as shown.
Which looks longer, toothpick A or B?

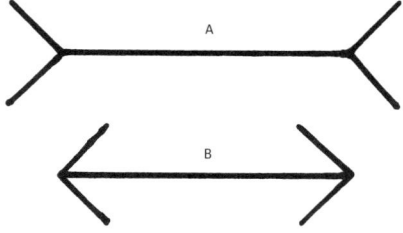

Square stopped writing to look at the whorls
of his fingertips, little miracles of line, their
repetition a swirling reification of his mother
and father and their mothers and fathers and
their mothers and fathers and their mothers and
fathers and their mothers and fathers and their
mothers and fathers and their mothers and
fathers and their mothers and fathers and their
mothers and fathers back through 125,000
generations to the ape, written in a language of
four base letters, AGCT, which combined into
words—CAC|ATA|AGG—the words forming
double-helix sentences of genes which filled
pages of chromosomes within the cells which
made up the book of his body. And he marveled
at the malleability of the system—people,
orchids, amoebas, elk—all cognate.

Square considered the letters of his name
written on the hospital form, little miracles
of line, their bowls and strokes a reification
of his elementary-school teacher, hand on his,
as she was of hers, who was of his, an unbroken
string of hands on hands—mostly unaware—
through clerks and writing masters back to
medieval scribes, the dead working through him
as if his hand were the pallet of a Ouija board
forming words without separation, sentences
coagulating into cells on pages, pages making
up sacred books of mysteries serene as the
Primum Mobile with their gilt capitals and
luminous illustrations worked out in detail so
fine they had been painted with an eyelash,
their ornaments and wonders—shimmering
portals of thought embodied—displayed on
high altars for the adoration of the faithful.

Body text once had body

a asectompCons
Wetheundersignedl
bandWifebothbeingo
enpearsofagereques
thatDoctorSilverste
ssistantsofhischoice
formupon
bilateralVasectompa
administeranpanest
echoose](thasbeener)
tousthatthisoperatic
intendedtoresultinst
Weunderstandthata
personisnotcapableo
comingaparent.Wea
understandthattheo)
tionsmapnotresultii
terilitpandthatnogua
nteeofsterilitphasbe
ibentoeitherofus.We
untarilprequesttheo

Couldn't it again?

What would it look like if it did?

Mayan pyramids also being at once shelter, altar, calendar and encyclopedia

Towers of children's alphabet blocks, as well

The world was written differently then,
Creation one continuous expression of Divine
Letters–Proportions–Harmony–Laws–Spheres
without separation, the symmetry of a snail's
shell, of a flower's bell, of an inner ear, a
breaking wave, a moth's flight or comet's tail all
features of a single face which You, Our God,
scribes copied, wisely reveal in Your Book,
our firmament, so that we may discern Your
Unity as the mold of all things although we
perceive it yet in signs and times and in days
and years while the angels and the blessed pass
their non-time reading a language without
syllables, the only mystery of the world being
the visible and how it revealed this design,
not the design itself which was invisible,
unequivocal and terrible in its clarity because
it was the face of the Word itself.

Has anyone ever seen an ionic bond?

Birth of a nation.

Babel?....

Just before the Fourth of July, Square took
Oval down to the mall to buy sparklers. As
they moved about the rows of red-white-and-
blue bunting (Made in China), he couldn't help
but wonder if the thing that bothered him
about having the "procedure" was the cliché
called Hitler. He'd feel stupid offering that alibi
to Circle, though. She'd hand it back in shreds.
But as she said herself, 'I can't not know what
I know' and what he knew was that The Fourth
of July was also the anniversary of the Nazi's
sterilization program. He'd learned that fact in
high school because his government teacher
demonstrated the inherent good of democracy
by pointing out that Germans passed the
Sterilization Act on July 4, 1933, revoking the
rights of "undesirables" to protest their
sterilization—on the very day that Americans
were "celebrating the Land of Free Choice."
Manifestations of this mindset are with us even
today, even in the smallest details, the teacher
had explained, using as proof the fact that
only in America could people choose between
hundreds of salad dressings.

Ever since, the fluorescent lights of grocery
stores, shining down harshly upon row
after row of salad dressings always
reminded Square of stark labs where
cripples were sterilized by Nazi doctors
wearing monocles, scar on one cheek,who
knew only of vinegar and oil and
couldn't even imagine another option.

Of course, Square's government teacher probably forgot (or never knew) what Square had only learned much later: that forced sterilization (and other forced surgeries) had been legalized in "The Land of Free Choice" twenty-six years before the Germans got around to it. Here as there, it was used to cure epilepsy, to improve will power, and to prevent moral degenerates, idiots, imbeciles, habitual masturbaters, and those who were otherwise "unfit" from passing their traits on to their offspring.

A slap on the buttocks
and Female Infant—Oval hadn't yet had a
name—screamed, her purple body taking on
fleshy color—like a flower absorbing dye
before his eyes.

The "Unfit" also including those who contributed to industrial inefficiency... ...and those with VD...

On the way home from the mall,
sparklers and a Doctor Barbie in the bag
on Oval's lap, they drove down a stretch
of expressway that bisected an affluent suburb,
a corridor lined with billboards advertising
expensive suburban vehicles, Luxury Vans,
Landrovers—shiny toys.

"Look," Oval said, "balloons."

...and the civicly unrightous...

Who's the Father? Call 1-800-DNA-TYPE,
said the billboard she'd meant, its background
a pattern of sperms, drawn to resemble party
balloons. A baby shower? The office party
where conception took place?...

As only a woman-child could, Oval mixed talk
of her friend Lisa's birthday party with "health
studies": anonymous sperm donors, pin the
tail on the donkey, surrogate mothers,
musical chairs...

Square felt profoundly the shock of her
body, legs that had been kid skinny only
moments ago suddenly having enough
womanly shape to transform her jumper
into a miniskirt. Ovaries and a womb were
also abruptly present, though unseen, as
naturally as nature, as invisible as the
billboard had been, though he must
have driven past it a hundred times.

*When an individual becomes so well-adjusted to the hospital milieu that
he knows of no other way of life, he is said to have become "institutionalized."*

MENTAL HYGIENE
JAN 1960.

Still, how could a government
teacher forget a law like that?
How could the governed?

At first it seemed ludicrous to say that a people
could write things that they didn't know they
were writing (as if a hand was the pallet of an
Ouija board). But the cross-outs on his rough
drafts, the arrows and additions mocked him.
He tried to tell himself that the final draft,
the version that would appear fixed in print
would be the real thing, the thing he wanted
to say. But once he x'ed out the first word,
wasn't what was left revisionist history?
And wasn't history, revisionist or otherwise,
as much an act of selective forgetting
as it was remembering?

The way the men who wrote "We the People"
forgot to include Hottentots.

*Or the way George/Christine Jorgensen, Flatland's first transsexual, had
to forget his/her body in order to remember her/his body.*

Dear Sir or Madam:

The problem in writing a story, like making
a diorama, was in trying to make sense of
a pool of ideas.

A C
G

A G C G A
A TC G
AT G CG G
T T G
AG T T TG

CT T T TTT A G
CG CG GG G

Well, maybe not forgot, Square wrote,
trying to get sCATTerings to AGGlutinATe.

G C G T AAA
C C CCT G GG AAA AT A
AT TA A
CCA

CA ATA TT A AA
A CC CCC CG C GG T A
AA T

TTT ATC
ACT A TGG GG GGT AC
AAGCC TTTTA C T
ATCCG T GT T
BITS AND

AATAC GCG
ACC AACT CCCA AG
CGCTCGATAATA
BITS AND

ATTC**astrati**
TTATACTCTGAATTC
AATATTTT**S he**
BITS AND

FRAGMENTS
COME TOGETHER
LIKE NUCLEOTIDES
SOME SPLIT APART AND DIE
OTHERS HOLD

LINKING UP
INTO DOUBLE HELIXES
CGGGCTCTCCA
TATTAGTT

GTATAGTT
ACGATAGAAAA
ATTATTTACATGGT
ATTGCTTTCTTCT
GTGTCTGCCC

ATAGCCCCT
TTTTGTGTGATG
CGGACTACGACAG
TTAGGAT

ACCGTC
AGATTTACTA
TGGGACCCCTG

TAATAC
CCCTCGGG

It's in the language.

Words being both the material and message
of language

**National Christian
League for the Promotion
of (Racial) Purity**

And if it's in the language, it's in the thoughts.

**French Academy for Promotion
of (Language) Purity**

And that's what worried him.

A legacy.
(often unawares)

1970 laws carrying on 1907 traditions

Of hidden histories.
**Like the Y chromosome
traceable to a single ancestor**

The unseen.

188,000 years ago.

*Societies of ants going back
100,000,000 years*

Mollusks going back 550,000,000 years

science Rocks

EXPERIMENT No.103 **RECESSIVE GENES**

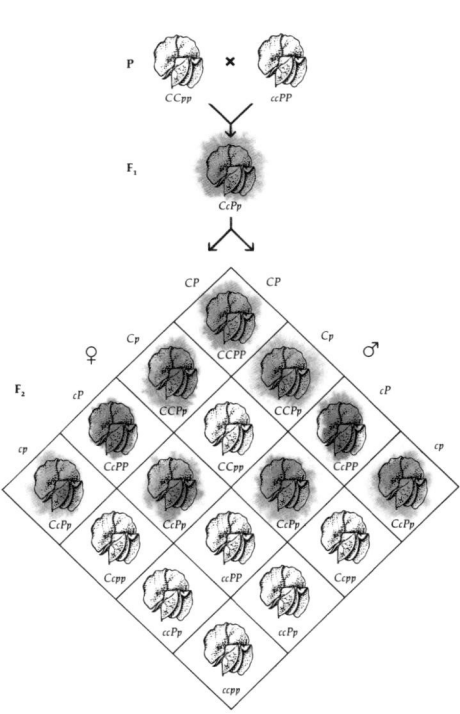

A Common Ancestor

| fader | vader | faoir | vater | pater | pere | padre |
| Gothic | Dutch | Old Norse | German | Greek | French | Spanish |

The unconsidered.

One English family,
the **Temple-Nugent-Ascot-Bridges-Chandos-Chenvilles (now extinct)**
had a family shield with 719 symbols, each an icon of their
blood tie to another aristocratic lineage.

Or their parents.
(billions of parents)

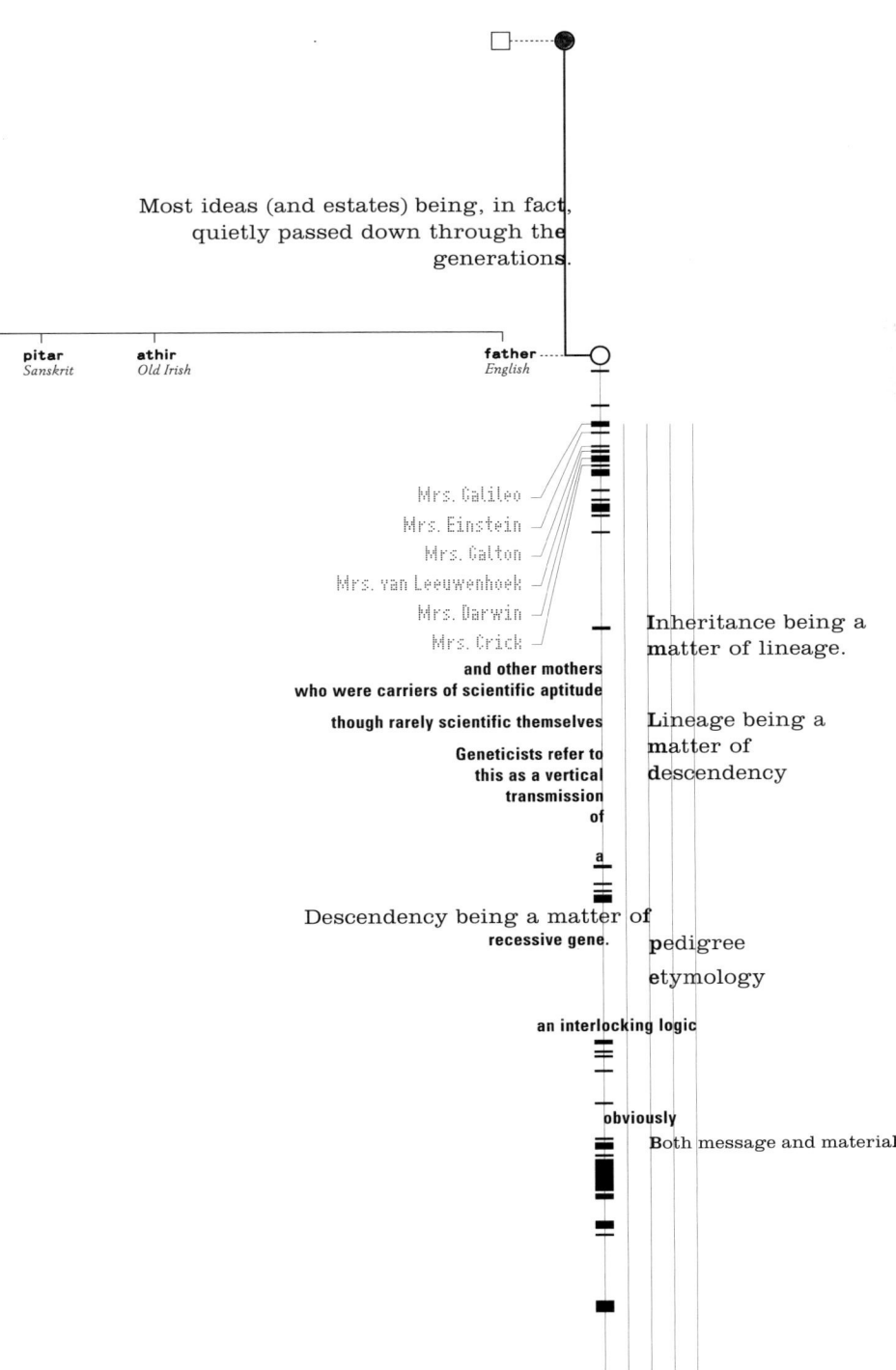

Most ideas (and estates) being, in fact, quietly passed down through the generations.

pitar
Sanskrit

athir
Old Irish

father
English

Mrs. Galileo
Mrs. Einstein
Mrs. Galton
Mrs. van Leeuwenhoek
Mrs. Darwin
Mrs. Crick

**and other mothers
who were carriers of scientific aptitude**

though rarely scientific themselves

**Geneticists refer to
this as a vertical
transmission
of**

Inheritance being a matter of lineage.

Lineage being a matter of descendency

a

Descendency being a matter of
recessive gene.

pedigree

etymology

an interlocking logic

obviously

Both message and material

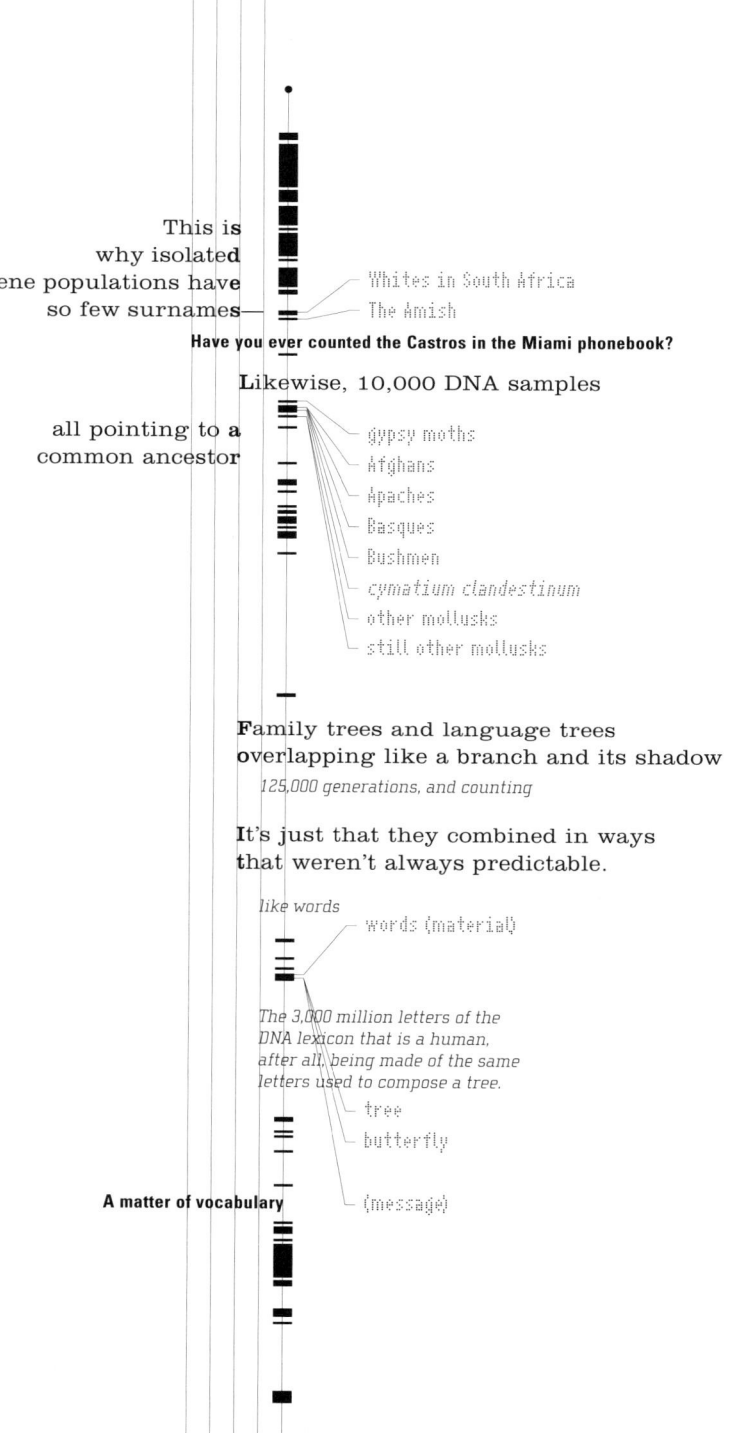

This is
why isolated
gene populations have
so few surnames—

Whites in South Africa

The Amish

Have you ever counted the Castros in the Miami phonebook?

Likewise, 10,000 DNA samples

all pointing to a
common ancestor

gypsy moths

Afghans

Apaches

Basques

Bushmen

cymatium clandestinum

other mollusks

still other mollusks

Family trees and language trees
overlapping like a branch and its shadow

125,000 generations, and counting

It's just that they combined in ways
that weren't always predictable.

like words

words (material)

*The 3,000 million letters of the
DNA lexicon that is a human,
after all, being made of the same
letters used to compose a tree.*

tree

butterfly

A matter of vocabulary

(message)

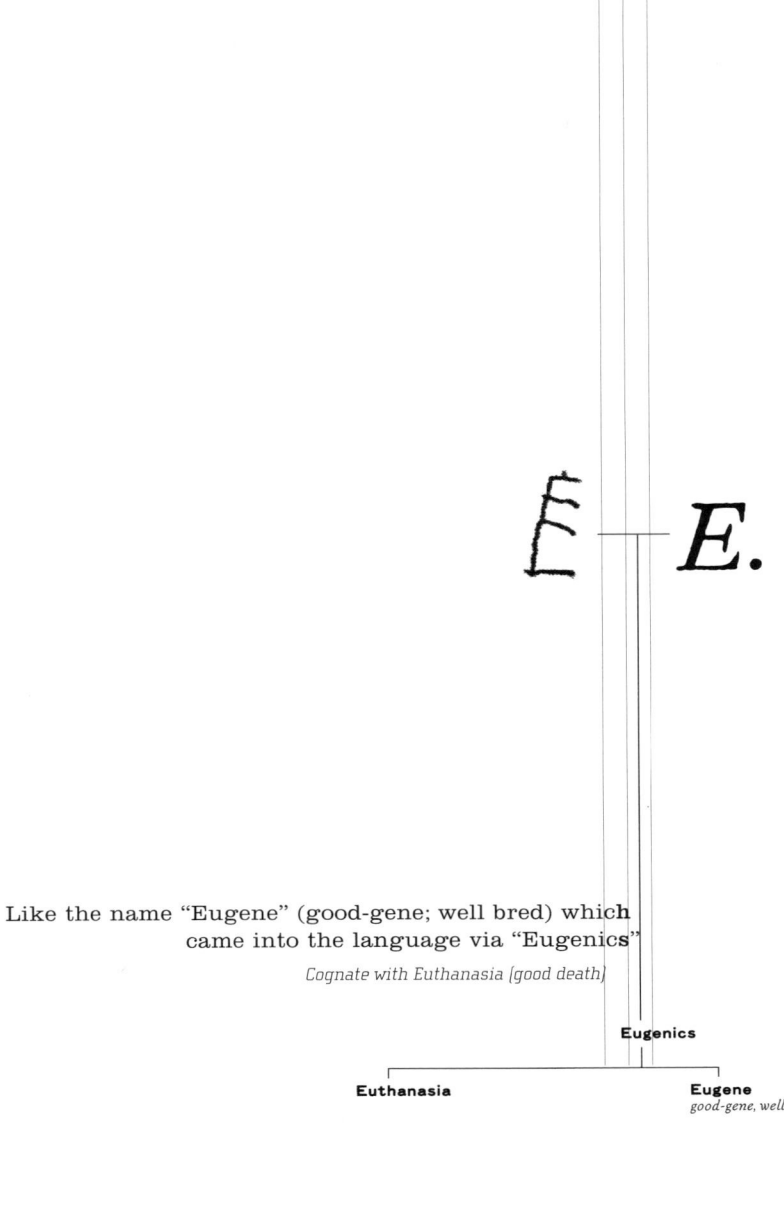

E.

Like the name "Eugene" (good-gene; well bred) which came into the language via "Eugenics"

Cognate with Euthanasia (good death)

Eugenics

Euthanasia

Eugene
good-gene, well bred

TABLE,

Showing the Average Slope of the Forehead, as obtained from the measurement of the facial angle of Jacquart.

RACES AND FAMILIES.	°s. of Slope.
CAUCASIAN GROUP.	
Men,	134°
Women,	138°
Children,	137°
(10-15 *years of age*)	
New-born infants,	141°
. . . . . .	
CHINESE FAMILY.	} 142°
USBECK FAMILY.	
NEGROES.	144°
CHIMPANZEE.	149°
ORANGUTANGS.	174°

M. DE QUATREFAGES *DE L'ANGLE PARIETAL, 1858*

Statistics are a wonderful tool to reveal untold histories.

the figure in the carpet

Likewise, by reading court convictions it can be concluded that no white man in America ever raped a black woman before 1957.

10,000,000,000,000,000 ants on earth

A common ancestor

a chromosome mutation differentiating humans from chimps.

Five million years of sweaty breeding

Any repetitious act will gradually mutate.

Caterpillar (Acherontia atropos)

Surnames die out

Pupa

For lack of a nail...

Even kingdoms

Animalia

The Final Solution **(a theory)**

originally invented for the

Homosexual Problem

(another theory)

since not all men

Cynthia cardui (Painted Lady)

Like Einar Wegener

Germany's first transsexual have male children.

Who have male children.

Like George Washington

Like George Jorgensen

Who have male children.

When a man dies without a son, the living brother shall go to the widow
and perform the duty of a brother-in-law to continue the line of the
deceased brother, that his name may not be blotted out from Israel.

DUETERONOMY 25:5

(theory again)

ACA | AAA | ATA | ACT | CTG | ACG | ACC | GAC | GCC | TTG | GAA | AAA | GTT | ATG |

Eugenes

Think of it—parents still name their sons
after a sterilization program.

(though often unawares)
Surnames passed on through the Y chromosome, obviously.

Haven't you ever played Chinese telephones?

Good-nature and good-sense must ever join;
To err is human, to forgive, divine...
Which we can see doesn't rhyme
Unless 6 generations ago
Alexander Pope pronounced join as jine

So goes vowels.
and ants

A sequence of letters

*I am convinced that in the next century millions will cut each other's throats
because of one or two degrees difference in the slope of their foreheads*

CA | ACA | CAC | ACT | CCC | AAC | TTA | TTT | CTC | AAA | GENETIC | WORD | MADE | FLESH | TAA | ACT | CAA | CCA | CAA | CAC | CCA

JOSEPH GOBINEW
1854

Given some 3 billion nucleotides within each cell,
and a thousand million cells per body

you can see how typos could add up.
That's 3,000,000,000,000,000,000,000 AGCTs

50,000 species of mollusks
identified by the shape

A theory
of their

shells

heads

Mostly random

Sort of like the thousand typing monkeys
who would eventually reproduce an
exact copy of *Don Quixote*
(only in reverse)

If alive today, Chaucer would be illiterate.

§68.   *In fact, if you run*
English's mutations in fast forward, you can watch it evolve:

Nu, broþerr, broþerr min & broþerr min i Crifftenn-
dom, wiþþ þohht, wiþþ word, wiþþ dede he fpaak unto
yemmuch in biwordes and faid, On a tijm y fouer went
forth to foow, and whil he was in foowing fumm fel
bi y wais fijd, and y birds cam and devoured it. Thee
ignorant wyl imagine, that thee passage was nothing
craggye but if fom one well learned and as laborious a
man, wold gather all the ideas held within these words
he wold open vnto vs their naturall force. Verily, we
do not mean all we write, which proceeds from divers
fuperfluous meanings that occur in many of our
words. Yet whether such unnecessary meanings choke
good seed or inrich their soil is a consideration that
admits of various censures, according to the different
fancies of men.

In other words,

men and mutations—

as inseparable as seed and cell

Theories as well

Nature or Nurture?

Cypraea cinerea
Cypraea pulchra
Cypraea lurida

Walking through a library, have you ever gotten the creepy sensation of walking through a vast Victorian collection of mollusks?

Even harder to tell apart than people.

Persians/Iranians
Cypraea cinerea
Jews/Arabs

Cypraea Isabella

Those most similar in genes being most similar in articulation

Even more so with ants

Myrmecia gulosa

Though, sadly, often most hostile to one other.

Hutu/Tutsi
Greeks/Turks
Cambodians/Cambodians
Serbs/Croats
Northerners/Southerners
Ponerinae

An ant colony's most dangerous threat being another ant colony.

330   PROPORTIONS OF THE FACE.   [Chap. v.

These are manifestly at variance with those laid down by Art, and we have been obliged to give them approximately only. But they refer exclusively to Belgians, and it would be necessary that the same proportions should be established with reference to all races as well as to their individual variations. Then artists should know the physiological limits beyond which they ought not to go.

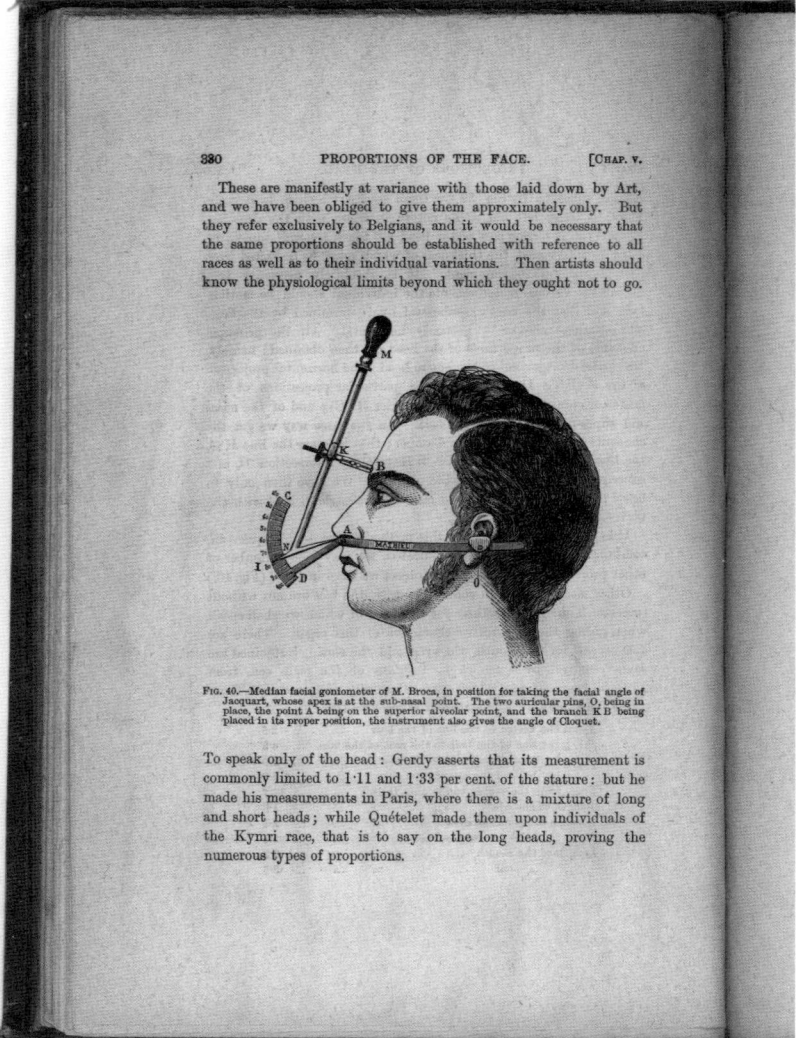

FIG. 40.—Median facial goniometer of M. Broca, in position for taking the facial angle of Jacquart, whose apex is at the sub-nasal point. The two auricular pins, O, being in place, the point A being on the superior alveolar point, and the branch K B being placed in its proper position, the instrument also gives the angle of Cloquet.

To speak only of the head: Gerdy asserts that its measurement is commonly limited to 1·11 and 1·33 per cent. of the stature: but he made his measurements in Paris, where there is a mixture of long and short heads; while Quételet made them upon individuals of the Kymri race, that is to say on the long heads, proving the numerous types of proportions.

From the mountains he had
once seen canyons. From the canyons,
mountains. But now, living in Flatland,
the Y Mountains (he once looked up to) or
the X Canyons (he once looked down into)
were so distant that they seemed to be
no more than distant fictions.

rumors of difference

*Ant societies, with castes,
hunting, gathering, agriculture
and slavery, able to organize
themselves into fierce armies.*

The driver and legionary ants are the Huns and Tartars of the Insect world.

WILLIAM MORTON WHEELER
ANTS: THEIR STRUCTURE, DEVELOPMENT AND BEHAVIOR, 1910

In the Land of Fat Free Salad
Dressing—Have it your way!—
31 Flavors, not Wagner

*Or if you prefer,
"Ants, driven by their
genes, organize
themselves into
patterns for
survival."*

and certainly not Nietzsche.
Especially in flatlands of free choice

**Jackie Robinson switch hitting
in the baseball league of the other gene pool.**

where theories were fed on as if they were bread

options as well

Choice being mainly a matter
of eliminating options.

We used LSD on 89 children from Jan 1961 to July 1965 and found that it is one of the most effective methods of treatment we have for childhood schizophrenia.

LAURETTA BENDER, M.D.
NATIONAL INSTITUTE OF MENTAL HEALTH

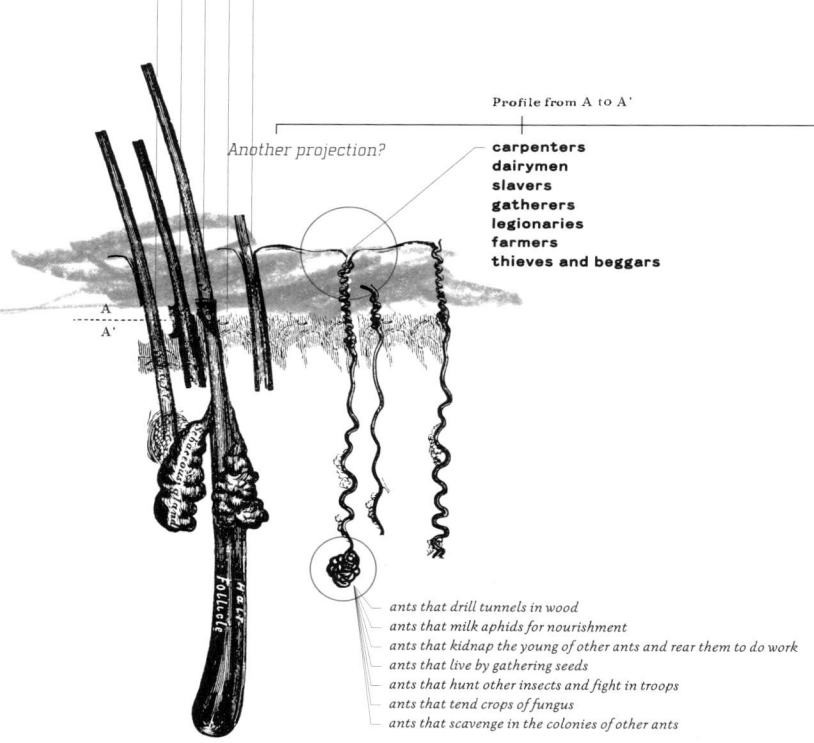

Profile from A to A'

Another projection?

carpenters
dairymen
slavers
gatherers
legionaries
farmers
thieves and beggars

A
A'

— *ants that drill tunnels in wood*
— *ants that milk aphids for nourishment*
— *ants that kidnap the young of other ants and rear them to do work*
— *ants that live by gathering seeds*
— *ants that hunt other insects and fight in troops*
— *ants that tend crops of fungus*
— *ants that scavenge in the colonies of other ants*

FIG. 676.—A sectional view

Were the number of salad
dressings in Flatland one of the
reasons some people found it
so hard to leave institutions?

Where dinner bells and schedules
made choices like that for them?

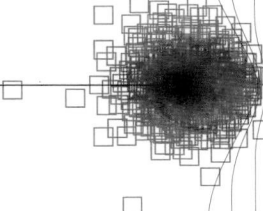

FIG. 677. (magnified)
*A single female ant is
sometimes swarmed by
so many males that
they form a solid ball
around her in their
frantic attempts to
copulate.*

Paradoxically, confusion
and refinement both being proportional to choice

The behavior of insects is sometimes very instructive

In fact, that's how science—a history
of failed theories—progresses.

Classification of mollusks

of ants

A simple story
[if at times confusing]

of fish

of mice and—

THE MATERIAL

2002

Collecting Blood Samples for the Human Genome Diversity Project

Not at all like sitting 1,000 monkeys before
typewriters and hoping they will produce
Don Quixote.

Thousands of species

Progress being like any linear plot

dorylus

Darwin's Plots

cymatium parthenopeum

*not Cervante's
(and certainly not Shahrazad's!)*

Thus the Human Genome Diversity Project
calls on geneticists to systematically collect
10,000 blood samples   **like butterflies**

from as many as possible of the 5,000
populations with distinct languages.

Becoming

rare

5,000 languages being a decrease from
the 6,500 that existed in 1992

Linear plots not being the only
model for change, of course.

parataxis

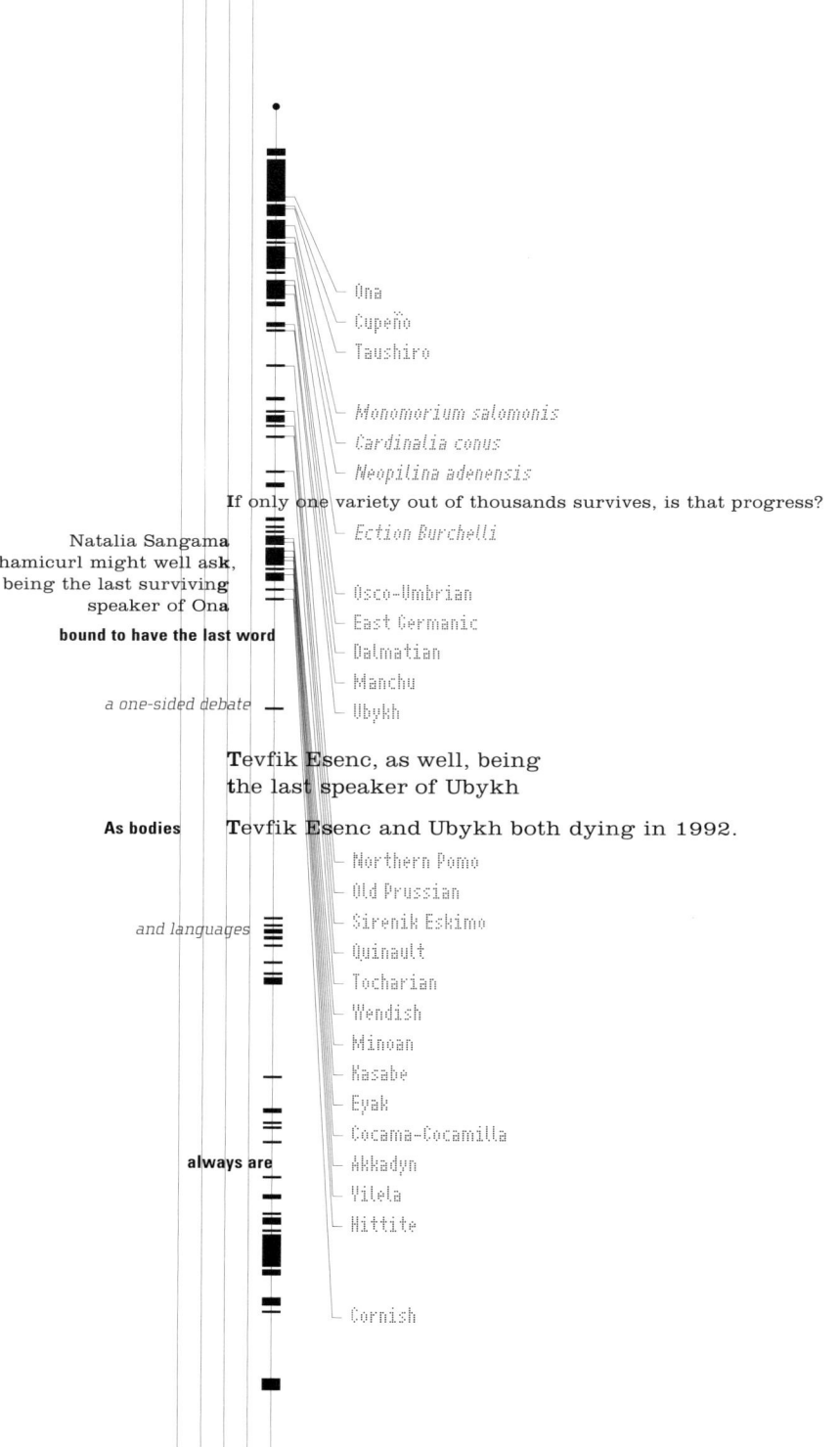

Ona
Cupeño
Taushiro

Monomorium salomonis
Cardinalia conus
Neopilina adenensis

If only one variety out of thousands survives, is that progress?

Ection Burchelli

Natalia Sangama
Chamicurl might well ask,
being the last surviving
speaker of Ona

bound to have the last word

Osco-Umbrian
East Germanic
Dalmatian
Manchu
Ubykh

a one-sided debate

Tevfik Esenc, as well, being
the last speaker of Ubykh

As bodies   Tevfik Esenc and Ubykh both dying in 1992.

Northern Pomo
Old Prussian
and languages   Sirenik Eskimo
Quinault
Tocharian
Wendish
Minoan
Kasabe
Eyak
Cocama-Cocamilla
always are   Akkadyn
Yilela
Hittite

Cornish

Within 90 years, another 3,000
languages are expected to be found
nowhere but in museum display cases

Roscinda Nolasquez (age 94)
and Cupeño (age 20,000) dying
together in California in 1987.

When Truganini died, the Tasmanian
language died with him.

Ishi and Yahi, same deal.

Likewise, only God speaks Kamas,

Ms. Klavdiya Zakharovna Plotnikova,
Kamas's last speaker, having died on
the 20th of September, 1989. ...

Almost 300 a year.

Did English murder Irish?

A victim a day
keeps the linguist away
(and the taxidermist busy)

In the parish cemetery of St. Paul, a grave marker commemorates the death of both Cornish and Dorthy Pentreah, this mother's last native tongue.

Each the equivalent of 1,000 Louvres.

Clichés too

and identity

CWRA PERTHI DE TAZ HA OF MAM....

(forgotten knowledge)

Flatlanders not believing like Medievals that time was the "always ever present."

**The *Neopilina adenensis*
mollusk thought to be extinct**
Survival of the fittest?

**Until a single living member was
found in 1952**

Nor do we believe, like Ovid, that progress
was a steady state of decline.

from a Golden Age...

**Eaten by the
fisherman
who found it**

...when trees had not yet been hollowed out to visit other shores...

Nor do we, as do 648 million Hindus
(among others) order our affairs as if
the universe moved through cycles.

The Neopilina adenensis going extinct (again)

...and men were content at home...

§01.   *A language only being as important as its speakers*:

3.8 Million years ago, an Australopithecus man, woman and child walked across a plain in Tanzania, leaving footprints in ash that hardened, preserving their passage as if to mirror our own... .

100,000 years ago, fifty humans walked out of Africa

[goes one theory]   and colonized Europe.

Like ants

Two thirds of all scientists worldwide now writing in English secreting systems

1864, First words transmitted over the telegraph (English): "What hath God wrought?"

What would science be in a culture that thought the universe was winding down like a watch?

[or a body]   *[or swung like a pendulum]*

1969, First words transmitted over the Internet (English, again): "Log in."

Practically all international business—English

DNA testing
and linguistic   **Eighty** percent of the world's electronically
reconstruction on   retrievable information—English
both sides of
the Bering Strait
show reverse
migrations.

:

... sometimes the man or the woman carried the child, sometimes they leaned against each other for support as they walked through a rain, turning to look back, from time to time, at?—

What?—

As if in doubt

Hard to imagine.

DNA and syllables
always in agreement.

**Lot's Wife (name unknown) not being
a very popular role model**

Ideas of progress

Pillars of society

as ingrained in us as they are.

conservatism.

**Every body needs some
at least .2%**

Even whole societies

Concerning the Inhabitants of Flatland

*The birth of a True Equilateral Triangle from Isosceles parents is the subject
of rejoicing in our country for many furlongs round. After a strict examination
conducted by the Sanitary and Social Board, the infant, if certified as
Regular, is with solemn ceremonial admitted into the class of Equilaterals.
He is then immediately taken from his proud yet sorrowing parents and
adopted by some childless Equilateral, who is bound by oath never to permit
the child henceforth to enter his former home or so much as to look upon his
relations again, for fear lest the freshly developed organism may, by force of
unconscious imitation, fall back again into his hereditary level.*

EDWIN A. ABBOTT
FLATLAND: A ROMANCE OF MANY DIMENSIONS, 1884

SCIENCE ROCKS

EXPERIMENT No.9 **GROWING REGULAR CRYSTALS**

Leave a paper clip suspended in a glass full of water saturated with salt. After a few days, look at it again, especially the new growths. Can you tell what you've created?

Why look back?
Science being as familiar as it is to us.

Change ≠ Life   *Salt flats being the flattest of lands*

Unlike fossilized
     lake beds
        phager
     Latin....

Progress in science
being as familiar as it is to us—a pattern.

*Living language is to unchanging Latin as swimming
fish is to the fossilized outline of a phager*

L ⊃ C
Patterns constituting the fastest vehicles for change.

**Sea turtles always come
ashore with tears in their eyes**

We—the pattern-making monkey—
just assume it—take it for nature, even.

excreting

Like the following sentence—

Try to mutate the word **APE** into the word **MAN**.

—whose words can be arranged into 3,628,800 combinations, only two of which make sense
both symmetrical

human tears
that colorless blood

Think of it, 90% of the languages used today–vanished.

also tasting of salt

Even if a million monkeys banged away randomly on a million typewriters they couldn't pull it off.

leaving only the fossils.

ClNaClNaClNaClNaClNaClNaClNaClNaClNaClNaClNaClNaClNaClNaClNaCl
NaClNaClNaClNaClNaClNaClNaClNaClNaClNaClNaClNaClNaClNaClNaClNa
ClNaClNaClNaClNaClNaClNaClNaClNaClNaClNaClNaClNaClNaClNaClNaCl
NaClNaClNaClNaClNaClNaClNaClNaClNaClNaClNaClNaClNaClNaClNaClNa
ClNaClNaClNaClNaClNaClNaClNaClNaClNaClNaClNaClNaClNaClNaClNaCl
NaClNaClNaClNaClNaClNaClNaClNaClNaClNaClNaClNaClNaClNaClNaClNa
ClNaClNaClNaClNaClNaClNaClNaClNaClNaClNaClNaClNaClNaClNaClNaCl
NaClNaClNaClNaClNaClNaClNaClNaClNaClNaClNaClNaClNaClNaClNaClNa
NaClNaClNaClNaClNaClNaClNaClNaClNaClNaClNaClNaClNaClNaClNaClNa
ClNaClNaClNaClNaClNaClNaClNaClNaClNaClNaClNaClNaClNaClNaClNaCl
ClNaClNaClNaClNaClNaClNaClNaClNaClNaClNaClNaClNaClNaClNaClNaCl
NaClNaClNaClNaClNaClNaClNaClNaClNaClNaClNaClNaClNaClNaClNaClNa
ClNaClNaClNaClNaClNaClNaClNaClNaClNaClNaClNaClNaClNaClNaClNaCl
NaClNaClNaClNaClNaClNaClNaClNaClNaClNaClNaClNaClNaClNaClNaClNa
ClNaClNaClNaClNaClNaClNaClNaClNaClNaClNaClNaClNaClNaClNaClNaCl
NaClNaClNaClNaClNaClNaClNaClNaClNaClNaClNaClNaClNaClNaClNaClNa
ClNaClNaClNaClNaClNaClNaClNaClNaClNaClNaClNaClNaClNaClNaClNaClN
ClNaClNaClNaClNaClNaClNaClNaClNaClNaClNaClNaClNaClNaClNaClNaCl
NaClNaClNaClNaClNaClNaClNaClNaClNaClNaClNaClNaClNaClNaClNaClNa
NaClNaClNaClNaClNaClNaClNaClNaClNaClNaClNaClNaClNaClNaClNaClNa
ClNaClNaClNaClNaClNaClNaClNaClNaClNaClNaClNaClNaClNaClNaClNaCl
NaClNaClNaClNaClNaClNa

5'... ClNaClNaClNaClNaClNa **A LINEAR PLOT...**   **APE   ARE**   *BONG*

ClNaClNaClNaClNaClNaClNaClNaClNaClNaClNaClNaClNaClNaClNaClNaCl
NaClNaClNaClNaClNaClNaClNaClNaClNaClNaClNaClNaClNaClNaClNaClNa
ClNaClNaClNaClNaClNaClNaClNaClNaClNaClNaClNaClNaClNaClNaClNaCl
NaClNaClNaClNaClNaClNaClNaClNaClNaClNaClNaClNaClNaClNaClNaClNa
ClNaClNaClNaClNaClNaClNaClNaClNaClNaClNaClNaClNaClNaClNaClNaCl
NaClNaClNaClNaClNaClNaClNaClNaClNaClNaClNaClNaClNaClNaClNaClNa
ClNaClNaClNaClNaClNaClNaClNaClNaClNaClNaClNaClNaClNaClNaClNaCl
NaClNaClNaClNaClNaClNaClNaClNaClNaClNaClNaClNaClNaClNaClNaClNa
ClNaClNaClNaClNaClNaClNaClNaClNaClNaClNaClNaClNaClNaClNaClNaCl
NaClNaClNaClNaClNaClNaClNaClNaClNaClNaClNaClNaClNaClNaClNaClNa
ClNaClNaClNaClNaClNaClNaClNaClNaClNaClNaClNaClNaClNaClNaClNaCl
NaClNaClNaClNaClNaClNaClNaClNaClNaClNaClNaClNaClNaClNaClNaClNa
ClNaClNaClNaClNaClNaClNaClNaClNaClNaClNaClNaClNaClNaClNaClNaCl

Cliches

Progress in science, that is, achieved
by eliminating from study those problems
that do not have scientific solutions.

Cradle to grave

But if every intermediate step must make sense

an interlocking logic

III.	*IIII.*	*V.*	*VI.*	*VII.*	*VIII.*	
ARM	**AIM**	**DIM**	**DAM**	**RAM**	**RAN**	**MAN.** ...3'

then the change can be made in eight generations

History being written by the victor, of course.

In this case?

Homoerectus?

A pattern **Science?**

English?

Did I mention that 437 animal species exhibit homosexual behavior?

(presumably this would include typing monkeys)

People, too, of course.

Not mollusks

Alice learned this in Wonderland.

This is why it was so important to preserve
in petri dishes a cross section of the genetic
material of vanishing tribes.

Mollusks being hermaphrodites

10,000 blood samples

symmetry
again

Among other things.

5,000 languages

Scientific solutions being those that could
be demonstrated objectively.

Is it possible to step outside your own diorama?

Bodies being as amendable as they are.

Your own plot?

The history-making animal
the Larynx-using animal

salty, sweaty, stink

Objectivity being the elimination of personal bias.

*Dioramas about tool makers always saying
more about makers of dioramas*

A pattern

And institutional bias.

And racial bias. And class prejudices.
And religious beliefs. And gender predispositions.
And national sentiment. And social standing.
And peer pressure. And monetary considerations.
And historical bias (such as a belief in progress)
or concern for personal recognition—even those
operating unconsciously.

Especially those operating unconsciously.

When the Hottentot Venus died, the brighter minds among us had the foresight to preserve her materials for future study.

GEORGES CUVIER
FATHER OF NATURAL HISTORY

This is the problem in identifying the gene(s) that
causes homosexuality.[1] Or the gene(s) that causes
laziness[2] or aggression, lack of empathy and

---

[1] Hamer, Dean H., et. al. "Evidence for Homosexuality Gene" in *Science*, July 16, 1993.

[2] Concar, David. "High Anxiety and Lazy Genes" in *New Science*, December 7, 1996.

foresight[3] or I.Q.[4] or sociability of women[5] or
sexual assault against women[6] or general
criminal tendencies[7] or scholastic achievement[8]
or defective personalities[9] or flexibility[10] or
obesity[11] or broad thumbs[12] or shyness[13] or
academic honesty[14] or intelligence[17] or altrusim[18]
or sexual infidelity[19] or meanness[20] or zest for
life[21] or industrial inefficiency[22] or frequency of
copulation[23] or selfishness[24] or social and economic

[3] Whitney, Glayde in *Mankind Quarterly*, 1995.

[4] Constance, Holden. "On the Trail of Genes for I.Q." in *Science*, Vol. 253, 1991.

[5] Skuse, David et al. "Evidence from Turner's Syndrome of an Imprinted X-linked Locus Affecting Cognitive Functions" in *Nature*, June 12, 1997.

[6] Thornhill, Randy. *A Natural History of Rape: Biological Bases of Sexual Coercion.* Cambridge: MIT Press, 2000.

[7] Bohman, M. et al. "Clear Evidence of Genes Associated with Criminal Behavior" in *Archive of Genetic Psychiatry*, Vol. 39. 1982. Bock, G.R. and J.A. Goode. *Genetics of Criminal and Antisocial Behavior.* Chinchester, UK: Wiley, 1996.

[8] Petrill, Stephen A. and Lee Anne Thompson. "The Phenotypic and Genetic Relationship Among Measures of Cognitive Ability, Temperament and Scholastic Achievement" in *Behavior Genetics*, Vol. 23, No. 6, 1993.

[9] Cloninger, R.C. et al., "Predisposition to Petty Criminality in Swedish Adoptees. II. Cross-Fostering Analysis of Gene-Environment Interaction" in *Archive of Genetic Psychiatry*, Vol. 39, 1982.

[10] Rusalov, V.M. and S.D. Biryukov "Human Behavior Flexibility: A Psychogenetic Study" in *Behavior Genetics*, Vol. 23, No. 5, 1993.

[11] Cummings, David E. et al. "Genetically Lean Mice and Morbid Human Obesity" in *Nature*, August 1996.

[12] "Genetic Regulation Defect" in *Nature*, August 1995.

[13] Brunner, H.G. et al. "Shyness and Hay Fever Linked" in *Science*, 1993. Cherney, S.S. and Monoamine Chen, D.W. Faulker, et al. "Continuity and Change in Infant Shyness" in *Behavior Genetics*, Vol. 24, No. 4, 1994.

[14] Footnotes always a ventriloquist act that speaks authority/truth.[15]

[15] Unless they are used to undermine a claim to "authority/truth."[16]

[16] (quote marks, same deal (as are parenthesis)).

[17] Jensen, A. R. "How Much Can We Boost IQ and Scholastic Achievement?" in *Harvard Educational Review*, Vol. 33, 1969.

[18] Hamilton, W.D. "Genes and Altruism" in *The Cambridge Encyclopedia of Human Evolution.* Steve Jones, ed. Cambridge: Cambridge University Press, 1992.

[19] Trivers, Robert. "The Evolution of Reciprocal Altruism" in *Quarterly Review of Biology*, Vol. 46, 1971.

[20] Hen, Rene. "Mean Genes" in *Neuron*, Vol. 16, 1996.

[21] Hur, Yoon-mi and Thomas J. Bouchard, Jr. "The Genetic Correlation Between Impulsivity and Sensation Seeking Traits" in *Behavior Genetics*, Vol. 27, No. 5, 1997.

[22] Aschaffenburg, Gustav. *Das Verbrechen und seine Bekämpfung.* Heidelberg, 1906.

[23] Bogaert, Anthony F. and William A. Fisher. "Predictors of University Men's Number of Sexual Partners" in *The Journal of Sex Research*, Vol. 32, 1995. See also Hamer and Copeland and Wright.

Isn't it odd how footnotes make a thing seem more scientific?—just the way phrenologists gave all their concepts Latinate names in the hopes that their narratives would morph into classical learning?

[24] Dawkins, R. *The Selfish Gene*, 2nd ed. Oxford: Oxford University Press, 1989.

standing[25] or novelty seeking/traditionalism[26] or
rape[27] or pauperism and shiftlessness[28] or sexual
promiscuity[29] or drapetomania (pathological
running away among slaves) or nomadism[30] or
smoking[31] or drinking among Orientals[32] or
church attendance[33] or humanness[34] or errors in
math homework[35] or positive emotionality[36] or
gambling[37] or divorce[38] or homelessness[39] or direction
of shell spiral in mollusks[40] or schizophrenia[41] or

[25] Burt, Cyril Lodowic, Sir. *The Subnormal Mind*, Oxford University Press, 1935.

[26] Koopmans, Judith R. and Dorret I. Boomsma, Andrew C. Heath, et al. "A Multivariant Genetic Analysis of Sensation Seeking" in *Behavior Genetics*, Vol. 25, No. 4, 1995.

[27] Hook, E.B. "Behavioral Implications of the Human XYY Genotype" in *Science*, Vol. 179, 1973.

[28] Goddard, Henry Herbert. *The Kallikak Family, A Study of the Heredity of Feeble-Mindedness.* NY: Pantheon, 1912.

[29] Wright, Robert. *The Moral Animal.* NY: Pantheon, 1994.

[30] Davenport, Charles, pres. *A Decade of Progress in Eugenics: Scientific Papers of the Third International Congress of Eugenics Held at American Museum of Natural History.* Baltimore. Williams & Williams, 1934. See also the records of the Eugenics Records Office, Charles Davenport, Professor of Evolutionary Biology, Harvard.

[31] Heath, Andrew C., et al. "Personality and the Inheritance of Smoking Behavior: A Genetic Perspective" in *Behavior Genetics*, Vol. 25, No. 2, March 1995.

[32] Guang-Chou Tu and Yedy Israel "Alcohol Consumption by Orientals in North America is Predicted Largely by a Single Gene" in *Behavior Genetics*, Vol. 25, Jan. 1995.

[33] Loehlin, John C. "Nature, Nurture and Conservatism in the Australian Twin Study" in *Behavior Genetics*, Vol. 23, No. 3, 1993.

[34] Gibbons, Ann. "Which of Our Genes Makes Us Human" in *Science*, Sept 4, 1998.

[35] Knopick, Valerie, Maricela Alarocon and John C. DeFries. "Comonbidity Mathematics and Reading Deficists: Evidence for a Genetic Etiology" in *Behavior Genetics*, Vol. 27, No. 5, 1997.

[36] Depue, Richard A. and Monica Luciana, et al. "Dopamine and the Structure of Personality: Relation of Agonist-Induced Dopamine Activity to Positive Emotionality" in *Journal of Personality and Social Psychology*, Vol. 67, 1994.

[37] Blaszczynski, A.P., et al. "Sensation Seeking and Pathological Gambling" in *British Journal of Addiction*, Vol. 81, 1986.

[38] Hamer, Dean and Peter Copeland. *Living with Our Genes.* NY: Doubleday, 1998.

[39] Koshland, Daniel E., Jr. "Sequences and Consequences of the Human Genome" in *Science*, Oct 13, 1989.

[40] Vermeij, George J. *A Natural History of Shells.* Princeton University Press, 1993.

[41] Defined variously as "incomplete personality" or "too many personalities" or "mastabatory insanity" or as a catch word for "anyone undesirable," caused by "nature" (genes) or "nurture" (culture). Kallmann, Franz, [who also fled Nazis] "The Genetic Theory of Schizophrenia," in *American Journal of Psychiatry*, Vol. 103, 1946. Over the years other candidates have been proposed.[42]

[42] Marshall, Richard. "The Genetics of Schizophrenia Revisited" in *Bulletin of the British Psychological Society*, Vol. 37, 1984.

[43] Entine, Jon. *Taboo: Why Black Atheletes Dominate Sports and Why We're Afraid to Talk about It.* NY: Public Affairs, 2000.

[44] Thomassen, H.R. et al. "Alcohol and Aldehyde Dehydrogenase Genotypes and Alcoholism in Chinese Men" in *American Journal of Human Genetics*, Vol. 48, 1991.

Explaining why so few sea captains are women, Charles Davenport, Director of the Eugenics Record Office in New York, demonstrated in 1919 that the ability to be a naval officer was inherited from 2 genes: a "thalassophilia gene," the love of the sea, and a "hyperkineticism gene" for wanderlust.

Of course the wanderlust gene failed to explain why so few runaway slaves became sea captains.

rather, the question was never asked

a matter of selection

Amaaea raricostata

When Mr. Bakewell demonstrated that the volume of a skull varied within races more than between races, he moved on to more meaningful criteria: arm length, the peritoneum, the ileo-caecal appendix, the larynx, and especially Blood globules...

a matter of larynx

DR. PAUL TOPINARD

butterflies

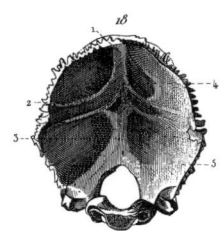

TABLE,

Showing the Size of the Brain in cubic inches, as obtained from the measurement of 623 Crania of various Races and Families of Man.

RACES AND FAMILIES.	No. of Skulls.	Largest I. C.	Smallest I. C.	Mean.
MODERN CAUCASIAN GROUP.				
TEUTONIC FAMILY.				
Germans,	18	114	70	} 92
English,	5	105	91	
Anglo-Americans,	7	97	82	
PELASGIC FAMILY.				
Persians,	} 10	94	75	
Armenians,				
Circassians,				
CELTIC FAMILY.				
Native Irish,	6	97	78	
INDOSTANIC FAMILY.				
Bengalees, &c.	32	91	67	
SEMITIC FAMILY.				
Arabs,	3	98	84	
NILOTIC FAMILY.				
Fellahs, ...	17	96	66	
ANCIENT CAUCASIAN GROUP.				
From the Catacombs. PELASGIC FAMILY. Græco-Egyptians,	18	97	74	
NILOTIC FAMILY. Egyptians,	55	96	68	
MONGOLIAN GROUP.				
CHINESE FAMILY.	6	91	70	
MALAY GROUP.				
MALAYAN FAMILY.	20	97	68	} 85
POLYNESIAN FAMILY.	3	84	82	
AMERICAN GROUP.				
TOLTECAN FAMILY.				
Peruvians,	155	101	58	} 79
Mexicans,	22	92	67	
BARBAROUS TRIBES.				
Iroquois,				
Lenapé,	161	104	70	
Cherokee,				
Shoshoné, &c.				
NEGRO GROUP.				
NATIVE AFRICAN FAMILY.	62	99	65	} 83
AMERICAN-BORN NEGROES.	12	89	73	
HOTTENTOT FAMILY.	1	83	68	
ALFORIAN FAMILY.				
Australians,	8	83	63	

Take schizophrenia, for example. Scientists have been unable to agree upon the gene(s) that cause(s) schizophrenia(s) because they have been unable to agree upon what symptom(s) they should call schizophrenia(s).

Every word was once an animal.

RALPH WALDO EMERSON

Repeatability (**a pattern**) being a tenant of objectivity, this is obviously a problem.

Patterns not always obvious

It's a matter of discriminating.

Between
    animals and words

    salt flats and syllables

Between good science and bad.

between a social construction and madness

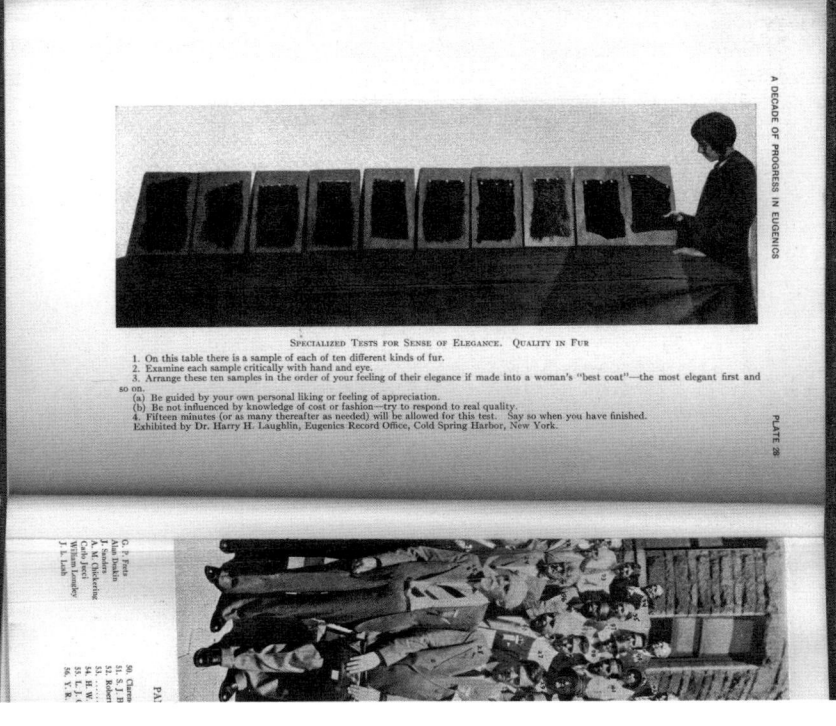

Specialized Tests for Sense of Elegance. Quality in Fur

1. On this table there is a sample of each of ten different kinds of fur.
2. Examine each sample critically with hand and eye.
3. Arrange these ten samples in the order of your feeling of their elegance if made into a woman's "best coat"—the most elegant first and so on.
(a) Be guided by your own personal liking or feeling of appreciation.
(b) Be not influenced by knowledge of cost or fashion—try to respond to real quality.
4. Fifteen minutes (or as many thereafter as needed) will be allowed for this test. Say so when you have finished.
Exhibited by Dr. Harry H. Laughlin, Eugenics Record Office, Cold Spring Harbor, New York.

PLATE 26

And old science and new.

The rapid growth of the feeble-minded classes coupled as it is with steady reduction among all superior stocks constitutes a race danger which should be cut off before another year has passed.

WINSTON CHURCHILL

And new science and politics.

And scientists and politicians from organs
of their century.

Limpieza de Sangre (Purification of the Blood)
was what the Kings of Spain called keeping Spain
Spanish
    i.e. ~~Moors~~
~~Jews.~~

Surely there are fashions in thought.
    Just as there are fashions in neckties.
Ethnic cleansing, another age might call it.
    Negative eugenics.

A pattern
old snakes in new skins

And rewriting your body seemed natural, suddenly.

    (the future, also)

By delet——

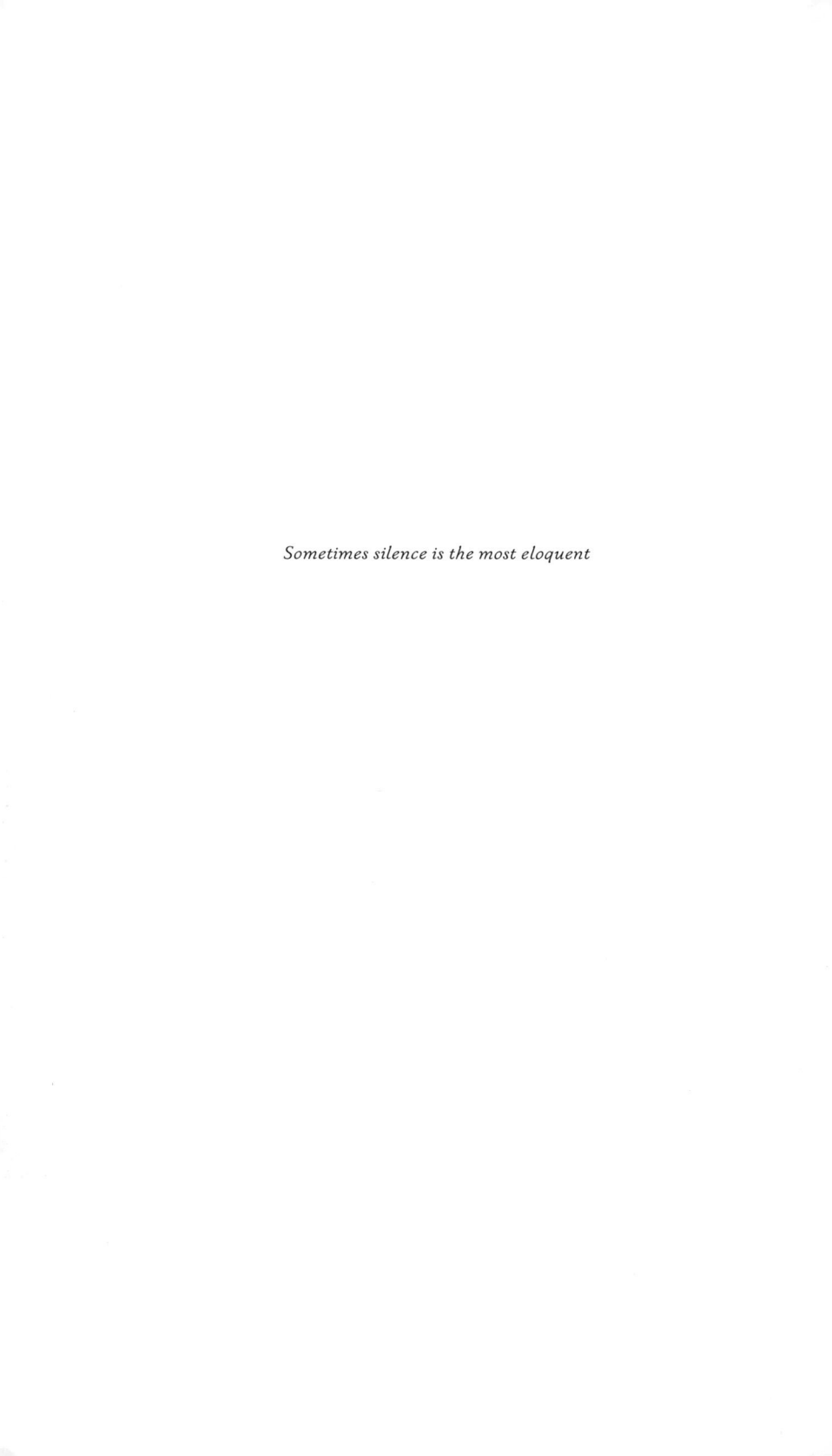

Sometimes silence is the most eloquent

I. **spake**

II.

III.

IIII.

V.

VI.

Old words die out.

Races too

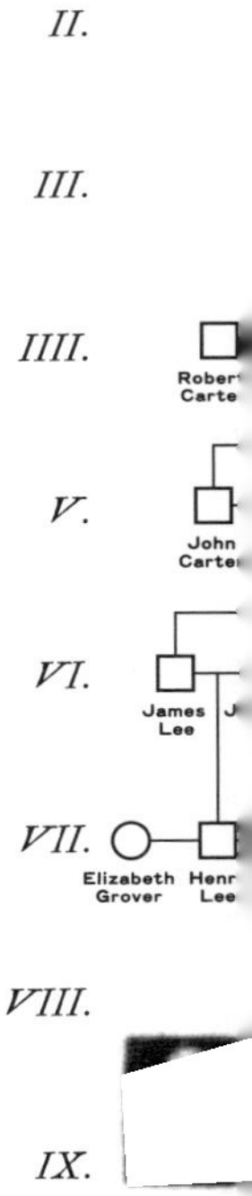

VII.

VIII.

IX.

New
words,
like
fools,
rush
in.   *insert fig. A*

Existing words change their meaning
[the material]
insert fig. C

Mainly unconsciously.
A pattern

So maybe instead of a fashion, I should have
called it an involuntary tic
[or institutionalization]

Ideas only being as important as their languages.

How else explain the fact that the sciences are
chock full of Latinate terms with their connotations
of classical wisdom?
insert fig. G

How else explain the fact that the study of humans
became chock full of math with its connotations
of objectivity?
insert fig. T

Jarvic Heart

fig. A

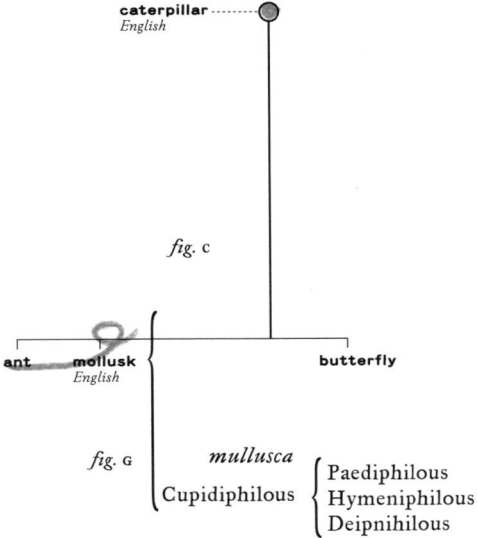

caterpillar
English

fig. C

ant **mollusk**
English

butterfly

fig. G

$$\left\{ \begin{array}{l} \textit{mullusca} \\ \text{Cupidiphilous} \end{array} \right. \left\{ \begin{array}{l} \text{Paediphilous} \\ \text{Hymeniphilous} \\ \text{Deipnihilous} \end{array} \right.$$

$$\text{SOCIAL COOPERATION} = p \, \frac{dx}{A} \cdot dU \, \frac{(x,t)}{dt}$$

fig. T

How else explain the many simultaneous and
independent discoveries in science?

Or Periods in Art?

Or the Great Vowel Shift

Like a mass rumba step

that made Chaucer's English a foreign language
to our ear?

A Common Ancestor

*A common
pattern*

Or the fact that so many nations adopted
forced sterilization at about the same time:

XIII.	Iceland	Estonia	Finland	Sweden	Denmark	Norway	Cana
	(1938)	(1936)	(1935)	(1934)	(1934)	(1934)	(1933)
	x	x	x	x	x	x	x

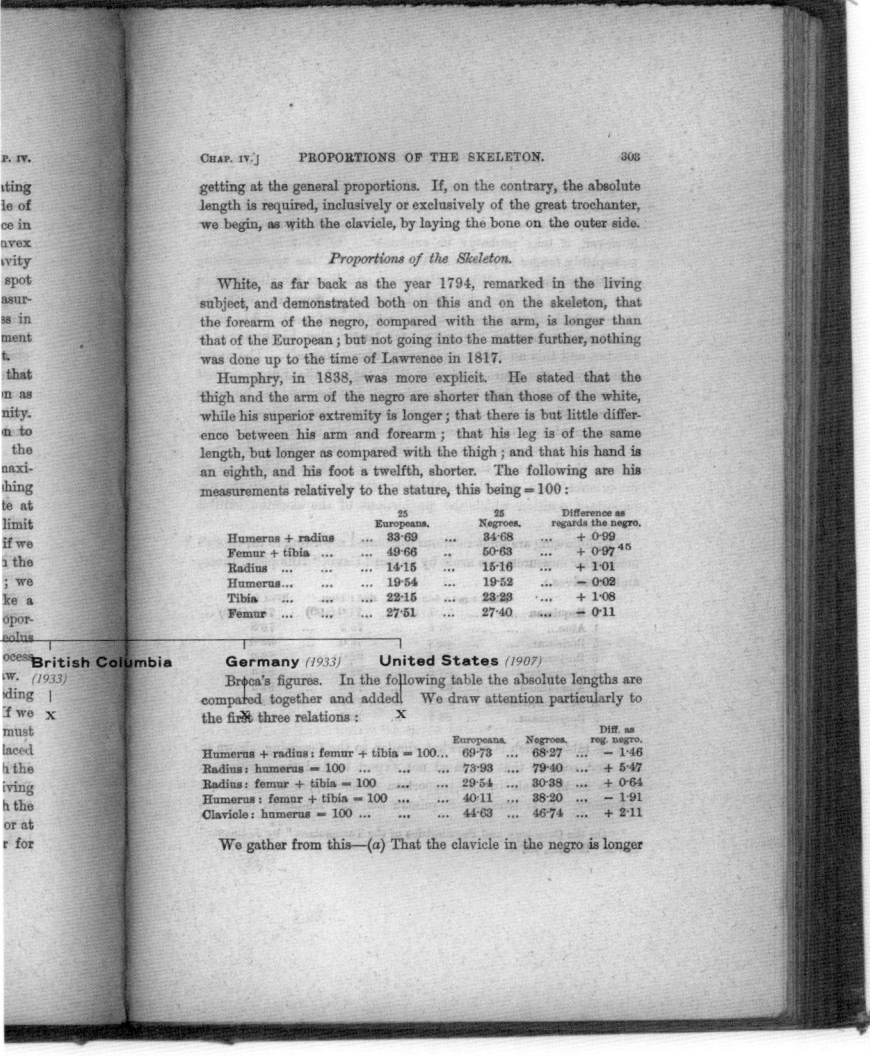

getting at the general proportions. If, on the contrary, the absolute length is required, inclusively or exclusively of the great trochanter, we begin, as with the clavicle, by laying the bone on the outer side.

Proportions of the Skeleton.

White, as far back as the year 1794, remarked in the living subject, and demonstrated both on this and on the skeleton, that the forearm of the negro, compared with the arm, is longer than that of the European; but not going into the matter further, nothing was done up to the time of Lawrence in 1817.

Humphry, in 1838, was more explicit. He stated that the thigh and the arm of the negro are shorter than those of the white, while his superior extremity is longer; that there is but little difference between his arm and forearm; that his leg is of the same length, but longer as compared with the thigh; and that his hand is an eighth, and his foot a twelfth, shorter. The following are his measurements relatively to the stature, this being = 100:

	25 Europeans.	25 Negroes.	Difference as regards the negro.
Humerus + radius	33·69	34·68	+ 0·99
Femur + tibia	49·66	50·63	+ 0·97 [45]
Radius	14·15	15·16	+ 1·01
Humerus	19·54	19·52	− 0·02
Tibia	22·15	23·23	+ 1·08
Femur	27·51	27·40	− 0·11

British Columbia *(1933)*   **Germany** *(1933)*   **United States** *(1907)*

Broca's figures. In the following table the absolute lengths are compared together and added. We draw attention particularly to the first three relations:

	Europeans.	Negroes.	Diff. as reg. negro.
Humerus + radius : femur + tibia = 100...	69·73	68·27	− 1·46
Radius : humerus = 100	73·93	79·40	+ 5·47
Radius : femur + tibia = 100	29·54	30·38	+ 0·64
Humerus : femur + tibia = 100	40·11	38·20	− 1·91
Clavicle : humerus = 100	44·63	46·74	+ 2·11

We gather from this—(a) That the clavicle in the negro is longer

---

[45] *Note:* Difference as regards the Hottentot Venus, + 1·21.

Forced sterilization seemed
like the scientific thing to do

to improve the gene pool.

The gene pool needing improvement, obviously.

right from the beginning

The immediate objectives are the total destruction and devastation of [Indian] settlements. It will be essential to ruin their crops in the ground and prevent their planting more.

PRESIDENT GEORGE WASHINGTON
SLAVE OWNER

Adam being an amoebae

FAMILY
PEDIGREE SHO

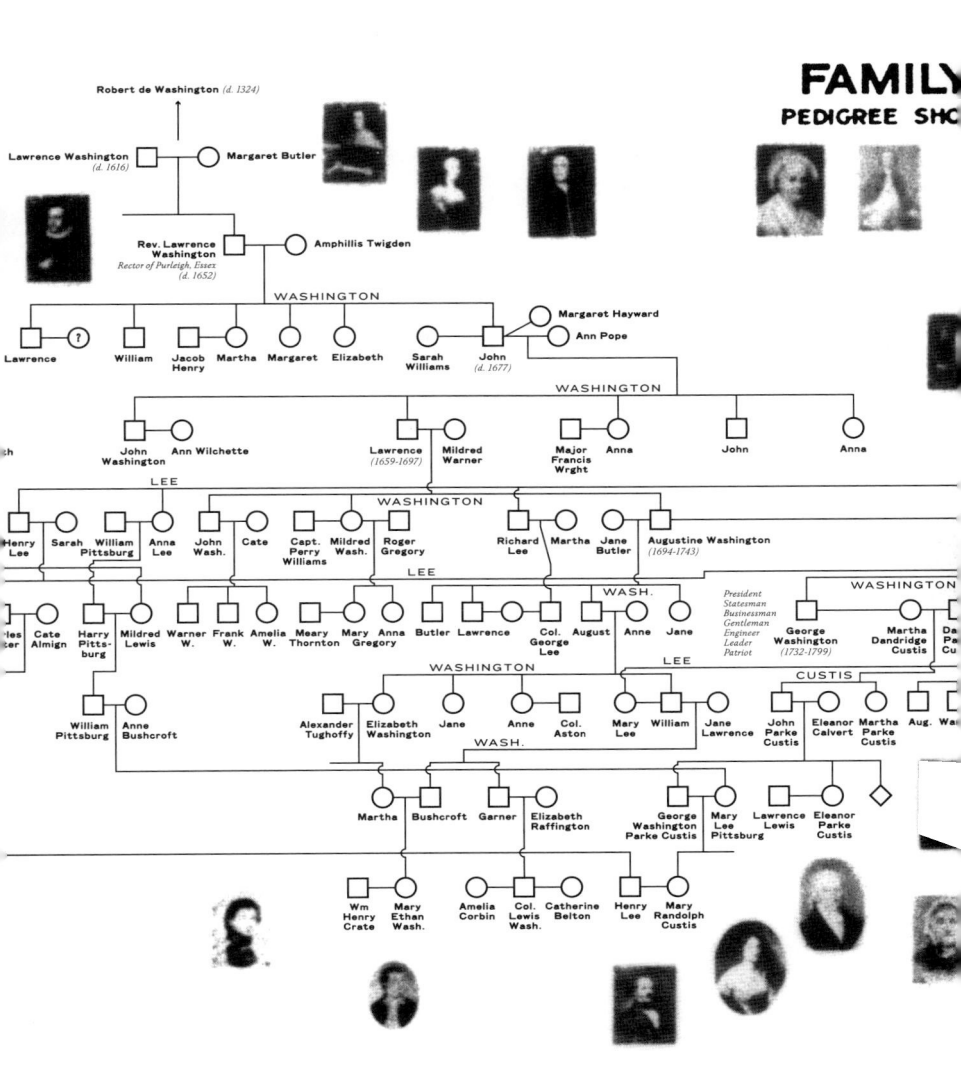

Robert de Washington *(d. 1324)*

Lawrence Washington *(d. 1616)* — Margaret Butler

Rev. Lawrence Washington *Rector of Purleigh, Essex (d. 1652)* — Amphillis Twigden

WASHINGTON

Lawrence | William | Jacob Henry | Martha | Margaret | Elizabeth | Sarah Williams | John *(d. 1677)* — Margaret Hayward / Ann Pope

WASHINGTON

John Washington — Ann Wilchette | Lawrence *(1659-1697)* — Mildred Warner | Major Francis Wrght — Anna | John | Anna

LEE
WASHINGTON

Henry Lee | Sarah — William Pittsburg | Anna Lee | John Wash. — Cate | Capt. Perry Williams — Mildred Wash. | Roger Gregory | Richard Lee | Martha — Jane Butler | Augustine Washington *(1694-1743)*

LEE
WASH.
WASHINGTON

President Statesman Businessman Gentleman Engineer Leader Patriot

rles ter | Cate Almign | Harry Pitts-burg | Mildred Lewis | Warner W. | Frank W. | Amelia | Meary Thornton | Mary Gregory | Anna | Butler | Lawrence | Col. George Lee | August | Anne | Jane | George Washington *(1732-1799)* | Martha Dandridge Custis | Da Pa Cu

WASHINGTON
LEE
CUSTIS

William Pittsburg — Anne Bushcroft | Alexander Tughoffy | Elizabeth Washington | Jane | Anne | Col. Aston | Mary Lee | William | Jane Lawrence | John Parke Custis | Eleanor Calvert | Martha Parke Custis | Aug. Wa

WASH.

Martha | Bushcroft | Garner | Elizabeth Raffington | George Washington Parke Custis | Mary Lee Pittsburg | Lawrence Lewis | Eleanor Parke Custis

Wm Henry Crate | Mary Ethan Wash. | Amelia Corbin | Col. Lewis Wash. | Catherine Belton | Henry Lee | Mary Randolph Custis

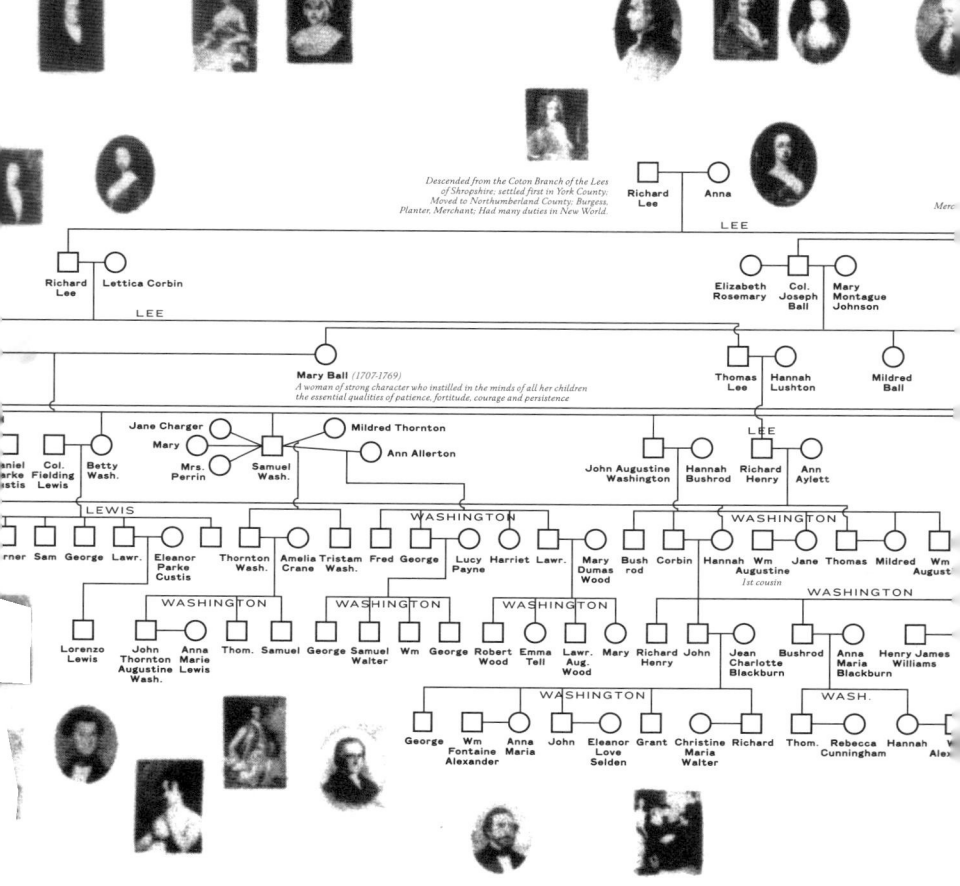

Y STOCK OF GEORGE WASHINGTON

OWING THE HEREDITARY STUFF OUT OF WHICH HIS FAMILY WAS MADE

Descended from the Coton Branch of the Lees of Shropshire; settled first in York County; Moved to Northumberland County; Burgess, Planter, Merchant; Had many duties in New World.

Richard Lee — Anna

LEE

Richard Lee — Lettica Corbin

LEE

Elizabeth Rosemary — Col. Joseph Ball — Mary Montague Johnson

Mary Ball *(1707-1769)*
A woman of strong character who instilled in the minds of all her children the essential qualities of patience, fortitude, courage and persistence

Thomas Lee — Hannah Lushton

Mildred Ball

Jane Charger — Mary — Mrs. Perrin — Samuel Wash.

Mildred Thornton — Ann Allerton

John Augustine Washington — Hannah Bushrod — Richard Henry — Ann Aylett

LEE

LEWIS

aniel arke ustis — Col. Fielding Lewis — Betty Wash.

WASHINGTON

rner Sam — George — Lawr. — Eleanor Parke Custis — Thornton Wash. — Amelia Crane — Tristam Wash. — Fred — George — Lucy Payne — Harriet — Lawr. — Mary Dumas Wood — Bush rod — Corbin — Hannah — Wm Augustine *1st cousin* — Jane — Thomas — Mildred — Wm August

WASHINGTON

WASHINGTON

Lorenzo Lewis — John Thornton Augustine Wash. — Anna Marie Lewis — Thom. — Samuel — George — Samuel Walter — Wm — George — Robert Wood — Emma Tell — Lawr. Aug. Wood — Mary — Richard Henry — John — Jean Charlotte Blackburn — Bushrod — Anna Maria Blackburn — Henry James Williams

WASHINGTON

WASH.

George — Wm Fontaine Alexander — Anna Maria — John — Eleanor Love Selden — Grant — Christine Maria Walter — Richard — Thom. — Rebecca Cunningham — Hannah — Alex

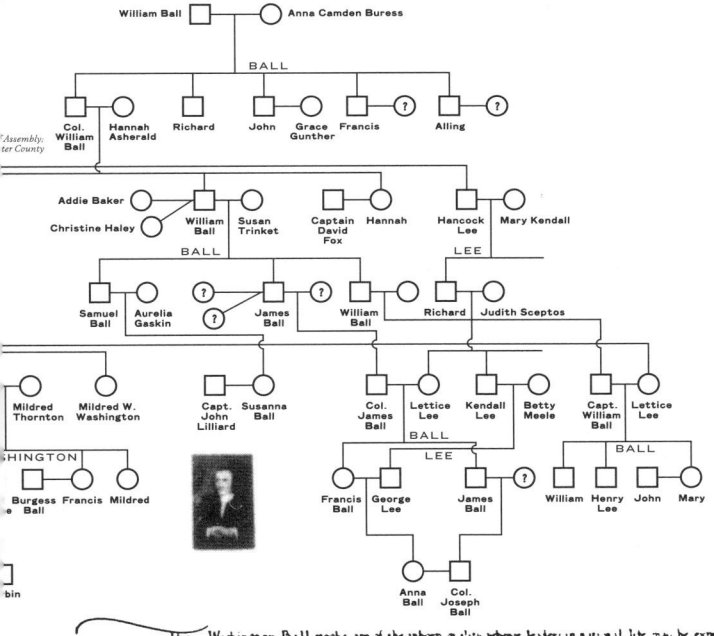

William Ball □——○ Anna Camden Buress

BALL

Col. William Ball — Hannah Asherald | Richard | John — Grace Gunther | Francis — (?) | Alling — (?)

Addie Baker / Christine Haley — William Ball — Susan Trinket | Captain David Fox — Hannah | Hancock Lee — Mary Kendall

BALL **LEE**

Samuel Ball — Aurelia Gaskin | (?) — James Ball — (?) | William Ball | Richard — Judith Sceptos

Mildred Thornton | Mildred W. Washington | Capt. John Lilliard — Susanna Ball | Col. James Ball — Lettice Lee | Kendall Lee | Betty Meele | Capt. William Ball — Lettice Lee

HINGTON **BALL** **LEE** **BALL**

Burgess Ball | Francis | Mildred e Ball | Francis Ball | George Lee | James Ball — (?) | William | Henry Lee | John | Mary

bin

Anna Ball — Col. Joseph Ball

The Washington-Ball stocks are of the inborn quality whence leaders in national life may be expected to arise. that is such stocks as carr... the essential elements which in rare and fortunate combinations produce high capacity. No man appreciated family stock values more highly th... did George Washington. This is exemplified by his prizing and utilizing superior seeds and plant stock for his fields and orchards and by his acqui... and increasing the best bred livestock which he could secure in America and Europe. He valued in his fellow men the qualities of fortitude, honesty, courage, common sense, good business ability, initiative, faith sacrifice, patriotism, love of nature, the manly spor... physical prowess and skill, and elegant living,- in short, character and intelligence. These qualities come basically from sound and superi... human stocks,- regardless of present fortunes. these are the inborn traits upon which education and opportunity must build in order... make effective men. Eugenics is concerned with the increase of such inborn capacities in the family stocks of future generations.

Dog howls.

Fire engines wailed, their bells clanging
furiously out of sync with the walking-pace
of the engines themselves. Main Street in Red,
White and Blue. All up and down, the parade
route was aflutter with toy-sized American flags—
Statistically proven nothing at all like the gargantuan banners of
Nazi Germany. Square couldn't even remember
the last time he'd seen soldiers in a Fourth of
July parade. Instead, these once-upon-a-time
displays of curiosities and wonders—G.I. Joes
who had actually stormed Iwo Jima, cowboys
on horseback—had become a celebration
of cornball, a sign of security in this, one
of the few suburbs in Flatland wealthy and
educated enough to keep up the tradition
(with a wink) of small-town spectacles turned
oxymoronic (by satellites and cell phones).

Native Americans jingled by in rain dance,
the applause they received louder every year in
proportion to the increasing value of their stock.
A people only being as important as their language.

Unlike Shriners who over the years were
increasingly watched in uncomprehending
silence, Shriners becoming iffy with their
cult-like hats and goofiness.

1st National Bank said the balloon Square had
gotten down the block, its stars and stripes
The language of already shrinking from loss of air. He waved it in
bankers still more front of Circle who smiled her too-sweet smile,
important than then grabbed it away and looked straight ahead,
smoke signals. arms crossed as if she'd just confiscated a toy
from a child.

The dog behind them snarled at a clown on a unicycle. White fangs, ears pinned back: a pure-bred without a collar. Every few minutes, the boy who owned the dog put it in a headlock to keep it from going after a float.

Around them, five million glands per body sweat. Because her blood had been "low," Mother had stayed home, too tired to make the effort. Oval wilted on the curb, fanning herself with an I'm a Jan Fan! It had been stuck in her hand by one of the dozens of cheerleaders (nothing at all like Hitler's brown-shirted youths) wearing *I'm a Jan Fan!* tee-shirts as they worked the curb, marching alongside Jan Liebowitz, Congresswoman District 23, waving and smiling the straight-toothed grin of a Fitter-Family contestant.

Another float for Jesus rolled by, all tissue rainbows and hallelujahs (nothing at all like missiles pulled by military trucks). Applause rose up from the far side of the street but no one near Square and Circle clapped. It didn't seem as if Fourth of July parades used to have so many politicians. Or preachers. But all of the gross features of the past had been overgrown by the present: across the street, weathered brick work still spelled out Civic Opera House high above the modern facade of an 8-Plex. And in place of Judy's Beauty Salon there was now a Tattoo and Body Piercing Parlor. It wasn't as if the street had gone seedy, though. The tattoo parlor was more franchise-clean than the adjoining 31 Flavors. While next door to that, in a building that a Flatland Historical Society plaque said once housed the formaldehyde stink and cigar smoke of old Doc Eastwood, there was now the corporately-sleek Family Center for Reproductive Services.

When Square first moved to Flatland, he used
to play a game with himself whenever he drove
past: he'd try to guess from the people coming and
going if the place was a fertility or an abortion
clinic. Then he and Circle had been referred, and
he was one of those people, reading a *People* in a
reception room of a clinic that offered both of those
services—and a lot more. Why had he thought the
two incompatible? Wasn't the clinic just an
extension of the hospital down the street?
—where the parade began?....

The sound of drums drew nearer.
A story that was downright pedestrian

"Live music," Square said, trying to interest Oval.
As if to confirm that "it wouldn't be as good as TV,"
previous bands had simply mimicked MTV in lock-
step to music that blared from enormous speakers
on trailers they pulled behind like tails. But
now the trill of fifes pierced the heat. A wave of
applause—three thousand hands slapping—carried
a banner into view: *Flatland Women's League*.
Behind it marched women in period costume,
Susan B. Anthony, said the sign one carried.
Women's Suffrage, said another. *Elaine Showalter*.
They threw candy.

lition that
rmal con-

e family.
acteristic,
increasing
by night
ation was

lear. An
not marry
of retini-
k, cousins,
no means

alopia). —
no loss of
et the af-
king. Ar-
s very in-
ce in guid-
trains, the
a retinitis.
in and not
l purple of

Nettleship
that is the
ny disease.
roduced in
(colored)

rmals lack
be duplex

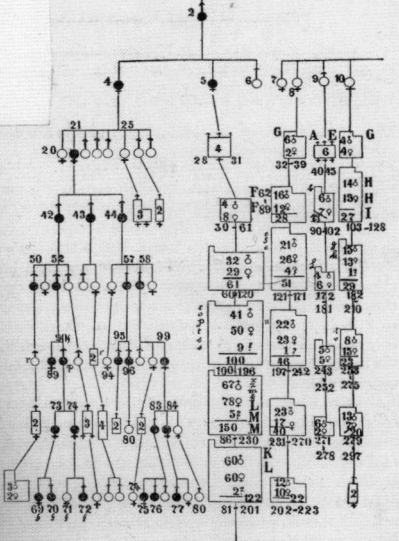

Fig. 86.—Pedigree of chart of an European strain with night blindness (black symbols). The rectangles indicate numerous normal individuals. Two normal parents have only normal children. Nettleship, 1907, from Grüber and Rudin, 1911.

Circle put the balloon under her arms so she could add her applause to the clapping of those around her. The crowd on the opposite side of the street remained mute this time, though it seemed to be the same mix of white-haired ladies in lawn chairs and middle managers and their families that surrounded Square and his.

"When will it be over?" Oval sighed. A Tootsie-Roll skidded up to the candy already at her feet. Candy littered the street, the throwing of candy having evolved into another empty form, the kids who used to dart out from the curb to scoop it up another casualty of prosperity and changing times. In fact, there hardly were any kids younger than Oval. And even her.... She sat with her ankles crossed, legs a wishbone, reminding Square that he'd meant to speak to Circle. Wasn't it time their daughter started sitting like a lady?

I'm a Dan Fan, said tee-shirts worn by the next group, tumblers passing out Dan Rosstenkowski (Republican) fans.

Then the Flatland Theater Troupe turned the street into a "hippie-in." They swung love beads, chasing each other in Dashikis and other period costumes. Enormous papier-mâchè heads. One with a bong flew in circles with the aid of a pulley contraption set high on scaffolding.

Hair.

A Pro-Choice float, another crowd pleaser, followed and again the people on Square's side of the street applauded loudly. A few boos came from across the street this time, anxiety causing the nostrils and mouth to pucker and the expiration of breath to sound the vowel 'O'. But the boos only increased the pitch of those who were cheering, their own determination to stand their ground contracting all the muscles of the body in a manner that often caused defecation, drawn lips, transforming howls into screeches as a signal to unify the troop into an "attack shadow" behind the actual combatants.

Once, Circle would have whistled her approval, putting fingers to lips to do so. Now Square couldn't help but notice how polite her applause had become—indistinguishable from the way she applauded Special Olympians, or the city librarians pushing book carts in serpentine patterns (nothing at all like interlocked goose-stepping formations). It wasn't as if she'd changed her politics, he knew, it was just that after having had the procedure done to her, it no longer seemed like a thing to cheer about. Even if she was glad it was legal.

The dog growled, barking and snapping at the noise.

Suddenly the people on the far side of the street began to cheer too. Cheer wildly. **RESPECT LIFE** For the good of society. loomed up, the huge letters erected on the flatbed of a truck that honked a deafening air horn, hoots and displays of bared teeth or the penis being reciprocal threat gestures. As the truck slowly rolled by, the back of the float revealed itself to be a gigantic papier-mâché fetus with a bulbous head. A man dressed like the Grim Reaper pantomimed hacking through its umbilical cord with a scythe.

"Ugh! That's such bad taste," Circle said. The people around Square were the ones who were booing now—Angrily—their escalation of vocal displays nearing the threshold where chest beating could crest into the throwing of feces.

An explosion of water drenched the Grim Reaper. Someone had lofted a water balloon at him and he had turned just in time to receive it full in the face. Dripping blond hair, the way he shook made him look like an angry duck. People laughed, including Circle. Then her face froze. The Grim Reaper was pointing his scythe directly at the balloon in her hand. "Who threw that!" he yelled, hoping off the float. Candy rained down on the people around Square like a volley of Brazil nuts pitched from trees on the far side of the street. "Ouch!" "Hey, that hurt!"

The Grim Reaper raised his scythe menacingly as he approached.

Circle went as rigid as the rabbit that has been shaded by the hawk, or the deer startled by the snap of a twig. On the cusp of fight or flight, her muscles contracted, fists clenching, her abdomen flattening to protect inner organs, her face going pale to reduce bleeding from wounds to come. "Do something!" she yelled at Square.

And in that swirling moment of candy and scythes, he said, "Huh?"

Oval snatched up the candy at her feet. With a windup
that shocked Square for its maleness, she pitched it
at the man, stunning him into a shielding posture.
Following as a troop the first movement of its
dominant leaders, people on both sides of the street
began shouting. More firecrackers. The dog launched
itself into the Grim Reaper's black robes. Snarling,
it shook him violently.

Regarding mollusks, there are over 100,000 varieties.

Regarding people, as Hermann Muller,
geneticist and 1962 Nobel Laureate put it:

*Probably close to 20 percent of the population... have inherited a genetic
defect. ... To avoid genetic degeneration, then, that 20 percent should not
be allowed to reach sexual maturity.*

The difference being that differences in mollusks were
seen as variation not deformity and classifying them—

As J.B.S. Haldane said of eliminating human variation,

*Once you deem it desirable to begin, it is a little difficult to know where
you are to stop.*[45]

---

[45] *Heredity and Politics*. London: n.p., 1938.

"**W**ell what did you want me to do?" Square
protested on the way home.

"**N**othing. The next time a lunatic with an ax…"

"**I**t was cardboard—"

"…**c**omes after me…

"**A**nd it was a scythe, not an ax."

"…**j**ust sit on your thumb!"

Oval snapped her gum, looking out vacantly at
the passing Flatland-side.

In fact, The Committee for the Scientific Treatment
of Severe Genetically Determined Illness began, in
1939, to "relieve the suffering" of deformed mollusks
up to the age of three….

For the good of the patients.

…**b**ut by 1941 it became apparent that they had been
over cautious and broadened their guidelines
to include four to seventeen-year-olds.

In America, the Land of 1001 Salad Dressings,
elimination of difference was left up to the states.

Only 30 out of 49 adopted forced sterilization.

the rest carrying on without a law
just as classifying mollusks was neither illegal nor legal.

it's only natural

Often, mollusks were even given a choice.

Scalpel/padded cell.

(an unseen history)

As for today?—

I have no idea about the number of sterilizations approved by courts today because there is no reporting mechanism.

CALIFORNIA STATE COMMISSION ON STERILIZATION OF PEOPLE
WITH MENTAL DISABILITIES *1995*

The Virginia law was even challenged.

All the way to the Supreme Court.

Which agreed with the inhabitants of Edwin Abbott's
Flatland that the toleration of an Irregularity
was incompatible with the sobriety of the State.

And that sterilization was like vaccination.

And that mental-health facilities should
continue vaccinating those who failed an IQ test...

...as well as epileptics...
Aplacophra

...and the antisocial:
Polyplacophora

unwed mothers,
prostitutes,

Monoplocophora
alcoholics,
Scaphopoda the sexually promiscuous,

Gastropoda
petty criminals, *Palmontala*
children with disciplinary problems,

over 25 thousand and other hereditary diseases.
customers

snipped in the bud
For the good of the patients.

"   "   "   " society.

40,000 species of snails alone

Numerous investigations have shown that this group makes a very slight contribution to the lists of genius.

STATE COMMISSIONER OF CALIFORNIA

Smart people had figured it out.

The "homeless" didn't yet exist.

Geniuses, even.

Mensa: A society of geniuses

says IQ tests.

variations on a theme

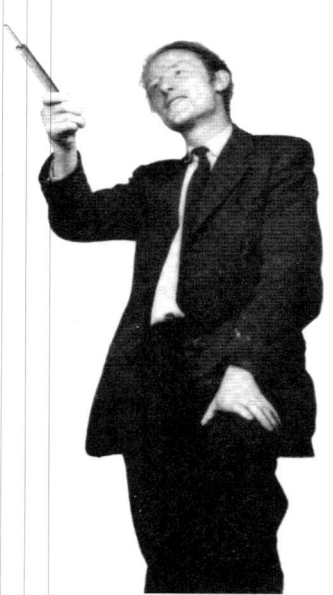

It would not be difficult for governments to add something to the food supply which would prevent procreation. ...The government could keep another substance at hand which would counteract the effects of the first one, and only people whose procreation is desired could receive it...

DR. FRANCIS CRICK
Nobel laureate and co-discoverer of DNA

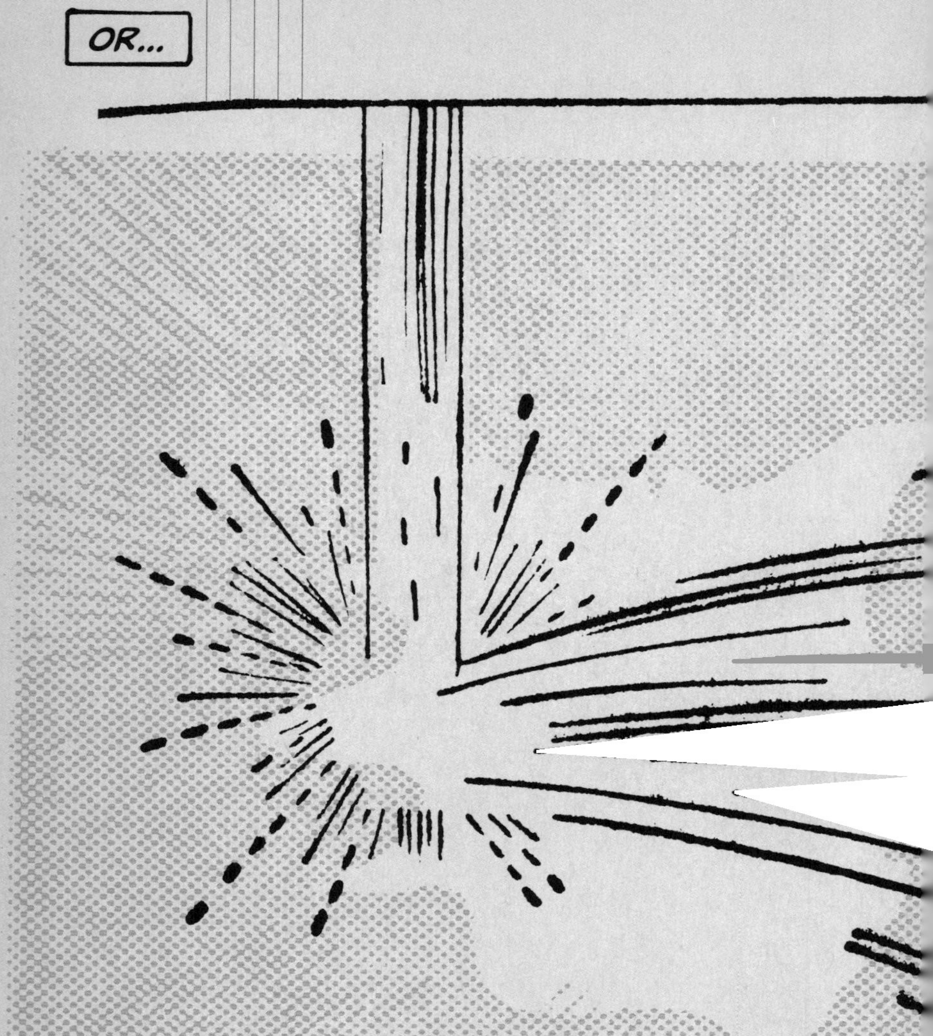
OR...

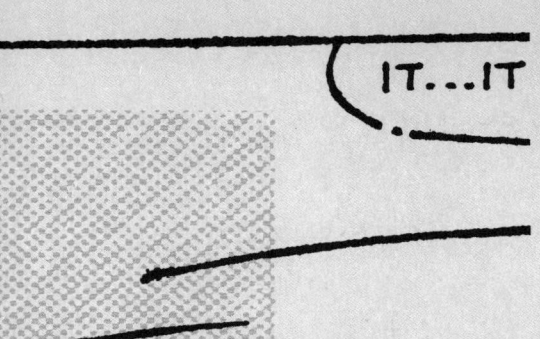

IT...IT

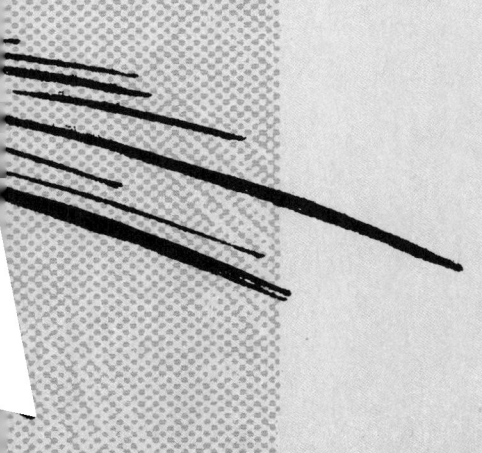

IT WOULD **NOT BE DIFFICULT** FOR GOVERNMENTS TO ADD SOMETHING TO THE FOOD SUPPLY WHICH WOULD **PREVENT PROCREATION**--THE GOVERNMENT COULD KEEP ANOTHER SUBSTANCE AT HAND WHICH WOULD **COUNTERACT** THE EFFECTS OF THE FIRST ONE, AND ONLY PEOPLE WHOSE PROCREATION IS **DESIRED** COULD RECEIVE IT!...

CONTINUED ON FOLLOWING PAGE

A tremendous step forward.

each individual carrying its house on its back

Mensa's Mission: *To identify and foster human intelligence for the benefit of humanity.*

each house also being its skeleton

a pillar of society

For the good of society.

though some mollusks take up residence in the empty shells of the dead

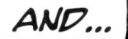

What he meant was that the good of the patient and the good of the society were one and the same.

As any cost/benefit analysis would show. ...

the same shell being reused

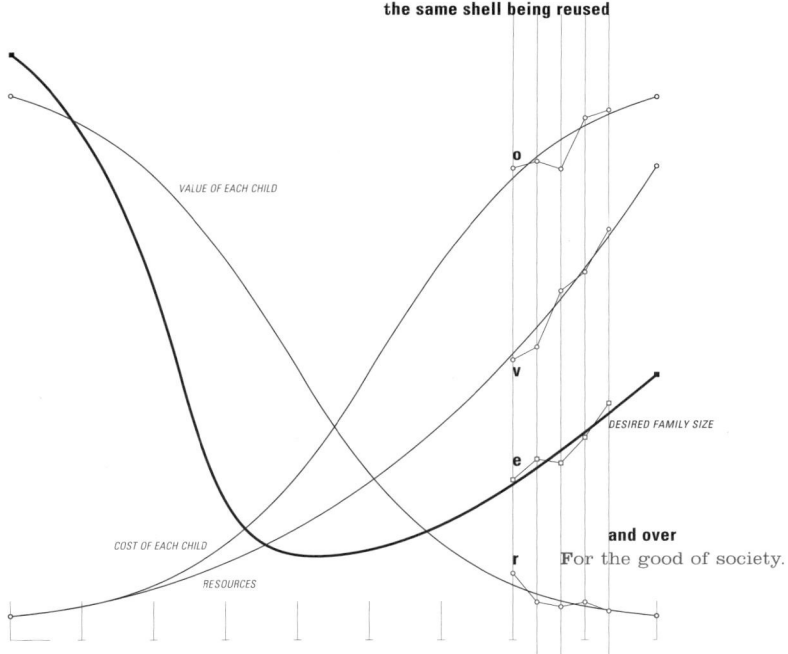

VALUE OF EACH CHILD

o

v

e

DESIRED FAMILY SIZE

COST OF EACH CHILD

RESOURCES

r

and over
For the good of society.

That's why British Mensa members
were once asked how to improve society.

In 1962, 47% recommended the legalized killing of "sufficiently unhealthy or subnormal infants."

Mollusks without shells being the most vulnerable.

over and over

With the scalpel inserted up a nostril, twist it around and around until the frontal lobe is reduced to the consistency of mashed potatoes; patients may exhibit an "apathetic attitude" for some time, but this effect is only temporary.

DR. EGAS MONIZ
NOBEL LAUREATE IN MEDICINE, 1949, AND INVENTOR OF FRONTAL LOBOTOMY

In 1994, Mensa members advocated the extermination of the homeless, retarded and elderly.

Mollusks with shells being the most likely to survive,

obviously.

over and over

Still, in America, we believe in choice.

Even if shells straight-jacket movement

This is why State Institutions often
sought out "volunteers."

and growth

**the living shells of mollusks always
growing in a clockwise spiral**

except for deviants

German diagnostic techniques being more advanced, German researchers were able to identify more subtle pathologies

the same pattern

counterclockwise

only different

such as "endogenous work-shyness"

whereby genetically lazy

or unemployed people

No one has written more idealistically about mankind than Dr. Goebbels.

KNUT HAMSUN
NOBEL LAUREATE IN LITERATURE, 1920.

(another genius)

were marked for removal from society.

over and over

Also those with

"camouflaged feeblemindedness,"
a type of
feeblemindedness that hides behind
a mask of cleverness.

Clockwise: *laciniaria*

counterclockwise: *radix peregra*

clockwise: *partula*

350,000 sterilizations.
Over 10 years

Each shell growing outward like rings of a tree—

(surely a fad as passé as wide neckties)

—a record of daily life, made as
it is by the mollusk's daily diet

1998:
Would-be immigrants to Germany must submit to
a genetic test to verify their claim of Germanness.

A lot of daily records forming a story of sea life, as well

Along with their application, a saliva sample
is taken for such purposes.

A mollusk shell growing by spiraling outward at a constant angle.

"Germanness" in Germany being genetic,
obviously.

a timeline of sorts,

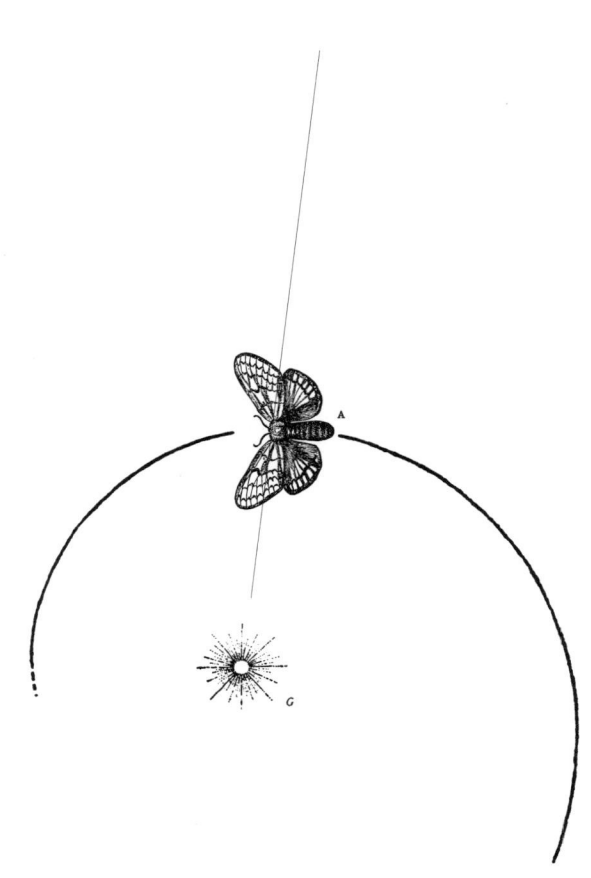

only coiled

Like a clock spring spiraling out from its shaft.

Of course, there is always a danger that one
group of people might begin to see the entire
world through the lens of their specialization?

**The way moths navigate by fixing
their eyes at an 80° angle to the sun.**

over and over   Just as there is always the danger that makers
of dioramas might see the world through the
lens of their time?

Even when the "sun" is actually a candle flame.

Was it just a coincidence that both Michelangelo and Kepler
placed the Son/Sun at the center of a geometric universe?

Candle flames and suns sometimes appearing the same size

over and over

Specialization

to a moth

being a function of history, of course.

Is this why Einstein claimed space was curved?

Unless it's biology.

**Even as their fixed and unvarying
system for navigation causes
them to spiral in.**

over and over

Is this why Pope Paul V refused to look through Galileo's telescope?

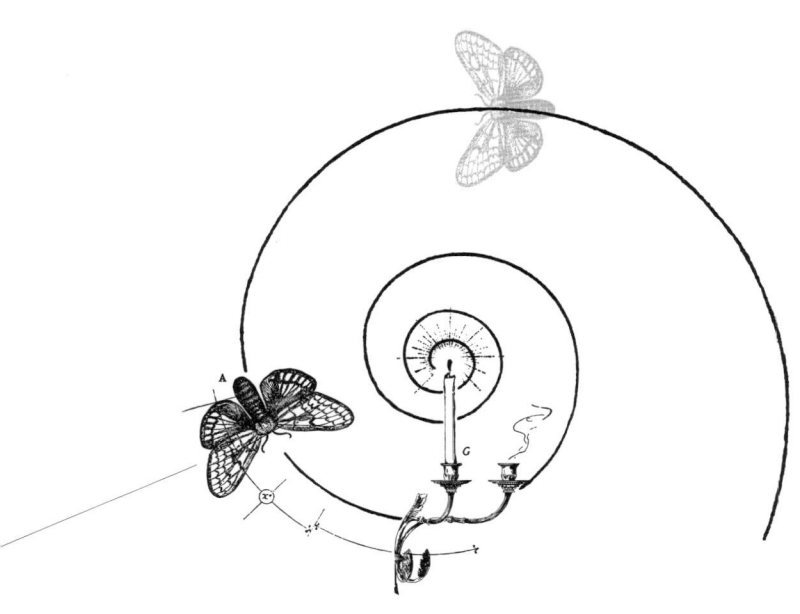

Like one U.S. Health Department
proposal to assign all children a personal
computer code number by which they
could be tracked for the rest of their life.
*Since the expectation is that every child will be found to have at
least one of the 3,548 mental illnesses listed in the reference book,
it said, there is no code for normal.*

Normal being men in white lab coats.

**But if space was curved, later astronomers determined,
parallel rays of light would eventually cross.**

If the number of normal children were graphed, their lin

A rocket travelling in a straight line would return to its origin.

Since
**parallel rays don't and rockets can't,
those astronomers concluded,
the universe**

must be

uld look less like

flat.

than

OR...   A FLAT LINE

*After all,
if a person turned Galileo's telescope
end-for-end and looked through it, wouldn't an
elephant appear to be the size of an ant?*

Still, It Moves

In a flatland.

Doubtless, there are many flatlands.

EPPUR, SI MU○VE

Aprile An: M DCXIII · à GALILEO G.L.

"Hello," Circle said, answering the phone in the
kitchen. Then her face went motionless (nature),
the way it had when the Grim Reaper hopped off
his truck to come after her. Her breath froze
(as they say in novels). She became so focused on
the tiny electronic voice in her ear that Square
also went oblivious to the noise of Oval playing
in the next room, the blare of the TV. His mouth
dried at the sudden fear in her eyes—that ancient
hello between hunter and hunted. But since
technology had placed a screen between her
and whatever was in pursuit this time, she fixed
her gaze on him, her hormones also putting his
on alert through a crystallization of purpose,
her tone flashing news of danger faster than
words. In the doorway, the cat arched its back.
Square got up from his sandwich and went closer,
tightening their troop of two. Circle held her
composure, the way she did whenever there
was a real problem (culture).

"Yes. Yes," she said, maintaining a professional
steadiness. "Yes, I understand. We'll be right there.
Thank you."

She hung up. "Mother's in the hospital."

Proving the existence of ant-sized elephants?
As well as

garden-variety

stars?

...of bodies changed to different forms...

OVID, *METAMORPHOSES*

How odd, thought Square, to realize that your mother-in-law is a cyborg.

She rested comfortably in her hospital bed, receiving a transfusion to "get my blood up" after having fainted in a mall. She'd never fainted before. Then to do so in the scary open-endedness of a public place.... Circle and Oval stood at the sides of her bed, each holding a hand as pale as the sheets Mother lay swaddled in while they looked down to her with the tableau pity of an eighteenth-century painting: *The Cyborg.*

(some things never change)

"I told you there was something wrong with my blood," Mother chirped, happy that the fainting spell had vindicated her. She still wore her makeup and the pallor of her face made her red lips look artificial and stuck on. Mrs. Potato Head. "Now maybe you'll see what I was talking about."

"Mom," Circle said, "we never thought there wasn't something wrong."

"But you never believed me when I said it was serious."

She hadn't always been a cyborg. Her body had
gone through most of its useful life without any
machine parts. Then Square was reading about
a future where the brains of people were infused the stones became
with nanobots the size of blood cells that made men and women...
whole libraries of digital information part of their our bones proof of what
mind's neurobiology. Robots, for increased dexterity, we have come from...
received human hands grown from the bellies of
hogs, and all of this the natural flowering of
the first cyborg,[46] a lab rat fitted with a tiny
pump that injected a continuous flow of
chemicals: an enhancement any human would
need to survive the hostile environment of deep
space. Or the Blood Ward of a hospital.

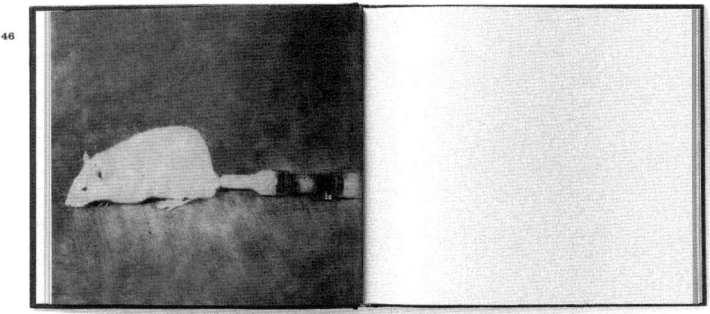

46

"Now maybe I've got your attention."

Before she'd become a cyborg, Mother's continual
testing and blood treatments had been torture.
Her arms were mottled with bruises inflicted by
nurses puncturing them over and over to find
her hair-line veins. Her platelet IV would leak,
wet the tape that held it in place, then fall out
and the ordeal would begin again. Sometimes
she couldn't even sleep for fear of getting "pin-
cushioned" (Pavlov's dog). Then one sunny morning,
the doctor stopped in, not with any explanation for
her "bad blood," but with a new offer: a synthetic
sponginess that could be surgically implanted
in her shoulder to serve as an interface between
her body and the equipment they used to draw
blood from and put chemicals into her veins.
Then, Oh happy day! After the operation, getting
her blood up, having it drawn and replaced via
an IV or any machine was as easy as plugging
an extension cord into an outlet. And even though
she was now part machine, it had been so natural.
So welcome.

The IV pump purred, its digital readout
metering a drip that ran down tubing
and into her shoulder, the flesh color of
the implant making it difficult to tell where
it began and she ended.

...at first she could not
believe that these were
parts of her own body...

smart people had figured it out

This was how it always went, Square realized.
First a procedure was tried out on the dying
or otherwise desperate who were grateful
for the peace. Then everyone wanted it for
the convenience. For the improvement.
Pleasure, even. Recreational sex.

(like steroids)

"Christ, I miss my old body," he sighed
and everyone looked at him. "Nothing,"
he muttered.

Circle rolled her eyes—she wasn't going to baby
anyone who hadn't undergone any procedures,
he could see.

Still, looking at Mother and her synthetic port,
looking at Oval's young limbs, he felt like such
a dinosaur. With a dinosaur's biology.

Another Form:

Please indicate your gene pool:

White (not of Hispanic origin) □
Black (not of Hispanic origin) □
Asian or Pacific Islander □
American Indian or Alaskan Native □
Hispanic (including Black individuals whose origins are Hispanic) □

How many times have you filled out a form like this?
It becomes routine.

Even natural.

Forms, laws, attitudes, manners....
Coherence, no matter where you....

step
small steps

common as feet
logical too

Like testing to "prevent native morons from breeding,"
as the Department of Health put it in 1920.

Native morons being 89.0% black.
Or 47.3% of the whites in the army.

Testing to "keep out inferior foreign stock" as well.
Naturally.

a common sentiment.

The Foreign Feeble-Minded being:

87% of the Russians
83% of the Jews
80% of the Hungarians
79% of the Italians
according to IQ tests administered to immigrants at Ellis Island

§149. Square slowly drove up to the next intersection and killed the engine. The driver of the other car was already standing there, a pinched frown declaring that she was as fed up as he was with arguing over who would get to go first and for a moment he considered just giving in. But no, damn it, he'd already given in at the last three intersections and it was his turn. Before he managed to get out from behind the wheel, though, the other driver whined, "I was here first!" As if that gave her right of way. As if he was so stupid. And the bickering began: He was older, he said; she was younger, she answered; her car was newer; his was cleaner; she was cleaner; he had more money; she was in a bigger hurry; his blood pressure was higher; her blood was bluer....

Those walking past, the ones who had given up entirely on driving, mocked them. "Get a horse!" Still Square and the woman battled on. She said she had more taste; he said, it was in her mouth. Suddenly, horror of horror, a third car approached. They began bickering furiously, hoping the other would bend before the third party arrived and made the negotiations hopelessly complicated.

Looking down the street, Square could see another argument in full heat. And beyond that another. The din from these fights and the thousands like them that were surely being fought out at every street corner across the country seemed to rise like a blister between earth and sky and he longed to be able to move about without having to consider every permutation of every variable at every turn....

Suddenly he found himself——

Was he?—— He wasn't sure at first but each step confirmed that, yes, he was abandoning his car!

A great cheer went up from the walkers when they saw him coming their way. Instead of being glad that he was giving up, the woman began swearing at him violently, "Come back, you quitter and bed wetter!" Her hatred only made him walk faster. As he neared the curb, walkers reached out to shake his hand, he thought, and he extended his own hand to them only to find himself in the grip of dozens of hands pulling him up among them. Before he realized what was happening, he was at the center of a crowd, having his back slapped in congratulations. The great crush of walkers who were trying to touch him began to move down the sidewalk, carrying him along. As they did, a whole new world opened all around: a world of joggers and mail carriers, and hikers. An organ grinder and his monkey tipped their fezzes in greeting.

I wish very much that the many people could be prevented entirely from breeding... The emphasis should be laid on getting desirable people to breed.

PRESIDENT THEODORE ROOSEVELT

"If allowed to breed, they would clog the wheels of human progress," as Henry H. Goddard, a father of American IQ testing, put it.

and make the nation darker
Obviously.
Like a recessive gene that could reappear in later generations.

"Statistics make a marvelous lens for seeing social facts," he also said.

Another social fact being that the European peoples were mixtures of three original races: Nordics, a race of soldiers, organizers and aristocrats who were self-reliant, so usually Protestants; Alpines, who were submissive to authority, so usually Roman Catholics; and Mediterraneans, "The perfect slave, the ideal serf."

a global problem

Still is

A shared assumption.

As opposed to the much more recent Human Genome Diversity Project which found the European gene pool was comprised of 65% Chinese and 35% African genes.

A collection of blood samples.
(the material)

In fact, in 1995 the People's Republic of China instituted the Eugenic and Health Protection Act to eliminate "inferior births," a serious problem among "the old revolutionary base, ethnic minorities, the frontier and economically poor areas."

It's only natural.

The further he was carried along, though, the more he found himself among walkers who didn't know what a heroic thing he had done. Back on his own feet, he was jostled about like a leaf in a wind. Other walkers ran into him, walking as they did with their eyes bent down to the sidewalk against the wind. But Square didn't care. Moving within their chaos, each step on his toes, each stranger's rude shove made more apparent what a sham his old life had been. For though he had grown up believing he could drive anywhere, the open-endedness of walking made prison bars of the lines he had once been forced to drive between. He became drunk with walking, and wanted to do so everywhere he had never been able to drive——as if all his life he had believed the world to be flat and then, instead of falling off its edge when he crossed that curb, he had discovered himself to have always have been on a sphere! He went up staircases——more numerous than roads!——and down garden paths. He developed a vocabulary of ambles, strolls, canters, jogs, sprints——compared to the speeds he had been forced to maintain as a driver, as often as not by fellow drivers, tailgating him when he went too slow or getting in the way if he went too fast——and he wondered what it was that had made him think he'd been free at all. Buffeted about, his state of haphazard happiness remained unbroken until his feet carried him to his destination and he remembered why he had set out from home that day to begin with: Grace Funeral Parlor——and the arrangements for his mother's burial.

How is it that Flatlanders could come to take
1001 salad dressings as a given?

(that 1001 salad dressings could speak "freedom"?)

How can the natural way to test an adulterer's
guilt in Afghanistan come to be knocking a brick
wall on top of him?

...mineie Moe

if he lives
let him go!

That any assumptions can come together
to be more real than a gas law.

More common than black pipe.

More deadly than a shower head
designed to spray cyanide gas.

By 1924, the United States passed
the Immigration Restriction Act to
prevent those of inferior stock from
entering the country

always by steerage   Naturally

(a legacy that lasted until 1966).

Like the inertia of a great ship.

Unlike today when American companies lobby
congress to move foreign technicians needed
in the bio-tech industry to the top of restrictive
immigration quotas.

The jet track

The funeral director greeted him somberly at the door. Needlework pictures of the lost-then-found lamb, praying hands and other clichés lined the hall and Square was grateful for their comfort. Suddenly, the director swung open the door to the coffin show room, joking, "People are just dying to get in!" When Square didn't laugh, the director said, "Sorry, I wasn't sure how you wanted to play it. Some like to keep it light." He returned to his previous demeanor, and ushered Square into an office. Seated there behind a polished mahogany desk, the director pulled out a form and asked, "Eyes?"

"Sorry," Square replied, not sure if this was another joke.

"What shall we do about Mother's eyes?" The director ticked off the options: put coins on them, transplant them into another's body, sew them shut, prop them open. He asked similar questions for every organ, for the service itself: funeral pyre, mummification, shrunken head, death mask? "Antoni van Leeuwenhoek had a death mask made of his mother, then hung it over his marriage bed." Cannibalism, necrophelia, taxidermy, leave Mother on a scaffold so birds can peck away the flesh? Sew her mouth shut so that she cannot answer to her name and thus be turned into a zombie? "Or perhaps Mother would like to have her hide cured then used to bind a slim volume of nature verse, as was the choice of Japanese botanist Masaichi Fukushi?..."

Back in 1939, this was accomplished by issuing
skilled workers non-quota visas.

Like the one given to Dr. Gustav Aschafenburg,
a genetic researcher, and immigrant from Germany.

a parallel history

Dr. Aschafenburg having built a scientific
reputation by statistically demonstrating
the need for sterilizing the "vermin of the nation:
the chronically ill, the criminal, the handicapped,
the elderly, the alcoholic, the homeless and other
'incompletes,' i.e., burdens on society."

A common opinion.

As plain as the earth's orbit around the sun.

Scientifically backed up.

Righteously advocated.

As was the U.S. Immigration Restriction Act.

That shut the door to inferior stock.

Including refugees from Germany.

Such as Dr. Aschafenburg.

Most of the 220,000 German refugees who
applied for visas to the U.S. in 1938 being Jews,
like Dr. Aschafenburg.

"unproductive eaters"

Could commerce be destiny?

83% feeble minded

Almost all Jewish visa applicants being
gassed by 1940.

Could biology?

The way gravity is destiny for a man who steps off a ledge?

Square felt the flat earth of habit begin to wash out from under him and struggling to find something to grasp he asked, "Which works?"

"They all work. I just do what you tell me."

Square fidgeted. "Well, which is right?"

The director shrugged.

In the end, Square chose to have Mother propped up in a drive-up window. He'd been born a driver, because she'd been a driver, so he thought she would have wanted it that way, though he himself remained a walker and was nearly run over, going on foot as he did, in the line of cars waiting to pay their respects.

Indeed, the longer he remained a walker, the less chaotic walking became. No one showed him how to walk, but guided by thousands of little smiles, courtesies and frowns, he somehow began to fit in. People stepped on him less and less, then one day he realized that he had been walking for what must have been months without being stepped on at all. From eye-level his new world looked as it had when he was being knocked about. But one day, from the bird's-eye view of a skyscraper ledge [a place no one could ever drive], he saw that the only reason he had been stepped on at all wasn't because of some open-ended freedom, but because walkers only made right-hand turns. To turn left, one had to make a series of right turns. He had absorbed this knowledge, Square realized, by degrees, guided by the movements of others just as fish in schools learn to swim as one. By degrees, he had also absorbed other characteristics of his new life, the food processed so that it could be eaten with one hand from non-spill containers by those on the run and the fact that cripples did not exist among the walkers. Back down from the skyscraper, all of this again became invisible to him except when he reflected upon his new life, and the fact that what he had once understood to be the world, had only been a world of drivers.

But what fascinated him the most, what in fact became to him an idée fixe, was the nature of walking itself, the idea that once he had had a body that he put in a machine with wheels that carried it here and there. Now, his body carried him. He was his body, since he'd become a walker, and without his body he couldn't walk, that is he couldn't be.

Unlike Dr. Aschafenburg who was given
a non-quota visa and welcomed to America,
the land of the free

to continue his work...

The problem is in discriminating.

with our native-born moron problem.

Of stepping out of your diorama and looking
back at what you assume to be natural.

Do you say Phish or Fish?

or phager

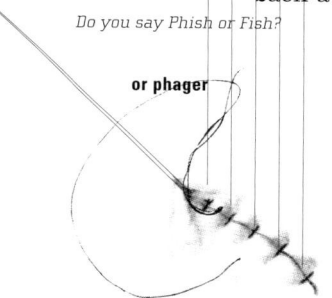

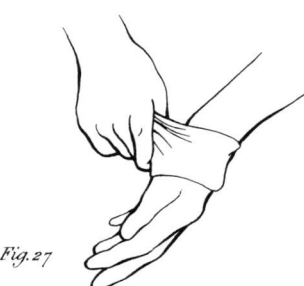

Fig. 27

In retrospect, the length of time it took Square to suspect he was Neanderthal, Square wrote, *proved that he was.*

How long ago had he first
heard the word 'Cyborg'?

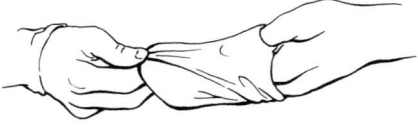

Fig.30

Inhabiting his Jurassic biology, he and his kind
ranged through a landscape of Technoflesh that
became increasingly alien. Antigen-nut trees
were alive with squirrels that urinated blood-
clotting agents; bushes had been injected with
the gene of a firefly to make their berries easy
to find at night, while people—

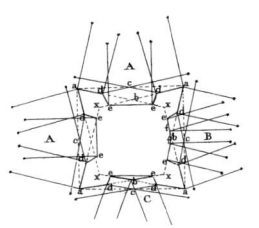

silently place a
glass on strings

$\overset{\rightharpoonup}{p}$ (⟨———⟩)

(Ped. I sempre)

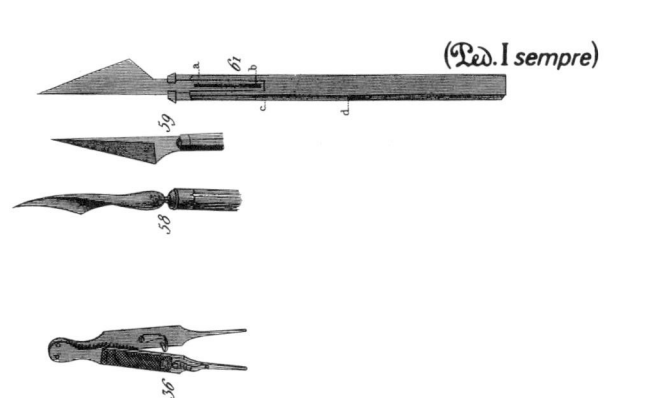

The corpse of the Australopithecus he had
killed lay nude before him. Using two flat
stones, he made a cradle to hold his music,
the thick book of mysteries he had found
in the weeds: *Grant's Anatomy and Dissector.*
He knelt down beside her, a cellist about to
perform. *Hold the scalpel like a cello bow,*
he read, gripping a sharpened clam shell.
Then—a quick check against the diagram
in the book—he pressed the shell's point
into the ape-woman's chest   he flesh yielded
easily, blood oozing out not as from a mortal
puncture but with no pressure or urgency,
as though it was okay, and he continued his
bow's stroke—the low opening of a requiem—
gaining confidence as he lengthened the
incision toward her *Mons Veneris* (*fig.* $\mathcal{A}$).
He wiped the sweat from his eyes. Since she
was more simian than a Neanderthal, he had
expected her hide to be at least as thick as
a callus so was surprised to find how much
like himself an Australopithecus could be.

Do we not have hands,
organs, dimensions?...

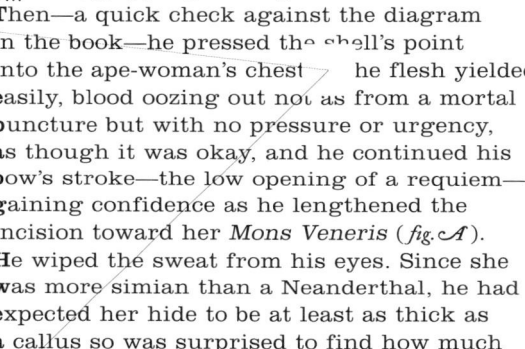

U.S. PATENT No. **5489742**

PROCESS FOR THE MANUFACTURE OF WHOLLY MICROFABRICATED BIOSENSORS

FH **D** 105

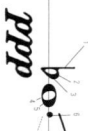

ppp

He took a deep breath, then began a second
long cut, curving around the other breast,
then the navel, duplicating the pattern
in the book till her torso was dominated
by a brilliant red **Y**.
...senses, affections, passions?—

As it said in *Grant's*, Square cut a "buttonhole"
near her navel. Hooking a finger through it,
he pulled the skin of her torso up and over her
face. Just as quick, she was transfigured before
him: a shimmering anatomical sculpture of ropy
muscles, pink and red with striations of yellow fat.
A scent of fresh meat wafted up, making his
nostrils twitch.

Are we not fed with the
same food, hurt with the
same weapons, subject to
the same diseases?...

In the book, transparent overlays, smooth
as membranes, presented the body as layers
where everything rhymed, and turning a leaf,
he wished it were that easy. His thumb left
a bloody smudge print on one stanza.
...*divide the pleura, being careful to*....

U.S. PATENT No. `5506131`

TRANSGENIC ANIMAL MODELS OF INFLAMMATORY DISEASE

ᴘᴡ B 36

...165'

Since he didn't have an anatomical hacksaw,
he used a heavy stone to break open the rib cage,
prying back the sternum to expose organs: a burst-
open watermelon with a vermilion heart, a pair of
blue sacs that were her lungs and mucussy tissue
like the insides of a fish.... He forced a finger into
what he thought was a pulmonary artery. But the
more he worked, the more confusing it became.
*Separate carotid and subclavian arteries of the
neck and upper chest...*

The salty stench of his own armpits thickened
with the exertion. *...Cut the larynx*—she didn't
have a larynx—*and esophagus from the pharynx...*
His fingernails became caked with dried blood
and skin cells (the material). *...With your left hand
under the right lung, lift and turn....* But where
was the?— He studied the confusion before him,
a mass of sea-slug slippery shapes. The body was
so clear in the book. *Knee bone connected to the
thigh bone.* In the flesh it was so different—
all snot and oysters—that he began to think that
the drawings had no more relation to real bodies
than medieval models of the cosmos had to actual
stars. Turning the heart over and over in his
hands, he was unable to tell up from down and
down from up. And yet, this glob had such
a haunting semblance to heartness that as he
studied it, holding it against the *lub dubbing*
within his own breast, an odd sense of recognition
began to come over him.

Through a stethoscope
an artificial heart goes
click clack

a metronome set
to waltz time

It wasn't so much that the heart in the book was as stylized as a valentine.... It was that the heart in his hand contained so much more than the drawing: fat from what this ape woman ate, a work-thickened parietal pericardium, and a thousand other idiosyncrasies composing her own personal book of hours, not the Every Man of *Grant's*, and he remembered trying to identify constellations by comparing dots on a chart to a sky-full of uncharted stars so that seeing the constellations, mentally connecting the dots the chart said to connect, was more of a matter of not seeing than seeing—of ignoring patterns that the makers of star charts said were not there in order to see the ones they claimed were.

He turned back to the organs before him. *Split lengthwise the Rectus Abdominis muscle, making the first incision at point 'G'.*... A belly-full of half digested mangos and snails spilled out, last lunches also not shown in anatomical models. Had she been a dog, she would have vomited out the parts that weren't good for her. But that wouldn't have shown in the diagrams either.... *Free the Ascending Colon and pull it out.*...

...healed by the same means?...

As he cut deeper, trying to not see what *Grant's* said wasn't there, laying bare recesses more intimate than even the ape-woman could have imagined, he began to worry that what he was after was also beyond the pictures in a book. Any book. *The liver 'D' stretches across the top, with its falciform ligament, 'E.'* He began to worry that even Cro-Mags with their 6,500 callouts for parts of the body hadn't identified what made him and the other Neanderthals Neanderthal while Cro-Mags had become?—

Intestines the beige of baloney—he took a bite, chewing thoughtfull⟩ ⟨s he worked, scraping out her insides as if he were hollowing a pumpkin. Haphazard skin tones, a shaggy body—all the qualities that were the luck of the draw for Neanderthals, and therefore something their society had worked hard at to make seem unimportant, had overnight become birth defects in the minds of Cro-Mags—*was his spleen this green?*—along with a whole encyclopedia of other traits: the ability to concentrate, to remember... Designer eye colors, wiry hair, pain threshold....

If you prick us, do we not bleed?

SHYLOCK

The deeper he dug, the more futile the whole
exercise became. *Marbled subdermal fat*....
Unlike the book, she only had one kidney.
Finally he removed the womb—the Origin—
a pink tissue bag that he knew was more
than it appeared. But this silky purse gave
up none of its secret and he dropped it back
into the cavity of her body, then stood,
arching his limbs, stiff. Switching reproduction
on and off like a light.

Distant thunder. No, on the horizon he could
make out the dust raised by a herd of centaurs
and he offered up a small prayer for the woman
they were surely running down. About him, the
mango grove was a deeper shade of green than
it had been the last time he had looked up.
He'd been so engrossed in his work that the day
had passed without his noticing and he knew he
had better get indoors before it got dark
(some things never change).

He took one last look at the book and the
disemboweled corpse beside it—all scarlet eruptions
like some kind of gigantic wild orchid of flesh,
then sighed and began trudging home.
Maybe he should have never left.

In the fading light, a Darwin's Moth (*Xanthopan morganii*) dipped it's twelve-inch tongue into the twelve-inch bell of another kind of orchid, moth and flower only having developed because each made the other possible. Mollusks and grubs churned up dead matter, making the earth seem new and green for the next generation, turning whole civilizations into dirt while the box turtle sighed. While the glo-weeds spread: after Cro-Mags got berry bushes to glow, they added in the genes of a salamander so the plants would crawl to sun themselves in the areas with the most light. But no one had expected the bushes to give off these descendants—weeds that glowed but bore no berries and would crawl, following the sun's path through the zodiac, like a green glacier on earth, over-running medicinal and edible varieties. In the rapidly dimming light, the pores that covered the weeds had begun opening to capture the night's dew and he walked a little faster.

Their tendrils were everywhere out here, climbing real trees instead of iron columns cast to look like trees. Above, the last rays of sunlight strained to filter down through a lattice of weed-choked branches—not iron ribs holding panes of industrial glass.

rw **D** 46

pp

Wood. Water. Rock.
To name was to impose an order, Square thought,
considering the greenhouses Cro-Mags had built
to experiment on their share of this interlocking
chaos. *Orchidaceae africanus.* Paper. Scissors.
To list was to catalog. *Rosa   nksiae, Caesalpinia
gilliesii.* To catalog was to see differently—as the
Cro-Mags must, the travois they dragged their
possessions on constructed of forty-seven different
kinds of woods: the strength of the Chestnut Oak
(Quercus prinus) going into its pegs; the velvety
Red Ash *(Fraxinus pennsylvanica)* for handles; its
checker-board hammock woven from strips of
Black Willow *(Salix nigra)* interlaced with White
Birch *(Betula pendula)*.... Could it be, somehow
that "Nature" wasn't shifting in their minds
toward "Inventory"?

mp (v.l.)

mp

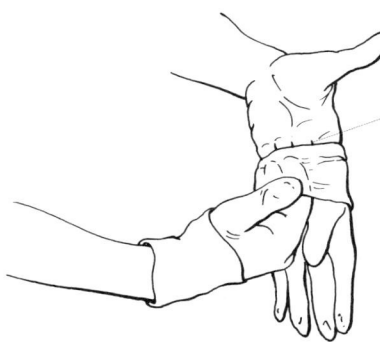

strike strings

3

A pool of tar stretched across the path. The bones of the woolly mammoth Square and the others had once trapped in it were still there, protruding from the dull, black surface. He used the mammoth's vertebrae as stepping stones, the great ribs arching around him like a cage as he used his own digits (*proximal, distal phalanges*) to reckon months.

Fig. 20

Back when they had killed the beast, the differences in Cro-Mags were so small that Neanderthals weren't even aware of themselves as Neanderthal. Thinking back on it now, though, Square saw that it was about then that the Cro-Mags had begun to remember the movements of animals better than Neanderthals. With their better memories, it had become logical for them to decide where to put the trenches while the dirtier, more dangerous job of digging the trenches and killing the beasts had fallen with equal ease to Neanderthals. Square hadn't even noticed the shift until the night ate half the third moon and it was time to scar the foreskins of the next initiates. To his surprise, every one of them assumed they would always be bearers of tar, not planners, their future as self-evident to them as the fate of the mammoth or the fact that women bore the children. Looking into their faces, flickering orange as they huddled with the elders and children around the clan's fire, Square saw the generations unfold— the way astronomers study the evolution of stars without seeing an iota of change in a single one— each more convinced of its place than the last, each in turn adding weight to the proof that it had never been nor would ever be any other way.

with palm

And it wouldn't have been any other way, Square now knew, trudging along within his squat frame, hunched shoulders matted with thick hair, if the Cro-Mags didn't come to believe that they were not just a superior species, but an altogether different animal.

Superior intelligence. Superior health. Superior beauty. True, his skull wasn't nearly as massive as the skull of that Australopithecus female back in the grove. But for Cro-Mags, even life span was eroding. Cro-Mag biologists at the University of California had pieced together the mechanics that allowed cells to "normally" divide fifty times before dying of old age and Cro-Mag corporations everywhere were racing to develop a mass-marketable end-run around this limit. When they did, when Cro-Mag life span increased to 125, then 500 years, when life span became like everything else about their bodies, a matter of choice, Neanderthals realized that their conception of time, their conception of God, of themselves, of life itself would....

(accel. - - - - -)

*fff*z

Individually, then in groups, Neanderthals began
to return to the forest their ancestors had once
abandoned. The 1952 novel *You Shall Know
Them*, a melodrama about a factory owner who
bred and kept a near-human species as his work
force, became a best seller—for both Neanderthals
and Cro-Mags.

Soon afterwards, a Neanderthal hunting party
had been tracking the carnivorous butterflies
that preyed on the young and old of their village
(as was cat nature). On the savanna they encountered
and were murdered by Cro-Mags. After that,
whenever a band of Neanderthals accidentally met
a band of Cro-Mags, Neanderthal males would pick
up heavy stones as their females fled in terror with
the young. The males would form a line between
their fleeing females and the beautiful Cro-Mags.
They'd beat their hairy chests and bellow, hoping
that the threat of unthinking animal ferocity could
level the advantage Cro-Mags gained from their
arrow heads and aerodynamic spears.

Them and their forty-seven kinds of woods....

molto energico!

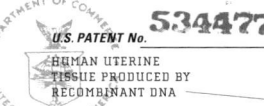

Still, unlike the others, Square never feared being carried into slavery—*You Shall Know Them* or not. The catastrophic consequences that seemed to follow each new Cro-Mag practice were just that, he believed—consequences—no more intended than the path he was walking on, worn into field grass—unawares—by coming and going until it no longer occurred to anyone to take another route, every other route now being harder. So when the Cro-Mags altered the mammoth's germ line to intensify its herding instinct, to create mammoths that would be as docile as a sloth and attracted to tar and then hunted them to extinction, the hunger that Neanderthals suffered truly did seem to be a consequence of Cro-Mag progress, not a pogrom directed at them.

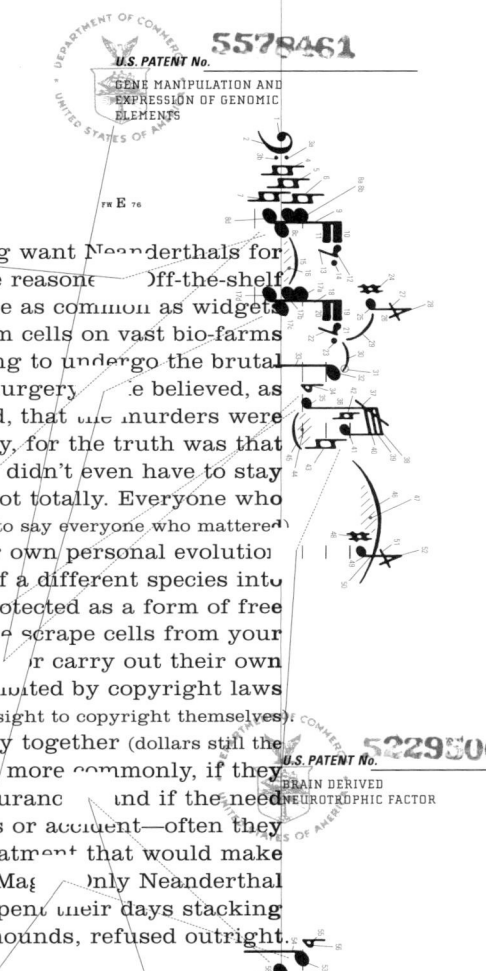

Nor would any Cro-Mag want Neanderthals for
their primitive organs, he reasoned — Off-the-shelf
Cro-Mag organs were as common as widgets,
grown from embryo stem cells on vast bio-farms
for those still willing to undergo the brutal
anachronism that was surgery — he believed, as
Cro-Mag chiefs said, that the murders were
isolated acts of bigotry, for the truth was that
Neanderthals like himself didn't even have to stay
Neanderthal. At least not totally. Everyone who
had the money (which is to say everyone who mattered)
could direct their own personal evolution
Incorporating the genes of a different species into
your own had been protected as a form of free
speech — having someone scrape cells from your
body in order to sell them or carry out their own
genetic project was promoted by copyright laws
(if a person had had the foresight to copyright themselves).
If they could get the money together (dollars still the
hardest subject to clone) or, more commonly, if they
had good health insurance and if the need
arose—through illness or accident—often they
would receive some treatment that would make
them at least partially Cro-Mag. Only Neanderthal
fanatics, the ones who spent their days stacking
stones into mysterious mounds, refused outright.

177

"So why don't you do it?" Circle asked once again, once he was home (flexing thyroarytenoids and the other forty-seven muscles of the larynx to do so).

Though she was also still a Neanderthal, nature had blessed her with so many Cro-Mag features that she could, in fact, easily pass among the most beautiful of them. "Don't you want what's best for your family?"

He himself couldn't explain this irrational attachment to his old body. It made no more sense than confusing himself with an old favorite hat, or refusing to let go a comfortable sweater that had a hole in one elbow—even though wearing it meant getting cold. And of course he wanted what was best for his family. Children engineered to repel mosquitoes, engineered to not develop an appendix, or wisdom teeth, or any anachronistic appendages—who could not want that for their descendants?—and all for the having by simply creating a litter of embryos from which they could select the one with the best genetic profile. When Oval was considering getting pregnant, he himself helped her go through the dizzying array of choices, taking copious notes on sperm banks, womb rentals—including the low-rent wombs of cadavers on life support—knocking out genes for spina bifida, colon cancer, schizophrenia, dialing in the standard gene clip that everyone (who could afford it) received for concentration and memory, for facial symmetry, for skin color.... Then there were the designer genes: genes from cod fish for increased tolerance to cold, genes from Gila monsters for increased tolerance to heat, and a thousand others....

The cat they had bought for Oval at a
bio-boutique flapped its wings, then hopped
up into Square's lap and barked happily
for him to play.

Composing a body as if it were a crossword
puzzle was natural for Oval. She was young
and didn't know any other way. But he couldn't
help but marvel at the species of free verse Darwin
had helped midwife, so long ago, intimating that
all life—not only men and apes but also the
bean stalk outside his window and the fruit fly
he swat a moment ago—all life spoke the same
language, written in the same genetic letters
and could be parsed like tenses.

When he looked to Oval, he could see an
etymology of himself within the dimensions
of her face. But what would she see looking at
her child with its five parents, four of whom
would be unknown to her?

"A super race?" Oval had answered, not even
looking up from her catalog. "Oh Look!
A gene set for sexual pleasure!"

(remove glass)

Fear of the unknown. Square realized he was suffering from that genetic disease called middle age and its main symptom: Fear of the Unknown. Not fear of the unknown bodies that might result, for surely seedless watermelons, hairless Chihuahuas—indeed every nature's freak that predated bio-engineering had been a creature of gene management. And familiarity had made them seem natural. Rather, it was the unknown attitudes that worried him—just as no one could have predicted that Darwin's leveling of men and animals would help make Animal Rights imaginable, as well as old people on pensions so meager that they ate dog food, and he couldn't help but wonder who and what he would see when he looked with Cro-Mag eyes at his wife, when he looked in the mirror and saw his own Cro-Mag face masking a brain that remembered what it had been to be Neanderthal.

To be your body, and not just have your body.

I can't not know what I know, Circle often said, and that, he decided, was all he wanted: for someone to acknowledge that it was okay to feel like you owed your body a fond farewell, a body he had lived in and had come to know over these seventeen thousand some years and now could only stand and wave goodbye to as it fled before him toward the East. Not that the band had to play *Auld Lang Syne*. Surely it was too late for that anyway, given the number of seasons that had passed since people began to take on second skins, often unawares. It's just that he wished Circle could see that momentous migrations were made with tiny steps. That the death of any language was a tragedy, and that his was surely going extinct since the speakers who knew the old meanings of fossils like "birth," "father," "daughter" were probably down to a handful. But in the face of whiter teeth, and fuller hair, not to mention increased IQ and sexual pleasure, how could he or anyone put that into words?... Words that didn't come off as sentimental fossils and nostalgia—the sure sign of an old Neanderthal fart.

Against this, against being of your time, the prospects of ending his story any other way than the way it would end seemed even to him sentimental and absurd.

He turned back to his notes:

Make Large Scale Changes to Genes in One Day!
said an ad for Stratagene's New Seamless Cloning Kit.

Scientists Make Part-Human, Part-Cow Cells
said another newspaper clipping.

Regeneration of Worn-Out Organs
said another.

Genetic Switch to Aging Discovered....
He looked down at the daily news—the daily fish
wrap, as Mother called it (the fossils that were her
metaphors coming from a strata when people had to clean
the fish they bought at the market)—and he wondered
how the marvelous had become so mundane
without his even noticing, the landscape exerting
itself on him as invisibly as subliminal advertising
(a '70s phenomenon). And like someone sitting in
a theater, coke in one hand, popcorn in the other,
who suddenly realizes that they bought into both
coke and popcorn only because ads had been
slipped in between the frames of a musical
comedy, he began to grow angry, the pressure,
suggestions, changes, even in who he was,
and all for the health of?—

The corner of an ad he hadn't seen before stuck
out from his papers: *Viagra. What An Uplifting
Experience!* It pictured a white-haired man
and woman dancing—*naturally, with the help
of a pill*—and the contradiction was disorienting.
How had this gotten into his notes?

Circle laughed in the next room.

Circle.

The sound of her levity coursed down
the canals of his ears and pounded their
drums. He picked up the Viagra ad and went
to her, cortex alive with anger and neural
activity—hot flashes through the amygdala,
then hypothalamus—their networks releasing
adrenaline, water on power lines contracting
his grip on the ad, digestion shutting down,
his anus pinching shut. As he entered the
room, her eyes widened on him, her smile
evaporating (as they put it in novels), nasalises
contracting for heavy breathing while his
own heart began to pound (novels, again),
mean arterial pressure rising.

"I'll call you back," she said into the phone,
then hung up.

He shoved the ad into her hands, speech lobes
of the brain in sympathy with its emotive region
charging nerves to make his chest cavity expand,
creating an air pressure difference between
the space they shared and the space that was
his alone, air rushing into the bellows of his
lungs which crumpled in a grip of muscle and
bone, his breath violently squeezed out through
the larynx, vagis nerves trilling vocal folds like
holes of a flute to produce the notes, muscles
morphing the throat—sax to trumpet—to
modulate the tone, the volume of air rushing
at the bell of his mouth, tongue flexed against
teeth to build up the air pressure that when
released pronounced the 't' then the rest of
"*This* isn't my problem! Or is fine tuning
always the next step!"

His shout hung in the void between them.

If you can curl the sides of your
tongue into a flute-shape, then at least
one of your parents could also do so,
and passed this talent on to your body.

words like fools rush in

*The cost of care of the handicapped vs. the cost of genetic consultations
of future parents demonstrates that genetic consultation increases
the 'vital property' of the family and the society.*

DR. MABUSE
HUMAN GENETIC CONSULTATION

And the patient.

A change in perspective

And the company.

People had figured it out.
Smart people.

Descartes

GenTech Inc.

And smart people, when given the facts,
will make intelligent choices.

Rationalism

**By manipulating a gene involved in learning,
researchers at Princeton University were able to
produce a strain of mice that outperform non-altered
mice on six intelligence tests.**

That is why in 1928, 20,000 U.S. students
were taking college courses in eugenics.

*If our knowledge of eugenics were applied, the defective classes would
disappear within a generation.*

CHARLES R. VAN HISE
PRESIDENT, UNIVERSITY OF WISCONSIN

Sheik, Ramses, Trojan-enz, Trojan-enz lubricated,
Trojan-enz with spermicide, Trojan-enz latex,
Natural Lamb, Fiesta Colors…. Standing before
a rack of 31 kinds of condoms, Square remembered
the first time he'd tried to manipulate these matters,
the sun-set colored boxes before him bearing perfect
romantic couples nothing at all like the medicinally
wrapped things locked up behind a counter in the
next town where the pharmacist couldn't distinguish
him from any other common-faced boy.

This is why bio-tech companies fund
biology labs in public schools.

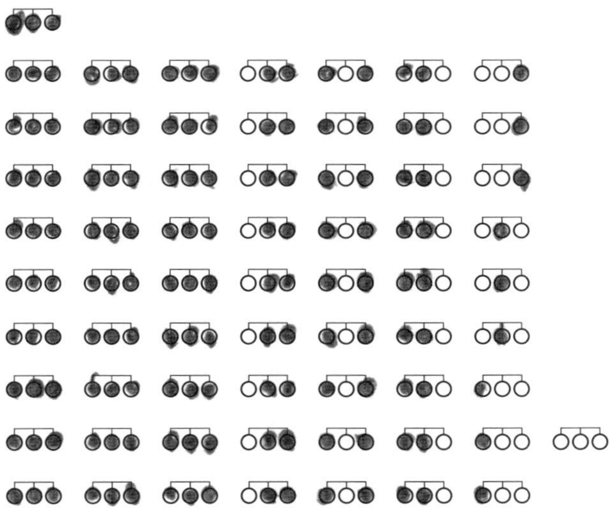

Concerning Irregular Figures

Throughout the previous pages I have been assuming—what perhaps should have been laid down at the beginning as a distinct and fundamental proposition—that every human being in Flatland is a Regular Figure, that is to say of regular construction.... It does not need much reflection, then, to see that the whole of the social life in Flatland rests upon the fundamental fact that Nature wills all Figures to have their sides equal. If our sides were unequal our angles might be unequal; in a word, civilization would relapse into barbarism.

Am I going too fast to carry my Readers with me to these obvious conclusions?

EDWIN A. ABBOTT
FLATLAND

The problem is that the facts keep changing.

While population increases geometrically, the food supply increases incrementally. Sanity dictates, then, that we encourage the lower classes to live near swamps and adopt unhygienic practices likely to breed typhoid.

THOMAS ROBERT MALTHUS, *1820*

Quantity control

Excepting in the case of man himself, hardly any one is so ignorant as to allow his worst animals to breed. Nor to see that this practice must be highly injurious to the race of man....

CHARLES DARWIN, *1871*

Quality control

Facts keep changing because the world keeps
changing since the time of Malthus,

and Darwin

When a fact was a fact.

Unlike centaurs

In fact, when talking about the prison
house of language men and women inhabit,
most people point to the fall at Babel where
Language shattered into languages. But
medieval cartographers and theologians
(for they were one and the same) used to refer to
an even more telling geography—Adam's
Peak—the highest point on earth and home
of Eden from where it was possible to view
the entire world at once—until Adam and
Eve were forced to leave and, like all of
their descendants, live out their days on
the flat land below.

Where a fact was a fact.

And Sir Francis Galton used a surveyor's sextant to
measure the dimensions of African buttocks.

turning numbers into

        Objectivity

categories

        quantitative assessment

If we don't check population by 1985, we will face global collapse.

THE LIMITS TO GROWTH

~~Nuclear~~ family

The problem with paradigms is that
they keep shifting.

**After Dalton proposed that atoms could
only combine in whole-number ratios,
the hard facts of chemistry began to
become whole-number ratios.**

Every generation's map becoming
the next generation's myth....

Doubtless there are millions of similar examples.

Terra incognita **always incognito**

Good news for textbook publishers.

Descartes, believing dogs were like
clocks, decided that they could feel no pain.

And that's not even considering the constant
that people with facts as good as their
intentions sometimes make bad decisions.

Here be dragons!

Cartesians, believing Descartes, nailed dogs'
paws to boards so they could vivisect them
and study the circulation of the blood.

And that was what was scaring him, he decided.

The shrieks of vivisectioned dogs only
being like the "boing" of clock springs.

unsprung.

The finality of story's end.

Tying off the vasa deferentia should be...

The fear of closure.

...considered...

end of the line

break in the chain

final things

gap in the sequence

...an irreversible procedure.

Walking away from a nature aligned to continue itself

Not that he was rewriting his body

transexuals

That was why the nation became engrossed
in cases like Karen Anne Quinlin's, one
of the first to have her life support system
shut off.

just a little editing.

Well, not technically the first.

"**If** *it is a female, discard it,*" one Hilarion wrote
on June 17, 1 BC to his wife Alis who was expecting.

Quality control sometimes spilling over into quantity control

A common sentiment.

A fine line

In fact, archeologists were surprised by DNA tests on hundreds of one to two day-old skeletons. The skeletons were found mixed among animal bones, potsherds, coins, and erotic figurines in a fourth century sewer. But contrary to expectations, many of the infants had been male—probably the unwanted offspring of courtesans who worked in a connected bath house.
(a buried history)

common people

But Karen was the first I had to deal with.

with a common problem

"I" meaning us.

Unless you're old enough to remember the Black Stork

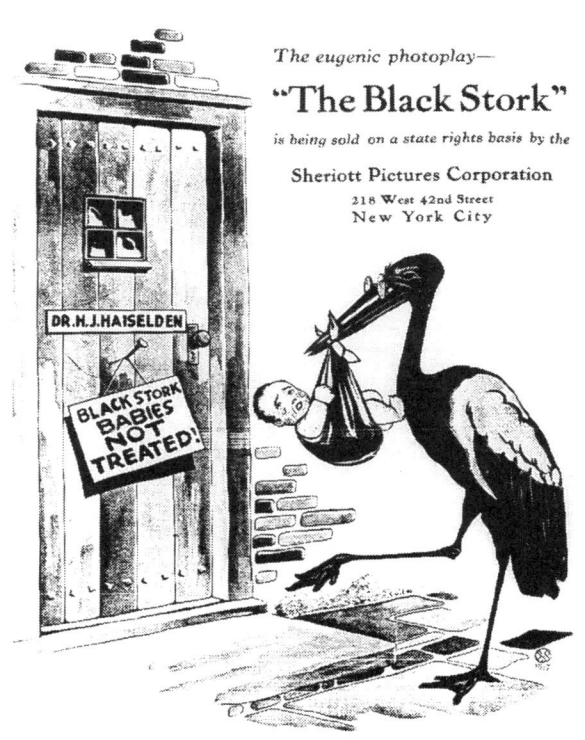

The eugenic photoplay—

"The Black Stork"

is being sold on a state rights basis by the

Sheriott Pictures Corporation

218 West 42nd Street
New York City

"Us" meaning those readers
who might ask themselves, "How would
I end her story if it was up to me?"

*The Black Stork being Dr. Harry Haiselden, a
pediatrician in the '30s who publicized the
defective newborns he helped die*

for the good of society.
*and the parents
and the infants themselves*

"Me" being someone with an aging
mother-in-law and a child and a wife and
who might actually have to make a decision
like this one day and was wondering how
he could be sure she wouldn't come out of
her coma and resume her life?

It had happened before.

Drowning victims

Brought back
to life 30 minutes
after the heart had
stopped

The "fact" of a stopped heart no longer being
synonymous with the fact of "death."

In fact, the only way to tell if a stopped
heart could be restarted was to try.

In situations such as Karen's (or the Black Stork's) who ever tried?

In the back of his mind he knew that Circle was thinking of their last unnamed fetus and would go through anything to not have to make that decision again. Not that it was the wrong decision; rather, it was that they both just wanted to live their common lives, do their common jobs, come home, maybe veg out in front of their low-definition TV and relax with their garden-variety family. Not be faced with decisions like that. Uncommon questions with no answers. And as bad as the last time had been, they both felt they had dodged a bullet (another cliché), the bullet being the possibility that the results would be negative, but the test itself would cause her to loose the child. Who could live with that? Still, some did —0.5 to 1.5% according to the legal disclaimer Circle had signed....

Out of 8,000 abortions performed in Bombay in 1985, 7,997 were of female fetuses.

Put another way, 0.04% were male.

An invisible history

And that's what scared him.

How could you be sure you weren't just acting like any other organ of your century?

Ease of habit

Vertical transmission.

Old wine in new bottles, as Mother would say.

Soon an endless number of lower races will have been eliminated by the higher civilized races.

CHARLES DARWIN

Even if you were aware
that you were drinking wine.

Which you wouldn't.

If Circle became pregnant again, screening
would be offered again, given her age. In fact,
it was required by their insurance company.
For information, only. Of course the counselor,
like the last one, would be very nice, no monocle,
no scar, probably a user of a variety of salad
dressings. In a pleasant office she'd pleasantly
say that she was only providing information—
that she was completely neutral.

It's not like they were one of those social
"undesirables" who only "chose" to be sterilized
because it was that or a straight jacket.

Or winos who
sold their blood

But didn't screening imply
screening for something bad?

And didn't the hospital know that no one
wanted their baby to be born with something

Ellis Island bad? And if something bad was found, didn't
the test imply that you should fix it? Why
screen if there wasn't a fix? And if the only
fix—say, for femaleness—was the procedure,
wasn't determining what kind of child should be
born the same as deciding what kind shouldn't?
Is not answering that question what the
counselor meant by neutral information?

Can questions predetermine answers?

The way stepping
off
a

ledge

predetermines
how you finish this sentence?

And why stop with a simple ☐ or like male/female?
○

Or was he just splitting hairs?

X or Y

A fine line

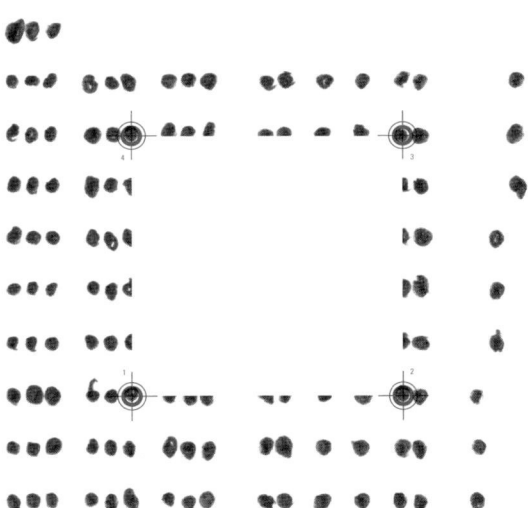

Common Nazis, of course,
having nothing to do with it.

In the land of free choice.

Nor garden-variety doctors in Peru,
offering two new dresses to any woman
who volunteers for a tubal ligation.

Neutral dresses

Since in Flatland there are only volunteers.

Like California mothers who are paid $200 for volunteering.
also IL mothers

Concerning the Women
*But here, perhaps, some of my younger readers may ask how a woman
in Flatland can make herself invisible.*

EDWIN ABBOTT
FLATLAND

and FL

In Peru, so far, 220,000 dresses have been given out.

Unlike CA where statistics are unavailable

MN

MI

PA

10,000 men signing up for tee-shirts, as well.

NH

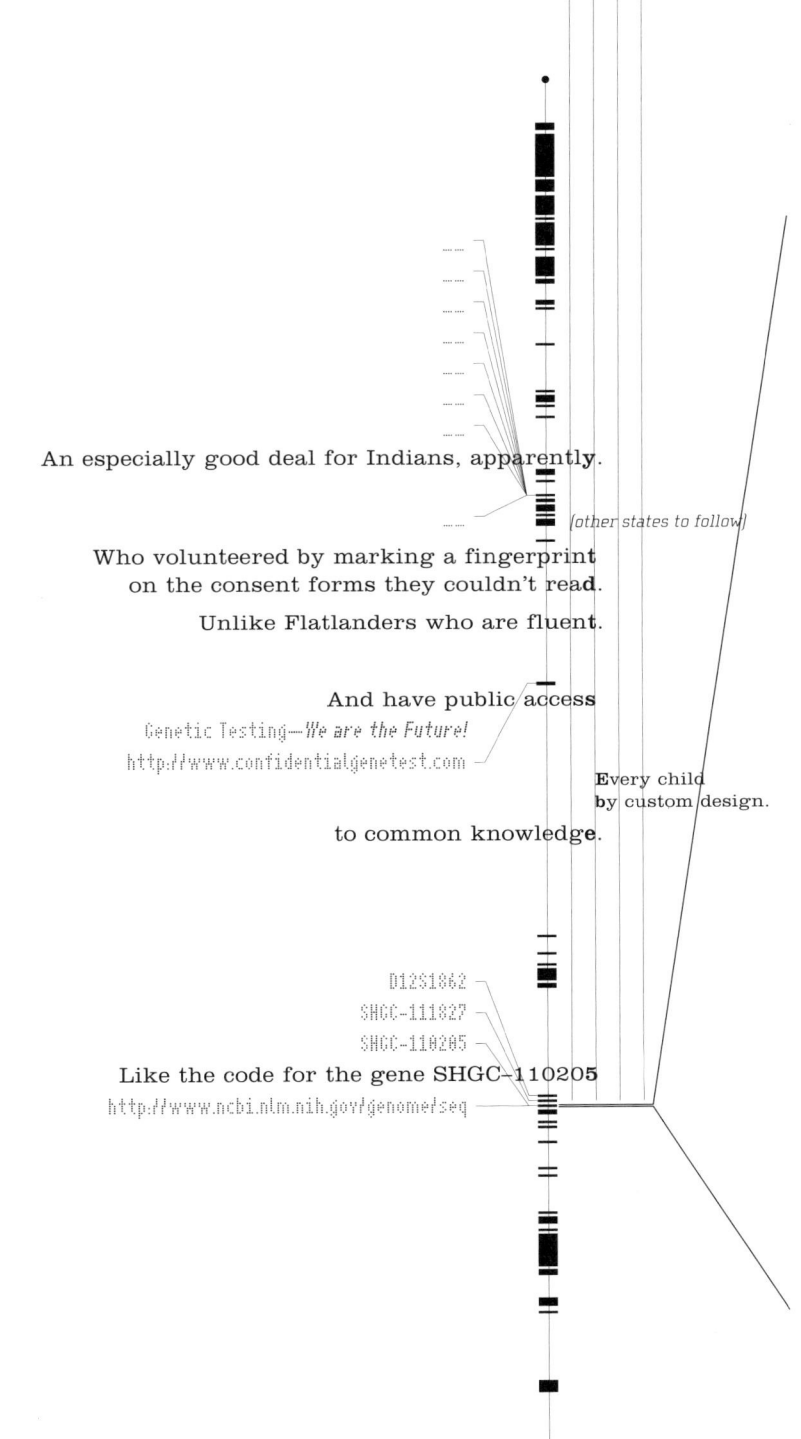

An especially good deal for Indians, apparently.

(other states to follow)

Who volunteered by marking a fingerprint
on the consent forms they couldn't read.

Unlike Flatlanders who are fluent.

And have public access

Genetic Testing—*We are the Future!*
http://www.confidentialgenetest.com

Every child
by custom design.

to common knowledge.

D12S1862
SHGC-111827
SHGC-110205

Like the code for the gene SHGC-110205

http://www.ncbi.nlm.nih.gov/genome/seq

5'... ACCCTGCCTGCCAAATTTTTTATATTTTCGGTAGAGACGGGGCTTCACTATGTTGGCCAGCGCTGGTC
TTGAACTCCTAACCTCAAGTGATCCACCTGCCTCAGCCTCCCACAGTGCTGGGATTACAGACGTGAG
CCACCGCACCCAGCTCACATGATGCTTTTATAACGCATAATACTTCACCAGACACTTTCTCAAACAT
CTCTTAATTCGGAACACAAACCTGTAAAGTTGATTACATTGTTCCTTTGTGTCCCTGAGGGCTCAGAG
AGGTTAGATGACATTTGCAAGGCCACATAGCCAATAGGTGGCAAAGAAAGAACCATAGCAAGATTTT
CAGCCAAAAAAATCCAGTGCTCTTCATATCAGAACTATTTCCAATTCCTTGGGGCTATGACCCATCA
CCATGGAACTATTAGCCTCATGAAACAAAGGTGAGAGGTCAGGGAGAGACTCGCAGATACCCAAGGT
GACTAGTGTTTGAGCCCTTGCTATGGCCTAGACACTGTGCTACATGCTGGTCATCCATCCTCTTCTT
GTCTACACACTAACTCTGCAGAATTTGATATTGTTCCCGTTTTTCAGGAGTTTAGACAAATTAGGCA
ACATGCTGAAAGATATGCTTGTTCTAGGGCAGAGGTAGGATTGAATTCAGACCTGTCTCGAACCCAAT
GTTGAATCTCCTACAATGTTCTGTTGTAAACAACGTTCTTGGAGAACGTAAACCTATGCCATGTTAT
GGGCTGCCTGAAATCGACCTATAAATGCAGTGGGATAAATTTACCCTCCACACCACATGAGGCTAAG
CTTTATGAATGTATGTACTTTATCCTGGTGTACATTAATGGGATTAGAATTCTTCCTACTGTTTGTT
TTTTAATTAATTAATTTATTTATGTATTTATTTTATTTATTGAGACAGAGTCTGACTCTGTCACCCAG
GCTAGAGTGCAGTGGTACAATCACAGCTCACTGCAACCTCAGACTCCTGGGCTCAGGTGACCCTCAC
ACCTCAGCCTCCCACATAGCCTGGGACTACAAACATGTGCCACCACACCTGACTAATTTTCTAATTTT
TATGGAGATGGGGTCTCGCCTAGGTTGCCCAGCTTGTCTCAAACTCCTAAGTTCAAGCAATCCTCCTG
CTTACTATTTTAGAAACAAAACGATGCAGAGGAGAAACTGGGAACTTCGTACCAAGTCTCTTCGTG
TGGCACAACTAACAATGCCTAAGAACTCTAGCTGCCATGGACTGAGTGTTTGAGATGTGCCAGGCTC
TGTTCTAGCACTTTGTGAGAATTATCTCATTAAAACCTCTCACCAACCTAATGAGGTAGTTACTCTT
GTTATCAACATTTTACTGATAATTTTTAGAAAGGGTAAGTAAATTTCCTGAGGTGTCAAGAATTCTG
GTTGCCCCATCCTAATGCTGCATCCCACTAAGACAAATTTATTAGGATATTTTATTTTATTTTATTT
TATTTTATTTTTTATTTTATTTTATTTTATTTCATTTATTTTATTTTATTTTATTTATTTTTTTTTA
TATTTTTTTTTTTTTTTATATTTTATTTTATATTTTATTTTTATTTTAGTTTTTCTTTNAAATTTAGTG
CGNTTAACCACAGTCGCGTCCAAAACGTAAAAACACTCATTTTGTGCTCATACAGATATGTAGTTCG
AAAACGAACGAATATTTTAATACTTTTTCAGATAATTGTGGCTTTCTTTATTTGATACTGTGCTCAA
ATTTGATAATAGTGTCTTAAAAGTTAGTGACAATGTGGAATCTGAAACCGAGTCAGTGGACTTTTTG
TACACTGTAACATTAAAATTTGATCTATCTTGCCTTTTGAGTCGGATCTTTTCCTGTGCGTGATTTTA
TAAGATCATCGCATTAGTCATGTGGAAAATATTGGTTCACTGAGTTACTCAGATCTTCCAAAATTTTCA
TACATTTTATTGTACAATATAAAAACAGTCACATTTGTCAATATCACCATCAATCTCAGATTAGGCT
TTAAATATGAGGAAGCCTGTCTCAAGGCTCATGGTGGTGGGGATACATGTGTTTCCAAAAATTCTAAGCTGTATT
TGAAAGCTTGAGTTTTATCACTGCCAACAAATACTATCAATTCTATTCTTTAAAGTGACAGAGATTCCC
TTCCTACTCAAGTCCGAATATTAATAGTCTGTCGGTCTTTCTACTAAAACTGGTCTTTCATAAAAAA
AAAAGTGTGGCTACTTCAGTATAACTCAATCACATGAGTACTTTTCTTCATGACAACTGTATTATAC
TTTGGTGTGGAGGAGAAATGGTCCATGTATACTTTCTATTTTTTATTTTTCTTGCTACTACAAATAT

```
TCAAATATTATAGCTATGAACATTCATATATAAATCTTATGCATTAGTACAAGAATTTCTCTATGTT
AGATACTCGAAGTGAAATTCCTGTCCTGTAGGGCAGACACGTGCTCAGATTTACTAGATGACCTCCA
GCTATTTTCCAAAGTAATTATACCAGTTTACCATTGCCCCTTTCCCCATCAACTCTTGGTGTTGATT
GATGTTTAAAATATAATCTTTCATAGCTGTGCTTTTCCCTAGTAAACCTCTACATCCTTGCGCCCCT
TTTATATCCTGTCAAACTACACGTAGAAAACTTCTACATAATTTAGTTTTGCCTTTGTCCCTCTGTT
TGATTTTTAATTTCTTTGAACCCAGAGCTTACCTTCTATCTCTTGGAAGCTGACCAGCATATGTAGA
GTAGCAGTTTGCAAGCAGTGAGTGTTGATGATCAGTGTTATTATGTGTTTCTCAAACATTAAGCTAT
TAATAAAGCACATGATTTGATATTGATAGCTGAAATGTACAGTCAAATACTCTAGCACACATTTTGT
GTGTGTTGTGTGTATGTATATTCACACGTGCACATTATTGAAAGAAGTCCTGTGCCTATTTTATGAT
TAATACATAGAATCAAGATTATTTTATTGTGTTACAATTGCAACATTTCTTATTAGGGAATAATAAG
ACCTTCTACTAATCTTAATAATGCCTTACATAAATTTAACACTTTGCAGTTTTGTTTTGTTTTTCCC
AAAGCGTTTCTCTGTTTGGGATTTGGTCACCAGTCAGTGCAAGCCCACAGTTGCATCTGCCTTTTCT
TATTATCCTCACTATCTACTTCTCTCACCCCTCCTTACCCCATGTCTTTGGTAAACCATAATTATTG
ACAGTGGTGATTTTCAAGTGCTTTGAATTTGGAATCTCTTTACTTGGTCATTTGAAGGCTATTACAT
GAAATGTCCTGGGCAGCTTTTGTGGGTCACAGGTAGTATCAACGTGGATAGGTAACATTGTAATATA
TAATCGATGGAAAAGATAATTGCTTTTGTGTTAATGTCAAGGTTTTCAGGTTTAAACCAGTGTTTTA
TAATTACTAGCCTTGAAAACTTAAAAACATAATGGAAAAATTGAAGAAACTTTCTTCCTAGTTTTTA
ACAAAAATAACTTCTGACATTTAAACAGCTCAATTAACTGTTTCCTTATAAATTCTAAACAAAATTA
TATTGCTTATCTACAGTCACTACAATATAATATAGGTCATTGGAAGAGACAGAGATTTTTTTGGGTC
TCATCCTTCATCGCTTTTCTCCATTGCTCTCCTTTTTCACCAGTCCCAGTTCTAAGACGCTCACATG
CCAAAGTCGCAGCCACATTTGGCCAGTAGTTATTATATCGCTTGTATTACCACTGCATTGCAAAGTG
GTATATTGATAAGAACAGTATAGTGCAGTAGTCACAGGCATTCTTAAATCTCAGCTTTGCCACTTAC
TGCCTGTCACACTAAGCCTCTGAGAGTCTGTTTACTCTCCTGCTAAGAAATATTATTATACCCACTT
ACCTCTTAGGATTAATAGGAACATTACATAAATTAATAAAATAATAAAAGTGCTTATTGACTTTTAG
TAAGCACCTTAGTGAATGTGGGTTGTTGTTGGTTTTTTTTTTTTTTTTTTAAATGAGACAGAGTCTC
ACTTTTTCACATAGCCTGGAGTGCAGTGGTGCGATCTCAGCTCACTGCAACCTCCATCTCCCGAGTT
CAAGTGATTCTCTTGCCTCAGCCTCCTGAGTAACTGGGATTACAGGTACGCACCACCACGCCTGGCT
AATTTTTGTATTTTTAGTAGAGACGGGGTTTCACCATGTGGGTCAGGCTGGCCTCAAACTCCTGACC
TTCTGATCTGCCCGCCTCGGCCTCCCAAAGTGCTGGGATTACAGATGTGAGCCACTGCACCCGGCTG
GTTGTTGTTTTTAATTGTTAAGCTGTTGTGATCACGGATTGGGTCAAGACCAAGGTGAGAGTTTTCCT
AATTTACTGCCTAGTAAATTAGCCAGTAAAAGCCTTTTGTATAAAACATAACTTTTTAGCCTGAGTCT
TTAAGCTTCCTAAGCGACCATTTCATATGGCAGAGGGGTTAAGACATTTCATTTTGAGAGCCTAGGTGT
ACAAAAGCCATAGAACAATGTAAGAGCCATATGTATCTCATAAAATAACGAGACGTTGGCGAGCTACAA
AGTAGTTTAATTTGTTCATTCTCACCAAGCTATTCTGAGGAACAAGTGAGATGAGATCTCTGAAATA
ACTTTCTAAGCTATCAAGCATTAAAACATGCCACTCTTTTTATATTCATTTCATTATCTGAACAAGT
```

```
AACAAAATCAAAAATCCACCGTAATATACCCAAATTGTCCCTGTAACAATATATATATTCACATAACAAT
TCCTCACAAAATAAAAACCCACTCCATACTTCCAACCCAACAATTTTCCTTACTCAAATCATAATTA
CGTTATAACATACCATTAACATCCATTTTATAATTTAAATTTCAATACCATATATTTTAGCCCACTAC
AAATTCATTTATTCAATCTCTCAATTCTGTTATCAAAAATTTATTCCATTAAAAATCATAATCCATC
ATTCTACCATTTCACCAATCATATCACCCTCTGTCAACTTCACCTTCCTCATCTCTAAATCTCTATC
TCATATTTTGTTGTAAACATTAATATCCACAACTCAAAATCCTCTTATTATTTTTTAATCAATTTCA
CTATACTTTAAAAACTCACTCTTCAAAAACCATCTATTCACTATAATATTTTGCTTCACATTCCATC
CCAACACCATAATAAAAATCAAAACTTTTAATAATAAAATATACTTACTCTTTTGCCTCTAAAAATT
ACAAACTCTCACTCCATTACATTCTTTTAAAAACAAACAAACTCCTTTCCCTACTTTTAAACAAAAT
TTAATTCTCTTTCATCTTTCTAATAATCCTCCTACATTTTCCTTAATTTTTTTCCCACAACCCAATT
TTAAACACTCCCTACTTCTTACCATATCTTTTTTCCCTTTTAAACACTCAAACTATCACCCCCCCC
CCATCCCTCATCTCTGTAATCCCACCACTTTCCTACCCCAACCCCCCCACATCACAACCTCACCACA
TCCACACCACCTTCCCCAACATCCTCAAACCCTCTCTCTACTAAAAATACAAAAAATTACCTCCCCA
TCCTCCCCCCCCCCTCTACTCTTACCTACTTCCCACCCTCACCCAAAAAATCCTCTCAACCCCCCA
CCTCCACCTTCCACTCACCCAATATTCTCCCCCTCCACTCCCCCCTCCCCCACACACCCACACTCCA
TCTCCAAAAACACTAATACATCATCTCCAACTCCCCTTTATCCCAACAATTCAACCTTCATTCACCA
TCTCAAAACTAATCAAATTATTAAATAAACCAAAAAAACTATATCAACATCTCAATACATCTACACA
AAATACCTCAAAAAATTTAATATCCATTCATCAATAAAAACATCCCCCCCCCACACTCCCTCACACCT
CTAATCCCACCACTTTCCCACCTCCCCCAGCCACACCCACTTCACCTCACCCACTTCAACACCACCCTC
CCCAACATCCTCAAACCTCATCTCTACTAAAAAATACAAAAAATTACCCACCCCTCCTTCCACCCACC
TCTACTCCCACCTACTCACAACCCTTCACCAACCCACAATCACTTCAACCCACCACCCACACCTTCCA
CTCACCCAACATTCCACCACCACTCTACCCCAACACACTCACACTCCATCTCAAATAAAAAAAAACC
AAACCAAACCAAATAAATACCCAACTCACAACCCACCCCCTACAAATCAACAATAAAAACACAATCT
ACTCCCACCTACTCACCACCCCAAACTCCACCACTCCTTAACCCCCACCACTTTCACACCCCCTCCC
CTACATACCAACACACCCCCCCCTTTTTAAAACATTAACTCTTAACTTTTATATCCTCTACTCTTC
TCACATCTCATTTCTTTTAATTTCACTTTCCCTTAAAAAAATTATAATATCCATCTTACACCTTTCT
CCCCAAATCTTTATCAATTCATACTATAAATTCCTTACCATCCTACCTCCCCCCTCTACCTACTCAC
TACATTTTACCTATTATAATTAATTTCAATTCTTCACCATTCTTTCATTTCAAATTTTTTTCTTACT
AAATTTTAAAACCATCATTATTATAAAACAAATACCATACAAATTCCATATTTTTTTTTTTTTTTTTT
TTCACACCCACTCTTCCTCTCTCCCCCACCCCCCACTCCCACTCCACTCCCCCAATCTCCCCTCAC
TCCAACCTCCCCTTCCCCCCTTCACCCCATTCTCCTCCCTCACCCTCCCCACTACCTCCCACTACAC
CCCCCCCCACCCCCCCCCCCCTAATTTTTTTTTCTATTTTTACTACACACCCCCTTTCACCTTCTTAC
CCACCATCCTCTCCATCTCCTCACCTCATCATCCACCCCCCCTCCCCCTCCCAAACTCCTCCCCATTAC
ACCCCTCACCCACCCCCCCCCCCCAAATTCCATATTTTTAAAAAATTATCTCTTTTACCCAAAACTT
TTTTCAAAATAAATAAAAATTACATATTTTCTACAAACTCAATCACCCCTAATCCTCTCCCTATTTT
```

```
GTATACGTAAATAATATATCAATTATATATATATCAACTATATATTATATATTTATATATTTATCAA
ATATATATTATATATTTATATATTTATCAAATATATATTTTATATATATAGTGTATATACACACAAT
ATATCATGATATTCATATCATGATATTCATATATAATTCATATATTATTCATATCATATATTATATA
CAATTCATATATTATATACCTATATAGCCTCATATTTTCAACTACAATATTTACCTACACAAAAGAAT
CTTCTCTAGCTAAATCTAGCTTAAAGCCAAAAATATTTTTTTATTCGAAATAATATAGTCGCTATCA
CATCAACATAAATGCCAGTTCTCGACTTTCGCATTAACTTAATTTTTTAATACATGTGCTCTAATCAT
TCCTTCACGTAACACAGAAATTCGATGAACATCGAAATTCGCGGATATTCACGACTCACCTATCTT
TTTTGATACTCTTCACCTCGACTTCTAAAATCGCACTCATACTTTATTGTACAATAAGTAATAATTC
TCATCGGCTGTCTATCCTTTACCGAAGAATAATAACCATGATGATGCTAGCAATTTAATCACCCGAACCT
ATCTTTCACAAATACAGTCGACCCATTCCCGTGCCCAAACTAATCTCGGCGTCGGACTCCACTTCCATC
AACCCGAACACACGAGCCACATATAGCGCACACGTCTTTCCTTCCTCATCTGTCGCCCTCCGCTCTCC
CCACTACAACACTCGGACACCCGCGACTCTCGCCGTTCCTTTTCGCCCTCAAAAATNCCCCTTCCCTCCGTTA
CGAAATCATTCAAGCCCGATTTCCTCTGTCCACCCTCGTTTACCCCTTATACATCTAGCGCGACGAATAAAC
CACCTCACCTAATCAATCCAAACAAACCATCTTCAGCTTACTCGCTCACATTACCTCTTTTCCTTCTTC
TCCACAATAGCAGCCCGTCTGCACTACTTAAGAGGCCGAATACGTTCCGAACAAACACAGAACTATCCT
TCAAAGTCACTCATCTCAAATATTTTAATATTCGCACAAATCATCACAGTACCACATCCTTCCTCGCC
TCTCTGTCACCACACTCCTCTGTCAAACTAAAACAACACCGATCTCTTCCTATATCCATCCAACACTTC
TTTTCGCCTATTCAAGTCACCCTCCCCGCTATATCTCATTTACAGTCCAAATCATTTATTTTTCTATTC
ATTCACTCACTTTTTACAACATCTGTCTCACATATCTTCCATATATCAATCACTCACACACAAAAATC
CTTTTTAGAGTATACATTTTAATCGGCGGTCGTTCCACTCAGCCACAGATAAGCATCACAATCTAAGCA
AATTATTTACTCTCTTCCACAACTAACCCCTATCGAAAGAAAATCATAACCAACATACCCAATATTC
CGAAACCGCTCAAATTTTAAATCGAATCCTCACACTACTCCTAATTAAGAAGCTCGATCTTCTCAAC
AAACACTTCAACCCCGCTACTAAACTATATCATCTCTCTGCACGAAACACTTCCACCCCAAAAGCCACACA
CTTCCTACACTAACCCTTTCCAACTCGGACCTCTCTCCCCTACTATCACATTCACTCTCATCTCTCCTCAA
ATCACCCACTCACAAAAACTACTACTACCCACCCACCCTCATATTACACTCTTTACAAAAAAACCTCCTTA
ACTCACACTTTTTTCTTCGCCTTCTACCTTAAAAATCATATAAATTTTATCTTATTAAAAATATACTCCC
TCACTACTTACCTAAATTTACCCATATTCAAATCTAATACTTTAAAAATCTACGACTCAGTATTTCA
CTCATACAATTTATATTAGTCTTTTATCTTTCACCAATAACTTTTTAACTTCTCTATTCTTAAACTA
CTACTTTTCAATTCTTTACAGAATCATTTCCAACAACTTCTACCTCAAATTCCCCATAACGACCAAA
ACATCCACAACCTTCAACCTTTATTACACAACACTAAACAAAATATTTCATTACTACAAAAAACAAAC
ACAACATCTTTATCCAAAAATTCAGCCTCCTCCAACCACACACTCCTCTTCTTAACCACTTACAACAA
AAAACCCATACACTACACACCACCAACTAACCTTCTAAAATATATTATATTTCTAAAAATTTACTTCTCT
CTCTCTAACTCTTACTAACTCCTTTATTTAAATCATTCTTCATTCTTCCTCTTTTTACCACATTTTA
ACTCTTATATATTTTTTCCCAAATACCATCTCATCTACCTTAACCACGTACCTTACTATTCTACTCAA
ACTTACTTAACATCATTTCACAAAGCAAAATTTCTCACTTCATCTCCCTCCATCTAACTTACTCTCA
```

```
CTATCAATAAATCATTTTACATTATTAGCTCACTGGAAAAACAGAAATATTAATAGTGCATGCTTGC
CTAATGGCATTTTGTCATGTTTAGAAAAAAGAATAATGAAATGTATTCATAAATTGAAGATATTAAT
CAAGTGTTAGTTTTTACTGTGTATTGATTAATATACAGACTTAACAGTAACATATTTTGATAAAGTA
TATGTCTTTGCATCATGTATAGCCAATAATAATTTTGATAAGTTGCCTTAATGTTCCAGCATTAAAA
TGTACTTTAGGAAAACTTTATAAAATTTACATAAATACATTTTCAAACAAAAAAGAATTTACAGTTG
CTTTTTTGGAAGAATTGTGTAATAAGACAGTTATTATCTAAATGACAAAATATTTAAAACAAACTAT
CAGAAAGCCATATCACTTTTCTAATTTTAGAATTAGAATATAACACATTTCCCCCCAAATTTCAAAG
TTAGTTTTGAAGAATTCTTTAGGTTAGTTTTTAGTTGTATACAACTTGATGTTGCTTATCATATAAA
TATGGTCAGGAAGCCCTGCATTCATTTTAAAGAATAAAATTAAAATAAATCTGTTTCTGGCCATATTG
GGATAGTTAATACCTATTTAGCCCTTCTACCATAAACACCAAGAAAAGTCGAAAAAATGTACAAGAC
TACTGTTTTCAGACATTCGACAATAGCCAGTCCAGCACTCTGCATCCCTGAGAGAAGAGAAGCAAGTG
ACATGAACTCTTTGACCACACTAACTTTTGATCCAGAGACATTTTCCAGACTGTGGCACCGCTTGCG
GGAATCTAAGGAAAGCCTGGTGGTCTTATTGAACCGAGGATGTGACATATTAAATTAAATTGAGAGA
CTGAAGTTCAGGGAGGTTAAGGCACATCGAATTTGTAGGGTAGGATACCAGAAAGGAAGGAGCAGTA
CAGAGAAAAAGCCTTCAGAAATCTGCTTAGGAATTCACTTGAGGCCTTTGTTCAATGCCAAGTTTTGTA
CTTGTAAAGTCGGATTCTATGAGCGCCAATGAATACTATCAAGGAGCTACAGCCTGAAAAATTACTAG
TGCCTTATACACGGCTCGGAAGCATGTTCAGGCGTTCCAGCCCAATCAGAAGAAAGATGTGGCTTGAAGCACTTG
GAGCTATTCAGCTAGACATATCAGCAAATGTCATACCTTAGGGAGGCGGCACTAACGCCTAAAACTAACCCTACA
GTAAAAGCCTGCCATACACCTCGACCTTTACGAAGTCTAAAAAAAGCAGACCTTAAAAGGCATCCAGTAGAACCA
CAAAAATATTAAATATGTGCTCGGGACAAAAACATTCTTTCGAAACAAGACAACAAAATCGAGACTGGTC
ACAATAAATAGTAAAAGAATTACTACACATCTGAACAAAACAGAAACAATCTGAGCCATGACGAGGACA
GAAATTATTCAGTGGGAACAGACCCTGAAGTAAGAGATGATCGGAGTCACCAGACAAGTACTTTAAAA
CAGCTCTTCAAATATGCTTATCGATAGAAACAAAAAACTATAATGATCGAGATAGCACTCGAAATGG
CTCGGTGCAGTAACTTGTGCCTGTAATCCCAGCTACTCTAGAGGCCTGAAGTGAAAGGCATCACTTGAG
CCTGGGAGTGAGCTATCACTGTGCTACTGCACTCCAGCCTGGGTGACGGAGTGAGACCCTGTCTCTT
AAAAAAAACAGAAATGGTAAAAAAAAAAATAAAAATAATTGAACTTTTTAGAGATAAAACAAAAATACC
GTCAAATGAAAATTTTATTGGATGTACTTAATAGATTAAGCCAAGTAGAAAGCAATATCAGTGAACGT
AAAAGACAGAGGCCAGTTGAAACTGTTCACAATGAAGTACAGAGCGGAAAAAAGCGATGCGGGAAAAAAACA
CAGTACCTTAGTGACCCCATGCGGATAGTATTATGTGAAGCCTAGGCATAAGTACAATTAATGTCACAGAAG
GGTCGGGACGAGGAAAATAGAAACTGCCTGAAAAAATTTTAATTTTTTAAAATTTCAATGCATGCAAA
TGAAAAAACTTTAATTTTTTGGTTAAAAACATGGTCAAAAAGCCTTGGTGAACTCAAAAGCAAGGTACA
TCAAAGAAATATCAAATGACTTCGGATTTCATCTAAATTAAAAAAAAAGTATGCTTTTCAAAAGATACC
ATTATGAAAATAAAAGCCCGTAACACAGAATGGGACAAAAACATTTGCAGTATGTGTATCTGACAATTC
AGAAATGCCCAGAATATATAAAGAAAAACTTATTACTTAACCAAATCAGTGATTGGCTGGAGTTAGAG
ATGGGATGGGAGGAATGAGTGGAGCAGCAGGGCCATGAGGAAACATTCTGGGCTAATGGAAATGTTCTTTA
```

```
TCTTGATTGTGGTGATGGCTAGTTAAATAAGTGTATGCATTCATCAAATCTCAAATTGTACAACTTA
AATTGAATGAATTTTATATAACTTACACCTCAATAATTTTAAAAGTAATATCAGTCTTTGAATTTAA
TGTTATTTCTTGGTATTTGACATACTATGTTGACATATTTTGCCAAGTGAATAATTTTACTTGAAAA
ATTTTGAGATAAACTATCATAAAGCACTTTAATATTCTCATGGTTCTTAAATTTAGGTTTCTGAATT
TTTGTTATGTCATTTGTGAACTTCACGATTAGTCTTACTTGTATAACAGGTAACTCAACTAACACAG
AAGCTGAAGAATCAGTCAGAAAGTCATAAACAAGCCCAGGAGAATTTGCATGACCACGTACAACAGC
AGAACGCACATCTTAGAGCCTGCACAAGACCGTGTCCTTTCCCTAGAAACTAGTGTCAATGAATTAAA
TAGTCAATTAAATGAAACCAACGAGAACGTCTCCCAGCTTGACATACACGGTAATATTAAATTTAATG
TTTGTGTAAAGCACCAGTTTTAGACACCGTCAAATGTTTTAAATTCTGTTTCTATCTCTTTTTACCTTG
CATATTAATTGAAAAAAATTTGAAATAAGAATTAGATAAAGCGCTATATCTAGATAATTTGTTGAACT
TTCCTGTTTGACTTTCTCCCCTGCTCCCCCTCTCTGTCTCTCCCTCCCTCCTCCCTTCTGCCTTCCT
CTCACTCTTCCTTTCTCCTCTCCCTCTCTCTCTCTGTCTCTGTCTCTCTCTGTCTCTGGCTCTTGCTCT
CAGGTGCGCTCTCTCTCTCCTCAAGCTACACCTAGTGAAATCACTAAATCTTTTAGATTTTCCTTGT
TTTGATCATGCCATGATTGTTTTTTACATTCAAATTAGTTAGATATTATACCATTACATTTCTATGC
TAAATATTTTTTTGACTTTGATTTTTTAAATCTTCCTTTAAAAGTCTGACTTCTGATTAAAAAAAAA
ATTCCCTTACATGGTGCCCGTATTCTTTCAGAATTCTATATAGCAGTCTTCCTCAATGAGTCAATCAT
GCGGTAAGCACTAAGACATAATTTTTTCTCCATTCTTACTATTGATTTCTTATTCTATGATATAGAA
TAGAAATTTATAGAAATAGTTCAACGCCTTGATTTTACTGTAAGATAATGATTCCACTCGAAAGACGG
AATATAATAATATAACTGGCATACTTACTAGAACTTCGAGAGAATATACATTTCTTTCTTTTTTAAA
AAATTATTTGCTAGATGAGTTATATGATAGATAACCTGTTTATGTGGATGTCAAATATAAGCGGGACG
CGAATGAGGACGGAATGCGAGTCTAGTCGACAATGTGAATGAACTAATATATTAGGGCAGTCTGTGAT
TCTTTCTGCATTGTAAGCTCCTTTCCTTTACAAAATATTGCTCTTCCACTGCTATTCATTTCAGAAC
TAGTTCCAGCAATGAGATCAGCCCATTTTTTTGTTACTATCATTGCTCCCATTATCACCTTGACAGT
AACTTCTTCTTTGCCATTACTCTGAAAAATATTACCTGTAGATATTTTTTAAGTTTTTGAGGCTTTT
TTCAAAACTACTTTAACTTCTTTATGAGCTAGTGTTAGTTCATAAAGTAGGATGTATGGCCTTACTT
TTCTTTTGAGAATTAGGACTCTGAGAAAAACCTAGTGCTTTAAGTGATATTATTAATAAAAGAATGT
CAACCAAAAGTGCTTAGCCAAAGGGTATTAGCTGTAGCCAGCTGTAGCTTAACTGTTAAGGTAATGT
TTTTTTCTGGAGTGTCCCTTTAACTATACAAATGACGCCTTTTAAGCTGTTTCTCAGTTTAAAGTTCC
ATAATACACCTTTTGATCTCTACTTCCACGGTACTTCCTTGTGTGCATGATCAGGACAGCATCAAGG
TACATTATTATCGCACATGTATCGAGCGCACTTCACTGCTTTTACTGTTTTAAGGGCTTTAATGCAAAA
GTTGCAACAATTGTAGCCTTGTAGTAATTGGTACTTAGTCATTGCCTATAAAAAGGGCAAACAGAGG
GGCTGGCTATATGAATAGCCACATTTCCCCCCCCGCCCCCCATCAGAAGCCTTTCTAAAATAAGGCA
AACTAGTGGAGCCAATTACTTAATTTCCCCCAAACTTTCTTTATATGCTACATGATTTTGGAATATAC
ATATATTACATTAGTTGAACCATGCTGTATAAAAAGATCATCAGTCGATTATCATATGTTAAAATAT
TTCATGAGTTTTTGGTTCCTCAGATAGATGAAATGCCCGTATGTAAATAAACCTGACTTCTGCAAAAA
```

```
TATATTTGTAGTCTATGCTATATATTCATCAGTATAGATTTACTATGTGTAGTTTAAAGGGAAGATT
TCTTTAGTTTTCGCCTTTAAATCAATGTCAATGTATATACCTTGATGTAACTATTATTTCTGTGAAA
ATTAAGTATTTTGATATTGAGAAAAAATTATCTGAATTTTTCCTTCAGCCCGTAATTAACAAAACAA
TGTAAATCTTAGATTTCTTATGATCATTGATCCTCTCTTCAACCAGATAAAAGAATGCACCCCCCAT
TTTTACTGTTTTCTCAAAAATATGTTAATTTTAAATACATGTTCTTACATAAATTCTTTTTTTGCAA
TCATTCTCTCAAGATTTTGTATGAGACAGATTTTGGCCGTCGCCGCCCGCAAAGGGCGGTTTTTTCT
AAAATTCCATCCCCAGCCTGTTTGAGGGCGCCGATCTAGCTCACTGCAGCCTCCACCTCCCAGGTTCA
AGGATTCTTCTGCCTCAGCCTCCTGAGTAGCTGGACTACAGGTGCATGCCACCATGCCCAGCCTAATT
TTTGTATTTTTAGTAGACATGGGGTTTCACCACATTGGCCAGGATAGTCTCGATCGCCTTGACCTTGT
GATCTGTCTGCCTTGGCCTCCCAAAGTGCTGGGATTACAGGTGTGAGCCACCGCACTTGGCCTATTT
TTTGCTTTTCGTATTCGAGGTGAGTTGTACTAAAGGTATTCCAACACTTAAAGGTGTTACTTTTGAT
AACAAGATACATCTTTTTGCTTGTTTGATTTTATTGGCAGCCTTGAATTTTTAATATTTAATATTTT
GACTGTGAGCTTCAAAAATAAAACCCTTTAAGTGACAAGTTATCACGGAATACTGAATTTTACAAAG
TGCCAGTTGTGCTGGCTGTTTTGAGTCATTGAATTCTGTAATTCTTGATTATCTTCGGAGTAATCAT
TTTTTGGGGCATGGTTATTTACTTTATCATAATAGTGGCAGACTTTCAGATACTCAGTTCTGAAAAT
ACAGTGGCCTTTTTTGGAAAAAAAGTGTACCTTTTCTTTCTTAGCAAAGGAATACTAAAGTGTTTTG
GAATCACATGAGGATATCTTTTTATTATTTATCCAGCATTATTAGGAGTCTTCTCCCCTATCATTCC
TATTTTGGCGATTTTCACATACATATTTTTCAATATATAAATCCATATGTTTTTGCCAAGGACTTAA
TTTTTAAATAGTTTGTTTAGTCACAAAACGAGTGTGCCGTTCAAGCAAGAGGAAATCAAGAACTAAAT
ATAAATTAAATAATTTGTAAATGCTGTTACAGATTAAAGCCCAAAACCGAACTATTACTATCAGCAGA
AGCAGCAAAAACTGCTCAAAGAGCCTGATCTTCAGAATCATTTCGACACAGCCTCAAAATGCATTACAA
GATAAACACCACGTAGGGAAACACATGCAATTTCATACTATCACCTAGTGCTTTGCTAGATAAATAA
ATTGCAAACATGTAAAGCATGATACCCACTTTTGTATAATCTTGTCATAGACTTGCTTATCCCCCTTA
ATTTCTCCATGAGTTCCAGTTGAGTAGTAAAAGTGCGGGTCACATAGATGGAGATAAAAATAACAGCC
TTTGTTTTTGATAAATTTCTACTAGTGTGCAGGTGTGGTTGGTTTCCTGATATTGTCCTTCTCCCCT
AGCCTAGACCTTGGTGTAGACCAGTAATGTTTCCTCCTAAACTTTTGAATTGTTGCCCCATCCCTTCA
AGTGTTGGTGATTGGATGGGGCAGACCACCACACATTTGTTTTTAGTAGGTAGACTGGACCATGACCCA
AATGTACTTGCCACTTGGAAACAGGAAAAGAACACTGTATATTCTACCTCAGTTATAAGAGTTACTC
CTTTCTTGGTAATAGGAGGAAGTGAGGAGCTGGAGGGAATACAGAAGCCGATACTCTGGTAGAATAGA
AGCATCCTACTTTAGGGTCACGGTGAATGTTGCTGGTAGATTTTTCTTAGCCTTTTACTGGTAGAAAT
TTTTAAAATTTACTTGTTATTCAGGGAGTAATATTAGTTATTGGTCTTTTTTTTTTTTTAGATGGACT
TTTTTGCTCTTGTTACCCACGTTGGAGCGCAATGGTGTAATCTTGGCTCACTGAAACCTCCACCTGC
CGCGTTCAAGCAATTCTCCTGCCTCAGCCTCCCAAGTAGCTGGGATTACAAGCATGTGCCACCGTGC
CTGGCTAATTTTGTATTTTTAGTAGAGACAGGGTTTCACCATGTTGGTCAGGCTGGTCTCAAACTCC
GACTTCAGGTGATTCACCCACCTTGGCCTCCCAAAGTGCTGGGATTATAGGTGTGAGCCACCGCACC
```

```
TGGCTTTATTGGTCCATTTTTTAAAAAACAATACACAAGTATATCAACTTAAAAAACACAACAAAAC
AGTTTTCTATATTTACCCTTTATGAAAAGCCCATTTGAATGGAATCTTTGCTGTTAAATTTGGTATG
TGTCCTACTTTTGGTACATAGTAGATTTACTAGTAATTTTTATTTTATTTTTTTTTTTTTTTGTGCAAC
TGGATATTCCAAATGAATTGAAAAGCATCATAAATCTAAACACTGTAATATTTTTAAAAAATAGTTT
TAAAAATTGGTGTGTCTTGAACATTGAAAATATTTAATTATAATATAAAAGTGTTATTTTATTATTAGC
CTGGCTAATATTTGGCTCCTAAAATAATTCTTCCTAGATAAACATTGAAAAGTTATTAAACTGTTAT
ACATATAAAACTTAGGATCTCAGACTATGCAAGAATTTAGTTCATGTCGTTTATATTGGTAGGTAAGT
ATAGCCCTCTGATATATCATTAGATTTATCTGAGCTCTTACTCCAAATATTTTTTTAAATAAAATTAG
AGTTTTCAATTTTACGTTGAACATTTGGCCACTACAATATAGTAAACCTTACCAAAGTTTTCTTCAA
TTGTACTTTTCTAAAGCAGTTAAATAAGATTACTACTCAGTTGCATCAGGTCACTGCAAAGTTACAA
GACAAGCAAGAACATTGCAGTCAGCTGCAAAGTCATCTTAAAGAATATAAAGCAGAAATACCTCTCTT
TAGAACACAAAACCGAAGACCTAGAAGCGTCAAATTAAGGTTTGTATAAAAGCAGTTGAATTTAGTCA
TATTTTCTACTTCAGTAGCAATGGAATCTCATGACCTACATGCAATCAAAGATTTTTAGTTAACAAA
GAAACGTGAAGTTGTGGTATAAAATTTTTAAAAAATTGCTTGTAATTTTTCATGTGTCTTAAGTTTGAA
TTCTATCTTTATTTTTAAATGTCTCCCTTAATGCAGCATCTTTTATAAATGACAGTCAACTTACATACT
GATTCCATTGTAATGTGTTACTTTTTCCAAAGCACAGATAACCAGGTATCTACTCTACCATTACAAGG
AACTTCTCAATTTTTTGTTGTGAAGTCTCTTCTGTTCCTTCATTCTTCCATCTCTTACCAACTTACT
CCAATATCACATTTCAGATATGGTAGACTTTTCCTTTTTAGAACTTTATACCCTTTGGATTTTGCTT
CTAATTTAAAAACACATTGACACTATGATAAACTGTATCTTACTTTAACACAACTCCATATGAATGT
GTTGATTTACTGAACAGATAAGATGATTAGACATCTCAGCAAGCGATTTGACCTGAGTTTTTGTGTCCT
TCAAATTAGCAACCCGCTTGCTGCTTAACTGCCCTTTGGCTAAAAATAAAAAAAAAAACCATTTTTAAAA
ATTGAGCTACTATCAGTTAAACAAAAACTTCTCAAGTTACTATATATGTAACTTATACTTCCTCACC
CCGGTGAAGCCGTGTGTGTATAAGTTTAGAGAAAAGAAATGAATATATGTACATACATACCAATATAG
TATCGGCGAATAATTACATTTACAATTCTGTTTATAGGTTCCTTTTTCTTTATGACAAACGATAATA
GCAAAGCCAGCGTACTTTAGGCCATCGTTAAAAATAACAGAAGTATTATTTTACTGAAAAGTGTCTAA
TGAGAATTCTTTTTGGGTACCTATTAAAAATAGTGGTTATTTAGAACTGAGTTTTTATTGTTTTTAT
CAGCTCTAACACTTTGTAATTATCATTTTAGGGACTATCATATTTTTTATATAGACATGTATAATTA
ATTTAGCTACATCAAATATCTTTTATTTAATGAATATTTTCAGTGTAGGTCAATGGTAAGCGCTACA
GATACCAATCAGTTTATAAAATATTTAGTGTGCCAAAATCACTACCACTGCAAGCGAAATGCATTGTGT
AAAGCCTTTTCAAACTTATATTCAACAGTTTGATTTTGTAAGTTTGTAAAAAATACACACATAATTACA
TGTATACATGTGAGCATGCCAAACTATATTCTGAACAACAACAATGTCATCTAGTCCAAGAGATTAAAG
AAGCAAAATCAGGAACTTAATTGGCTTTATATTTACGATCAATAGGTGTTAATGAGAAGCGAGTACGT
GACAACTTCATTTTTAGTTTTAAATATCTTATAATTACATCAGTGTTTTTAAACTGTGACTATAAAAGA
TAATATGTTTTAAGTGAGTAGACATCAGTGAACCTGTTAACTTATTTTTTTCATACTTGAGTTAATAACT
TTTACTGAGATAATAACTATTTATGTTTCTATGTTTCTTTTAAGTTGATTGTTTCATTCACAATTAA
```

```
TTTTTTTTTTTTTTTGACATGGAGTCTCATTCTGTTGCCCAGGCTGGAGTGTAGTGGTGCCATCTCAG
CTCGCTGCAACCTCTGCCTCCCAGGTTCAAGCCGTTCTCCTGCCTCGGCGTCTTGAGTAGCTGGGAC
TTCAGCCACCGGCCACCACGCCTGGCTAATTTTTTTTTTTTTTTTTTTTTTTTAGTACAGATAAGGTTT
CACCATGTTGGCCAGGCTGGTCTCGAACTTCTGACCTCAAGTGATCTGCCTGCCTCTGCCTCCCAA
GGTGCTGGGATTACAGGCGGTGAGCCACCGCGCGCCCAGCCCAGAATTATTTTTAAACCCCACCCCTT
AGTGGCAGTCTATCATCTATAAAGCTTTCTGCTGGGGTCCTCTCGAAAAGATTTTAAAAATAAATAAC
ACCCTTTAGTAATCGTTTCACAATATGTTTTTTATATAAATAAATTTTTTTTTCTAATGTCACACCTG
TTTCAATATAAACAAAAAATGTTATACTATTTAATAATAAATTATAATACTAAANTATTAAAATGGC
TGCCATATCATATTTCTTTCATACAAACTACAAGCTGATAGTCTTCAAGTTAAAGCAAGCAAGGAGC
AGCCTTTGCAAGATCTACAACAGCAAAGACAGCTGAACACACAGATTTAGAGCCTCAGAGCCACAGAATT
CAGTAAACAACTTCAAATGGAGAAGCAAATGTAAGCTAAACCACTTTACTTACAAATTAAGCGAAAA
GATTGTGAACTAAGTATTAAAATTTCCTTCAGATTTAAATTTTGCTATCGTAGTGCTTAAAGACTTA
TTAGATATTTATTTTGTGTTCATTTTATAAACTGATCTTAATGTGAATCAAAAAATAAAGCCATCAT
AATAGCGTTAAACTTCTCTACAAAACGACTGAAAACTTAGTTTTATAAAATTTCGGTCATCCACTTTC
TTTTCAACAATGATATCGTGCTCATTTCTCTGGCATAAACCTTGCTTTTATGTTGTTCACAAATTTCA
ATAAATTACTGTAAAATTAAAAAATTCGGGGATATTTATGTGTTACCCAAAAGTAGTTAGCCCTTCTA
GCTATACCAAATACGGAATGGATTCTTTCTTATAAGAAGTGATCTTCTCAGCCTCGGCTAGCCATAGCA
AGATTGCTTGAGCCTTGGGAGGTCGAGGCTGTCACACCACTGCACTCCAGCCCTCGGGCGACAAAGTGAT
ACTCTATCTCAAAAAGCAAAAAAAAAAAAAAAATAACCTCAGCTTTGTGATCCATTTTGGCAGATTCT
CTATGTTTATGAGCACAAAGCAAACACAAAAACCAGTGTGCCTTCTTGTTTTTCTTATTGATGCCAA
ATTCACACATAGTTAAATGCACAGATTTTACATATGTACTTTGAGTTTTAATCAGTGTATATTCTGT
GTATCTGTGGATCTAGCCACAGCACCATATAGGACATTGTCATCACTCCAGGAGTTTTCTCACTTGC
CCTTCTAGTCAATACCTTCCTTATCCTTTTCCTGTAGACAACCACAGTCTATGTGTCTATATGGTAT
CCTGACACCAGTATCATGGTATTGGTACCTAAATATCATAGTATCTAATATCATAATTATGATATTCA
AAGTCATAAATGTAGCCTAAGTTGGTGTGCCATAACACACAAAGCAAACCAGAAGATATTTTTAATAT
ACCATAAAATGGTATATTTTTAATGTAGCCTTTATGATATTAGATATTAATCCTTCTCCTTTATTATT
TTTCAAGATTGTCTTGACTCTTCTAAGTTCATTGCTTTTCCATACACATTTTTGTATTAACTTGTAC
ATGTCTACAAATAAAACTGTTGTATTTTCATTAGAATTCCCTTGAAACTATAAATCAATTTGGGGAG
AAATGACATCTTAACAACATTGACTCTTCTAATACACAAACATATGTCTCTTTATCTACTTGGGCCT
TCTTTAATTTCTCTGAGCAGTATTTTATGGTTTTTAACATAGACATCTTGTACATCTTTTGTTAAAT
TTATTCCTGAATATTTTTTTAATGCTATTGTAAATGTAATTGTTTTTTAAATTTAATTTTCCACTTA
TGACTAGTATAAAAATAGAATTTTTAAATATATATTGACTTTTCTGCCTATAACCTTGCTCAATTTA
CTTTTTAGTTTTAGTTGTTGTTTGTACAGTTCTTGATGTTTTCTAACTAGACATTCATGTTATCTGT
GAATAGACACAAAATTTACTTCTTCCTTTCCAACCTATAGGCCTTTTATATCTTTTTTCTTGCTGCCT
GGGACATCCAGTAACATTGTGAATGTAAACAGTATTGGCAAATATCTTTGCATTATTTCTAATCTTA
```

```
GGCAGGAAATATTAAATCTTTCATCATTAAGTTTGAGGTTAGCTGTAGGTTTTTCTGAGATTCCCTT
TATCAGATTGAAGACATTACCTTTGATACCTAGTTATATATAAAAAAAAAATTATCGGCCTTGTGGC
TCATGCCTGTAATCCTAGAAATTTGGGAGGCTGAGGCAGGCAGATCATCTGAAGTCAGGAGTTCGAG
ACCAGCCTGGCCAACAGGGTGAAACCTCGTCTCCACTAAAAATACAAAAATCAGCAGGGGATGGTGG
CACACGCCTGTAATCTCAGCTACTCGGGAGGCTGAGGCATGAGAATTGCTTGAACCTGGGAGGCACA
AGTTTCAGTGAGCTGAGATCATGCCACTGCACTCCAGTGCCACTGCACTCCAACCTGGGCGACAGAG
CGAGACTCCGTCTCAAAAAAAAAATAATTATTAAAAAACAAAAATTACCGTGCTTGGATTGAATTTT
ATCACCTTTTTTCCTGTATCTGTTGATGTGATCATATGGATTTTCTGTTTTATTCTGTTAATATGGT
CAGTTACATTGATTGATTTACTGTTAAACCAACCTTGCTTTCCTGGGATAAATTAACTTGACCATGC
TGTATTACCTTTTTGTATATTGCTGTTTTTGATTTGATAATACTTTGTTAAAAATGTTTCATATATT
TATGAGGGGTATTGGTCTGTAGTATTCTTTTAATATCATTGTCAGGTTTTGATATCAGAGTTATACT
GGCCTTAAAAAGGAATTGAGAAGTATTTCCTCCTCCTTTCTGAAATAGTTTGTATGAGATGGATATT
ATTTGTTTCTTAAAAGTTTGATGGAATTCACTAGTGAACTGGCTAGCCTTAGAGTTCTCTTTCTGGA
TTGTTTCATTTGGGGTTCAATTCATTTAATAGACACATAGAGCCTATTCTAATTTCCTGATTTTTTTTC
TTGAGTCAGTTTTGGTACATTGTGTCTTTCAGAAATGGGTTCATTTCCTCTAAACTTCAAGTTTATT
GGCAGTTGTTCATAATATTACACTTTTAAGGTCTGTTAGCGATCTGTAGTAGTGTTCCTCCTTTATTC
TTAATCATGCTAATTTGTCTTTTTAAAAAATCAATTTAATTAGAGATTTATCAGTTTTATCAGACTAT
TGTAAAAAGCTTTTGATTTATTTTGTCAGTTTTCTATCTTATTTATTTCTCCTCTTTATTGTTTCCA
TCTTTAGACCTTATTACTTTGCTTTTTTTTAATAGCTTTTAAATGTGAAAGCCGTCACTGTGTCTGTC
TACATTTTGTAGTATCTGTTTCTTTTTTTTCAGTTACCCACTTTTCACTTGTCAATGCTAGATGTAAG
ATTTCTGCAGATGGTAGTATGTAGCCTTATTCTAATAAAATCAGTGTATTATGACAGTTTTGCCACA
GATGGAATAAATTATCTTGAAAGACGGTATCTTTTTTCTAATTTGCACTAAAGTGCTCAATGGATTC
ATGCCACCTCTGAGTATAAGGGTGGATTGGTTTAGAAGTTATTGGGACCTATACGATTTATTAGTAT
ATGAAATTTCAAATGTCTCTGGTGGCAGAATGGGCATGTGCTTCTGAACATATATAGCCATAGAAGT
GCTTAGCTGCAGCATCATTCGTTCACTCCCAAGGTAGAATTAGTCTCTTGCCCAGCTTATCCTTGAT
GTTGATGCTGAATTTGGGTCCTGCCATGATGAGATCTTCAATGAACACATCACTCACCATTATTTTG
ATGGATAAAAATCAGTTCCACCCAATTCATTTGAATGTCTTCATATAACTGGTTACATTTGAGTACA
TTTTGTCTTTAAACATCAAATCACCTGCTCTGACTGAGTTGATGGACTTGACTTGTGTCAAGGGGAT
GAGGGCTCTTGACTGTTCCAGTAGTAAAGGTAGAGACTAACGAACCTGAGAAAAGTCCTCTTCAGAAA
GGTGAAATAAAACCCATCAGAGTTGATGATTAAGTTGTTTCACACACTTCATGGTTTTCATCCTTGTT
TGGGCATATGATGGTGAAAATATTCTCATTTTCATATCTAGTAAATTGGGTCCTGATGCTTTGAATC
GGAGCTTATAGAATTGCATCTTGTGCCTCAGGTGGCATTCCTCCTCACGGTAGTTTCCAGTGCCTAG
CTATTTGACGAGCATATCTGATCCATTACACTTACCAACCAAATGGTTCATCATTATCTCTAGAATGC
AGGGCATCAGTCCATGAAGATCATCTCCGAGATGGCTTTTGTTCTGTTCCTCAAAAACTCTGCAGGCC
CAATGGTTCTTTCTGTTTCCAATGGGCCCAATGGAAGTGGACCCATTTTCATTCTATGTTCTAATCT
```

```
CATCGTTCAGAATTCACTTACAGGGCTCCCACATCCTATTGGGGTAGGAAAACCTTTAAGATCTTTC
TTGCCTATGTACTTTGTACATACATTTCTCCTCTGAGGTCTTCTCACATTTCTGGAGTACTACCTAG
GCAAGGAGGGCTGGGGTCCCTTCTGCTCTTATATCAGATAAACATATAGAGACTTTGACTAAACCCC
ACCCATGAGCCCAGGGCTTAGCCCAAATAACAGGATACAGGGCTCCCCTTTTTGAGGGCCCCCTTAC
ATTTATACACCCAATGTTTCCCTCCCATCTTACAATGTATTTTCATTCCTCTGCAGTTTAATATATT
TTCTGATTTCCTTTGTGATTCCTTCTTTAATGTGTAGGTTATAAGTATGTTTACTTTCCAAATATTG
AGGCTTTCCTAGGTATATTATTCTTACTGATTTTTTTTTTTTTTTTTTTTTTTTGAGACAGAGTCTCA
CTCTGTCGCCCAGGCTGGAATGCAGTGGCGTGATCTCGGCTCACTGCAACCTCTGCCACCTGGGTTC
AAGCGATTCTCCTGCTTCAGCCTCACGAGTAGCTGGGATTACAGGTGCCTGCCATCATGCCTGGCTA
ATTTTTGCGTTTTTAGTAAAGATGGGGGTTTCACTGTGTTAGCCAGGCTGGTCTCGATCTCCTGACC
TTGTGATCCGCCCACCTTGGCCTCCCACAGTGCTGGGATTACAGGCGTGAGCCACCGTGCCTGGCCC
TAATTTCTAATTTAATTTTATGGCGGGCCAGAGAACATTCTTGGTAAAATTCAAACTTTTGAAAGTAA
GTCTTATTTAAGCCCCAGCATATCGCTTATCATAATTAATTTTCCATGTGCACATATATGCACTCTG
TGTTATTGGGCGGAGTGGCTATAAATAACAATTACAGGGCTCGTTCTTATTCNCTATNATCTTGCCAC
TTCCATCCTCTGGTTGCCCTATCAGTTTCCAAAAAGACATATTATAGGTTTCAACTATGATTGTGGA
CTTGTTATTTCTTCCCTAGTTACTTAAAAAAAACCAGAAGGTGTCACAGTGACTATGTAAGCCTCCT
ACTCCCTTTGGGCTTTTCTTGAGTCACCAAGTTCTGATGATTCGGTAAATAATTTCAAAAAGTTAAG
CAGCATAGTAAATAAATATATCAAGTCTTAATTCTAAGGGTGCTTAACACGGATTTTAACTATATTA
AAATGTAAAATAATATTAGTATAATGACTTTTCCATTTCGGACCTTTAAAAATCAACGAGGAATAATA
TCTTGTGAACCTATTAAGCCTTTAACATCTTTTCCAGCCTATTTTTTAGGAGGTAAAAGTGTGTTTCTA
GAACTAAAAAATTACATTTCGAGGTATAAATACAGTTTTGATATTGTATTAATACACAATTTCAAAT
ACTTTATTAGTACATCTTTTAACAACCTCCCTTTAACATATTGACTTATTTTTATTGGTTACAAATT
TATTCTGATTACATTGGAACTAGTGTGCATTCTAGAAATACTGTTACTTAGCATCTGGTTTTGACTT
TTAAAATGCCTGTTATTTATAGTGTATTGAGGGTTTTGCTGTATAATTTGCATAGTTCCTTTTATCA
AAACAATAAAGTCTATAGCTTTCTAAAGCTATAACTTTATTTCTTCATTCTTGTTGCTTTTTGTCA
TTCATCGTATAAGAGAACTATATTAAGGAACAAATGATAACAAATCCTTTGTATAATCTGCTAGCTTC
TAGGGTTAAAGTAAATCATTTGTCTTCCCTCTATATTGTAAATAAAATATTTTTTTAATTTTCTTTC
TTTGATTTTTTTCTGGGTTAACCATAAATATTTTGAAGCCTAAGAACTCTCACACATAAATGTGTTTC
ATGTTTTCAAGGAAAGAGACAAAGTTCTCTCTGTCGTTGGAGAACTAACATAATGAATAGATTCTTTA
TGGAAAAACGTTTCTGGCTGTTATAGAGTAGAGGGCTCTGTCGATACATAGTTTTTTTCCTCGGGATTA
GTTGTCGCCGACAAAAATGGATTAAGTCAGGAAGCCTTAGATAGTTTTGTCTTCACTACTAACTTATT
TGACTTGGGAAAAATAATCTACATCTGTTAAATGATCAAATGAGATGTTCTAAAGTATTTTTCAGTG
GTGCGATTTTATCAAATTAAATTATTTTTACTTGTGAACTATACAAAAAAGTTTCAGAACTCAGTAA
TTGTTTGTGATTAATTTTGAATGGTAAATTAGAAGTGGTAAATTATGTGTTATTTAAAAACATTGTT
TTTTAAATATTAGAGTANGCAGTACACANGNTTCGCTCAAACATCGGGTGATTGTATTCTAGTTGTTGA
```

```
TTGAAACCACACTTGTGTTGTAGATGCCAGCCATGTAACTAGCAAAATTATAATTGCTTCATGCCCA
AGTTCTGAATCAACATTGTTCAAATTTATATCCTGGCTATGCCATTTATTAGCTATGCCATTTCGCC
ATCTTTTAGACCAAATACTTAATCTCTGTGCCTCTAGTTTCTATATGATAGAGTCTATATGAATCTAT
GTGATAGAGTTATTGTGAGAAATAAATGGGTTAATATCTTTAAAGTACTCAGTACACTGACTATAAT
AAAGTAAATGCTCATGCTAGTTATTATTTTATCATTGGTTATATCATATATCATCCTTATTGTCATA
CTCTCTGACTCCTGTTTTGCATAAAAATATTTTGCTATTCATTGTGGAGATAAGCTGAGACGTCTAT
ATATAACACTAACATTTTTTCAAAAGTAACTTTGGATATGGTCAAATGCTTGAATGTAATGCTAGGT
TCTTAGTAAAATATGCATAGAACATGAAAACATGACTTTGGTTGGAGGGTGGGAGATAATAGTGGTT
TACCTTGGTGACAGAGGAACTTCAGTGTGACTTCTGTATGATGTCTGAATTTGAACAGAAACATATC
CTAGTGGATTGTACAAACAAGGTAGTAGTAAAATATGCCCCAGATCTCTAAATGAGGTAACTATTCT
ACAGTGTATTATTATTATTTTAAACAGAGTCTCGCTCTGTCAGCCAAGCTGGAGTGCAGTGGCG
CAATCTCGGCTCACTGCAACCTCCACCTCCTAAGTTCAAGCGATTCTCCTGCCTCAGCCTCCCAAGT
AGCTGGGATTACAGGTGCCTGCCACCACGCCTGGCTAATTTTTGTATTTTTAGTAGAGACAGGCTTC
ACCATGTTGCCCAGGCTGGTCTCGAGCTCCTGACCTCAAGTAACCTGCCCGCGTTGGCCTCCAAAAG
TGCTGGGATTATAGGCGTGAGCCACCTGGCCTGTGCAGTGTAATTTAATGTCATCAGACAGATACTAA
ATGTATTTTCTGAAAAGTGATTTTGTTTTTATCATAGTTACTATAGAGCTATTCTTTGCGACAACTG
TGGCCAATAGGCTTAGTGGCATATGAGAATTTTTTTTTTTAATTATTATTTTTTGAGATGGAGTCTC
TTGCTCTGTTGCCCAGGCTGGAGTGCAGTGGCACGATCTCGGCTCACTGCAAGCTCTGCCTCCTGGG
TTCACACCATTCTCCTGCCTCAACCTCCCGAGTAGCTGGGACTACAGGCACCTGCCACCACACCCGG
CTAATTTTTTTGTATTTTTAGTAGAGATGGGGTTTCACTGTGTTAGCCAGGATGGTCTCGATCTCCT
GACCTCGTGATCCTCCCGCCTCAGCCTCCCAAAGTGCTGGGATTACAGGTGTGAGCCACCGTGCCTG
GCCCGAGAATATTCTTCAAAGACAGTTGACATCCAACAATTTAGACATTGATGTTGACATACCTATTT
TCCATAATACAAGAGAATACTAATGTAGATCATTTACAAGCTGTAACTATACAATTATAAGTCAAAA
AGAAAGCTAGTGTTAAAAAAAATAATAAAGATTAATCCAGCATGTCACCTAATAGTGAATAGTGTTG
GTTATGAAACCAATATGACGGCCAGCTATCTTTACTAATTATCTGTAGCCAACAGCCTCAGTAATTTC
TTCCTACAGTAGTGCCTGGAGTGTAGTAGTTACTCAGTAAATTGTCTTTTGAATGAACAAATGAAGG
CTAAATACATTTTTTTTTTCTAGTTACTCAGTACATCGTCTTTTGAATGAACAAATGAAGGCTAAATA
GATTTTTTTTTTCTTTCAGGCTTCTCATCAGTTGAAATTGGAACTCAATTCAATGCAGGAACAACTT
ATACAGGCCCCAGAATACTTTAAAACAAAATGAAAAGGAGGAGCCAACAACTTCAGCGGGAACTAAATG
AGCTAAAGCAATCAAGTGAACAGAAGAAAAAACAAATTGAAGCCACTCCAACGAGAGCCTTAAAATTGC
TGTTTTACAGAACGTAGTGATATATTTGTTTACTTTTTATAGCAAGAAAAACTTGGCAATTAAGAAA
ATAGTATGATGATTAATACAGATGCATAAGTTGCAACATTGAAAAGTTTTACATAAGCTAATTTTTTT
CTAAGTTTAATATATGAAAGCATTTGACTATATTATCAAATACCTGAGTCTGGATTTCCATTCACTA
TAACTCTCTTGTCAGATAATTGTTATTTAAAATTATTGTACTAATCATTTGATAGACATGAAACTAT
CTTATTAAAAATAATATATAACTGGCCGGGCACAGTGGCTCACGCCTTGTAATCTCAGCACTCCAAGG
```

```
CACGCAGATCACCTGAGGTCAGGAGTTCAAGACCAGCCTGGCCAACATGGTGAAACCCCGTCTCTAC
TAAAAATACACAAATTAGCTGGGCGTGGTGGTGCATTCCTGTAATCCCAGCTACTCAGGAAGCTGAG
GCAGGAGGCAGAGGTTGCAGTGAGCTGAGATCATGCCGCTGCACTTCAGCCTGGGCGACAGAGCGTAC
TCTCTCTCAAAAAAAAATAATAATAATAATAATGTAACACTTAAGCAAATAATTTATGCAACATTCA
TCCTGTATTAGAAAAATTTAAAGCAATTTAAAATAAATCATTCTTATTAACGGCTAAGAATAAAAAT
TACAAAGTCGGATATCTTAAAAAACATTCACTAGTGTAAAGCCTTCATATACTTTTAATTATTAATATT
TTAAGTTACACTGTAATGGTTTCCATTTCCAAATCTATTCTAATTTATTATTGAGCATATTTTTTAT
TCTTAAGTGTTTTAATACTTGTCCAGACCAAGAGTTGGTAAAAATGGATTATACTTAATATGAAATA
TTTGAGCACAATGAGTTCCTTCTCTACTGTTAGTATGTCCATGTTAATTGGTCTATGGAGAAGATAG
TAGAATCCCTCCTATGTAGAATAAACTAAATATATCATGCCATTAAGAGTTGGCTTTCATACTGCTA
AAGTACAAAGTATATAAATTAAAACAATCAAAAATACACATTTTATGTTGACCACTGTTTTTGTAGC
TATTATTATGCTGCTTTACAAAATAGTAGTTCTTTAATAATACAACCAAGAGTAGACAAATGTGTCT
ATTCTTTTGTTTTTCTTACCATATATAATCAAAAGTCAACATGTAATTATCACAGTGCATACTTTGT
TGTATGCTTTCATATCCTGAGGTCATTTTCTTCAAAATATACTAGCCTTGTATCCAAATATTTACAA
AATCTTCGTTTTTATAGCATCGTAACTTAGTGAAATAAAAAACACAAGTATTTTTAGCATGTTTTCT
TATTTAAAAATTATGAGTTATAATAATATTTCTTTTGGATTTGTGATTAATATATATTCCCTGTACA
GTTGACCCTCCATATCTGTAGATTCTGTAACTGCCACTTCGACTTGAAAATATTTGCGACAAGAAAAC
CAATAAAAAGTAACAGTACAGTATTAAAAAATAATACAAAATTGCCTGCGTGCCAGTGCCTCACACCT
GTAATCCCAGCCACTTTGGGAGGCTGAGGTAGGCACAGCATTACTTAAGGTCAGGAGTTCGAGACCAGCCT
GGCCAACATGGTGAAATCCTGTCTCTACTAAAAATACAAAAATTAGCTGGGCATGGTGGTGTGCCACC
TGTAGTCCCAGCTACTCCGAAGGCTGAGGCAGGAGACTCGCTTGAACCCCAGAGGCGAGAGGTTGCAG
TGAGCCAAGATCGTGCCACTGCACTCCAGCCTGGGCAACAGAGCTGAGACTCCATCTCAAAAAACCAA
AACAAAACAAAACCAAAACACCCAAAATTTAAAATACAGTAAAACAACTATTTACATAGCCATTTACA
TTGTATTAGGTATTGTAAGTAATCTAGAGATGTTCAAGCCAGCCAGATCTGAATGCAAATTTTGTTT
AATTTTGTTAAATTTGCACACACATTAACTTACTCGTCATAGAGAAATGATTCATCTTTCTGAGCTC
AATTTAATGCAGTCATAGAGTTCTTGTGTAAAGATTGAGATAATGTATTTAAAGTTTCTAGTACTGTGA
CTCATACAAATCTGGAAGTAAAATAGTTGTTCGGATATTATATGGAAGTATAGCAAACTCTGACCTGAG
AATGTCAGTCTGTATATGGTAGACCATGTAATAATAGCCCATGACAAAGTTATCATTGTCACTGGCCCA
TGGTCAAGTAGGCAAAACAAGGATAATGTCTTTAAATGGGTATAGATGTGTGTGTGTGTACACACTTAAAT
ATATATATAAAACATAAAAATATGTATACACACATTATGTCTACATATGTACTTTTATATCTATAGC
TATAGAGTTATATATATAAGTAGATATCTATAGATATATAGTTTTTCCACATTGAAGGTCATAATGCA
CTTACACATTTTTCTGCATATATATATATATAAATAAAAAGTAATACTACACGCATTAAAAATACCAAAAT
TTAAAATACAGTAAAAACAACTATTTACATAGCCATTTATATTGTTAATGCTATGTTACCTAATGGTA
TTGTAAGTAATCTAAAGATGATTTAAAACATTATATATAGCCATAAGACTATTCGGGAGTTACTGATC
TAGAATCAAGAAAGCCATGCTGTTAAGTCAACAATCCCTCACCAACTTTGCTCAAAATCTAATGTGGA
```

```
AATATAAAGTGAATAGGATATGCCCCCTTATTTTCAAGCACCTTATAATTTAATGAGAAAGCAAAAT
GTAAAGCAAAACAAAACTGTATTATATAATGGAGCAGTTATCAAACTGTTGCATTTATCTGTTTTTT
TTTTCATTTAACTTCTTCACTAATGGATTTGAGTTCCTCAAAGACAGAGAATTTTGTCTTTTCTAGC
AAATAAGCTCTTAATCATTTTAAAAAAATGAATGAATGAGTTTGTCAAAGCAAAAATATTGAAAGCC
CAAACATGAGCCCAAAGAGCTATTATGGCCATTATTGAGACTTCACAGAGAGCCTTAGTTAAGAGTCA
GAACAATAATTAAAGAGTTAAGAAACCTAGATTTGTGAAAAAAGTTAAAGAAAAGAAGCAGTATTTT
AGAAAAGAAATCTGTAGGTGCATTATGACCGTCAATGTGAAAACATATCCAGGAATTCTTCAATGTG
AATTGGAAGAAGAACTCTATGAAAGGAGGATGGCATGGGATGTTATCAGATACTGTATAGGGACATC
AGCTCTCTGCTCCCCGATAGGCAGTTAGGACCACCAATTCCTATCATTCTGTCTCCTAGCTTTCTTGAAT
CCATCCTTCTCATTTTCCACTGCTACAGCCTTAGTCCAGACTTTCTTTTTCTCTTATCTAGGCTGTT
AATATAGCCTAATAAATGTTCCGGGCCCTCCAGTCTATTTGTCATTCAATCACTTGTTTGAGAAATA
TTACTAGGCACTTATTTTATGCCATGGCACAATTCTAGGTGCTGAAGACGACACAGCTGCGAATAAA
ACAGACATGGGACCTGTTCTTGTGGAGCTTATACTTTAGTGCGTAGAGAAACTAAACACAGACGGTAT
GAAAGATAGTGATGGGACATAATTCTACTGAAGGTTGGGTGATCAAAGAAGCTTTGCTGAAGAGATT
TGAGTTGATGTTGGTATTTTCTAAAAACAGATGACCAATATGGTTAAATTTGGTTCTGAGGGAGAAG
GTAACATGAGATGAGCTCAGATAATTAGACAGCGCCCCAGATCATTTATATGCAAATTAGATTATGAG
ATAACAGAATGCTATATTTTATTCTAAGGGCAATTGGACTCTATTGGAGAATTTAGAACAGAGAATG
CTGCGCTTTGACTAAACGGAAAATAAAGGATTTTGTGAATGATTATAATGATTTGTGAATATATTTT
GGAACTTGCATCATCACGGACTTTCTGATAGATTCAAAAGTGAGAGGTAATAGGAAGAGGATCAAGCA
TAAACTGGGTTTGTGCATGTGGGTAGTTGGTAATGCCATTTATTGGGGGAAGTAGGAGCTTTTTTTT
TTCTTTTATTTAAGTTCTAGTTTACATGTACAGAACATGCAGGTTTGATACATAGGTATACATGTGC
CATGTTGGTTTGCTGCACCCATCAACTCATCATTTACATTAGGTATTTCTTCTAATGATATCCCTCC
CCCAGCCCCCCACCCCCTTTGTTTGAGTTCTTTGTAGATTCTGGATATTAGCCTTTTGTCACATGGG
GAGATTGCAAAAATTTTCTCCCATTCTGTAGGTTGCCTGTTCGCTCTGATGGTAGTTTCTTTTGCCG
TGCGGAAGCTCTTTAGTTTAATTAGATCCCATTTGTCTATTTTGTCTTTTGTTGTCATTGCTTTTGG
TGTTTTAGTCATGAAGTCCTTGCAATGCAGCCTCTTTTTTCGGTTCCATATGAACTTTAAAGTAGTTT
TTTCCGATTCTATGAAGAAAGTCATTGGTAGGCTTGATGGTGATGCCATTGAATCTATAAATTACTTT
GGGCACTAAGGTCATTTTCATGATATTGATTTTTTCCTATCCATGACCATGGAATATTCTTCCATTTG
TTTGTGTCCTCTTCTATTTCATTGAGCAGTAGTTTGTAGCCTGTCCTTGAAGATGTCCTTCACATCCC
TTGTAAGTTGGATTCCTAGGTATTTTATTCTCTTTGTACCAATTGTGAATGGGAGTTCACTCATGAT
TTGGCTCTCAGTTTGTCTGTTAATAGTGTATAGGAATGCTTGTGATTTTTGCACATTGATTTTGTAT
CCTGAGACTTTGCTGAAGTTGCTTATCAGCTTAAGGAGATTTTGGGACTGAGACAATGGGGTTTTCTA
AATATACAATCATGTCATCTGCAAACAGGGACAATTTGACTTCCTGTTTTCCTAATTGAATACCCTT
TATTTCTTTCTCTTGCCTGATTGCCCTGGCCAGAACTTCCAACACTATGTTGAATAGGAGTGGTGAG
AGAGGGCATCCTTGTCTTGTGCCCGTTTTTAAAGGGAATGCTTCCAGTTTTTGCCCATTCAGTATGA
```

```
TATTGGCTGTGGGTTTACTATAAGTAGTTCTTGTTATTTTCAGATACGTTCCCTCAATATCTAGTTT
GTTGAGAGTTTTTAGCATGAAGGCTGTTGAATTTTGTCGAGGGCCTTTTCTGCATCTATTGAGATAC
CATGTGGTTTTTGTCGTTGGTTCTGTTTATGTGACGGATTACATTTATTGATTTGCATATGTTGAAC
CAGCATTGCATCCCAGGGATGAAGCTAACTTGATTGTGGTGGATAAGCTTTTTGATGTGCTGCTGGA
TTCGGTTTGCCAGTATTTTATTTGAGGATTTTCGGATCGATGTTCATCAGGGATATTGACCTCAAAT
TCTCTTTTTTAGTTGTGTCTCTTCTGGGCTTTGGTATCAGGATGATGTTGGCCTCATAAAATTAGTT
AGGAAGGATTCCCTCTTTTTCTGCTGATTGGAATAGTTTCAAAAGGAATGGTACCAGCTCCTCTTTG
TATCTCTGGTAGAATTCAGCTGAGAATCTGCCTGGTCCTGGACTTTTTTTGGTTGGTAGGCTATTAA
TGATTTCCTCAATTTCAGATCCTGATATTGGGCTATTCAGAGATTCAACTTCTTCCTGGTTTAGTCT
TGGGACGGTGTATCTGTCCAGGAATTTATTGATTTCTTCTAGAAATTTTCTAGTTTATTTGTGTAGA
GGTGTTTATAGTATTCTCTGATGGTAGTTTGTATTTCTGTGGGATCGGTGGTGATATCCCCTTTATC
ATTTTTTTATTGCATCTATTTGATTCTTCTCTCTTTTCTTCTTTATTAATCTTGCTAGCAGTCTATC
AATTTTGTTGATCTTTTCAAAAAACCAGCTCCTGCATTCATTGAATTTTTTTGAAAGGTTTTTTTTG
TGTCTCTATCTCCTTCATTTCTGCTCTGATCTTAGTTATTTCTTGCCTTGTGCCTTGCTTGTGAATTT
GTTTGCTCTTGCTTCTTTAGTTCTTTTAATTGTGATGTTAGGGTGTCGATTTTAGTTCTTTCTTGCT
TTCTGTTGTGGGCATTTAGTGCTATAAATTTCCCTCTACACACTGCTTTAAATGTGTCCCACAGATT
CTGGTATGTTGTGTCTTTGTTCTCATTGGTTTCAAACAACATCTTTATTTCTGCCCTAATTTTGTTA
TTTACCCAGTAGTCATTCAGGAGCAAGTTGTTCAGTTTTCATGTAGTTCTGCGGTTTTCAGTGAGTT
TCTTAATCCTGAATTCTAATTTGATGGCACTGTGATCTGAGAGACAGTTTGTTGTGATTTCTGTTCT
TTTACATTTGCTGAGGACTGCTTTACTTCCAATTATGTGGTCAATTTTACAATAAGTGTGATGTGGT
GCTGAGAAGAATCTATATTCTGTTGATTTGGGGTGGAGAGTTCTGTAGATCTCTGTTAGGTCTGCTT
GTTGCAGAGCTGAGTTCAGATCCTGGATATCCTTGTTAACCTCTGTCTCGTTGATCTGTCTAAATATT
GACAGCGAGGTGTTAAAGTCTCCCATTATTATTGTGTGGGAGTCTAGGTCTCTTTGTAGGTCTCTAA
GGACTTGCTTTATGATTCTGGGTGCTCCTGTATTGGGTGCATATACATTTAGGATAGTTAGCTCTTC
TTGTTGAACTGATCCCTTTAACATTATGTAATGGCCTCTTTGTCTCTTTTCATCTTTGTTGGTTTAA
AGTGTGTTTTATCAGAGACTAGGATTGCAACCCCTGGTGTTTTTTTGCTTTCCATTTGCTTGGTAGA
TCTTCCTCCATCCCTTTATTTTGAGCCTATATGCGTCTTTGCATGTGAGATGGGTGTCTTCGAATACA
GCACACTGATGGGTCTTGACTCTTTATCCAATTTGCCAGTCTGTGTCTTTTAATTGGGGCATTTAGC
CCATTTATATTTAAGGTTAATATTGTTATGTGTGAATTTGATCCTGTCATTATGATGTTCGCTGCTT
ATTTTGCCCCGTTAATTAATGCAGTTTCTTCATAGCCATCAATGGTCTTTACAATTGGCCCTGTTTTTG
CAGTGGCTGGTACCGGTTGTACCTTTCCATGTTTAGTGCTTCCTTCAGGGAGCTCTTGTAAAGCAGCC
CTGGTGGTGACAAAATCTCTCAGCCATTGCTCATCTGTAAAGGATTTTATTTCTCTTTCAGTTTTGA
AGCTTAGTTTGGCTGGATATGAAATTCTGGGTTCAAAATTGTTTTCTTTAAGAAAGTTGAATATTGG
CCCCCACTCTCTTCTGGCTTGTAGGGTTTCTGTCGAGAGATCTGCTGTTAGTCTGATGGGCTTCCCT
TTGTGGGTAACCCGACCTTTCTCTCTGGCTGCCCTTAACATTTTTTCCTTCATTTCAACCTTGGTGA
```

```
ATCTGACAATTATCTGTCTTGGAGTTGCTCTTCTTGAGGAGTATCTTTGTGGTGTTCTCTGTATTTC
CTGAATTTGAATGTTGGCCTGCCTTGCTAGCCTTCGGGAAGTTCTCCTGGGTAATATCCTGAAGAGTG
TTTTCCAACTTGGTTCCATTCTCCCCATCACCTTCAGGTACACCAATCAAATGTAGATTTGGTCTTT
TCACACAGTCCATATTTCTTGGAGGCTTTGTTCATTTCTTTTTACTCTAACCTTGTCTTCTTGCTTT
ATTTTGTTCATTTGATCTTCAATCACTGATACCCTTTCTTCCACTTGATCGAATCACCTGTTGAAGC
TTGTGCATGTGTCATGAAGTTCTCGTGCCATGGTTTTCAGCTCCATCTCTACACTGTTTATTCTAGT
TAGCCATTCATCATTCAAAAAGGTTGAAAAAACCTTTTTTCAAGGTTTTTAGCTTCCTTGCGATGGG
TTCGAACATCCTCCTTTAGCCTCGGAGAAGTTCGTTATTACCAACCTTCTGAAGCCCTACATCTGTCAA
CTCGTCAAAGTTATTCTCCATCCAGCTTTGTTCTGTTGCTGGCGAGGAGCTGTGATCTTTTGGAGGA
GAAGAGGTGCTCTGATTTTTAGAATTTTCAGCTTTTCTGCTCTGGTTTCTCCCCATCTTTGTGGTTT
TATCTACCTTTGGTCTTTGATGTTGGTGACCTACAGGTGGAGTTTTGGTGTAGATGACCTTTTTGTT
GATGTTGATGTTATTCCTTTCTGTTTGTTAGTTTTCCTTCTAACAGGTCCCTCAGCTGCAGATCTGT
TGGAGTTCCACTCCAGACTCTGTTTGCCTGGGTATCACCAGCCGAGCCTGCAGAACAGTGAATATTG
CACAACAGCAAATATTGCTGCCTGATCCTTCCTCTGGAAGCTTCGTCCCAGAGGGGCAGCTGCCCTAT
ATCAGGTGTCTGTTGGCCCCTATTGGGAGGTGTCTCCCAGTTAGGCTACTCAGGGGTCAGGGACCCA
CTTGAGGATGCAGTCTGTCCGTTCTCAGAGCTCAAACGCCATCCTGGGACAACCACTGCTCTCTTCA
GAGCTGTCAGACAGGGACGTTTAAGTCTGCACGAAGTTGTCTGCTGCCTTTTGCTTAGCTATGCCCTG
CCCCCAGAGGTGGAGTCTAGAGGGCAGTAGGGCTTGTTGAGCTGTGGTGGGCTCCACCCAGTTCGAGC
TTCCTGGCCACTTTGTTTACCTACTCAAGCCTCAGCAATGGCAGACCCCCCTCTCCGAGCCCAGGCTC
AGAAGTAACAGCTTTTTGATGCTCGTGGCTACTCTCAGCAATCCACATTTCTGCTTGAGATAGGTAT
GTCAGTCATTCAAGTGGAGACATCAGCGAAGATACATGGATATAAGCAACCCACAGTTCAGATGGACAG
GTTGCAGTTAGCAGACATAAGTTTGGGAGTCAGTTGTAAAGCAATATCTTTAAAGCCTGGGACTAGTTG
AGATCTGGGTTTTTTTTTCTTTTCTTTTTCTTTCTCTTTTTCTTTTCTTTCTTTCTTTTTTTTTTTGA
GATGGGGTCTCTCTGTTGCCCAGGATGGAGTGCAGTGGTGCGATCTCGGCTCACTGCAACATCCACC
TCCTGTGTTCAGGCGATTCTTCTGCCTCAGCCTCCTGAGTAGCTGGGATTACAAGTGTCCACCACCA
TGCCCAGCTAATTTTTGTATTTTTAGTAGAGGCGGGGTTTCACCATGTTGGTCAGGCTGGTCTCGAA
CTCCTGACCTCAGGTGATCACCCACCTCAGCCTTCCGAAGTGTTGGGATTACAGGTGTGAGCCACCA
TGCCCCGGCCCTAGTTGAGATCTTCTAAAGAGAGAGTGTATGGATTAAAAGAGGGGCCAGCAATAGAAC
TCTGGGCTGTCTCAACATTCACAGAAGTAGCAGACGAAAAGCAGCCTAGTAAAAGATTTTGAGAAGTT
ATCACCAGTAAGGTAGGAAGACGAACCTAAAATATAAAGTACTTTCGAAACCAGTTGAAGAAAGTGTT
TCTAGAAGGAGACAGATAATCAACTATATCAGGTACAACTTGACAGGTCAAGTAAGACATTGACAAGCA
TAAGAATATAGGATTTTGGAACATGGCAGTCACTAATGACTTCAACAGCAATTTTATTGAAGGTAGT
ATATTTTGAAAGTCAAATACCTATTTTTCATACTATCGCATATGCTATATGTTTTAACTATGTCATAAT
TTGTGCATATCTCCTGAATCTTCTTGAAGACTAAAGACAAGTTTAGAGTTTAGAGGGACCTTTAAAAC
TTTGTGACATTTTCTTTTTCTGCCTTGATATTTAATTAACGATGACCTGTAGAAATTTCCTAAGTTATT
```

```
CTTGAATTTCCAAGAGTAGAAACTATATATTAATACTTCAACAAAGTAATCGCTTCTTACTTTCTTT
CATGTACAAGTTTCCCTTAGTTCCACCTTAAATTACCTCACCTGACGCATCTACCACTCCATGCTCC
CTCACAATGTAGTTGTTACTCTTTCTCCCGAGACCTGATAGTACTTCCCAGTGAAATGCCTTTTTAA
AAAAAAAAAAAAATTAATTACTTTTGTATTTTATGTTCTTTAAATTCACACTTCTTACATTTTGTAA
TTCTTTGACTTTATAAGTAATTTACCCTATTGAGGTAGAAATTTCGGCGCATAAGTACAGTTCATCTT
ATTGTTTGGAATTTTCTTCTAGTTGTCTCGGATTTTACTTTATATTTGTAATTGGTTTTTGGAATGCA
TACTGTTTTAAATAACTATTGTATGTTTCAGACAGACCTTGACAATAAACTACACCACCAGTTAACA
CACCCAGCCCACGAACTTCCACCACAGAAAGACAAAATATCACTATTACAAAACAACTATGAAAAAA
GTCACGAAACTTTCAAACACCTTCAATCTCATTTCTATGGGAGGGAATCTGAACTTCTAGCCACCAG
GCAAGATCTTAAGGTATAGTAAACTATACTGTACCATAAAGTCTCAGTAAGTTTTATAGACATTTAT
TAAATGATCTATTTGAATCCAAATGGGCAAGCAAATGTTAGTATTTGTGGAATAGTGTGCTGTTTTC
TATTAAAATTGTTATTTTGTATTACCATGCTTTAAAAAAATTGTTTAAAATGTGGGCATTTTAAAATGA
CATATTTATAATAGTAAGCATAATTTCGGATATATCTTAATTGCGACACTGTTAACTTATGTAAGTATT
ATGCTGTCTTTGTGTGTGAATAACTTTAAAGATAGCCTGCTGTTAAGTTTTAAATGTAAACCACTTG
TGAAAAAATCCAAGCAATTTTACCATTGCTTGTCAGCCAATTCTGACATTAGTTATAATATTTGTCA
AGTTCCCAATATTACTGGATTGCCTAATGATTAAAATTAGGAGATTATAGCCTCAAAATAAACTTACC
CTTAATTATATAACAATGTATAGAAATTTTGTCTTTGGTAATGTTATTTGATTAGATAAAGTATCAA
CTTTATTAAATTGAACGATAATGGGCAAAACGCCTAAACAATTTTTAGGTCACACCGAAGGTACCAGTTT
TCTAAGCAAAATGGAATATTTGTGTTCTGTCACACGAGGATTCACCCAGTTTTTTTTCTGTCTCTCTT
TTTGTTAAGCGGCAAATGCTTTATCTGTTTCTTTTCCTATGTCTTTGGGATTTTGTTTATTTAAAGTGGCAT
ATTCCAAAATTCTGACAATGCAAAGCAATATTTAAAATGTTTTATTTAGATAGCGCAGCCATATATTTTATC
CATAGGCTGCTTATAAGGAATTATGAAGGAGGTGGGACTTGATTAGGTCCTCGAATTTGAATACACAGA
GACTCCCGAGAAAACGGTCATTTTATTCAGCGGGCACATTTCAGAAAAGCTGCCATAGTCACAATCAATA
AAGCAAGCAGACAGTTAACATAATTGCCTTGCTGGCGTACTAGTTTATGTTTGGAATTAAGCTTTAA
AAGCTTGGATCTAAATTGTCAAGTATCTTACATGCCTAGCAAAGATCATTGGATTTTATATTTCACG
GCAAAAAGCTGAAAAGCGTCTAAATAGAGCAGTAAAATGAAGAAAATAGTACTTTTAGCAAAAACAACCTGG
TAGTGGTTTGCAGACAGCCTTGGATTGCACCTGGGATAGACTAGTGCTGGAGACATGAGCTTAAGCAGGGT
TACTAACTTCCTTTCTCCATAAATTCTAATAGTCGAGGTATGAGTTGATTAGAACTGGGCATGAACAT
TAAAGAGGGATCAAAATAGAGCATTAATGGGACACAGAGAGACAAACAAAAGCACTCAACCCCATACCTGCC
TGCAAGGCATTTGACAGACACATACGAAAATTGGGTGAAAGCAATTTTCATAGTCCCCAGTACAATATCTATG
TATCTATCTATGTATCTATCTGTTTATCTGGACGTAAAAATTAGCCAATAGTTGTTATTAAGAAAATA
GTACCACACATGATTTAGGTAGTGTTAAATTATTATTATTTGACCTTACAACACTATTGAAAGTATT
GAAAGTCAAGCAAGCTTTGTCGGACCACTTTCGGCCTTAGCCTAAGAACACTGACGAACCACTAAAGCG
AGTTACTTACATTTGTATTTTAGGCAAATGACTCACTCCACGAGATTCAGCGAATGAGAAACACGGCTGAA
TCTGAAGACCAGAAGACTTTCCAGTAGTCTAAGTCCAACACCATGCTGGTGTGGGCTGCTAATAGCA
```

```
ACCATCCACAAAACTCCATCAATTTCAACCATATTTAAATCATACAACACATCAAACTTAATCTTTC
ATTCCAAAACTCTTATACAAATCACACTCTTTCCATATCCATCTCATTTACCCAAACCATAACCTAC
TAACACCAACCAACATTAAATTAATCAATCTTAATTCATTTCATTCATATTCTTTCATTAACCCACC
CATTTTTATTATCCTTCAAACCTATCTTCTCTACTAATAATTTCATACATCAAACAATAACTCAAAT
CTAAATATCCCCAAAAACACAAACCTCACCCACAACCCTCCCATACACTTTTACAACTCTTAACCCA
CCTTCCATACATCCTCTATTCCAAACCTTCCTTTTCCCAAACACACCACCCCCACTCCTTCCTTTTC
CACACAACACACCCCTACTCCTCTACAATAACACAACCATCCTTAAATCTTACTTCTCATTCAAACT
CTCCCATTCTTTCATCATTTCACTATAATTTTTTAACAAAATAAAACATTCCTAAATTTTATATAAA
ATCCTTTTAAAATCACAACTCTATCAACTACTTAACAACCTAATTAAAAAAAATACTCAATTCCTAC
CCAACTTCACATCATATTTATACACTACCATAACACATCCCTATCACTTATTATTTTTCTTTTCCTT
CAATCATCTTCCATCCTCTTCTCTATAACACACACAACACCCACACATTCACACCCTTCTAACATCAT
ACCTAACTACTTCAACCCTATCTACCATCCCTTCACACTCTACACCATCCCCTAACACTCTATATAC
CTACACACCACTACAATCCAACCTACCCTCCCCTCATCTATCCCTTTACCCCCATCTCCTCCATTAT
TTATCAACTACTTAACTTTCTTCACTCCATATTTCACATTCCCTATCCTCTCTACACCACTCTTTCTTC
TCCACCAAACCTACACCTACAATTTAACTCTAAAATTTACACCCTCACTCAACTCAAAATTCTACCA
TAATACATTTACAATTAAATATAAATCTTCTTACCCTACTACTCTATATCATTTCATCACAAATCAA
CAAAAAACAACTAAAAATATCAACTTTTTTTTTTTTTTTTTTTAACAAACTATCCCAAAACTTCCTCAAT
ACACAAAAACAACACCTACCATCCAACACTCCACAAATCATTTCTTTACTCCCCTCCTATAATCTCA
TTCCCATAATCACCCTCAACCTTCCTATTTCATCCATTTACCCCATTTCCCTATTTCAACCCCACTAC
ATCCCTTACACATACTCCCAACAAACCATCCAATCCCACACACCCCTTCTCCCACCCAACACATCCT
CACCACACCAAATAATATCCAATATTATTATAATCTCCAATAACAAACATCAAAACAACATTTAAAA
TCCATCCCACTATAAATCTTCATCTATCTCATTCAATCATCTACATCAAACTTCACACCCACCCCAA
AACATCTCTTCCCATCTTCACAAACCCATTTCATCCACCACTCCAAATTTTCACCTTCACTTTAAAAA
ATCACTCACTCCCTTTTCTCACTTTAACATTTTATACCCTCTTATTTAAACCATCCCCTTTTTCCAA
ATCTTCTCCTTACACCTTACCCTTCCTTTCCACCCTCTACCAACCCTTCCTATTTTTAAACATTACA
TCACCATCTCTATTAACTAATTATACTTCCTCTACACTCTTTCAACTCCACTTTCTCAACTTTTCTC
CTTTTTTATCTCAAATCACTCTCACCCTTTCTCACATATACCTCACTTCCCACATCTCCTATACACC
CTTCTCTAAACCCCACTCCACACCATCTCACACTCACTCTTTTTCTCTCCATTTCCCACACATACCCTA
TACTCTCCTCCCCTCTCTACCTTCCATTTTACATCCCTCTTCTCCTTTTTCCCCCATCTACTCAACT
CCCTTAACTCAAACACCACCTTCTACCCTCCTCTCTTCTCTCTTACCACTCCTCTCTCAATTAATCCTTAC
CTCCTCCATTACTCAACAACTACCTCATCTTAATTCTTCCCTCAAAAACCCTCAACCCCTTTACCCT
TCTACTCCCACTCATTCAAATTAACATTTTAATTATATCACAAACACCTAACTCCCTTACTCCTAAC
AAACTAAACTTTATATTTCATCTATTCTCATAAATTCCATAAATTTTACCCAAATTTTCAAATATTT
ACTATCAACCATCATTTATTTTTCCCCCTACTTTTTCAACACCACATAACAAATCTTAAACATCCTA
AACACCTTCTAATTCACCACAAATTACAACTTCAACCAAAACCCACTCCCTCAACCCACCTCTTCA
```

```
ACAGGAGAACAGAAATCACCACATACTAAAACACCAGGTGAAAAACGAAGAACAACGACCTGAACAAA
GAATTTATTGACAAACAAGCTAAGTTGGTCAGTCAGTTAATCGGGGGAAGTGTGTTTTCCAGTAGAG
CTTTAAATCAATCCAGTGAGAGGACTGTTCTACTTATAAGATCTGATTGAAATGCTTTCCTAACATT
TTAGTTTTTGATTAAGGAAGGAGATCTGATTTATTTACATAGCTGACATGTGGTTGGAAATATTTTA
CCCTGTAACCATAATTCTGTTTTTATAAGTGAACATTGAAATGAAATAAAATTAAAAAATTTTTTTT
GTTTTTTAAGTGTCAGAAGCTAAACAACCCCACAACTACGTAGATCTGGTAAATGGTGTGAATGCTA
GTCATGTTAAACCCATTTGTTGGGTCAAAACGAATGTTGATAAGGGGGAGCCGAAACTTGAGTTTCA
AATTATGATGAACAAAGTCTGCTTTTCCTTTCCTAAGTTGCACATGCCAAATGGGAAGCATCTGGCT
TTCCTCTGTTGAATTAAGTCCAAATATGCCCAGATAACTTGCCCATTGAATATTTTAGTTGAAGAGT
TTCAATTTTAACTTCAAACAGTCATTTGAAGGTTTCATAATGGTTTTTGGCAGACTGATAGAGAAAA
GAAAGCATATGGAATTGGGACGAATAAGGAAATTTCAGCCTTTGTCTCTAGGGCACCTTGCTATCCCT
AACCATATGTGTCTTTCCTGCCTCTGGTGGAGAAGAAGAAAGATCTCACATTGTGTCACTTTAGCTCA
CCATCATGATGGTCACTATCCATCATTTCAGCATTTTGACCTTTGAGCCAATTCATATTACATAGAT
GCTTGTGGAATCAGTTTTATTAATGTGTAATGAAATATGTTCTCCTGCCTCCATTCCCGAACAAGCA
AATTGCCAGTATTTTAAATGTAATAAATCACTTACATTTATTTTGCACTACTTTTGTAATAGATTTC
CCCCCAACTTTTCCTTTTTTTCAGCCATTCCGAAATAAAAGAAAAGGAAGTAGGAATGAAGAAGCATG
AAGAAAATGAGGGCTAAACTTACCATGCAGATTACAGCCATTAAATGAAAACTTAGGCCACTGTGAAGAA
GGAGTCGCCAATCTAGTCAACGGAGAGCTTAGTGAGCCTTGAGAAACAAAACGGATGACTTACGGGGTGAA
ATTGCAGTATTAGAAGCCAACGGTTCAGAATAATCAAGATGAAAGGAGACGACTACTGGAAAGGTGAT
TCATATCTACTAAAATTAGTTTATTTCCATTGTAAGTGATAAAAAGATTGTCATATTCCATAGTTTT
TAAAAATAGAAGAATCTTGAGAAAAGTGCATAAGCCTCTATAGGTATTTAAGTAGCCATTTAAAAAT
TAACCTGTAAAACAATCAGATAGTCAAAATTAATGTATCATATATTTTAAATTACTAAAGTAGTCCA
TTATCTATACCCTAGAAGCGTCTTTAAATGATTTTCTAAAAAATTAATTACCTCTTTGCAATCTATT
CCAGATGTCTTAAACGAGAAGGTGAAATAGAAAAACCTTCAAACCAAAGTATTAGAATTGCAAAGAAA
GCTGCATAATACAACTGCAGCAGTGCAGGAGCCTGGGCAGAGAAAAACCAATCACTTCAGGTCAGTCAC
CTATCGATATGAAGCAGTTTTTTAGTCTAGAATTGGCTTATTAGTGAAAAGCATATTTTTACCTTTT
AAAAAATCTCATGTTTTATAAATACTTTCAAATAGCTACTCTCTGTTTAGCAGTATTGTAGGTTTTG
TCGATAATTAAATATAAAACTAAACAACTTGTTTCAGAGACCTCAGAGATTCATTAGAAAGCCATGT
CATTCATTAATTGTTAGTATATGGAAAGAACTACAAAATTCAAGAATACCAAAGAATATATGAGTCA
GTATCTCTTAAAGAAGCCGATCTGAGTATATTCTCAGAGTCACCAGCGGAAAATTCATCATTATGTTTA
GAATGGATTGGAAATCAGCAAAGGTTAGCAAGATATTTCAGGGAATAAAATTCAATTAATTTTATTTT
GTCATTCAGATTTATGAGTATAGCCTACTTTTGACAATAGAAGCCTGACCAGTGTATTTCTGATTTTTA
AAATTTTATTTCATGGGTCATATAGTCAAAATTTTATAGAACTCTGCCAGCCAAGTTAGAAATAATCT
AGCATTCTTTAAAATGTTGAATACTATAATATATCGATACTTCTTTAAAAAACAGATCAAACATACA
CAAGCCTTGAATAGAAAGTCGGCCCGAAGACAATGAAGTACAAAACTGTATGCCCTGTGGGAAAGGCT
```

```
TTTCAGTAACAGTGACACGCGTAAATAATTTTCTTCATCTAACTATCTTTCTGGATTTCATTTGTCA
CTCATAATTAATGTTTTAACCATCAAAATAGTCCTTCATTTGACAGAATAATTTTCTGTTTATCAGT
AAACTTTAACAACAACATAGAATAACTTCATGCAGTCTAGCCTTTTGGTTAGCATATCTGTTTGAATT
TTACTTTTAAATTCAGTCCTTGTCTTCCAACTTAGTTACTGTCTGGGACAATCATTTTCTGAATCAG
TGCACCAATATTAAACTCATGTTTTAGTAATCATTGGGTTCTTTAAAGGAAGAAAAAGCAGAGGTAT
TTTAAAAATATATTCTAAATACTACCATTCTGTTAATGACTTAAGTTTATATTTCTTTTGGAGAGCCA
TTAGTGCCTCGAAACATTTGGCTGATAGGAATAGTTTTTCATTTGATAGAGATACTTTATAAAAACTT
TTTTAATGCCTCCTCTGGTTCTTTTGAGTAGTTCCATAATAAAATTCTATGTAAAATGTTTAGCCATAG
TGTTTGATAAATAGGAAGCATTCAATGTAGATTATAGCAGAGATTAAGCTAACATATTGAAACATAT
CATTAAATAATATACCAATGACTTGAAAGCTAAAGTACCTTCATAATGTAGCATGCTGGTATTCATG
TAGATTCATAATACTTTTGGCATAGATTCTATTCTTGAAATTGTTTAATTTTTGGCATTTACAGCAT
CACTGCCGACAGTGTCGGAATATCTTCTGCGCTGAATGGTCAGACAAAGATGCCTTAACTCCTTCCTA
CAAGAAGCCTGCCTCCTGTGTGTTTTGCATGTTTCAATGACTTGCAAGGATAATGGGTTATCACAAC
TTCACAGTAATATTACACTAACATTAGATTTTTAATAAATGTACTTAATAGAGGTCTTCGGACTACTA
TTTGGTTTGGACACTGGTTGCAATACTAGATTTTTTAGGCAATTAGTATATATTTTGGAATGTTATGGAT
ATCAAGTAAAACTCTTCTATTTTTGTGAGACTTGGGCTTATCATCTTTCATTACTTTTTTTCCCATTT
AGCCCCTGGGAATAGCTTTCATGCCCAAGTTTACAAATTAGCCAATGAAATGTAAATAAACTTTGGAC
ACAAAATAGCAATCTATTTTTTTAATATAATTTCATTATTCACAAATGAAGAATGCCATTCCATAGC
TTACTTCTTTCTCCTAAATTTAATGTACAAAAATGTACATGCATGCATATTATCACCTGTTGCTGTTT
TTGTTGCACAATAGCACATTAATTATATTAAATATTCTCTTTGTGAAGTTATGCACAGAACTGCAAC
ACTTTCCTCTGCCTTTTTCTCTTATATGTGGGTTCATGGTTCAGTTGCATTGTTATGCTATGAATTT
ACTATCACAGATTATACTCATAACAATCTAAACATCATAATTCCCAAATTCTACTACAAAAAATAAA
GTCTGTTAATGAGAGGCCATAAAATTCTGTCCAGCTTCTCTGCAGCCGACAGGACTTAAACCTATTAA
AATGACTTTCTGGGGAAAAAAAAAAAAAGCTGGCTGTGTTTTACTCTCTAATTCTTTGCCTTATAAA
TTCCCTGTAGCAACTGAGCCTTTAAAGATCAGGTCATTGTTCTTGGCTGGTTTTTGGAATTCATTTT
CCTCAAAAACTATAATTGTACTTCCAGCGTTATTCCAGGCATCCTTGCTTCATTTGGTTTGTAGTATG
GGTACAAGGGACTTTATAAATAAAAGCACCTGCTAAGCTAGGCCTGTAAAATACAATTTGGAGAGAG
TATAATATACAGGCAAGAATAGCTCTTTTTTTTACTGACATTCTAATACAATAACTGACACAATTTTA
AAAGCATTTTCTATCTATTCGGGCACCATACTATGTTTTTTTCTCTATATAGCAACCCTGTGAGATAGG
TCAGCTAATTCCTACTTGTAAATGAGGAAACATATTAATTTTTCCAAGGTCACAGAGCCTTATAAATG
ATATAGCCACGATTTCGAATTAGGTCTGTCACTCCAGAGCCTCAATCTCTCTCTTGTCCTCATTTACT
CTTTCCTGTTCTATAGCCTGCTCTGCCCATGTACTGTATCTAATTAGTCAAGTTAATAGGCCCGAGGA
ATGAGAAAAATATTTTTAAAAGGAACAAGAGAATGCTAGTTACAAATCAGAAAATAAAAAAGCTGGAA
GCATAGTTGTTTTGTTTTTGCTTTTTGAGACAGAGTCTCACTCCATCACCCAGGCTGGAGTGCAGTC
GTGCGACCTTGGCTCACTGCAACCTCTGCCTTCTGGGTTAAGTGATTCTCCTGCCTTTGTCTCCCC
```

```
AGTAGCTGGAATTACAGGTGTGTGCCACCACGCCTGGCTATTTTTTTTGTATTTTTTCACCACGTTT
GCCAGGCTGGTCTTGAACTCCTGACCTCAAGTGATTTGCCCGCCTCAGCCTACCAAAGTACTGGGAT
TACAGGCGTAAGCCCACCCAATGCCCGGCCAACCCTATCTTTTAAAAAAATTCAAAATAAAAAATTAG
CAGCATTCCCTGTAGTCCCAGCTACTGGGGAGGCTAAGGCAAGAGGACCACTTGAGCCCCAGGGAGTTT
GAGATCAGCCTTGATATAGCAAGACCTAATCCCAATAAAATTATATATATATAATCTTCTATTGTATT
GTGTGTGTATATATATATTTCACACTTCAATAGAACATACACAATCTCACAAAGAAGTAAAAAAAA
TTTAAGAGTATCCTACCCACCAAAGACTAAATATTCTATTGACCTCCTATTTCAACTATTAATGACT
GAAATCATCCAAAAATGTCTACAGACCTTTAAAGCAAAATACCATGTTGCAAGAATTCCATGCCCTG
CACATGTGATAGCAAAATAAAGTCATTTTGGGGTATGAAACAGCCTCAGAATATGTACTACCTAGAAA
CTTTTCCTAAATAAATACCTCAGAAATATTGAAAGATATCAAGATGCATTGATATTAATCTGATAGT
CACCTTTTTTTGTTTTGGTTTGTTTTTGAGAGACAGGATCTTTCTCTGTCACCCAGACTGCAGTACA
GTGGCATGATCACCGCTCACTGCAACCTCAGCCCCAAGCATTCCTCCCACTTCAGCCTCCCAAGTAGC
TGGGACTACAGGTGCCCAACACCACACCCAACTAATTTTTGTATTTTTTGTGGAGACGGGGTTTCAG
CATGTTGCCCAGGCTGGTCCCAAACTCCTGGGCTCAATCAGTCTGCCCACCTTGGCCTTCCAAAGTG
CTGGGATTACAGGCATCAGCCACTGTGCCCAGCTATATTAATCATTGTAAATATGGTACAACTGAAT
TTTTGTAGCCCTAAAACCTAAAAGCAAGCCTCAAATAAATCTCATACCTCTTTTCAACAACTAGAAAG
AAAATATCTTTTAGGAATTTGCCAATTCAAAGCCATAAAGTAAGCAAACCAGGATCTCATCTTTTAG
CATAGACATACTTTTTAAGGTATACTTTTTATTGAACCAAAGCATACATAAACCTAAAACTACACAC
AGGCAAAAAATGCTGAGCGCGAGCTGCTCCCTCTGCGATATTGGAGAGCCACCTCCATGTGTCATCTGA
GAAAGGGCCACAGTGAGGTTGCCCCAGGTTCTTAAAGCGAAAAGCTGACTCTGGGGTGTCCCTTCCCC
ACCCAAAATGCCTCCCTGTTGCCATCTCCTTGACAAATCAGATGGAGGTGGCACATTTTTTTCCGTG
ATAATCTTTTGTGACCTTTCTATAAGACTCTTAATTTCCTTCTTGAAGTTACAACCAGAGGTTGCAA
GTTTTTGCATTGGGATCAAGTATTCCATTATCATTATCCCCTAGGAGAGACAGCCTTTACAATCCCAT
GTGCCGTGAGCGCATTGGTAGAAAAGAGTATGACCTTCCTTCCACAAAACTAAAAGCTAAAAGACTTTA
TTCATTTTTTTTCCTTCCCAAATTCAAGCAATTCACTTCTAGACATCCTTGGCAGGAGCTCAGAACTG
TTTATGCAGGCTCCACGCAGGCAAAATATTTTTTGATATCCTGCTTTTGGTTGAGTCATGGTAATGT
TGGCAATGGTGGTGAGGGCAGGAGATCAAGTCATTTTTCAAAGTTCTAAGTAAATGATGTTCTAGTA
AGATCAATATGAGAGAATTAAAGACTAATATAAAGTTTATCGCAAGGGCCACCATCTATAAGTTAGA
CCTTTTTTTTCTTTTCCTCTAAGGGCAGTGTTCTCAAATTTTAACCCATGTAAGAATCACCTGGAAGT
CTTGTTAAACACAGACTTCTGCCTGGGCACAGTGGCTCACACCTGTAATCCCAGCACTTTGGGAGGC
CGAAGTGCGTGGACCACCTGAGGTCAGGAGTTCGGACAGCCTGACCAATATGGTGAAACCCCGTCTG
TACTAAAAATACAAAAGTTAGCCAAGTGTGGTGGTGTGCACCTGTAGTCCCAGCTACTCAGGAAGCT
GAGACAGAAGAATCGCTTCAACCCAGGAGGTGGAGGTTGCAGTGAGCTGACATCGTGCCACTGCACT
CCAGCCTGAGTGACAGAGTGAGACCCTGTCTCAAAAAAAAAACCACGGACTTCTGACCCCATCCCAGA
GTTCCAGGCGTTGGAGAGCATGGAGCGGGGAAGATTTTTTCCTTTCTAACAAGTTCTCAAGTCATAGTG
```

```
ATACTGCTGGTCCAGGCACCCTACTTTAAGAACTACCGACCTCAGGGAACCTTCACAGTAAGTATCT
GTAATGAGTCCAATCAATGAAAACTTCAGTGAATTAGACTTCATTAGAATTACTTCAACTTTGTTTT
GGGAAAGTCTATAGACATTTTTGTTTAATGCTGCATACATATGCATTATCTCCACCTACGGCATCAAA
TAAATATTCTTTGGGGTACTGATCTAATGAGAATACTGGTAGATATAAATGCTCTTCCATTTGCATT
TTAATTATTTGAAAACTAATGTTCACAAATTCACTCCCTGGTGCTCTAATCATTTCCTCTACTATTC
AATGCTTATCAAAGCAAGTCATTAATAAAATAGATCAACACAAAATGTTTTATGATGTGAACAAAGT
AGAGTCCCAAAGAATGCCATCTCACAACCTTAGACAAAATAAATGAAATAGAAACCTACAACTGCTTC
ACTGAACTATGAGTGATGATTTGTTGAATGCCTCAACAGGAAGTAAAAAGTTACATTTGCATCATTT
CTGTATTTGATCAGCCGTTGTTTACCTGACTTGTTCTTAGGCTGCCTTAGATTCTGAGCTGCCTTCC
CTTTAGGCTTTTTCATAAACAAATAACTGGAAATGTCTCTAAGGAGGGGAGAGACCAGTTCCTCATT
GCAGCTGGTAGCAAGGTTGCTTTCACTCAGCCAGGAGGACCCATTGTTACAGGTGTGGAACTTGTTG
CTCCGAGCCCTCGCCTGGCAGCTCACTCTGGATCTGCGGGTTCTGAGGAGCCTCGGGACCCACCTGG
GTGCAGTTGCCTTCAGGGACAGAGACCATCTTACAGGTATTAAAGCCAACATTCAGCTGCTTTCTGGGT
TTCTCTCTTGCACTTTCCTTTTGTCCTATTGCTATCAGTTTCGCTTGTTTTGCTGATCTCTCCAGGT
CTCATTAGAATTACTGAATCATTAACCTGCAATGGTTTCATTTCTAGTACAGTGAGATGGCTTCCCC
AACACTGTGCGTGGGTGTTTGCTGGATTCTCAAAGCTTGGAAGGTCAAAGGTTGGTGAATTTTCTTT
ATGCTGACCATGTATTAATTTCCTCTTTTAAACATAAAGAAGAGTTAGCCATGAATGGATTGACTTGT
TAACTTTTGATTCTACCAGATCCACTCGGTGTAGTCATTTAGGGAAAGCTTCCCAGGAGCCCTTAGCC
ATTATCTCATTTAATTTCTGCAACAGGCCTGTGAGCGAGGTTCTTTGATGTCCTCTTGGTAAATGCT
GCATGCCAGTTGGCAGAGGCACAAGTGGCTTGTCCTAGGTCACACAGCCAATTGGCCGTGATACTGGA
AGAGAAACCAGACCCATTTCTTCTGGTGCTTGAGCTCTTCCTGCCTTTCTGCAAACCACCTCCCTAA
GCCCTGCTGTTTTTAAAGTTTCTCCATTTCCGCAGTGCATCATGTCGGCAGTTACTATTGCCTTGGT
TCCAATATTTAAGACAGTGGCTAATAAATAATTCTTACCGATGTGAATCCTATTGGCCATAAATAAC
TTCCTACCAGCAGCTACACCCCTGTGTCTCAACGACTACAAAGGAAACCCAAAGCCGTATCCTAACC
CCTCAAAAGAGGAGAGGAAAAGCCCAGAAGGACAGAGGGGAAACCCAAAGACTAAGAAATCTGATCT
AACTATTATGCAAGTCCCTATGCAAATATACTGAATTCCTTTAACATTGTTGCTGCCTAGAACTTGG
ACAGTCTTCTAAAGCAGAAAAATAATAGAACGGCCCTGATTGTATGTATGTGTGAAAGTACCTATTG
ATTCAAAATTAGCTGGGTGGGGTGGTAAGCCATCCATAGCCCCAACTACTCAGCAGCACTCCACCATG
AGGATTCTGTGAGGCTAGGAGTTTGAGGTTACAGTGCGATATGATCACACCTCTCGCACTCAGCCTGG
GCGACACAGACCCAGACTCCATCTCTAAAAACAAAAAAAAAAAGAAACAAAGTACCTATAGATTTGATG
CTCAGCTCAGCATTTGTTTGTTCGGAGAATGAGGAACTGCCCTCTCCATGTAGCAACAATGTACCTT
ATTTTATCAATGGTAGGGAGGGACCCATTTCATACCTCTCCAGCAATGTTGCTATCAACCTTCAGAGC
AGCCTCCAGGAATTACCAATCTAAAAACCAAAACTAGTACAATCTCACCTTAACTGAACATAAGTTTC
CTAAACTGGCATTGCCCTCTTTCCTCCACTCTGCAAAAAGGGTACCTCATGGGTTTTAGTTCTACA
TGTGAAGTTCTATAACAATTGAGTCCTCAGCCTCAAAATAAAGCAAACACAACATTAAGAATTTTAGA
```

```
ATGCAAATGTGTCACCAATAAGTCCAATGTATTTGCTACTTCTTGCTCACTGGATCCAATCAGCATA
ATGTCATCAGTCTAATGGACCAGTGTGCATATCTTGCCGAGCCGAAAAGCCGATCAAGGTCTCTCCGAA
TAAGATTATGACACAAAGCTAGAGCAGTTGATATACCCCTGAGGCAGGACAGTAATGGTATATTGCTG
GCCTTGCTAGCTGAAGGCAAATTGCTTCTGGTGGGCCTTATGGACAAGAATGGAGAAAAAGGCATTC
GCCAAGTCACTGGCTGCATACCGGTACCAGGAGATGTGTTCATTGGCTCAAGCAATGAAACCACATC
TGGTACAGCAGCTGCAATTGGAGTCACCACTTGGTTAAGCTTACAATAATTCACTGTCATTCTCCAA
GATCCATTTGTCTTCTGCACAGGCCAAATGGGACAGTTGAACAGGGATGTGGTGGGAATCACCACCC
CTGCGTCTTTCGAGTCCTTGATGGTAGCATTAATTTCCACAATCCCTCCAGGGATGCGATTTTTTTT
TATTTACTATTTTTCTAGCTAGAGGTAGCTCTAAATGGCTTCCATTTTGCCTTTCCCTCCGTAATAG
CCCTCACCCTACCAGTCAGGAAGCCAATGTGGGGGTTCTGCCAGCTGCTAAGTATGTCTATGCCAAT
TATATACTCTGGTCCTGGAAAAATGACCACAGATGAGTCTGGGCACCCACTGGACTCACTGTAAGT
CAGACCTGAGCTAAAACTCCATTAATTACCTGACCTCCATAAGCCCCTACTTTAACTGGAGGACCAC
AATGATGTTTTGGGTTCCCTGGAATCAACCTCAGCTCAAAGCCAGTGTCCAGTAGTCCCCAAAATGT
CTGATCATTTCCCTTTCCCCAGTACACAGTTACCTTGGTAAAAGGCCAGAGGTCTCCATAGGGAAGG
ATGGGAAAAAGATTCACGGCATAGTGAATTGAGATCGCACCACTGCACTCCAGCCTGGACGGCAGAG
CAAGGCTGCATATCAAAAAAAGATTCACTACATAAATTGTCAGTAATGTAGTGGGGTCCTTCCTCAA
GGGGACCTGGCCTTCCCTTTATTCAAGCGGTTCTGGGTTTGTAAACTGGCTCAAGTCTGGAAATTCA
TTGAGGGGCCGTGATTCTGTTTTTACAATTCAAATTAGTCTTGTCCATTCAAACCTAGAAGTTTTCTG
CTTATGAAAATTAGGTAGGAATGTAGTAGGCTTCCTATCAATTTTAATTCTAGGAACACTGTAATTA
ATTAGCCAGTGCCAGCACTCTACAGGAGTCAGTCTATTCTGATTGCCGCTTTGCCTCTTCCGTCCAT
TATGGTAGCTACACCCACCTTGCCTTTGATGGTTGAGTGCTGCCACCTGGCCTCTGCCACCTTGGGA
TCCAATTATTCCCATTGTATTTAAATTTTGTAGTTGAGTGACTGCAGTTCCCACTGTTAGATCTGAC
ATACAGAGAAGAGCCAATTACAGGGCCTCTTCAAAAATGCAGGTCCTGCCCTCACAAATCTATTTCACA
AGGCATTGGTCAAGGGTGTATCTTCTGACCCTCTCTACTGGGATGAGTAGGTCTAAAGTGACTAATC
CACTCCACCATCCCAATCTCCCTAAGCCTTTGGATCCCTTCCTCTACATTAAAACTGAGCGAGATGAG
GCATTTCCAGCTCACTCACAGTGGGCTATCTTTTAATCCATATTTTAGCTAACCAAGAAATAAACTC
TTCGACCCTTTTTTAACTCCCCAAGCTCAGACATTAAATGCAGAGTCCCTATTTAGTGGGCCCAAAT
CAATAAATTCAGCCTGATCCAACTCTATCTTCCTTCCACCATTATCCCACACCCTTAATATCAATTC
CCATGCCTGTTCTCCAGATTTCTGTTTATATAAATTAGAAAACTCAAGCAGTTATTTTCAAGTGTAG
GACCCCTCCTCATGGGTCACACTCTCAAACCTTACCTCTAGGTGCCTGCCGGGACTTTAGTCCAGTTA
CAGGTCTAGAGGCAAACAAGGTTGTTGGGGGTGGCTCCTCGAGAACAATCAACATTATCTTGCCTGCC
AACTGCCTCAAGCGAGCCCATCACTATTGCCTCAGCCAGTGCAGGCTTTATCTCCCCAGACAAAGGT
GGAAAGGCTGATGGCAGCATGGGTCAGGGTGGGGATGTTGCCACTACTGGGGATGGGAAGCCTGTTT
TTTTCTAGCAAAAAGCATTGTCAGCAATTTACAAACTCAGTGTCCCCAGCTTCATCAGCGTCCTCCCG
GGCATCCTATTCCAAGTTGCAGGGTCTCATTCTTTTTCCAATCAATGCCCTCACTTTAACAGTAGGCA
```

```
CCTCGTGGGGCTGTGCATGCACCTTTCATTGCAGGTCAGCTACTCACATAATAAGAGCTTGTGTCTA
TTTTTCAACAATTTCAGCTCTTTCTCTACAACAGATAAGACTGTCACTCACGGCAATCTTAGCAAAT
TTTCAGGCTCAGTGTCTGCTTCTGAAGCCAGGAGTTAGAATCCCTGAGTTCATCATTTTCTCTCAAC
ACTTTGTCTACTGAACTTAGGAGCACCCAACCAGCTTTGTTATGTTCCTTGGTTCTCCACATATGTC
AAAGGTATTATGTATAGAGTCACTAAACTTGCCTGTCACAAGCAGTGAATCAGGAGTGTCAAATGCA
TTTATGTTGCATAACTCTCCAAACGGTTCACACCAAGGACTATCAGTGTTCTCCATACTATTAGAAG
TAGAGTCCTTAGCATTTTTCGGTCTAATCATATGAAGCAGCCAACTCCACAAGCCCCAAAACCAATG
AAAGAACTCCATCCTTAATACTCTGTTCCTCTACAACCACTCCTTGTACCAAAATCTGTATTAGTCA
GAGTTCTCTACAGGAACAGAACTAATGGGATAGATAGATAGATAGATAGATAGATAGATAGATAGAT
ACATAGATAAAGAGTTTATTAAGTATTAACTCACATGATCACCAGGTCCCACAATAGGCTGTCTGCC
AGCTGCCGGAGCAAGCAGAGCCAGTCAGAGTTCCAAAGCTGAAGAACTTGGAGTCCAATGTTCGAGCG
CAGGAAGCATCCAGCATGGGAGAAAGACCTACGCCTCGGAGCGTAAGCCAATCTCAGATCTTCACGTT
TTTCTGCCTGCTTTAGATTTGCTGGCAGCTGATTAGATGGTGCCCACCCAGATTAAGCGTGGGTCTG
CCTTCCCCCGCCCACTGACTGATATGTTAATCTCTTTTGGCAACACCTTCACAGATACACCCAGGAT
CAATACTTTGCATCCTTCAATCCAATCAAGTTGATACTCAGTATTAACCATCACAAGATTCTTACAT
TACTACTAATAAACAAGAACTGAAAACAAAAACAAAAACAAAAACAAACCGAGACACACATCCCCCATT
TGTCTCTCTTCACTCCCTCTTCTCTTCTTCCACATGTCTCTCTGCAGTCTTTTCTGCAGCCAGCCATTTG
TTCAAACAGCCCCACTTCCTTGAACAGCCTGCTTGCCAGGCTGCATGCTCATATAATGTTAGGTGAAGA
GTCAAGAGCCTCTGCATGAGCGCCCCACTGTCTATCTAAGAGCCAACGGTTCTTGCCTCAAAAAAAAAAAA
AAAAAAAAAAAAGGCCTATCAAATGGTATAAACTAGGATTTAGCAAACTATGGCCCATAACCTGTTTC
TGTTAATAAAGCTTTATTGGAACACACCAACCCCCACTCATTTGTGCATTGCCTGTGCCTGTTTCAA
CATTCTAATGCCACAATTGCAAGAGACTGCATGGCCCACAAACCCTAAAATGTTTACTATCTGTCTC
TTTACAGAAAAGGTGTGTCGACCCCTGGCCTATACAATTAAGAAATGCTTGCCTCTGTGGCTTCCAA
TCACAGCAAAATTTTTTGTCTTGCAGAATAGATATGAAACCTTTTTCAAAAATACTGATTCTTCTAT
TACAGTCGTTTTGGGGTTTTTTTGTTTTGTTTTGTTTTGTTTTGTTTTTTTTGAGACAGAGTCTTGC
TCTGTCACTCAGGCTGGAGTGCATTGGTACAATCTCAGCTCACTGAAATCTCTGCCTCCTGGGTTCA
AGTGATTCTCTTGTCTCAGCCTCCCGAG | **THE FACTS** | ACACGGTGTGCACCACCACACCCGGCTAA
TTTTTGTGTTTTTAGTAGAGACAGGATTTCGTCATTGTTGGCCAGGCTGGCCTCAAACTCCTGACCT
CAAGTCGTCCACCCTCCTTGCCCTCCCAAATGCTGGGATTACAGGTATTACAGTGTTTTAACCTGTA
ATATATGTAACCTGACAATGTGTAAGTGACAAGTGCCCAATATACTCTTAGTTCTGAAATTGGCTAA
CTGGAAACCCTTGCTCTCACGTTTTTCTTTGTGAACTCGTTCTTCCTGCCATTCCCTCTCTCATTC
TGTAATATTTAAGTGAACTCATACTCACTTCAAACCTTCCTCTGTTATCACTAGAATATGGCCTCTG
GAAAAAAATCTTCACAATTCATTCTTACACAAGTGTGAGGGAATTTAGCCTTAAGCGGATATACACT
CTCATCTTTCCAAGTACAGCCAGTACATTTCTCCCTTTTGGGTTTCCCCGCATCTTATAAATGTCTC
CATCATAATTTCTAAAACACTATATTGTGTTTCTTTTAAATTCATCTGCCCCCAAGAATCAAAACCT
```

```
TCCTGAGAGCAGAGACTGCTTCTTATTTATCTTTGAACCTCTAGCATCCAGTACCCAGAAGAGTCT
ACTTCCAAAAGATGAATGGAAGAAGCAAGACAGGCAGGTTGGCAGGCTTCTTGGATTACCGTTCCA
CTTATCTATCCCCAATGCATTTGCATTTTAACAAAAGACAGCCTTGAAGCCAAGCAGTGAAACTGTGT
TGGTGGAAATTTTAAACATCAGAAGCAAGTCAGGGGAGATGCTTTTGTGGATAGGGAAACATTCCTAG
CATCCCTTCAATTTTATATTCATAGGAAGCATCCATCTTACCTAATTTTCAGGTCAGCCCTGAAAGA
GACAACAGAAACGTACATGCTACATTTCTATAAGACTATAGACTAACCTTCCAATGCTCAAATAGAA
AGTACCAGAAAAATTAAATACATCCATATTACCCACTCGGGCAACACTAACATGAAAGCCAACTGAT
GAGATATTTGAAAGTTTGTCTTGAGGAAAAAACAAACAAAGAAAGTATTAAATGCCAGTAAAACTTC
CCCCAAAGTCAGAGTCATCTGGGGTTACCAATAGGGGGCAGCCAGGACCTGGAGTTAAAATCTACTGG
AGTCAAACTCCCTGAATTTAAATCCTAGCTCCACTTCTCTGTGGCAACAAGATCTTGCACAATTTCC
TTAACCACTTGAAACTTCGATGTTTTTAATCCACAAAGTGCAGACACAAATACAGTCAGCCACTGTA
TTAATCATGCTTTTCTCAACAATCGGCCTCATATACAATAGTGGTCCCGTAAGATTATCATAACGTA
CTTTTGCTCTACCTAGTTTATGTTTAGATACACAAATACTTCCCATTCTGTTACTGCTGCCCTACATT
ATTCAGTACCATAACACGGTGTACAGGTTTGTAGCCTGGGAACCCCAGTGACACCTTACAGCCTAG
GTGTGTAGTAGGCTACACACCATTGAGGTTTGTGTAAGTTCACTCTGTGATGTTCACACAATGACAA
AATTCCCTGAGGATGCATTTCTCAGAACGTATCCCCATCATTAAGCAATGCACACCTGTAGTGTTCC
TCTCACAGGTGTCTTTCTTTTGAACTGGTTAATAATATAACTCAAATAGTAGCTATGGTTATTCTTAGA
GAAACCATTCATTCAGCACCTCCCACATGTAAGTCATTGACTTATCCTTTCTAAAATTTTCTAACCC
CAGAGCTAAATATTCTAACATCAGGCACATCAAATGTAATGTATCTGACCTTTAGGTTCAATAGAAT
ATTATACCCCACAGGCTTTTATTTAAAACCCCTTATGTCCCTAGCACTGTCTGTTAACTGTAGAACA
TACTAGAGGAGAAGACTCTGTCAGCCTTCTTCGGGGCTTTAAGGCTTGTTGGACAGGATTCAGAGACT
ACTAGCCAGTGTACTGCTCATTACTCAAAAGCAGAGACTGCAGCCTTGGGGAGCCTTCCTCGATATGG
GCATGCTGCAAGCGGAACCACGTGCCCACTCTTCCAGCAGCCATCAGCCTCATCTGTTAGCCTGGTGCAA
AAGTAATTACGGGTTTTGCCATTACTTTTAATTGCGTCAAAAACTGCAATTACATTTGCACCAACCT
AATAGAATGTAAGTTCCAGGAAAGTGGGATTTTCATCTGTTTTGTTTATTGCCTTATCCCCGGTACC
TAGAACACTGCCTGGCACTTAGTAGGTGTCCAATAAATGTTTAAGCAAAGAAAAACAAAAGCAAAAAG
GAAATTGATTGGTAGTTGGGTTTCGACATGCCTTTTAGGGAAAAATTGTATGGTCCCCTTTTGTTTC
GTGTATTTTCTCCTCCAAACTATTTATCTGACTCCCTCCAGCTCCTCTTGACCTCCTCGATCTTCCTT
ATAGTTTTCTGCTTGTCTCTCGAGTGTACTTTCGGGTTTGTGGGATTTGTACAAATATTGCTTAATCC
CACAAGCGAGTATGTTGAGTGTTTTCCATAAAAAACAGTAACCTAGAAAGAAGCGTCAGATTTCTGGG
CAGTTGCCAGCAGTTACCATGGTGCTCTGAACACACCGTCNCAAAAAATATTACTGATTTGACCCCA
CAGCCACAGTACATGCTATTTCTCACACATCGATGAGACTCTTAAGAGCCATCTCTGTTCTGTGTTCA
AACTGATGTATAGGGTACAAGTCTTCCATTTGTTCACTCTGCATTTATGAGAAATCGCCATCATAGT
ACCGGATTCCAGCGCGGTAAACTAGAAGCTCATCATCCTATCTGCTTCTCATTTGCGTTTCCAACAAA
TGGAATACTTTGATAGAAACGTGAATTGGAAACCATAGTCGAACCCTATTGGTAACCCCAGATGACT ... 3'
```

```
LOCUS       12737473     92866 bp    DNA          PRI       10-FEB-2001
DEFINITION  Src from: Homo sapiens chromosome 12 working draft sequence segment.
ACCESSION   12737473
VERSION     12737473
KEYWORDS    .
SOURCE      human.
  ORGANISM  Homo sapiens
            Eukaryota; Metazoa; Chordata; Craniata; Vertebrata; Euteleostomi;
            Mammalia; Eutheria; Primates; Catarrhini; Hominidae; Homo.
```

REFERENCE 1 (bases 307629 to 322268)
  AUTHORS   Muzny,D.M., Adams,C., Adio-Oduola,B., Ali-osman,F.R., Allen,C., Alsbrooks,S.L., Amaratunge,H.C.,
            Are,T.R., Banks,T., Barbaria,J., Benton,J., Bimage,K., Blankenburg,K., Bonnin,D., Bouck,J., Bowie,S., Brieva,M.,
            Brown,E., Brown,M., Bryant,N.P., Buhay,C., Burch,P., Burkett,C., Burrell,K.L., Byrd,N.C., Carron,T.F., Carter,M.,
            Cavazos,S., Chacko,J., Chavez,D., Chen,C., Chen,R., Chen,Z., Chowdhry,I., Christopoulos,C., Cleveland,C.D., Cox,C.,
            Coyle,M.D., Dathorne,S.R., David,R., Davila,M., Davis,C., Davy-Carroll,L., Dederich,D.A., Delaney,K.R., Delgado,O.,
            Denn,A.L., Ding,Y., Dinh,H.H., Douthwaite,K.T., Draper,H., Dugan-Rocha,S., Durbin,K.T., Earnhart,C., Edgar,D.,
            Edwards,C., Elhaj,C., Escotto,M., Falls,T.A., Farrell,S., Ferraguto,D., Flagg,N., Ford,T., Foster,P., Frantz,P.,
            Gabisi,A., Gao,T.C., Garcia,A.A., Garner,T., Garza,N., Gill,R., Correll,T.H., Guevara,W., Gunaratne,P., Hale,S.,
            Hamilton,K., Harris,C., Harris,K., Hart,M., Havlak,P., Hawes,A., Hernandez,J., Hernandez,O., Hodgson,A.,
            Hogues,M., Holloway,C., Hollins,B., Homsi,F., Howard,S., Huber,T., Hulyk,S., Hume,T., Jackson,L.E., Jacobson,B.,
            Jia,Y., Johnson,R., Jolivet,S., Joudah,S., Karlsson,E., Kelly,S., Khan,U., King,L., Korvah,T., Kovar,C., Kratovic,T.,
            Kureshi,A.A., Landry,N., Leal,B.C., Lewis,L.C., Lewis,L.T., Li,T., Li,Z., Lichtarge,O.A., Lieu,C., Liu,T., Liu,W.,
            Loulseged,H., Lozado,R.T., Lu,X., Lucier,A.T., Lucier,R., Luna,R., Ma,T., Maheshwari,M., Mapua,P., Martin,R.,
            Martindale,A., Martinez,E., Massey,E., Mawhiney,E., McLeod,M.P., Meador,M., Mei,C., Metzker,M., Miner,C.,
            Miner,Z., Mitchell,T., Mohabbat,K., Morgan,M., Morris,S., Moser,M., Neal,D., Newtson,T., Newtson,N.,
            Nguyen,A., Nguyen,N., Nguyen,N., Nickerson,E., Nwokenkwo,S., Oguh,M., Okwuonu,C., Oragunye,N., Oviedo,R.,
            Pace,A., Payton,B., Peery,T., Perez,L., Peters,L., Pickens,R., Primus,E., Pu,L.L., Quiles,M., Ren,Y., Rives,M.,
            Rojas,A., Rojubokan,I., Rolfe,M.C., Ruiz,S., Savery,C., Scherer,S., Scott,G.A., Shen,H., Shooshtari,N., Sisson,I.,
            Sodergren,E., Sonaike,T., Sparks,A., Stanley,H.C., Stone,H., Sutton,A., Svatek,A., Tabor,P., Tamerisa,A.,
            Tamerisa,K., Tang,H., Tansey,J., Taylor,C., Taylor,T., Telfrod,B., Thomas,N., Thomas,S., Tomasula,S., Usmani,K.,
            Vasquez,L., Vera,Y., Villalon,D.C., Vinson,R., Wall,R., Wang,S., Ward-Moore,S., Warren,R., Washington,C.,
            Williams,C., Wleczyk,R., Wooden,S., Worley,K., Wu,C., Wu,Y., Wu,Y., Zhou,T., Zorrilla,S., Nelson,D. and Gibbs,R.
  TITLE   Direct Submission
  JOURNAL   unpublished Molecular and Human Genetics, Baylor College of Medicine, One Baylor Plaza,
            Houston, TX 77030, USA
REFERENCE 2 (bases 307629 to 322268)
  AUTHORS   International Human Genome Project collaborators.
  TITLE   Toward the complete sequence of the human genome
  JOURNAL   unpublished
REFERENCE 3 (bases 307629 to 322268)
  AUTHORS   Worley,K.C.
  TITLE   Direct Submission
  JOURNAL   Submitted (30-MAR-2000) Human Genome Sequencing Center, Department of Molecular and Human
            Genetics, Baylor College of Medicine, One Baylor Plaza, Houston, TX 77030, USA
COMMENT   GENOME ANNOTATION REFSEQ: NCBI contigs are derived from assembled genomic sequence data.
            They may include both draft and finished sequence. On Feb 10, 2001 this sequence version replaced
            gi:11440850. COMPLETENESS: not full length.

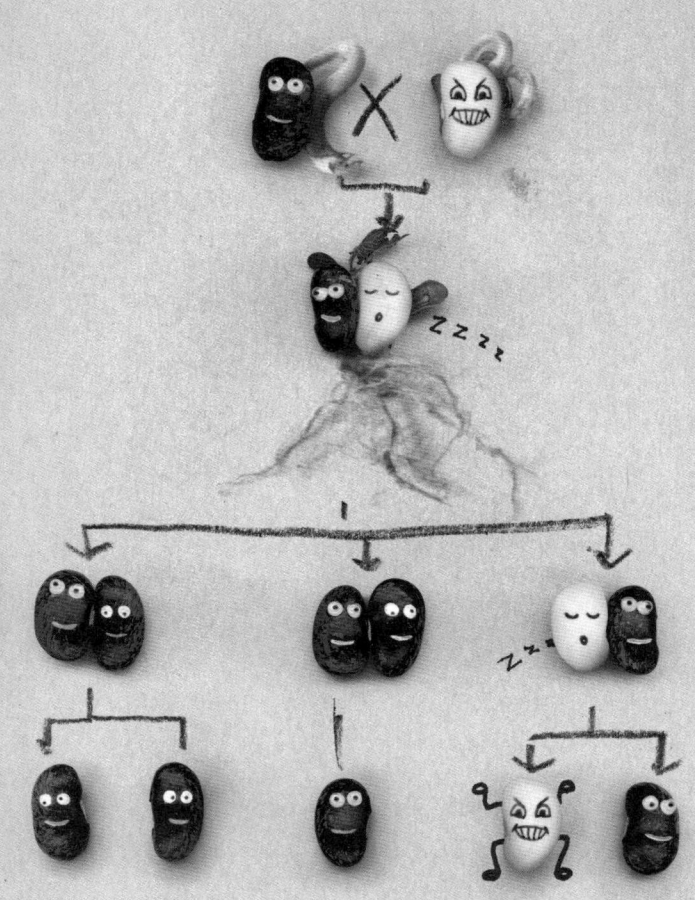

How the round gene
is passed on to create
round offspring

Of course, you would have to know
how to read the patterns.

self-directed evolution

Which isn't easy.

| |...
MICROSATELLITE|ANALYSIS|OF|THE|CELL|POPULATIONS|AND|THE|LAMBS|AT
FOUR|POLYMORPHIC|LOCI|CONFIRMED|THAT|EACH|LAMB|WAS|DERIVED|FROM
THE|CELL|POPULATION|USED|AS|NUCLEAR|DONOR|DURATION|OF|GESTATION
BEING|DETERMINED|BY|FETAL|GENOTYPE?   ...| |

Even for good readers.

Even if you supplied the beans.

Childhood versions of biology having
as much relation to contemporary
science as childhood versions of
religion had to do with theology.

Even if you owned...

**Only a two-chromosome difference between men
and chimpanzees—imagine!**

The Garden

How I Tried in Vain to Imagine a Dimension Not My Own
*'Why should the thirst for knowledge be aroused, only to be disappointed
and punished?' I repeated, unable to crack the nut of the phrase 'Upward but
not Northward.' What could this enigma possibly mean to regular figures,
bound as they are to the flat plane of their paper? I resolved to endeavor
a demonstration by setting before the public a clear view of the whole subject;
and for this purpose it seemed necessary to resort to writing.*

EDWIN ABBOTT
FLATLAND

Even if a person can't yet fully explain the
cause of some symptom, though, is that any
reason to stand by idly while the quality of
life can be improved for so many?

A thin line?

A utopia, really

All the difference in the world?
quality control

Can anyone really explain how
aspirin works?

In fact, aren't
doctors and scientists and technicians and
plain-ol' common folk obligated to act?

*The 'Adam's Apple' is a wooden ball fitted with straps which can be buckled
at the back of patient's head. Since the oral cavity of the patient is more
or less filled by this instrument, the patient can obviously utter only stifled
screams, which require a great effort and cause him to grow tired and
become quiet. This is actually the purpose of this device, which must
not be condemned as cruel, since its aim is to produce one of the most
healing restrictions.*

JOHANN CHRISTIAN HEINROTH *1818*
TEXTBOOK OF DISTURBANCES OF MENTAL LIFE AND THEIR TREATMENT

You can't fight city hall.

For the good of the patient?

**All of our assumptions, truths and aspirations preserved in the fossils
of our language**

our clichés

*In Succinylcholine Therapy, the subject remains fully conscious as he goes
through a sensation of suffocation akin to drowning. While the psychiatrist
intones reminders that the man's acting-out behavior has brought him to
this pass, the therapist assures the subject that he will be able to breathe
again and suggests group psychotherapy or other ways to amend the
behavior.*

MEDICAL WORLD NEWS 11:29–30 (OCT. 9) 1970

And the good of society?

like a ship of fools: a cliché from
the Middle Ages when towns would put idiots and other
social undesirables on a ship then send them away

morally obliged (as they say in novels)

That is, once you name a gene and know
how to test for it, maybe even manipulate it,
isn't your refusal to do so a judgment?

**No town ever allowing a ship of fools from
another town to dock**

No Exit.

Ellis Island

Even Helen Keller thought juries of
doctors should decide which defective
infants should be allowed to die.

Doctors' decisions based on facts, no doubt.

*That the <u>moral</u> qualities of mankind are <u>inherited</u> is now so firmly established
that we have difficulty in realizing the opposition early investigators
encountered in establishing this fact.*

R. A. FISHER
"The Evolution of the Conscience in Civilized Communities in
Special Relation to Sexual Vices" in *Eugenics in Race and State, Vol. II.
Scientific Papers of the Second International Congress of Eugenics.*
held at American Museum of Natural History, New York.
Sept. 22-28, 1921.

Collective decisions being more objective
than individual decisions.

obviously

For the good of society, the U. S. Public Health Service initiated a study of untreated syphilis. It was 1932 and researchers understood the insanity and death that resulted from untreated syphilis. They also knew how to cure it. What they wanted to know was the natural course of various ravaging symptoms.

To learn this, they selected 400 infected African-American males in the town of Tuskegee, Alabama [a controllable environment]. Spinal taps were administered to establish a base line of the neural damage already suffered by the subjects. In order to keep them in the study, the subjects were told that the placebos they received were treatments for the disease. Over the next 40 years, researchers collected data on the deterioration of the subject's bodies. They ensured that local physicians didn't corrupt the data by giving the subjects antibodies. Being conscientious researchers, they also compared the subjects to a control group of 200 who did not have the disease. The fact that nearly twice as large a proportion of the syphilitic individuals as the control group has died is striking, the National Institute of Health pointed out after reviewing the first ten years of data. At conferences, in journals and other public forums, the National Institute reported results such as the fact that, based on 23 years of data, 30 of the test group autopsied had died directly from advanced syphilitic lesions. Unfortunately, the study was concluded prematurely in 1972 due to sudden interest by the press which unfavorably compared it to the FBI Farm where corpses were left lying about fields and in ponds so that the rate of decomposition might be studied. At last word, eight test subjects were still alive. It is not known if they intend to donate their bodies to science.

That is, the story told by a collective
being more objective.

A collective story being a lot of little stories

(collected)
A history, really, of language.
Including mutations.

and in the language
such as Braille

of a lot of individuals.
A people   **Such as Helen Keller.**
begets

a history

That's why Esperanto
never   *begets*

a people

caught on.

begets
a history

begets   *a people begets*
a history begets
a people begets
       a history begets
a people begets
       a history begets
a people begets
       a history begets
a people begets
       a history begets
a people begets
       a history begets
a people begets
       a history begets
a people begets
       a history begets
a people, and so on....

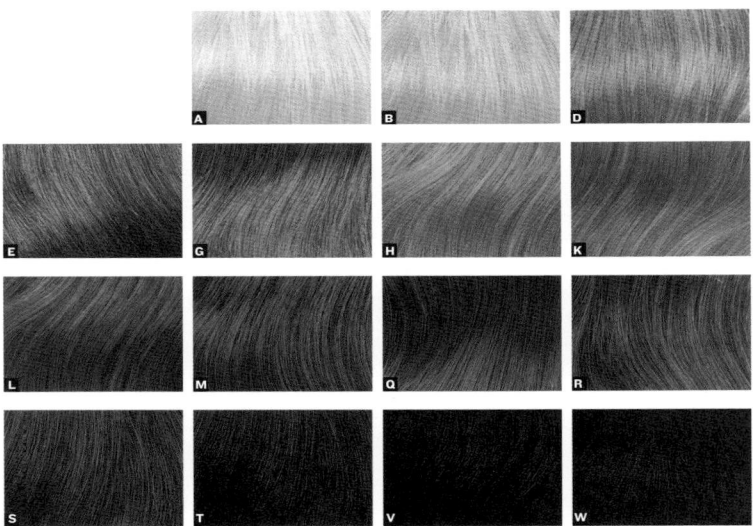

Make your selection now : ＿＿＿

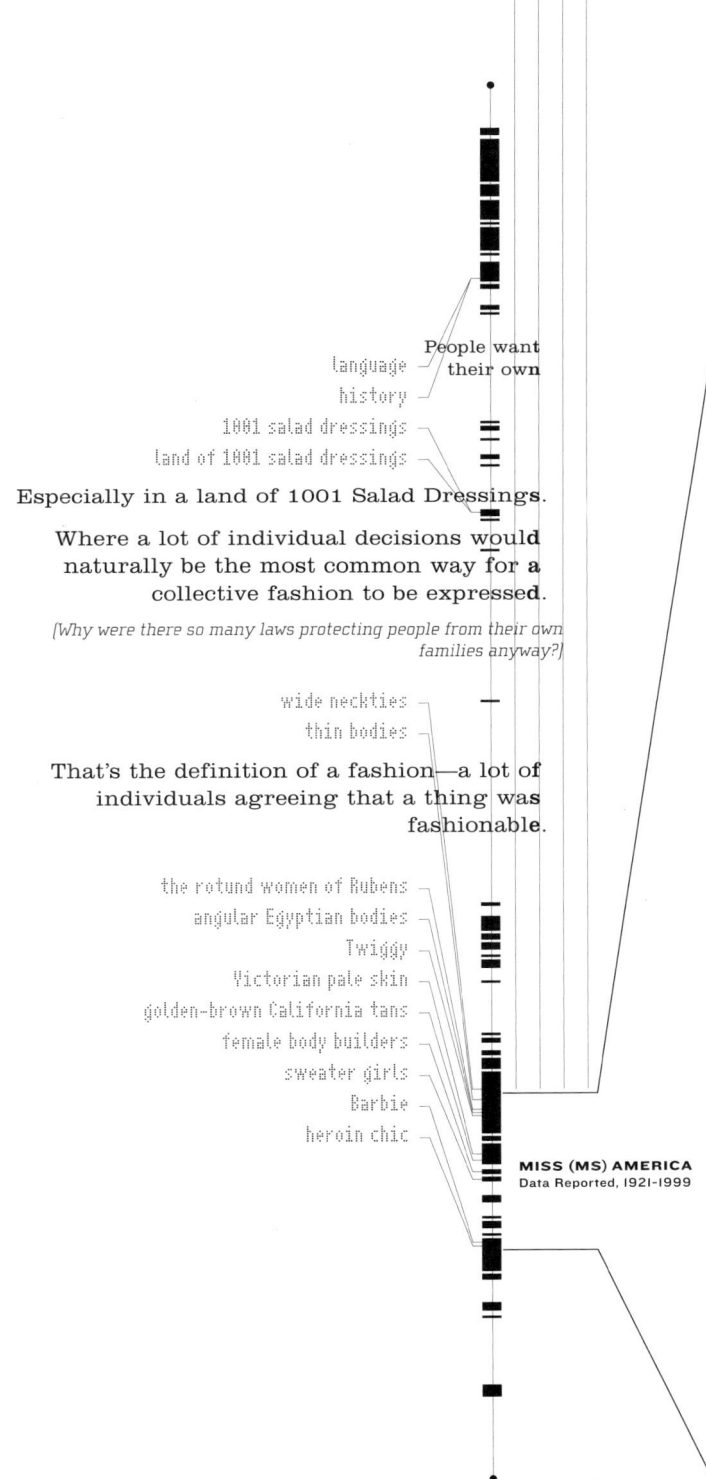

People want
their own

language —
history —

1001 salad dressings —
land of 1001 salad dressings —

Especially in a land of 1001 Salad Dressings.

Where a lot of individual decisions would
naturally be the most common way for a
collective fashion to be expressed.

*[Why were there so many laws protecting people from their own
families anyway?]*

wide neckties —
thin bodies —

That's the definition of a fashion—a lot of
individuals agreeing that a thing was
fashionable.

the rotund women of Rubens —
angular Egyptian bodies —
Twiggy —
Victorian pale skin —
golden-brown California tans —
female body builders —
sweater girls —
Barbie —
heroin chic —

MISS (MS) AMERICA
Data Reported, 1921-1999

Yr*	Name	Age	B-W-H	Ht	Wt	Neck (inches)	Upper Arm (inches)	Lower Arm (inches)	Wrist (inches)	Glove	Thigh (inches)	Calf (inches)	Ankle (inches)	Shoe
1921	Margaret Gorman	16												
1922	Mary Campbell	18		5'6"	135									
1923	Mary Campbell	19		5'6"	140									
1924	Ruth Malcomson	18		5'6"	132									
1925	Fay Lanphier	19			138									
1926	Norma Smallwood	18	33-24-33	4'4½"	118	12				6	19½	12½	7	
1927	Lois Delander	17												
1928														
1929														
1930	NO PAGEANT													
1931														
1932														
1933	Marian Bergeron	16												
1934														
1935	Henrietta Leaver	19	33-23-35											
1936	Rose Coyle	22	34-23-34	5'6"	114	11½	9½	8½	5½		19	13	8½	
1937	Bette Cooper	17		5'6½"	120									
1938	Marilyn Meseke													
1939	Patricia Donnelly			5'7"	126									
1940	Frances Burke	19												
1941	Rosemary LaPlanche	19	34-24-36	5'1½"	120	13	11	9	6		23	14	8	6½
1942	Jo-Carroll Dennison	18	34-24-34	5'5"	118									
1943	Jean Bartel	19	36-23-35	5'8"	130									
1944	Venus Ramey	19	36-25-37	5'7"	125						19½	13	8	
1945	Bess Myerson	21	35-25-35	5'10"	136	13½	9½		5½		20	14½	8½	
1946	Marilyn Buferd	21	35-25-36	5'8"	123	13					22½	13½	8½	8AAAA
1947	Barbara Walker	21	35-25-35	5'7"	130									
1948	BeBe Shopp	18	37-27-	5'9"	138									
1949	Jacque Mercer													
1950														
1951	Yolande Betbeze		35-24	5'5½"	119									
1952	Colleen Hutchins		36-24-36	5'10"	143									
1953	Neva Langley		35-23-35	5'6½"	128									
1954	Evelyn Ay		37-24-36	5'8"	132									
1955	Lee Meriwether		34-32-35	5'8½"	124					7				6AA
1956	Sharon Ritchie													
1957	Marian McKnight	19	35-23-35	5'5"	120					7½				8
1958	Marilyn Van Derbur		35-25-36	5'8½"	130					7				7B
1959	Mary Ann Mobley	21	34-22-35	5'5"	114									6AA
1960	Lynda Mead	20	36-24-36	5'7"	120					7				8
1961	Nancy Fleming	18	35-22-35	5'6"	116					6				7½
1962	Maria Fletcher	19	35-24-35	5'5½"	118									
1963	Jacquelyn Mayer	20												
1964	Donna Axum	22	35-23-35	5'6½"	124					7				7AAA
1965	Vonda Van Dyke	22	36-24-36	5'6"	124									
1966	Deborah Bryant	19	36-23-36	5'7"	115									
1967	Jane Jayroe	19	36-24-35	5'6"	116									
1968	Debra Barnes	20	36-24-39	5'9"	135									
1969	Judith Ford	18												
1970	Pam Eldred		34-21-34	5'5½"	110									
1971	Phyllis George	21	36-23-36	5'8"	121									
1972	Laurel Schaefer	22	36-24-34	5'7"	118									
1973	Terry Meeuwsen	23	36-25-36	5'8"	120									
1974	Rebecca King	23	36-24-36	5'9"	125									
1975	Shirley Cothran	21	36-23-36											
1976	Tawny Godin	18	36-24-36	5'10½"	128									
1977	Dorothy Benham	20	35-22-35	5'7½"										
1978	Susan Perkins													
1979	Kylene Barker	22	35-23-35	5'4"										
1980	Cheryl Prewitt	22		5'7"										
1981	Susan Powell	22		5'5"										
1982	Elizabeth Ward		36-24-36	5'9"										
1983	Debra Maffett	25	32-22-35	5'7"	115									
1984	~~Vanessa Williams~~	~~20~~	~~34-24-34~~	~~5'6"~~	~~110~~									
1984	Suzette Charles													
1985	Sharlene Wells	20	35-25-36	5'8"	120									
1986	Susan Akin	21	32-22-35	5'9"	114									
1987	Kellye Cash			5'8½"	116									10
1988	Kaye Lani Rae Rafko			5'10"	131									
1989	Gretchen Carlson													
1990	Debbye Turner			5'7½"	118									
1991	Marjorie Vincent	25												
1992	Carolyn Sapp	21												
1993	Leanza Cornett													
1994	Kimberly Aiken	18												
1995	Heather Whitestone													
1996	Shawntel Smith	24												
1997	Tara Dawn Holland	23												
1998	Kate Shindle			5'11"										
1999	Nicole Johnson													

Looking over the facts, it can be seen that the weight
of Miss America has decreased by 30% over the years.

If graphed, the years in which Miss America bust-hip-waist
measurements are given to the press forms a bell curve

It's a mindset.
ideas natural in their time   *A style*

waist

a fashion

Symmetry

though changing over time

breasts

can you see both?

an inheritance

---

*Additional material reported: 1922: "Typically American"; 1925: blonde with hazel colored eyes and fair skin; 1926: a figure that the judges considered almost perfect. 1927: light brown hair; 1933: natural blonde; 1935: talent competition added; 1937: blue eyes and blonde hair, as one would expect; 1939: light complexion; 1940: typical American girl; prefers tall men; doesn't care whether Franklin Roosevelt or Wendell Willkie wins election; 1947: curves in the right places; 1951: suntan complexion; 1952: blue-eyed blonde with ideal measurements; 1953: fair complexion; 1954: blonde with ideal measurements; 1957: blonde hair, blue eyes; 1962: forgot her knitting to flash a figure that won her the swim suit trophy; 1965: sang "Together," in the talent portion of the pageant, alternating her lovely voice with the voice she gave to a ventriloquist dummy; 1968: a pianist of impressive dimensions; 1971: fair complexion; 1974: hopes to be a juvenile court judge; 1977: blue-eyed blonde; 1979: keeps in shape through vigorous cheerleading; when asked about the Equal Rights Amendment, she replied, "I still enjoy total femininity"; 1980: winner predicted by statistics professor; 1982: a classic figure; drinks milkshakes to keep her weight up; 1983: deep California tan; 1984: first African-American winner; forced to resign crown for posing in nude photos; 1986: winner predicted by computer statistician; 1987: cites size 10 feet as her biggest fault; 1989: first classical violinist to become Miss America; 1990: third black to win; 1991: talent counted for 40% of a contestant's score; swimsuit 15%; 1992: wore a red ribbon as a symbol of solidarity with people who have AIDS; 1994: believes the controversial swimsuit competition should remain because "it's a tradition"; 1995: first handicapped (deaf) person to win; 1996: over a million viewers nationwide called and voted 4-to-1 to keep the swimsuit competition; 1997: during the talent competition, Holland dressed in a midriff-baring oriental costume to sing the operatic composition "Ou va la jeune Indoue"; 1998: for the first time contestants allowed to wear two-piece swimsuits.

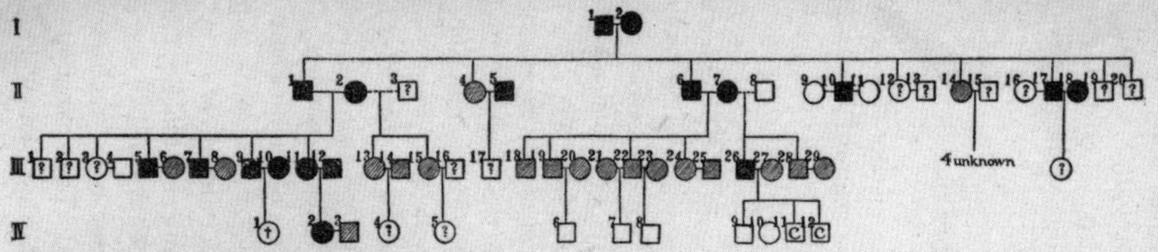

FIG. 48.—A fragment of the Jukes pedigree, being descendants of the elder daughter of "Ada Jukes." Showing occurrence of *shiftlessness* (black symbols) and partial shiftlessness (striated symbols).

I, 1, a lazy mulatto; I, 2, a non-industrious harlot, but temperate; II, 1, a frequent recipient of out door relief, in jail for assault; II, 2, lazy and a harlot; II, 4, twice recipient of out relief; II, 5, laziness, assault, vagrancy; II, 6, vagrant, out relief, jail; II, 7, vagrancy; II, 10, lazy, in poorhouse; II, 14, a harlot recipient of a little out relief; II, 17, lazy, licentious; II, 18, a harlot; II, 19, died young; II, 20, unknown; III, 1, 2, 3, little known; III, 5, 6, received out relief; III, 7, vagrant in jail; III, 8, received a little out relief; III, 9, soldier, pauper; III, 10, harlot, poorhouse inmate; III, 11, harlot, jail, out relief; III, 12, out relief; III, 18, bad boy; III, 19, licentious, pauper; III, 20, harlot; III, 22, licentious; III, 24, harlot, pauper; III, 26, pauper and drunkard; III, 28, basket-maker and pauper who later acquired some property; IV, 2, harlot; IV, 11, 12; criminalistic. DUGDALE, 1902, Chart II.

<pre>
                            THE
                         NORMAL
                       LAW OF ERROR
                    STANDS OUT IN THE
                  EXPERIENCE OF MANKIND
                AS ONE OF THE BROADEST
              GENERALIZATIONS OF NATURAL
            PHILOSOPHY ◆ IT SERVES AS THE
          GUIDING INSTRUMENT IN RESEARCHES
        IN THE PHYSICAL AND SOCIAL SCIENCES AND
      IN MEDICINE AGRICULTURE AND ENGINEERING ◆
    IT IS AN INDISPENSABLE TOOL FOR THE ANALYSIS AND THE
INTERPRETATION OF THE BASIC DATA OBTAINED BY OBSERVATION AND EXPERIMENT
</pre>

diabetes— 1 out of 80 people

Today, geneticists talk about 3,000 symptoms with a clear deviation from the average.

DR. MABUSE *1986*

cleft lip, 1 out of 675 people

Each with its own signature.

Science Rocks!

EXPERIMENT No.74 **AFTERIMAGES**

Stare at the flag for 15 seconds.
Now look onto the blank sheet of paper and you will continue
to see stripes and stars.

The image you see is called an
AFTERIMAGE

It is safe to predict that in the near future tests will bring tens of thousands of defectives under the surveillance and protection of society. This will ultimately result in the elimination of an enormous amount of crime, pauperism, and industrial inefficiency.

LEWIS TERMAN, *1916*

We should put our resources into the formation of a custodial state: a high-tech and more lavish version of the Indian reservation for some substantial minority of the nation's population where they can be prevented from breeding while the rest of America tries to go about its business.

A.R. JENSEN
Harvard Educational Review, 1969

Of course, Jensen was speaking of new
diseases, not old ones like homosexuality
or industrial inefficiency.

Or a ship of fools   *or the smallpox in blankets that the
U.S. Government once handed out to Indian mothers*

Even if history is much more objective,
that is repeatable, than science.

Unless it dies.
Like Latin.

This is why we have copyright
for works of culture (stories) and
registered trademarks for works
of nature (life).
A group consensus.

Gene sequence©, Blood Sample®

Mickey Mouse©, Oconomouse®—same deal.

In fact, it wasn't until the primate larynx
(nature) changed shape that humans were
able to make any articulate sounds
at all (culture).

Let alone tell stories.

In other words, a gram of oxygen would have
weighed the same in ancient China as it does
in contemporary America.

*The Oconomouse™ being a mouse genetically engineered
to have breast cancer.*
developed at Harvard

funded (and patented) by Dupont™

Had ancient Chinese a conception of oxygen.

And had they had a concept of grams.
Sometimes culture and bodies come together.

Mice and cancer...
It's a hybrid

The first cyborg also a mouse.

Lots of designer mice
Dial 1-800-Lab-Rats
and receive a catalog.

The point being that culture came after bodies.
not at all like the chicken/egg cliché.

...the elements of Mickey Mouse© as well...

Or the flying monkeys who carried
Dorothy to the Wicked Witch of the West
...existing in a state of nature...
unlike harpies
without language

...until people, smart as
chimps, figured out ways...
...to make products...
like rats
Minnie Mouse©, too

...of words... Enchanted Forest©

...**of** lives
Goofy©
The Cowardly Lion©

A mortal coil

Unless bodies follow culture

But the way I just phrased that last example
assumes that there is a thing called oxygen
waiting to be found.

What is looked for is what is found.

GLENDA©

Usually unconsciously.

The way a driver, pulling out into traffic
unconsciously goes with the flow.

rather than buck

the trend.

It's easier.

The way Flatlanders once lined up all over
the country to enter Fitter Family Contests.

Maybe I should have
Fitter Families Contests once embodying a said that the two
system of measurement shared by all cultures would have
agreed upon identical
Flatlanders weights had their
histories led them to
construct identical
systems of measure.

Held at state fairs.
First Kansas

KA

then 40 other states as well

OZ

Where whole families competed and
were judged like livestock.

Called "human stock"
KY
*A being who conceives of himself as a link in an evolutionary chain is going
to act differently than one who thinks of himself as that being who stole
fire from the gods.*

KENNETH BURKE

ND
SD
"human husbandry"

A practice that continues in their surviving
descendants: Miss Idaho, Miss Indiana,
Miss Ohio,

Miss IL

Ms. OR

NY

DC

FL

NH NM

think

differently too

NV WA

GA

IA

MI TX

PA **A** Legacy

prize different value CT

As well as a matter of good stock (nature).

AL

CA

SWIMSUIT COMPETITION

AR

Families being
considered the material of society.

...until it became Ms. America (culture)

GOOD LEGS :

MUSICAL ABILITY :

INTELLIGENCE :

People being considered the material of families.

PROPORTIONS :

FACIAL FEATURES :

SMILE :

SYMMETRY :

Genes being considered the material of people.

Could a Hottentot ever become Ms. America?

People sometimes being identified
as material as well, obviously.

Like the thousands of U.S. servicemen who
unawares participated in bio-medical experiments.

And the grade school boys who were invited (for the good of society)
by the National Institute of Health to join a science club and participate
in an experiment...

Material also often being found in prisons

...the experiment not actually being the model rockets the boys
made, but the radioactive oatmeal they were fed.

Like the inmates who "volunteered"
to have their testicles exposed to 20,000
X-rays worth of radiation.

Unlike Elie Metchnikof, who died injecting
himself with a bacteria to cure old age.

Or Werner Forseman, who threaded
a tube up a vein in his arm,
all the way to the heart.

And Clinics

where 820 pregnant women "volunteered" to drink
a "vitamin cocktail" containing radioactive iron.

For the good of society.

future children, as well

Society must look upon germ-plasm as belonging to everyone and not solely
to the individual who carries it.

THE AMERICAN [HUMAN] BREEDERS ASSOCIATION, *1914*.

Not that any commoner would
mistake people for their materials.

TIM HEIDLER

m (ME)   n (NO)   ŋ (SING)

Or a change in laryn**x**
as the difference
between people an**d**
chimp**s**.

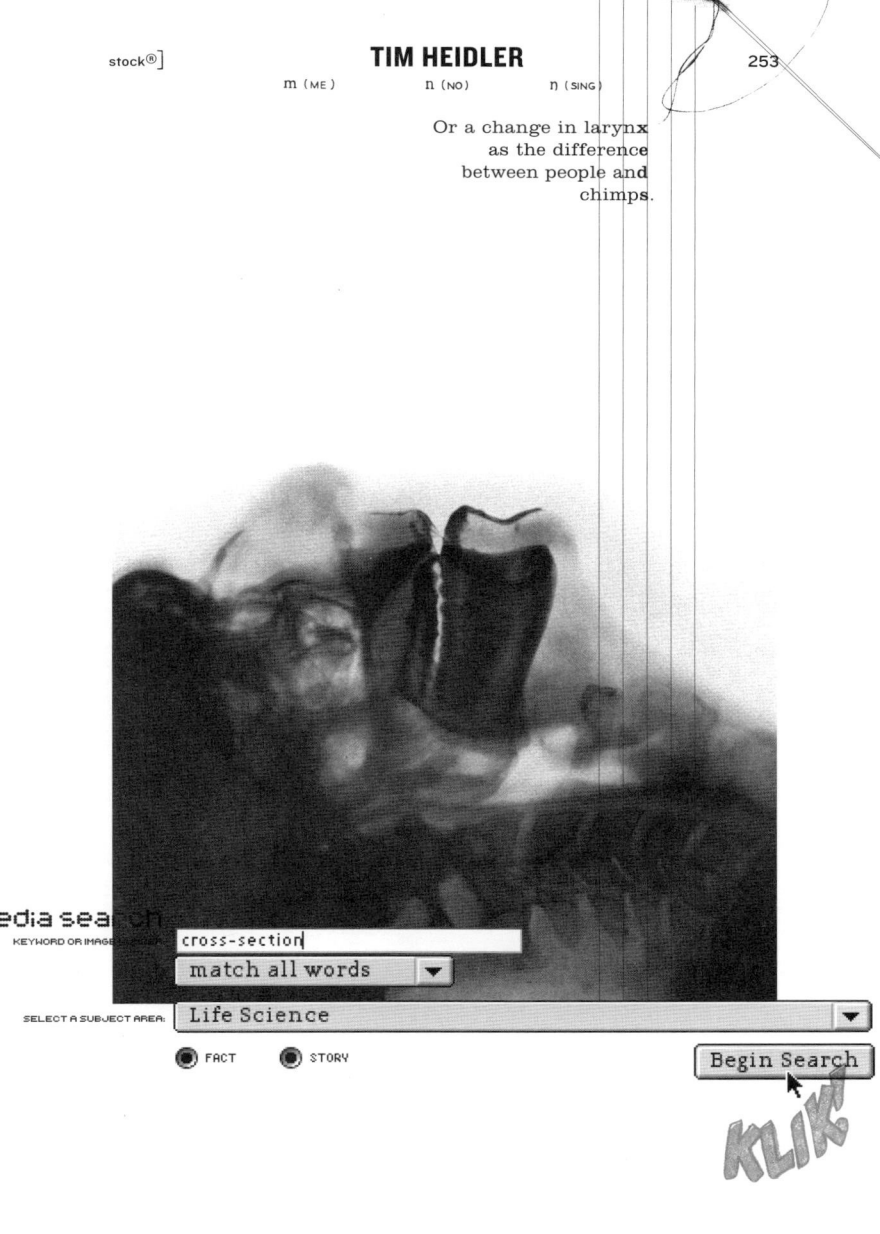

ɱedia search
KEYWORD OR IMAGE: cross-section

match all words ▼

SELECT A SUBJECT AREA: Life Science ▼

● FACT   ● STORY

Begin Search

KLIK!

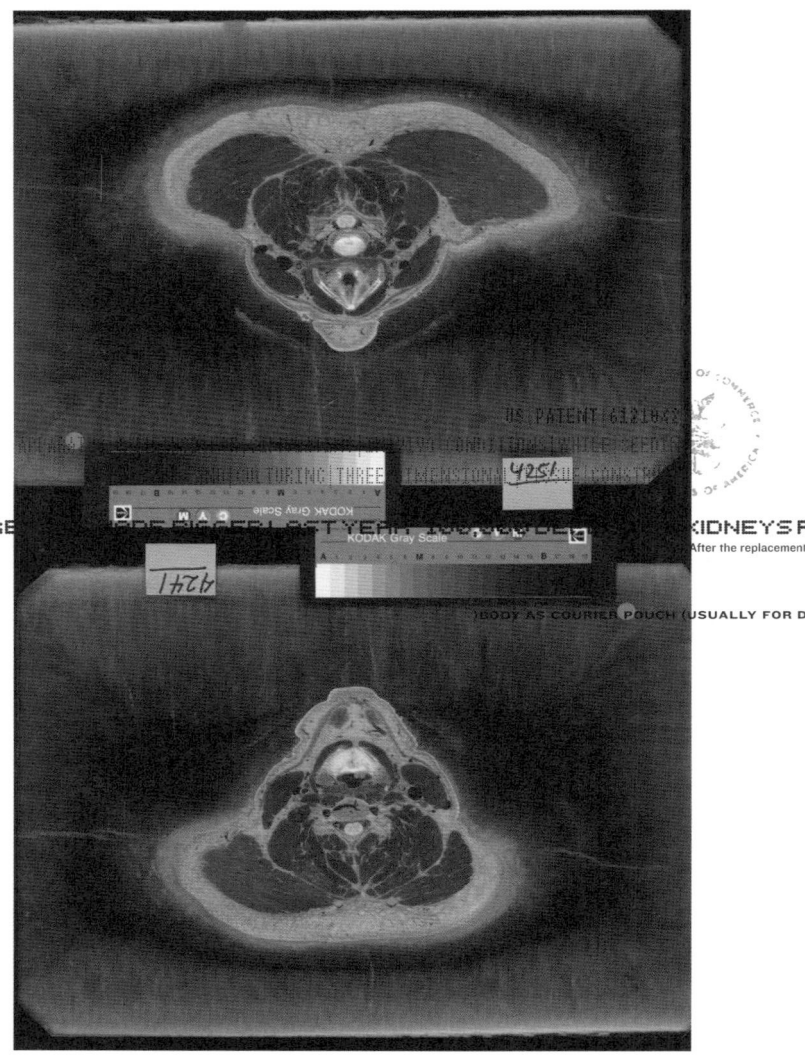

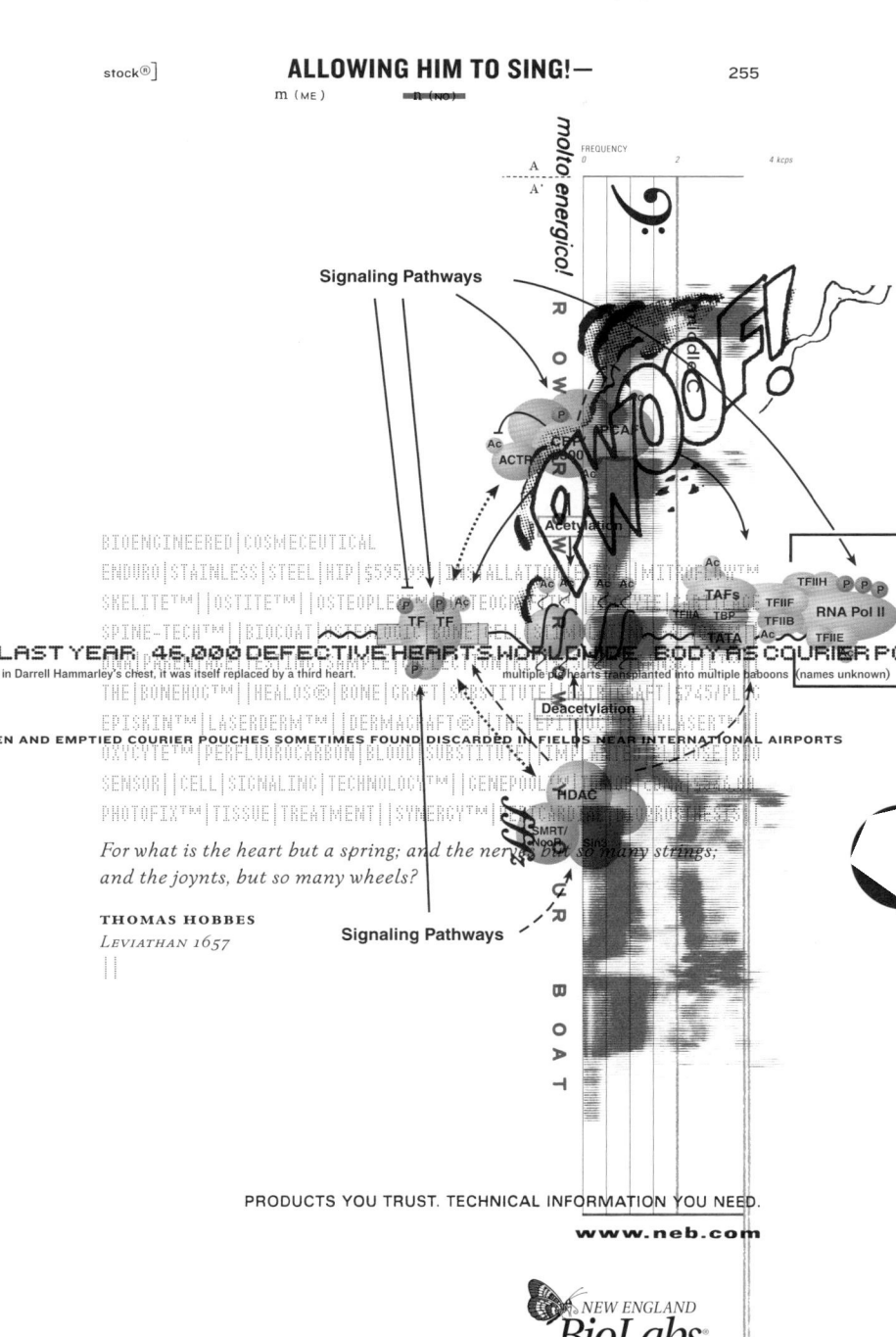

m (ME)   n (NO)

For what is the heart but a spring; and the nerves but so many strings; and the joynts, but so many wheels?

THOMAS HOBBES
LEVIATHAN 1657

PRODUCTS YOU TRUST. TECHNICAL INFORMATION YOU NEED.

www.neb.com

NEW ENGLAND
BioLabs Inc.
where science is the priority

A MUSICAL ROUND
ROW ROW ROW YOUR BOAT

[Human

Only **one doll** order per Profile please. Photocopies are acceptable for multiple orders.

Child's Name (Please Print) _____

Child's Age _____ **Birthdate** _____ / _____ / _____ **Phone (** _____ **)** _____

1. **Face Shape (Photo Required):** My Twinn has a wide range of face shapes for children ages 3-12 from which our artisans select the match which best resembles your child based on her/his photo(s). It is essential to enclose 1-2 nice color photo(s) with your order which we will use to select a face shape, hair style and overall look. **Don't worry about finding the perfect photograph. Write child's full name on back of each photo.** Do not send irreplaceable photos; occasionally photos are accidentally lost or damaged. In the case of vintage photographs, we recommend sending us a good photocopy. **Number of Photos Enclosed** _____

SYNTHETIC EMOTION and PROJECT

2. **Skin Tone:** Check box left of selection. (Refer to "Skin Tone Chart" on page 14.)
   ☐ Very Fair   ☐ Fair   ☐ Olive   ☐ Light Brown   ☐ Brown   ☐ Dark Brown

3. **Eye Color:** Circle closest eye color.

   A10   A17   A40   A50   C30   D10   D30   D37   D50   T07   T20   T40
   A20   A30   A60   C20   C40   D20   D34   D40   D60   T10   T30   T50

4. **Hair Color:** Check box left of closest overall color. (Refer to "Hair & Eyebrow Color Chart" on page 14.) Include a representative sample of hair with Order Form, if possible.
   ☐ L   ☐ M   ☐ Q   ☐ R   ☐ S   ☐

CH SYNTHETIC BONES   SYNTHETIC BONE MARROW   SYNTHETIC BLOOD   MECH

Elmer Deugebauer walking with the transplanted knees of a cor

5. **Eyelash Color:** Check box left of selection. (Available in colors noted.)
   ☐ Blonde   ☐ Golden Brown   ☐ Dark Brown   ☐ Black

6. **Eyebrows:** **Color:**
   ☐ A   ☐ B   ☐ D   ☐ E   ☐ G   ☐ H   ☐ K

   CARNAL KNOWLEDGE   CUT OPEN (TUMMY TUCK BREAST REDUCTION BUTTOCK LIFT)

   Check box left of selections (see Color Chart on page 14).
   ☐ L   ☐ N   ☐ S   ☐ T   ☐ V   ☐ W
   Shape: ☐ Straight   ☐ Slight arch   ☐ Arched   ☐ Other (Draw)
   Thickness: ☐ Thin   ☐ Moderate   ☐ Full

7. **Hair:** **Cut:** ☐ All one length   ☐ Tapered   ☐ Layered
   Check box left of "Cut" selection, and circle hair "Length" choice.
   Length: Ear length   Chin length   Shoulder length   High-back   Mid-back   Lower back

8. **Hair Style:** **Bangs:**
   ☐ Straight   ☐ Layered
   ☐ Very curly   ☐ Wispy
   ☐ Slightly curled under   ☐ None
   Check box left of selections that apply.
   Style:
   ☐ Bone straight   ☐ Loose curls all over   ☐ Ends curled under
   ☐ Straight with a little wave   ☐ Tight curls all over   ☐ Ponytail
   ☐ Wavy (permed)   ☐ Sides pulled back   ☐ Pigtails
   ☐ Ends curled up   ☐ Other (Describe below)

   Boys: (Photo Required.)
   ☐ Tapered cut in back   ☐ Block cut in back

9. **Birthmarks/Moles/Freckles:**
   Using a pen, please mark on faces at right where your doll should have freckles, birthmarks, moles or scars. Indicate dimples with a "D". Draw scars where applicable.

   Comments: _____
   _____
   _____

   Child's Right   Child's Left

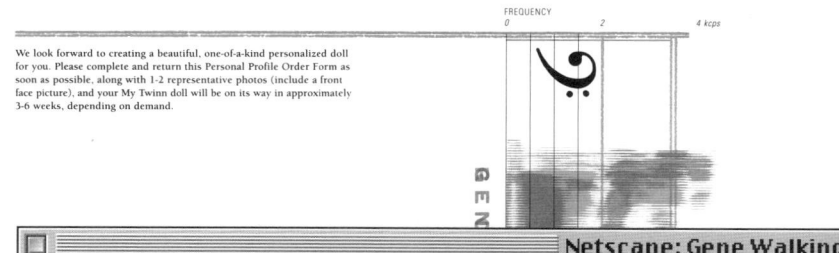

We look forward to creating a beautiful, one-of-a-kind personalized doll for you. Please complete and return this Personal Profile Order Form as soon as possible, along with 1-2 representative photos (include a front face picture), and your My Twinn doll will be on its way in approximately 3-6 weeks, depending on demand.

FREQUENCY
0   2   4 kcps

Netscape: Gene Walking

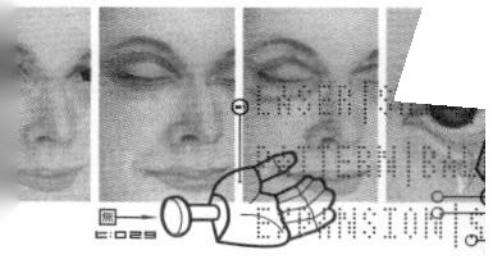

USCLES SYNTHE

Dr. Alexis Carrell, of the Rockefeller Institut

PEOPLE SEEN THROUG

LIPOSUCTION
NOPLASTY
$3,274 FOR 0
TREATMENT
TH ENDOSCOP
MICROSURGIC

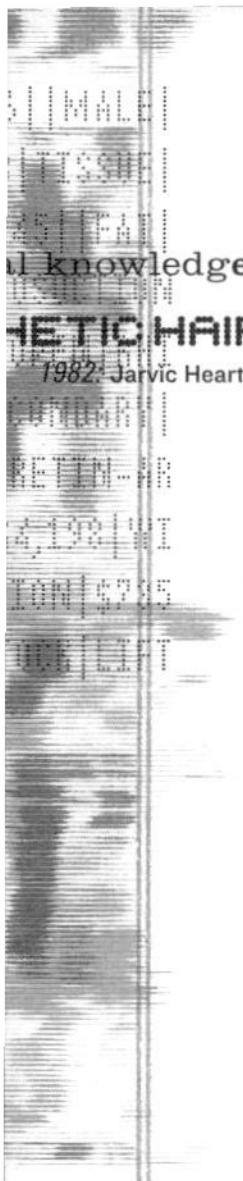

l knowledge

HETIC HAIR EARS G

1982: Jarvic Heart goes on the market.

FLYrSYr® A TOMATO WITH THE GENES OF THE COLD WATER OOD FISH TO MAKE IT RESISTANT TO FREEZING FRANKENFOOD

ARTHUR FINNIESTON CLINIC

PRODUCTS YOU TRUST. TECHNICAL INFORMATION YOU NEED.

www.pall.com

FINNIESTON GROUP*

MARAMED SYSTEMS*

BioSculptor®

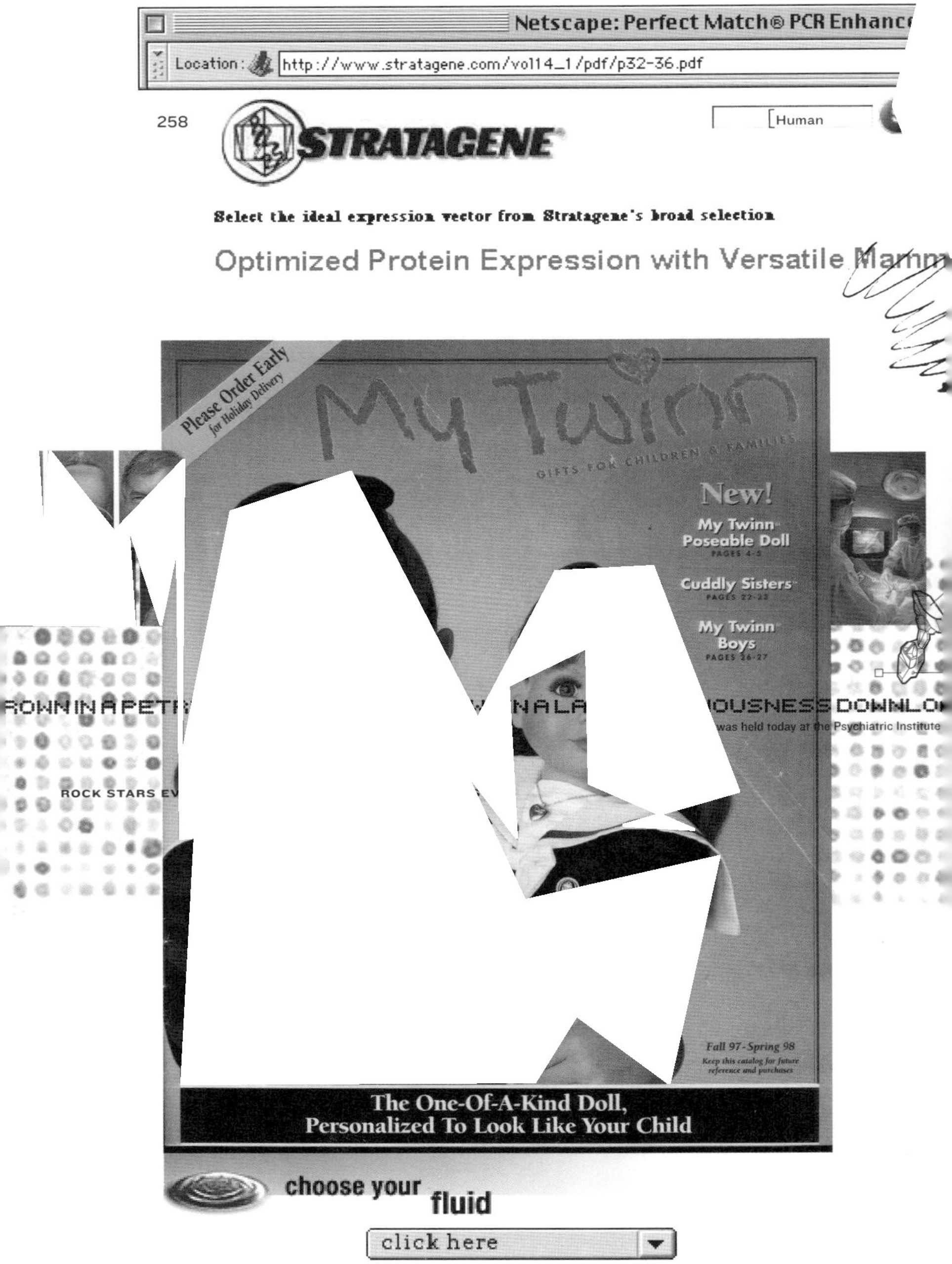

Netscape: Perfect Match® PCR Enhanc

Location: http://www.stratagene.com/vol14_1/pdf/p32-36.pdf

STRATAGENE

Human

Select the ideal expression vector from Stratagene's broad selection

Optimized Protein Expression with Versatile Mamm

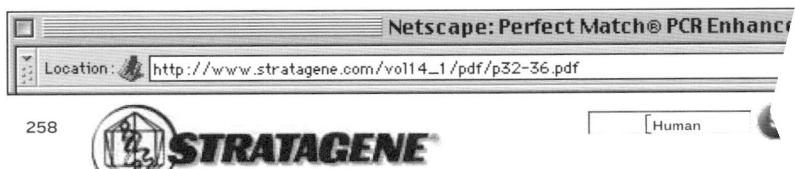

Please Order Early *for Holiday Delivery*

My Twinn

GIFTS FOR CHILDREN & FAMILIES

New!
My Twinn
Poseable Doll
PAGES 4-5

Cuddly Sisters
PAGES 22-23

My Twinn
Boys
PAGES 26-27

ROWN IN A PET

NALA

OUSNESS DOWNLO
was held today at the Psychiatric Institute

ROCK STARS EV

Fall 97–Spring 98
Keep this catalog for future
reference and purchases

The One-Of-A-Kind Doll,
Personalized To Look Like Your Child

choose your **fluid**

click here ▼

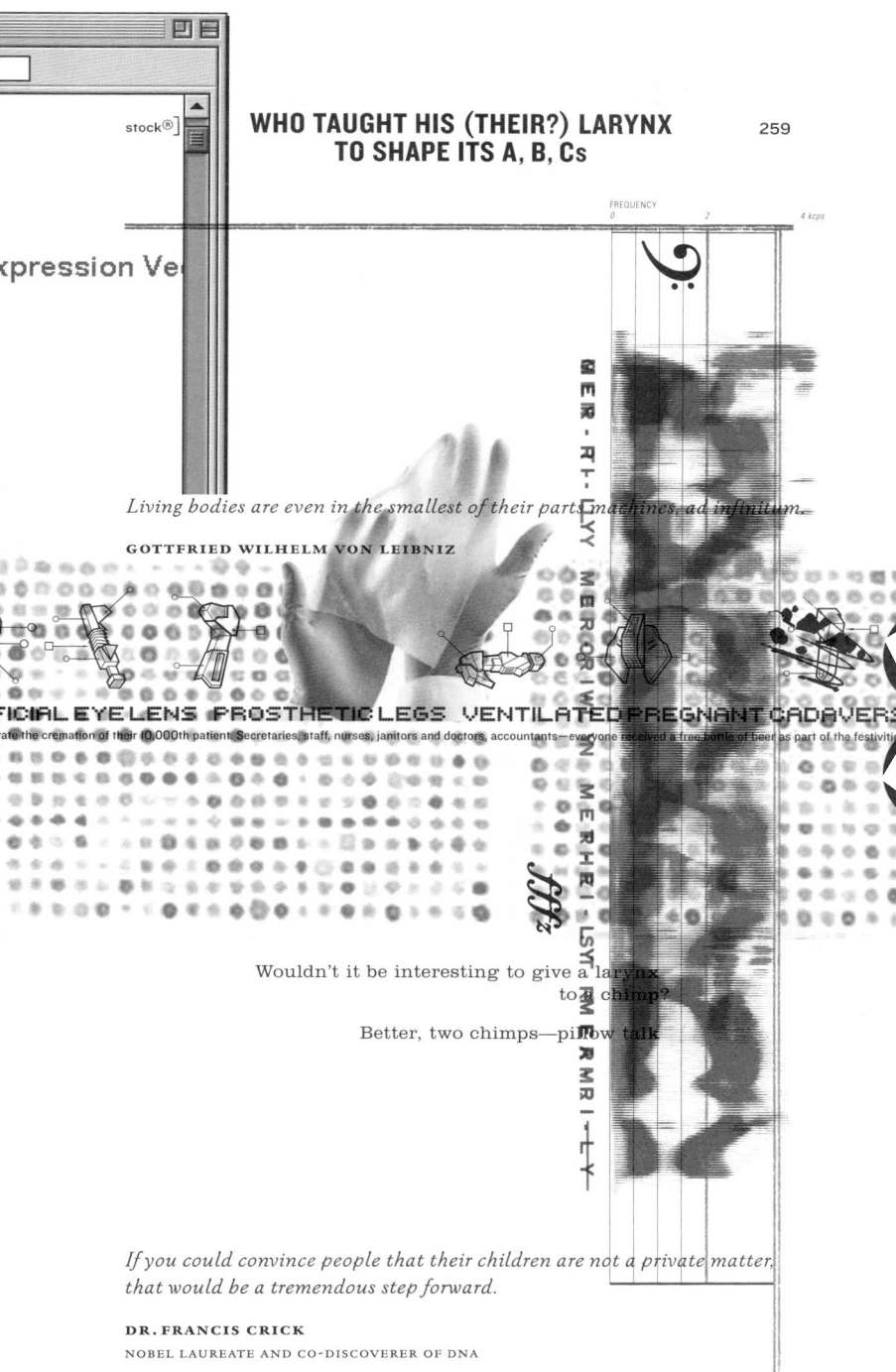

Living bodies are even in the smallest of their parts machines, ad infinitum.

GOTTFRIED WILHELM VON LEIBNIZ

FICIAL EYE LENS   PROSTHETIC LEGS   VENTILATED PREGNANT CADAVERS

ate the cremation of their 10,000th patient. Secretaries, staff, nurses, janitors and doctors, accountants—everyone received a free bottle of beer as part of the festivitie

Wouldn't it be interesting to give a larynx
to a chimp?

Better, two chimps—pillow talk

*If you could convince people that their children are not a private matter,
that would be a tremendous step forward.*

DR. FRANCIS CRICK
NOBEL LAUREATE AND CO-DISCOVERER OF DNA

STRATAGENE®

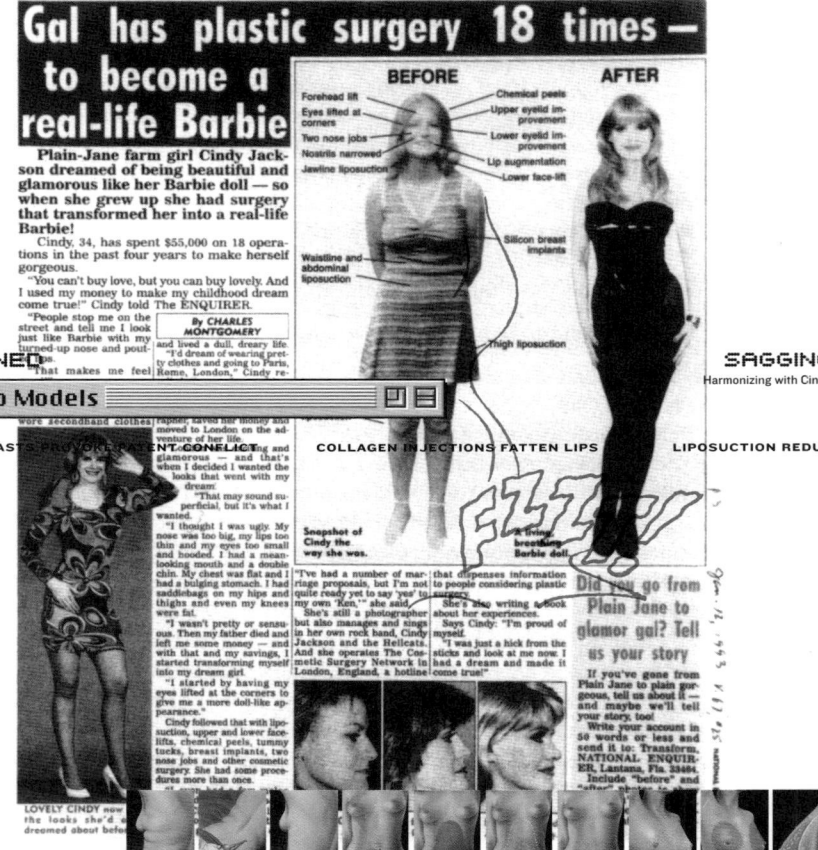

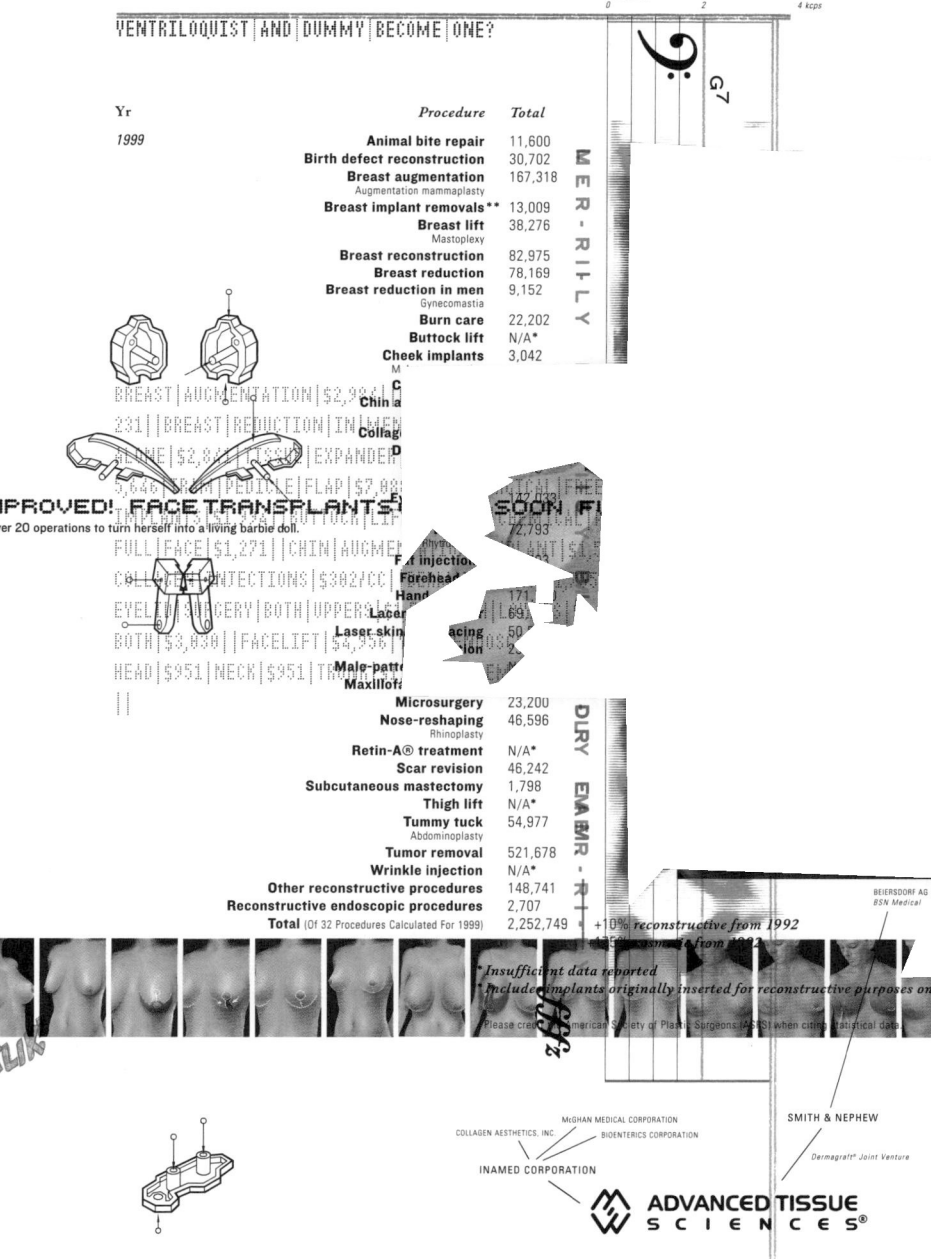

VENTRILOQUIST AND DUMMY BECOME ONE?

Yr	Procedure	Total
1999	Animal bite repair	11,600
	Birth defect reconstruction	30,702
	Breast augmentation Augmentation mammaplasty	167,318
	Breast implant removals**	13,009
	Breast lift Mastoplexy	38,276
	Breast reconstruction	82,975
	Breast reduction	78,169
	Breast reduction in men Gynecomastia	9,152
	Burn care	22,202
	Buttock lift	N/A*
	Cheek implants	3,042
	Chin a...	
	Collag...	
	...EXPANDER	
	Microsurgery	23,200
	Nose-reshaping Rhinoplasty	46,596
	Retin-A® treatment	N/A*
	Scar revision	46,242
	Subcutaneous mastectomy	1,798
	Thigh lift	N/A*
	Tummy tuck Abdominoplasty	54,977
	Tumor removal	521,678
	Wrinkle injection	N/A*
	Other reconstructive procedures	148,741
	Reconstructive endoscopic procedures	2,707
	Total (Of 32 Procedures Calculated For 1999)	2,252,749

IMPROVED! FACE TRANSPLANTS ... SOON (FI...

over 20 operations to turn herself into a living barbie doll.

FULL FACE $1,271 | CHIN AUGME...
COLLAGEN INJECTIONS $302/CC | Forehead...
EYELID SURGERY BOTH UPPER...
BOTH $3,630 | FACELIFT $4,956 |...
HEAD $951 | NECK $951 | TR...

+10% *reconstructive from 1992*

Insufficient data reported
Includes implants originally inserted for reconstructive purposes onl...

Please cred... ...merican Society of Plastic Surgeons (ASPS) when citing statistical data.

BEIERSDORF AG
BSN Medical

SMITH & NEPHEW

Dermagraft® Joint Venture

McGHAN MEDICAL CORPORATION
COLLAGEN AESTHETICS, INC.
BIOENTERICS CORPORATION
INAMED CORPORATION

ADVANCED TISSUE
S C I E N C E S®

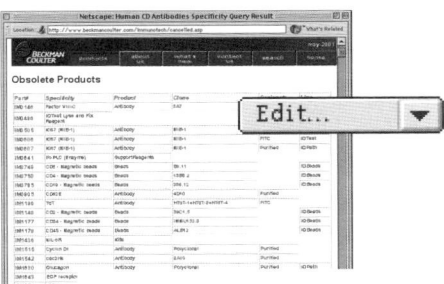

At <u>$2.80</u> *per base,* OPERON'S **DNA makes** *anything* <u>POSSIBLE.</u>

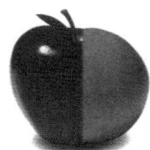 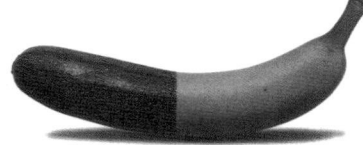

THE APPLORANGE THE ZUCCHANA CHICKEN GENE IMPL

1999: Matthew Scott receives hand transplant.

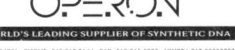

NUMBER OF INHERITABLE DISEASES: 3000 - 4000 NUMBER OF DISEASES POTENTIALLY CURABLE BY

$2.80 PER BASE DNA FROM OPERON

ANNOUNCING PRICE REDUCTIONS FROM THE WORLD'S LEADING SUPPLIER OF DNA.

Operon's price reductions present a whole new world of possibilities. Our custom DNA is now available for just $2.80 per base with a $20 set-up fee per sequence. So you can afford to do more experiments and get more results.

Operon consistently delivers precisely the product you need. On time. With unsurpassed purity. Backed by an unconditional guarantee. And, as you can see, at an extremely competitive price. We ship our custom-made sequences in two working days, on average. And that includes large orders and orders placed late in the day.

So don't let your budget limit your thinking. Call Operon, the company that makes anything possible. In terms of speed, purity, and savings, there are no bases for comparison.

CALL 1-800-688-2248 TODAY.

OPERON

WORLD'S LEADING SUPPLIER OF SYNTHETIC DNA

©1993 OPERON TECHNOLOGIES, INC., 1000 ATLANTIC AVENUE, SUITE 108, ALAMEDA, CA 94501. PHONE: 510-865-8644. FAX: 510-865-5255. NIHBPA 263-00033233

Circle No. 13 on Readers' Service Card

ELEMENTS OF HUMAN BODY | SULFER | POTASSIUM | SODIUM | CHLORINE | MAGNES becoming a quaint lis

* *Operon Technologies 2001 DNA Research Catalog-Recipes section:* Zucchana Bread: I egg, 3/4 cup sugar, 4 ripe Zucchanas I/3 cup butter, I-I/4 cup all-purpose flour, I-I/2 tsp baking powder, I tsp vanilla. Pre-heat oven to 350 degrees. Mash together butter, Zucchanas, egg and vanilla. Mix in sugar, flour and baking powder. Pour into greased loaf pan. Bake until an inserted toothpick comes out clean—approximately I hour. Cool 5 minutes. Loosen sides from pan and remove.

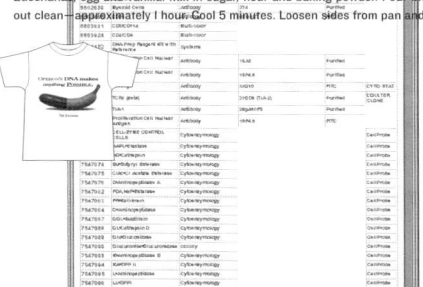

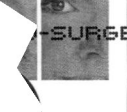

m (ME)   n (NO)

FREQUENCY
0   2   4 kcps

CAN|INFORMATION|BE|DESTINY?|THE|WAY|BIOLOGY|USED|TO|BE?

ff

Netscape: What's New

search
- GENOMIC SEGMENTS
- ALL BIOLOGICAL DATA
- PEOPLE
- CITATIONS

by
- NAME/GDB ID
- KEYWORD
- DNA SEQUENCE ID

Submit   Reset

N SALMON SHEEP GET GENE OF TOBACCO PLANT HUMANIZED MOUSE CO

s of the cadaver that donated a hand to Matthew Scott going into 22 other people.

INEERING: 3000-4000

Smile! Renaissance™ non-rad DNA labeling kits give you reproducible results, not high backgrounds.

MARKET FOR FETAL PRODUCTS: $11 BILLI

Are you repeating experiments just to reduce backgrounds? Then look into Renaissance™ non-radioactive DNA labeling and detection products from DuPont NEN® And get low backgrounds and reproducible results the first time, and every time.

- Sensitive HRP-luminol systems for colony plaque lifts and Northern, Southern, and Western blots
- Results in minutes
- Guaranteed one-year shelf life.
- Backed by full protocol and comprehensive technical service.
- Now available: Random Primer Fluorescein dUTP Labeling Kit and Oligonucleotide 3' End Labeling kit (Fluorescein dUTP)

DuPont gives you a choice of radioactive and non-radioactive labeling and detection products. For information, or orders call 1-800-551-2121. For information by fax call 1-800-666-652 and request number 9001.

DuPont NEN®

Thus, instead of a Social Security Card, a national repository would be created to hold blood samples of every man, woman and child, each identified by its DNA sequence which would be printed on an ID.

ONE PROPOSAL

Netscape: Beckman Cou

Location: http://www.beckmancoulter.com

st Victorian

given the gold mine that inheres in ACGTs

BECKMAN COULTER

A SIREN'S SONG?

Welcom

processes for

▶ **BEC**   36.99 -.01

Stock quote minimum 20 min. delayed

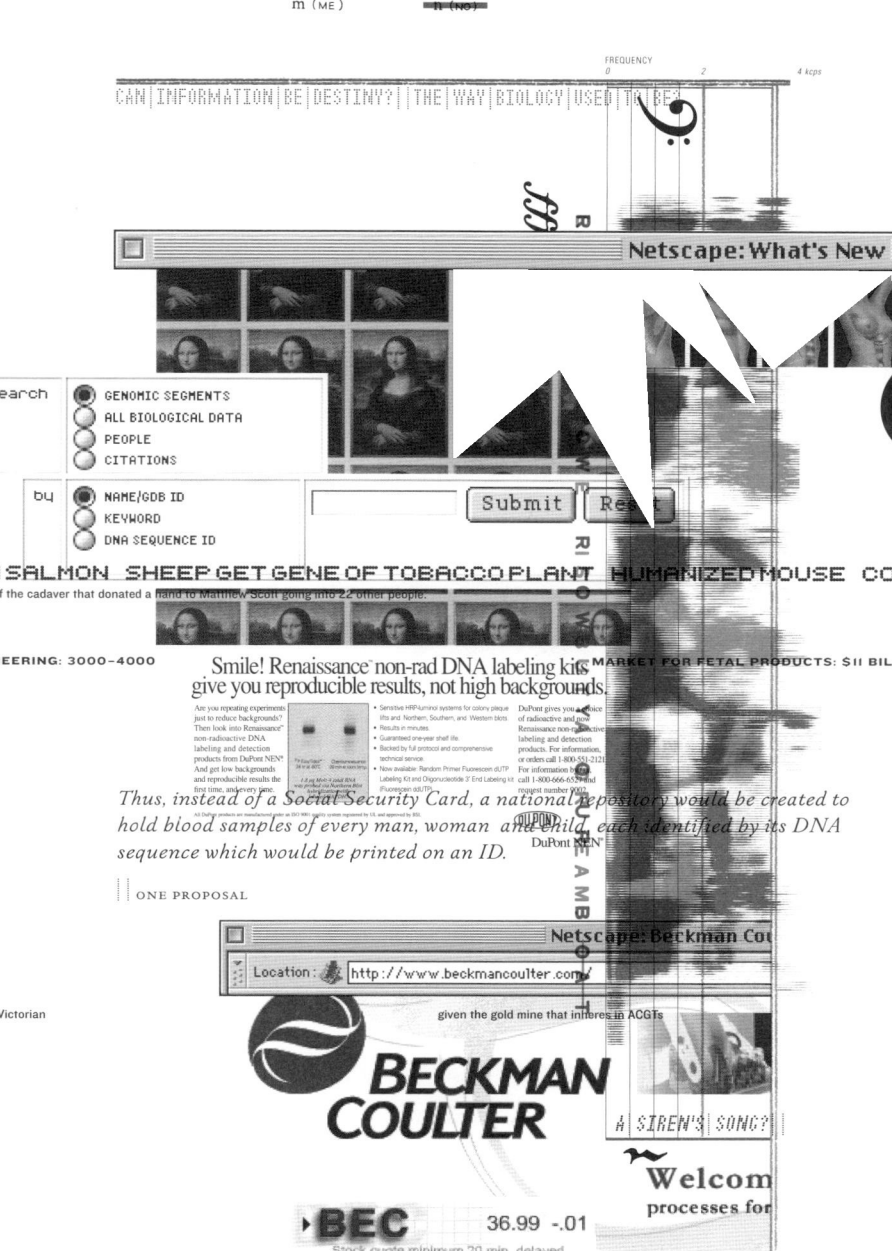

THUS YOUR PORTRAIT MIGHT LOOK LIKE

http://www.ronsangels.com/index2.html   Go

Rons Angels

[egg auction]

come up to beauty
come up to rons angels

starting bids: $15,000 – $150,000 US
in $1,000.00 increments

'S ANGELS

auction
m auction

mation

act
ID
ment
sidents

rmation

BICISE
for life

choices

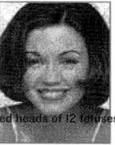 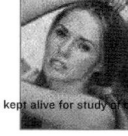 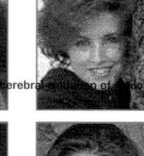 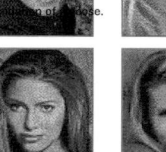 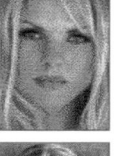

1973: Decapitated heads of 12 fetuses kept alive for study of cerebral circulation of glucose.

RESHAPE

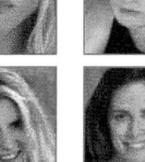 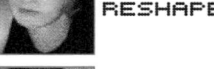

site summary

There are 6.1 million infertile women in America. Some are looking for eggs so they can have children. Many are opting for eggs from dissimilar donors. There was even an Asian couple who chose an egg from a blue–eyed blonde Scandinavian woman. Or you could choose the girl who most resembles you. A better looking version of you.

There are also millions of men from around the world who would love to have their genes combined with beautiful, healthy and intelligent women. Many men have substantial financial resources, yet are unable to find the genetic combinations that would impart beauty to their offspring.

Beauty is its own reward. This is the first society to truly comprehend how important beautiful genes are to our evolution. Just watch television and you will see that we are only interested in looking at beautiful people. From the network anchors, to supermodels that appear in most advertisements, our society is obsessed with youth and beauty. As our society grows older, we inevitably look to youth and beauty. The billion dollar cosmetic industry, including cosmetic surgery is proof of our obsession with beauty.

What is the significance of beauty? It has been reported that young babies prefer to look at a
symmetrical one. Beautiful people are usually given the job of

Cut off the head and the mind will follow.   Hearts as well   Scientists too

REVOLUTIONARIES

m (ME)   n (NO)   ŋ (SING)

FREQUENCY
0   2   4 kcps

PRINTED | OUT | YOUR | NAME | WOULD | BE | |D157; VNTR Genetic ID

http://www.ronsangels.com/index2.html   Go

Rons Angels

[sperm auction]

[model 89]

DDY TO OVERCOME THE NAGGING EFFECTS OF AGING, LIFESTYLE OR HEREDIT

8: First In Vitro Fertilization. A Modern Miracle.   1998: Biologists at Texas A&M receive $2,300,000 to clone Missy, the dead pet dog of an anonymous couple.

SLIDING | TOWARD | MODERN | ROUTINE

Why not?

LARRY AGENBROAD
PROJECT PALEONTOLOGIST, *WHEN ASKED WHY THE DISCOVERY CHANNEL HE WORKED FOR WAS TRYING TO CLONE A WOOLLY MAMMOTH:*

**minimum bid: $15,000
in $1,000 increments**

closing 3/01/2000

Please include your membership number when maki

A | POINTILLIST | PORTRAIT | OBVIOUSLY

PERFECT HEALTH, HETEROSEXUAL SUCCESSFUL BUSINESS MAN AND MALE MODEL

I am an honest sincere man who understands the needs of parents and the love a parent has for a child.

I'm single, in my 30's, 6'1" 180lbs., blue eyes, brown hair, and have a family business building custom homes for executive clients. I am one of 5 children—we are all one year apart. I am the middle child with 2 brothers and 2 sisters—all of us are in perfect health with no major illnesses a height and weight proportional. My parents were married after they graduated from the same

and their accountants

RESGEN™

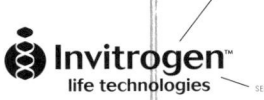

⊛ Invitrogen™
life technologies

SERVA™

FOR | SPEED | OF | PROCESSING | YOUR | ID | MIGHT | BE | REPRESENTED | LIKE | THIS

The Republican governor of New Jersey—home to dozens of biotechnology and pharmaceutical companies—has vetoed a bill that would give people a property right to their genetic information, warning that it could "chill" research in the state.

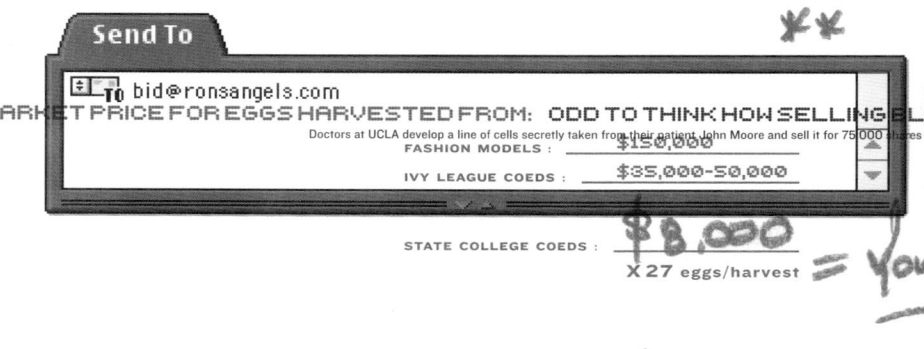

MARKET PRICE FOR EGGS HARVESTED FROM: ODD TO THINK HOW SELLING EL

Send To

bid@ronsangels.com

Doctors at UCLA develop a line of cells secretly taken from their patient John Moore and sell it for 75,000 shares

FASHION MODELS : $150,000

IVY LEAGUE COEDS : $35,000-50,000

STATE COLLEGE COEDS : $8,000

X 27 eggs/harvest = You

BLACK COEDS : $0.00

** −$1750 (*flat fee paid to donor per harvest*)

Until cloned, a gene's status in nature is no different from the wild beast or migratory waters: ferae naturae. *The claim that a fox owns itself would not lead to the development of products that enhance public health.*

RICHARD M. LEBOVITZ
MILEN, WHITE, ZELANO & BRANIGAN, ATTORNEYS

FREQUENCY
0　　　　2　　　　4 kcps

M·E·R·R·I·L·L·Y

Human blood is a commodity

FEDERAL TRADE COMMISSION *1964*

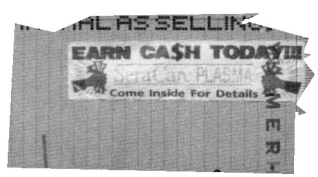

...L AS SELLIN...　　　...ONCE B...

EARN CA$H TODAY!!!
SeraCare PLASMA
Come Inside For Details

...; Jarvic Heart recall

E·R·R·I·L·L·Y

Netscape: INFOBIOGEN Home P...

*I implore travelers to nab bodies whenever they observe ... le involving
savages. Boil the bones in a solution of soda or caustic p...sh to rid them
of their flesh. This process takes several hours, but it wi...provide material
that is needed to complete anthropological collections.*

GEORGES CUVIER
FATHER OF ANTHROPOLOGY

PRODUCTS YOU TRUST. TECHNICAL INFORMATION YOU NEED.

www.bms.com

CONVATEC™
CLAIROL™
ZIMMER™

✿ **Bristol-Myers Squibb Company**

MEAD JOHNSON™

THE WAY GRAVITY CAN BE DESTINY?

[Human

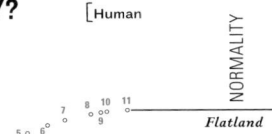

NORMALITY

7   8 10 11
5 ○ 6 ○ ○   ○ ○ ○
                9

Flatland

3 ○○ 4

MOST EXPENSIVE : $_2$○ AB—

CHEAPEST :   O+ 20^2 | SKIN | PER | PERSON | |

5.5 | QUARTS | BLOOD | PER | 154 | POUND | MAN | | 3.5 | QUARTS | BLOOD | PER | 110 | POUND
WOMAN | |

SACRED. BLOOD BANKS GENE BANKS PEOPLE TOO

Genetics used to screen employees

though that never kept mollusks from being bought and sold   *2,000,744:* Number

Gravity being a fiction to explain time/space.

ALBERT EINSTEIN   whose last breath is on display in a test tube in the Henry Ford Museum, Detroit

MUSEO DI STORIA DELLA SCIENZA IN FLORENCE GETTING ONE OF

BLONDES | HAVE | 140,000 | HAIRS | PER | HEAD
REDHEADS | HAVE | 90,000 | HAIRS | PER | HEAD

ODDITY

○1 *1785:* Woman artificially inseminated with husband's sperm

5,000 infants born per year by one of 16 alternative ways to conceive

FREQUENCY
0   2   4 kcps

THAT IS,

How to Create a Work of Permanent Art

Corpses impregnated with epoxy resin or polymerizing emulsion may be fully cured at 122°F (50°C). The curing of polyester-copolymers is initiated by UVA-light, followed by heat treatment at 122°F. Once curing is complete, specimens can be stored indefinitely at room temperature.

DR. GUNTHER VON HAGENS *1999*

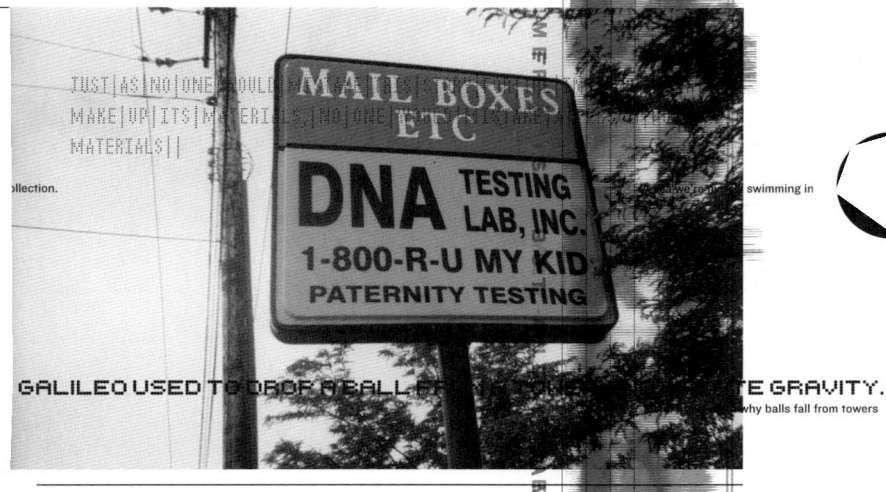

JUST AS NO ONE WOULD MAKE UP ITS MATERIALS, NO ONE MATERIALS

ollection.

swimming in

GALILEO USED TO DROP A BALL

E GRAVITY.

why balls fall from towers

Additional material reported: 2 *1890:* Woman artificially inseminated with non-husband sperm; 1952: Contraceptive pill; 4 *1953:* Frozen donor sperm; 5 *1972:* Screening sperm for desirable traits; 6 *1978:* Test-tube baby (Louise Jay Brown), a modern miracle; 7 *1983:* Surrogate womb rental; 8 *1989:* First genetic engineering; 9 *1991:* Embryo conceived to supply material for sister; 10 *1992:* Embryo with best genetic profile selected from among multiple transplants; 11 *1999:* Woman impregnated with sperm from a dead man.

PRODUCTS YOU TRUST. TECHNICAL INFORMATION YOU NEED.

www.incyte.com

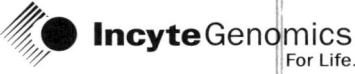

Incyte Genomics
For Life.

SUPPLY

... | | ABIDE | IN | ME | | EACH | BODY | SUPPLYING:
2 | CORNEAS | | 2 | INNER | EARS | | 1 | JAW | BONE | | 1 | HEART | VALVES | INCLUDED | | 2 |
LUNGS | | 1 | LIVER | | 2 | KIDNEYS | | 1 | PANCREAS | | 1 | STOMACH | | 206 | BONES | | 2 | HIP |

Netscape: Products and Services - Life Technologies

JOINTS | | 27 | LIGAMENTS | | 650 | MUSCLES | | 20″ | OF | SKIN | | 60,000 | MILES | OF |
BLOOD | VESSELS | | 90 | OUNCES | OF | BONE | MARROW | | AS | I | WITH | THEE | | ...

BLACK MARKET IN ORGANS   100,000 HUMAN GENES, AND ALL OF THEM COLL

206: Number of re-usable human bones   Anyone who thinks this is about the Nazis or other uncommon situations is missing the point.   *1952:* First frog c

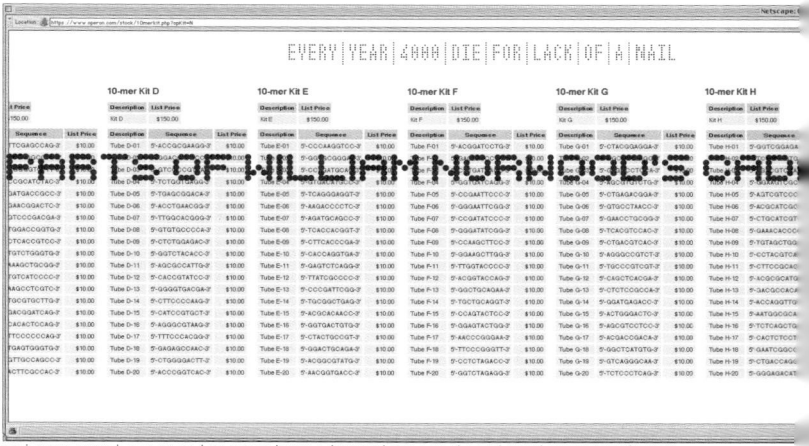

EVERY | YEAR | 4000 | DIE | FOR | LACK | OF | A | NAIL

BY | SUNDOWN | ANOTHER | ELEVEN | WILL | HAVE | FALLEN | OFF | THE | WAITING | LIST
| |

molto energico!

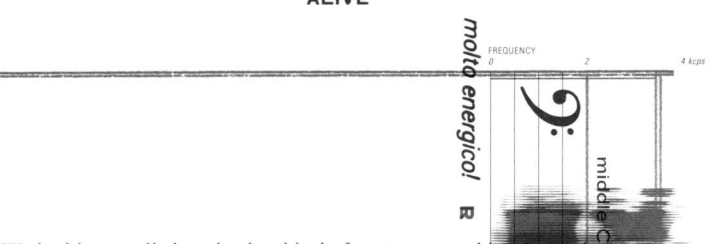

We had been called to the deathbed of a nine-year-old girl in order to see
if we could assist her. But once there, we saw that she was suffering from
very unusual symptoms. So we became extremely interested as scientists in
performing an autopsy. If she were alive at her father's return, which was set
for the next hour, I would have to hand her over; but if she were to die before,
we could do the autopsy. I ... played with the thought of extinguishing the
flickering light of her life with a small injection of morphine. While the
surgical nurse was having her dinner, I sat on the small bed with a full
syringe in my hand and wavered—should I or shouldn't I?

Netscape: GeneOp(R) Custom Gene Products

_E, TAGABLE, PROCESSABLE, SALEABLE... GOLD RUSH. A COMMON MARKET

Grave robbers cut off the hands of Juan Peron and hold them for $6 million ransom.

THE DIARY OF **DR. ALFRED E. HOCHE** *1937*

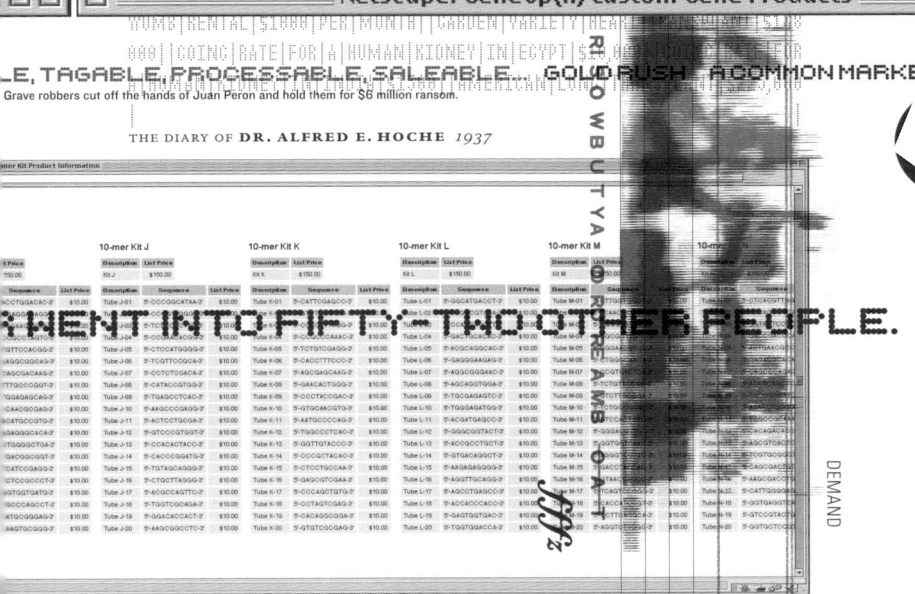

WENT INTO FIFTY-TWO OTHER PEOPLE.

PRODUCTS YOU TRUST. TECHNICAL INFORMATION YOU NEED.

www.biovalley.com

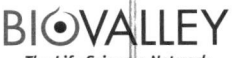

BI•VALLEY
The Life Sciences Network

OF COURSE, THIS IS ALL FLEXIBLE.
(AND NEGOTIABLE.)

[Human

100%

AS|DR.|HOCHE|DEMONSTRATED|CHANGING|HIS|MIND|ABOUT|SCIENTISTS|AND
THEIR|MATERIAL|AFTER|THE|ASHES|OF|A|NEPHEW||A|HOLOCAUST|VICTIM||
WERE|SENT|TO|HIM.

Organ/Procedure	1st recipient	51st recipient	nth recipient
Baboon heart	Baby Fae	*	*
Synthetic heart	Haskell Karp	*	*
Mechanical heart	Barney Clark not counting the TinoMan	*	*
Liver Transplant	Thomas Starzl	*	*
Plastic arteries	Michael DeKakey	*	*
Fetal tissue injections	Don Nelson's brain	*	*
Kidney transplant	William Grigsby	*	*
Lung transplant	John Russel	*	*
Heart transplant	Louis "I am a new Frankenstein" Washinsky donor: Denise Ann Darval, 25 and dead by auto accident	*	*

Insufficient data reported

75%

TIMING IS EVERYTHING

IT'S SORT OF LIKE WHETHE

50%

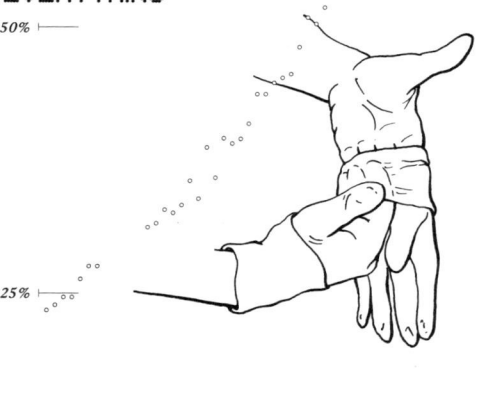

25%

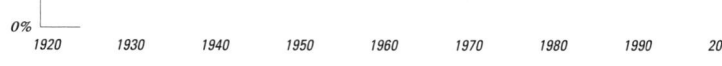

0%

1920 1930 1940 1950 1960 1970 1980 1990 2000

% OF BODY SURFACE AREA EXHIBITED IN PUBLIC BY MISS (MS.) AMERICA, 1921–1999

FREQUENCY
0   2   4 kcps

DEAD | (Japan) | A | STILL | HEART | | EVEN | IF | FROM | OUR | PERSPECTIVE | THE | BRAINS | DIE
IN | JAPAN | AS | SURELY | AS | THEY | DO | IN | FLATLAND

Not at the same time, of course.

It being impossible to be in these two states at once.

Unless you were—?—the first brain-dead body
(patient?) to be kept alive by procedures that
allowed its (his? her?) organs to be mined.

Elaine Esposito, in a coma
for 37 years, 111 days

Died but not dead

Bod

There app
Berkeley's mi
(but

In Ja
Dead Japa
side of Natu

T YOU BELIEVE A FLOWER CHANGES COLOR WHEN YOU PUT OUT THE LIGHTS.

Ask Karen Quinlin

THE | MATERIAL

In either case, it's culture—clearly—color, being much
like the sound of a tree falling in the forest
—or like everything if you're Bishop Berkeley,
who believed that nothing existed unless someone
was perceiving it in their mind's eye.

And yet,
conclude it i

Even if my conclud
be an enactment

IF BY "COLOR" YOU MEAN APPEARANCE (AN ARTIST'S CONCEPTION), THE ANSWER IS YES.

Or not yet living—non-viable

IF BY "COLOR" YOU MEAN CHLOROPHYLL (A BIOLOGIST'S UNDERSTANDING), THE ANSWER IS NO.
OBVIOUSLY.

viable material

stem cells

fetal brain tissue

Did that mean that Japan would vanish if all the
Japanese were asleep and no one in Europe was
thinking about it (and vice versa)?

No, answered Berkeley, because all was held
in the mind of God.

Or so Berkeley held in his mind.

Ptolemy, und
geometry, natur
The mat
Antoni va

Or what

DEAD | (Flatland) | **BRAIN | DEAD** | | BEATING-HEART | CADAVERS | SOMETIMES | KEPT |
ALIVE | FUNCTIONING | FOR | DAYS | THE | BRAIN-DEAD | BODY | BEING | THE | BEST | SITE
| TO | TEST | PHARMACEUTICALS | | DOUBLE | DEAD | **BRAIN | AND | BODY | DEAD** | | TRIPLE
DEAD | DOUBLE | DEAD | TOO | LONG | TO | SUPPLY | USEABLE | PARTS

BIOMEDICAL COMMUNICATIONS DEPARTMENT

BIOCHEMICAL

NUTRITION SCIENCES
PHARMACOLOGY

ENGINEERING DEPARTMENT

BIOMECHANICAL ENG
COMPUTER INFORMATION

MEDICAL CAMPUS

MOLECULAR BIOLOGY DEPARTMENT

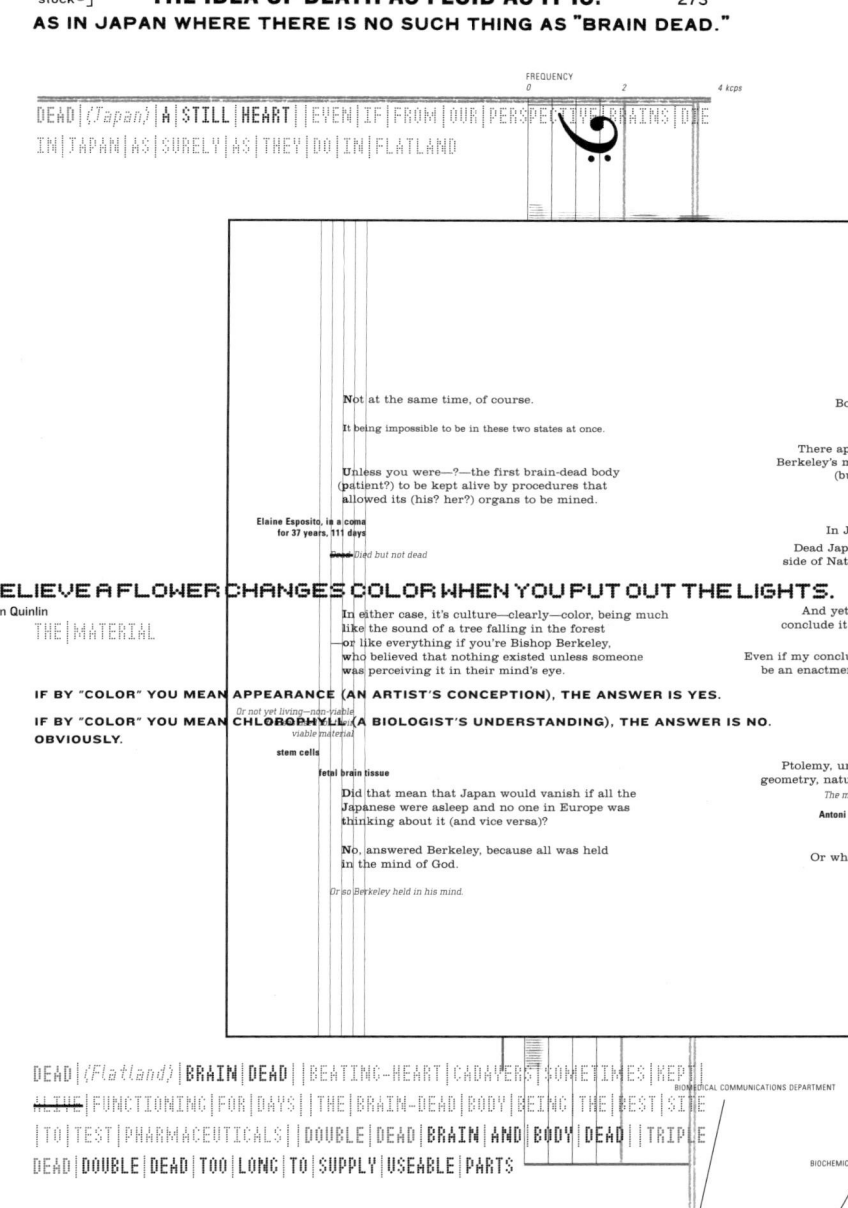

EVEN IN FLATLAND, DEATH VARIES BY STATE. [Human
LIFE ALSO, NECESSARILY.

DIFFERENT STATES HAVING DIFFERENT DEFINITIONS
A PERSON COULD BE DEAD IN AL AND ALIVE IN LA

at once.

lead body
es that
ined.

Bodies in Flatland dying as surely
as they do in Japan.

There apparently being no distinction in
Berkeley's mind between nature and culture
(but we've been through all of this—
so it must be nature)

In Japan, dead means "no heartbeat."
Dead Japanese bodies weighing in on the
side of Nature in the nature/culture debate

NO EXIT   OUT OF 3 OF YOU READING THIS WILL D

Audiences in 1933 thought that an actual giant ape had been killed to make King Kong. Of course, most of those people are dead now.   even if they were once Miss Ame

forest

Berkeley,
less someone

And if I had been raised on monster movies, I'd
conclude it is nature seems to indicate that
it was culture after all.

Even if my concluding that it is culture may just
be an enactment of the mindset of my moment
in history.

A heuristic.

ash if all the
Europe was

as held

Ptolemy, understanding the world through
geometry, naturally saw circles in the heavens. *Balls, said Galileo*
The man in the moon, through Georges Méliès's lens

Antoni van Leeuwenhoek, looking into the first microscope,
saw faces on spermatozoa

Or what is looked for is what is found.

NEWTON MOTIVE FORCES DARWIN *his own, no doubt* BELIEF IN PROGRESS THEN EINSTEIN
AND RELATIVITY AND MODERNISM AND FREUD AND SAUSSURE AND THE ATOM
IC AGE AND WATSON AND FOUCAULT AND CRICK AND DNA AND ALL THAT JAZZ

....

INDEED, THOUGH THE WEIGHT OF MISS (Ms.) AMERICAS
HAS DECREASED 30% OVER THE YEARS *(fashion)*, WAIST-
TO-HIP RATIO HAS REMAINED CONSTANT AT 0.7 *(biology)*.

FREQUENCY
0   2   4 kcps

1.0

0.7

...USE OF THE INHERITED STORY WITHIN YOU WORKING ITS WAY TO CONCLUSION...

The shells of mollusks derive their aesthetic appeal from the regularity of their form.

EVEN AS YOU MAKE YOUR WAY TO THE END OF THIS—

SO | IT | WAS | NATURE | AFTER | ALL | | AT | LEAST | IN | A | GENETIC | WAY
PATTERN | IN | THE | CARPET | | SYMMETRY | INDICATING | AN | ABILITY | TO | PLINAY
AND | BEAR | CHILDREN
| |

A Natural History of Shells

MER - RI - LLYY MER OR I WN W N M RHRI - LSYT RM E R MR I - Y

0.0

1920   1930   1940   1950   1960   1970   1980   1990   2000

NIAMS
NIAID
NIH NHLBI NICHE
NLM NCI NHGRI
NLM CIT FIC

NCBI

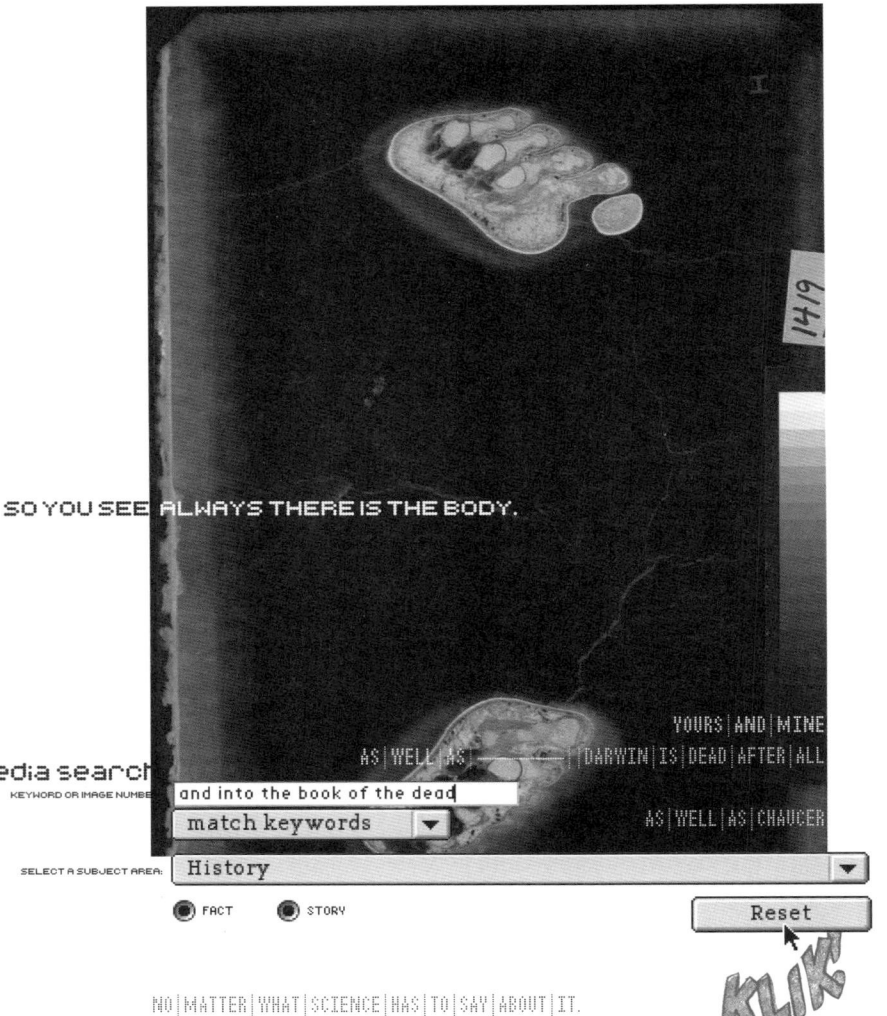

Every second, another 1.2 characters falls off the list

SO YOU SEE ALWAYS THERE IS THE BODY.

YOURS | AND | MINE

AS | WELL | AS | | DARWIN | IS | DEAD | AFTER | ALL

edia search

KEYWORD OR IMAGE NUMBE   and into the book of the dead

match keywords   ▼

AS | WELL | AS | CHAUCER

SELECT A SUBJECT AREA: History   ▼

⦿ FACT   ⦿ STORY   Reset

NO | MATTER | WHAT | SCIENCE | HAS | TO | SAY | ABOUT | IT.

KLIK

Square noticed, Square wrote, that
his signature on the form had faded to
the gray of a weathered bone.

The odd thing was how little it bothered him
considering that he had once killed a man over it.

It had been some four hundred years ago
when penmanship masters had rock-star
status. Printing presses had begun spewing
books, their mystery laid naked by division:
chapter headings, paragraphs, punctuation,
a separation of words ... That is, The Author,
but also many authors. Like the one on his
back beneath the Sistine Ceiling, giving
life to Adam and in so doing modeling
the clays of his pigments into you and I:
figures with individualized features rather
than the stylized gestures of Saint as
Stained Glass. With the solo, melodrama
became possible and Bravissimo! —
the birth of opera!

Wei-sing (Tawain)
can trace his lineage
back through Confucius
to the 8th century, B.C.

Of course, Wei-sing
would never refer to
it as B.C.

First by force, and then through rhetoric,
the Old Order fought to hold down the new.
One family (now extinct) required all of its
servants to bow before the 719 symbols on its
family shield: a graphic genealogy tree that
illustrated their pedigree (neutral information),
that is, their natural, God-given right to
wealth and position and respect that they
used as a club against new money: merchants
without coats of arms but financial levers
long enough to pry loose old grips on titles,
on who, in their carriage, should give way
to whom, on who should be the first to tip
their hat....

Chinese having
different systems
of measurement.

When THEY can read and write as well
as WE, went a common sentiment, literacy
as an index of status falls behind refinement
of expression. Or as George Bickman put it
in his 52 volume treatises on penmanship:

*Give in writing what we admire in fine Gentlemen; an Easiness of Gesture,
and the disengag'd Air which is imperceptibly caught from frequently
conversing with the Polite and Well-bred.*

Naturally

"Sprezzatura" was what the *Book of the
Courtier* called this disengag'd Air: (seemingly)
effortless elegance.

And Square sighed at the memory of it. He'd been filling out a lady's dance card when Master Ascot-Gevilles-Chandos-Temple, the last in a long line, laughed at his elaborate signature, mocking in actuality the claim to gentility it implied and the attendant presumption that he, Square—the son of a futures trader—could deign to dance with a lady of aristocratic lineage.

Impulsively, Square had replied by producing his card from the ruffles of his shirt cuff.

The room fell silent. All eyes were now on Monsieur A-G-C-T who hesitantly at first, and then in a passion, as though being presented a calling card by the son of a merchant (with only one last name) was as insulting to his ancestry as being told that an ape, by putting on a fine feathered hat, could ascend to the status of a lord. Confronted by the ape itself, grinning before him all in silk while society watched, he had no choice.

"Good day, Sir," was what was said, though the gravity of this exchange was more than clear.

The next morning, Square dispatched his intermediary who delivered a courteous challenge written in an elegant hand along with a gift of fine writing paper, but no pens.

A courteous reply of acceptance was received as well as a gift of quality writing quills, but no paper.

A time and place to courteously exchange pistol shots was arranged.

Though he had been totally unaware of such thoughts at the time, looking back at that appointed hour, Square could see himself behaving as exactly the kind of organ Goethe had in mind: An Individual, standing erect and alone within a highly structured time and place, delivered there by elegant handwriting, a lifetime of breeding concentrated into an ultimate moment.

Each of the duelist's seconds checked their master's opponent for holy relics or other charms; they ensured that the sun was evenly positioned along the line of fire and carried out the other rituals of their office.

Then the pistol (an arrangement of causes and effects) in Square's hand (another arrangement) exploded, a miniball putting a period to the line of A-G-C-Ts by shattering the skull of this last link. Days later, he was convicted by an aristocratic court for "patricide," then hung, and both deaths were recorded in a secretary hand, humanistic cursive, a descendent of the hand of the Biblical scribe which evolved into the business hand passed on to him through an archeology of marks, through secular instructors and technique still learned in grade school and which you reanimate, gentle reader, whenever you fashion an 'S' by drawing an ogee curve whose lower radius was slightly larger than the upper radius; a 'q' by making a downward stroke first and attaching a bowl one third the size of the upper curve on the 'S'; a 'u' by....

Small steps

fossils bearing knowledge

I suppose it would be natural to do a sex
scene in a story like this, Square wrote. But how
to depict it? Square peg in a round hole?

Pistil and stamen?

Albrecht Altdorfer never wondered, painting Lot
screwing his daughter. *Fucking* was dark back
in 1510. What made man animal—Pan copulating
with goats and anything else he could catch—not
spiritual, and so always man was shown mounting
the woman from behind (making the beast with two
backs, as Shakespeare had it), often upright: a thousand
years of authors and painters and clergymen and
just plain folks who were sure it was satyrs and
gardens and oysters and horny nature—

A fashion

among the common classes
—bestial—and could imagine it no other way
(though they themselves never fucked "doggie style"—how our
language dates us!). But today, where the main sexual
organ was the brain and making love was
as polysemous as language?....

Roses are Red
Violets are—

Who's on top?....

Unless forgiveness could be found, after all,
in four little letters—A-G-C-Ts of amino acids?—
bodies making what bodies always made of
language, the pre-larynx—

"Come," imprinted on a single partner (cementing
the pair bond). A softening in Circle's eyes, call it
dilation, indicating that she was receptive. Hearts
and flowers. And, 186,000 years of conditioning;
the Pavlovian dog within secretes catecholamines.

Estrodiol binds to estrogen receptors. Moonlit Serenade.
Likewise, testosterone washes cellular organization
of the male variety, hypothalamus, vaso-dilation
following strictly the double-helix letter of the law,
hearts beating with anticipation, vaso-congestion
of spongy tissue flowering within the law of the
letter, the alpha and omega of cells propagating
themselves—motive without mind—his bilateral
symmetry having subconsciously whispered to
hers a high probability of average gametes, average
being more desirable than Valentines for its lack
of irregularities, likewise, her clear complexion,
0.7 waist-to-hip ratio and sound teeth—a biology
of selection often pronounced by these apes,
naked, "love."

Afterwards, he lie hot, blood's pH balance
returning, breathing heavily though weak beside
her (nature), the two of them exhausted as if
they had swum in to shore from far out, a spent
Fiesta rubber (culture) on the floor murmuring
the unsaid thing between them: His Turn.

"Have you figured it out yet?" she asked, her voice
distant, still coming back from where ever they'd
been (a 3.6 million-year-old cliché in any case).

Salty tears,
that colorless blood

the fossil footprints of Laetoli, Tanzania

semen-matted pubic hair

her pink and white belly
salty sweat from pores

She had acted as if she'd meant the ending to
his story. But he could see that this was only a
way for her to segue into the question of his body.
So he began an answer, also mutating his story,
groping for a way to explain that it was taking
so long because the story had fused with his life,
that the story, a common story, had become
synonymous with the difficulty of making any
story real, not just seem real, but be real, the way
other narratives built worlds that came at you
as solidly as bricks.

—the Declaration of Independence

theories of evolution....

"Sometimes stories seem anachronistic," he said. He checked her face for recognition as he added, "So dumb." When there was none (was she just playing poker? The way she did in court?), he continued, "Unless...." He took from the night stand *Modern Art in the Common Culture*. The weight of the book surprised him, sex having drained him more than it used to. He ran a palm along its trimmed edges, breathed in the scent of its paper. He wanted to taste it, to put his ear to it like a sea shell so he could, as advised in all the books about "how to write stories," describe it by using all five senses, to make her (and you) experience the text as an object in the world, real as a brick. Only more so because it was more than its materials. Instead, he lie back against her sweaty flesh and read: "For conceptual art to have currency it must: 1) be living and available rather than concluded; 2) presuppose contact with lay audiences; and 3) reference the world beyond the gallery." He put aside the book and took up again the language of their bodies, Circle turning in his arms to join the conversation, her back to his chest, a grooming posture, the press of buttocks against his thighs a reconciliation. "I mean, what fits this criteria better," he said, "any story I could write or what you do in court? A funeral home in L.A. will put your loved one's corpse in a drive-up window so mourners can pay their respects without getting out of the car. What novel can say more about America than that? What sculpture could hope to compete with silicon breast implants? The first natural history museum in America began as an art gallery no one would have heard of if its owner didn't see the light. I mean, who needs fiction when you have Thomas Edison electrocuting elephants? Or Galileo's telescope? Or surgical?—"

"Procedures."

"But they never call it sterilization, do they?"

Then they lie there in silence, each a rhetorician,
her breasts (largest per body weight in the animal kingdom)
soft and shaped as though to fit his cupped hands,
the scent of her neck in his face, the organ above
her neck working through conclusions different
from his own, no doubt, 50,000 years of hunting
at odds with rearing young too helpless to even
hold on, His & Her gardens of nerves imprinted as
differently as calligraphy from cast lead. A vein
in her neck rose and fell with her pulse.

After a while, Square said, "I think that's why
your mother wants us to go to the opera."

He felt a tide of weariness swell within Circle.

"I know it's not going to be an antidote for
anything," he added, "but maybe there's
something— Maybe if we went to the opera—"

"My life has become an opera. Since this vast
thing came up we've been living a melodrama.
I just wish you'd end it."

"She only wants us to see things from a
different perspective; for her, the opera still
has the power to affect people and she
wants us to—"

"I don't want to be affected.
I want you to take your turn."

The odd thing about hearing her say "It's your turn"
was that he had gotten so used to hearing her say,
"Now, it's my turn." For years they had lived where
ever he found a job: in Sphereland, or so it had
seemed, even California. Circle had had the baby
and he had had the job and that was the way it
was or would ever be (he had been institutionalized,
he now realized). Then about the time that she
passed the bar, Square discovered that somehow
the professional class had gotten full up, at least
for Squares, and Circle found a better job than
his, in Flatland. "Now it's my turn," she had said.
So they came. Only by then, Oval was in school
so there was nothing for Square to do at home,
as there had been for Circle. So he did what
spouses of the-one-with-the-job have always done:
Gone boating. But since there weren't any oceans
in Flatland, his sail was a blank whiteness and
his oar a pen and he began to write, *First pain,
then knowledge....*

Of course, castration imagery came to mind....

private parts

and its various shadows

...his favorite being the stone testicles from a
statue of Oscar Wilde that adorned the author's
grave until broken off by ardent mourners
trying to pry back the statue's fig leaf,

the testicles becoming a paper weight
in the grounds keeper's office....

often mistaken for public property

Fossilized footprints
worn away by blowing sand, as well....

Not more than a faint impression, now, Square's
signature reminded him of Santerias who
protected their shadows as fiercely as they
guarded their nail clippings from falling into
the hands of voodoo priests. Once he had
guarded his signature as if its idiosycracies
contained something of him, the halts and
ill-formed loops of a five-year-old being a
true trace of nascent mind and musculature,
a similar loosening of grip betraying later in
life a nascent arthritis from writing too much.
Smart people had made a study of such marks.
Libraries were full of scholarly articles on
the criminal mind, the efficient and orderly
personality as revealed in handwriting....
According to the scholars, whole cultures could
be seen in the way individuals shaped their
names, a collective unconscious revealing itself
in slants and 'i' dots as surely as it appeared
in the way nations prepared their cuisine, or
ordered the bricks of their architecture, Arabs
writing from right to left, Aztecs in a spiral,
English characters looping as wildly as their
gardens while French handwriting was as
sculpted as Versailles and Square wondered if
others had noticed that all of the signatures
in his culture had become as ubiquitous and
as hard to outline as a breath in atmosphere....

Permeable as shade...

An e-mail signature
in mirrors and smoke

When Square tried to imagine the procedure,
it was all drums and fire light. Dr. Silverstein
danced into the examining room, his nude body
tattooed with medical diagrams. Women spoke in
tongues—"polymorphic loci"—and rolled on the
floor around Square, splayed atop a pyramid, a
jeweled ceremonial knife raised high over his
testicles, a scream, a plunge—

He shuddered.

How had his testicles become so solemn?
Instead of technique, they used to be the object
of jokes and limericks. *Can you tie 'em in a knot,
can you tie 'em in a bow?* All song and merriment:
"*Two silver balls, upon a string, You must be
playing with your own ding-a-ling.*" Even when
he added in the dark side, e.g.,"balls in a vice"—
or Oscar Wilde caught between Queenberrys
and a hard place—the core of the metaphor
was always a vulnerability that could make
Achilles' heel pale. He could imagine Achilles
on a talk show with the rest of them, glibly
discussing his balls.

"No fear of an undiplomatic pregnancy,"
agreed Benjamin Franklin.

"What better way to suspend the moment?"
added the Youth on Keats's *Grecian Urn*.

"I don't even have to worry about spills,"
Onan chimed in and a laugh track roared.
"Ah ha he ha hee!..."

Then Ephraim described the procedure—
"all I felt were two tugs." Samaria, dressed in
Old Testament chador, was on stage with the
other wives, joking about how much their
marriage had improved. Especially since they
no longer worried about bringing children
out to the slayer.

Square knew Circle would say they'd have
a better marriage.

If he didn't go through with it, would he even
have a marriage? And it would be his fault—
willing to risk her body so he could avoid
two tugs—after the number of times she'd
been flayed for him. Square shivered.
He'd say that and worse to her, he knew,
were it the other way around.

*For Those on a Diet: the average ejaculation, about one teaspoon,
contains approximately 123 calories.*

THE PLAYBOY ADVISOR

The Fourth of July had barely passed and Dr. Jack Kervorkian was at it again. Seeing him on television always got Mother going about the possibility that "someone"—some shadowy institution or family member—might "euthanize" her one day. "I don't even know how we got on the subject," Circle tearfully told Square afterwards. "She was just going on in her way about the opera and us having another baby and all when those frozen embryos came up." According to last Sunday's magazine section, embryos were accumulating in labs across the country. They'd been abandoned by couples who had gone through one of the many invitro fertilization programs: a harvesting of eggs, a teaspoon of fertilizer, cell division, then the replacement of a few of what were now embryos back into the womb. The leftover embryos were placed in straws like any kid could find around the house and stored in barrels of liquid nitrogen. Already there were hundreds of thousands of them because once a couple died, or divorced, or simply conceived, the extras were something they just didn't think about.

The article had gripped Square by the short hairs because when Circle had had a hard time conceiving, they had enrolled in such a program. But X-rays showed that her fallopian tubes weren't blocked so fertility drugs had been prescribed instead. Reading the article, though, Square was sure he would have been one of those fathers who simply didn't return calls because?—

Flush them down the toilet like guppies?
Expect Circle to bear them like puppies?
Sell them? Use them in experiments?
Let them die?

the material

*We should make a law which helps nature have its way with those too
helpless to care for themselves and burden both the creature with its own
existence and the family and the society with the burden of supporting it.*

DAS SCHWARZE KORPS *March 18, 1937*

If he didn't think of them they didn't exist.

Circle was far more pragmatic than
him and he could well imagine Mother's
reaction to her solution.

"One thing led to another," Circle
said, clutching a Kleenex, her eyes
glistening, "and the next thing I knew
she was accusing me."

Semiotics in even a tear, blood to
blood, he answered by coming near.
"She said you wanted to kill her?

"No, but of being capable of it."

"Where on earth did she get an idea like that?

Circle bit her knuckle. "Square," she said, a
leveling of tone. "I told her about the D&C."

He could feel emotion rearrange his
own tonal register. "Jesus, why?—"

"She kept talking about how heartless the parents of those embryos were—deciding that their children were 'lives not worth living'—and she wouldn't get off of it until she got onto people who have abortions, then people who decide that their senile parents deserve a 'death with dignity' when the parents aren't even lucid enough to know where they are so how can they be worried about dignity? Then she started to cry and say that the worst thing was that she'd want it that way because so many people would think it was natural that she'd begin to believe it too.

"It got crazy, like we should check the basement for pods. Like we're all being brainwashed and we'd think it was the normal way to go and she kept describing the people who have to make these decisions as if they were monsters but they're not. She may as well have been calling me a monster and I'm not. You're not. And I was trying to make her understand that sometimes circumstances— Sometimes the world— The more I tried to reason with her, the more she kept insisting that we needed to get to the opera. That I might have more empathy for people if I went to the opera and it was so absurd and I was sick of lying to her. And I thought that if she knew I had, that we had— Oh, I don't know what I thought."

He turned away. "Jesus, I can't believe you told her!..."

How I Had a Vision

... a drowsy sensation fell on me; but before my eyes closed I endeavored to reproduce the Third Dimension, and especially the process by which a Cube could be constructed by the motion of a Square. It was not so clear as I could have wished.

EDWIN A. ABBOTT
Flatland

He hadn't meant to take sides, Square thought, setting flame to the note Mother had left for Circle. They'd argued before about babies and always his gender had made him a Switzerland between them, biology being a woman's battleground (even if it was mainly occupied territory). Then he had been called to the front and suddenly his body had purchased him a right to opinion. To action, even. And here he was, burning Mother's note before Circle could find it.

Her handwriting became momentarily brilliant as the paper turned to ash. In the halts and loops of the ink he could hear the quiver of her aging larynx:

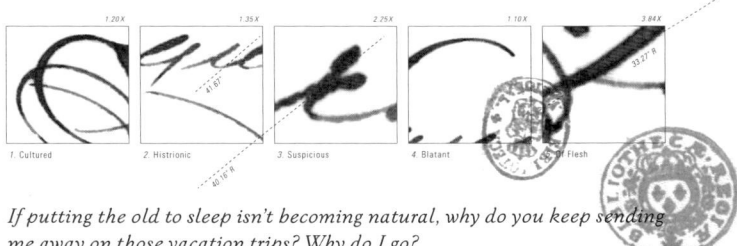

If putting the old to sleep isn't becoming natural, why do you keep sending me away on those vacation trips? Why do I go?
We've both read Freud you know.

Freud also able to
dispense with the body, of course.

And the couch

Not that he thought he would when he started.
Small steps

hypnosis   unconscious

he never liked them anyway

Far from it, being trained as a
doctor of the body, after all.

The talking cure

Neurosis, his specialty, being a disease of the nerves.
or so Victorians believed

Until Freud rewrote Psyche and
found he could do the same for his
patients, diagnosing their letters,
paintings and other traces.   **(triangulation)**

Even if they were dead.

Like Goethe.

Or Moses
like Adam

Psychoanalysis being a form of literary
criticism, of course.

A play on words

Like Anthropology.

ADAM being MAN in Hebrew

Once anthropologists,
like Freud, gave up the body.

Hebrew for MAN being GROUND
        mud

That is, once they stopped measuring
skulls and started reading garbage.
earth
Or funeral customs.

    the material

    molded

    clay

When the Hottentot Venus died,
caustic potash was used to
strip the flesh from her skeleton
which was put on display in
the Musée de l'Homme
(Display Case #33)

Same with sociology.

a mold of

Stop measuring,

her ape-like genitalia
start reading

People just kept getting lighter and lighter.

The Bronx Zoo got Ota Benga, an African pygmy

who was kept in a cage with an
orangutan (name unknown)...

Their representations keep getting
lighter that is—proliferating as they do.

X-rays making even clay vessels transparent

...until public outrage set Ota free...

As Descarte said, I am the representations
I make to myself of myself.

...not because a black man was caged like an animal,
but because the zoo exhibit Ota lived within depicted
him as part of an evolutionary chain.

...as opposed to an image of God....

a heresy

CAT scans painting pictures of thought

no strings or gears there

dominion over plants and animals

Economic
Man

Sexual Male
Person
African-American
Hero

[Human

Fractured

Hyphenated Lives
Celebrity

In fact, when it comes to representations of humans, we live in a period of hyperinflation.

Public Life   *Supply and demand*
Hyphenated Americans
middle class
master
race

Private lives

Schizophrenia
personality scale
I.Q.

Terminator
Country-Club Set
Mammogram
Sperminator
Brain dead

Virgin Birth
Eve in Stained glass
Adam in a Petri dish
Cell line

A bell curve
Son of Man
Naked Ape
Patent
pending
Infants with baboon hearts
Monkey's uncle
humanized mouse
Acres of

I contain multitudes.

Skin
Blood bank
The Material
The Subject
Virtual sex
Inflatable Suzie
Vinyl reality
Organ harvest
cow-humans
tomato-fish
Synthetic skulls
Consciousness download AFTERIMAGE
synthetic

nerves
Synthetic emotion
(a.k.a. Prosac)

Modern
Prometheus

mp

FREQUENCY

0   2   4 kcps

HOW | ODD | IT | MUST | BE | TO | STUDY | ANATOMY | THESE | DAYS | *So unlike the Enlightenment*
THE | BODY | BEING | A | FASHIONABLE | OBJECT | OF | INQUIRY | NOW | AS | IT | WAS | THEN

| OF | DRAMA | ALSO

When cadavers stunk
and had to be stolen
from graves...

a seller's market

or the gallows

Cadavers today just as likely to be virtual.

...dissection being an original form of deconstruction...

"Surgery theater"
unlike "Adam," not
meant as a pun

...of the soul, as well as of the person

the material

Unlike Alexis St. Martin, a fur trader
accidentally opened by a shotgun blast

...a deconstructed body... **that** exposed the inside of his stomach.

...impossible to reconstruct...

[so far from God]

William Beaumont, the army
surgeon who nursed him to health

...at the Resurrection...

Unresurrected, **peer**ing in and seeing what no one had seen before:
unreconstructed bodies

a miracle in red and pink,

unable to get into heaven

the first Visible Man,

doomed to their clay **but** still a man,
common clay **not** a cadaver or computer image or drawing,

This is why Enlightened anatomists drew their cadavers as if alive

but a living stomach, walls roiling,
slippery as wet clay,

posed classically

shimmering with digestive juices

even if holding their own skin

that sometimes stained the drawings
and notes Beaumont made over the
next eight years.

An antique notion, obviously

continental dollars

A matter of Supply

What I meant to write, Square wrote, *was that if there is nothing
backing a currency…*

Bodies once closely identified with
individual people

and Demand

God too, of course

$0 + 0 + 0 + 0 + 0 + 0 + 0 + 0 + 0 + 0 + 0 + 0 + 0 + 0 + 0 + 0 + 0 + 0 + 0 + 0 + 0 + 0 + 0 + 0 + 0 + 0 = X$

So much so that one
19th century anatomy
student in New York **Unlike** today's Visible Man:
set off a riot by waving **a** human body translated into computer images.
a cadaver's arm out the
window—"You-whooo!"— **a mortal coil**
at a passing boy **information**

rearrangable

Who?

animated

A reflection of culture as well
Telling the boy
it was his mother ON-LINE|EVEN||www.nlm.nih.gov

You! **W**hich happened to be true.

Twenty-two died in
the fighting

PIXELS|LIKE|THE|DOTS|OF|INK|THAT|MAKE|UP|THE|BODY|OF|THIS|TEXT
ANYTHING|DONE|REPEATEDLY|WILL|MUTATE||EVEN|OUR|OUTRAGES

That's why when people
are in zoos today,
as they were in Stockholm...

...zoo patrons protested, angry
because unlike the other animals
on display, the humans had a
screen they could go behind
to defecate or have sex...

(or do you say 'shit' and 'fuck'?)

Was it possible to keep the virtual body
and the non-virtual body apart in your mind?

...thus cheapening the **The** way we keep our mirror images
exhibit... distinct from ourselves?

And cleave history from story?

Or do you just not look?

...named Joseph Paul Jernigan when he was alive...

But that doesn't solve a sticky issue.

...and in the act of stealing a microwave oven...

If I am not my clay,.....
...or my image...

...and surprised by
Edward Hale, 75...

or my story?

What am I?

...whom he stabbed to death...

a word? *A form?*

...ATTACTTT

GTCAATAGCGTTAAACCAATTCGTTGCCTAACTGAAACTTACTTTTATAAAATTTGCGTCATCCACT
ACTCCATACTTT|MADE|FLESH|?...

Bodies always weigh in

This is why, once Galileo offered as
eye his telescope, only Flatlanders refused to look.

...and from remorse, or the hope of being
made into a Hollywood movie, or because
his family wouldn't pay for a funeral,

Histories varying as they do

donated his body to science,...

"Earth" meaning for all
previous history "fixed,
immovable position."

...which froze it solid, then
sliced it into 1,878 layers,
each the thinness of a
microscope-slide, *Terra firma*

Transparencies of an anatomy
textbook come to life

each photographed, and CAT scanned,
and MRIed and assembled into a virtual corpse,

freed into the ether...

Obviously circled by the sun.

(a metaphor for it's time?)
the material

resurrectable

on any computer...

Who would you believe,
Galileo's machine or your own eyes?

images proliferating throughout the world.

via modem.

Via telescope

New Worlds / New Jernigan
of light

and ones and zeros

lighter and lighter
manipulable

like clay

new clay

new pun

Whenever Square thought of himself as
a boy, he suffered something like the
anxiety monkeys raised in zoos must
feel when they find themselves suddenly
returned to the jungle, a vast and terrifying
openness all around, his skin tingling with
profound disbelief that the person he was
thinking about was the same as the one who
was thinking, his life sliced into birthdays
lived by a series of people so different from
one another that he didn't even know
which of them to ask, Who are you? *A perennial question*

Only asked because a mutation 800,000 years ago
allowed the larynx of a chimp to articulate sounds?

Addressed?–
Where?
Out there?

inside?

First grunts evolving into first doubts?
To "I" *But what was that?*

Tarzan might have wondered,
his ape-language failing him as he squat
beside the skeletons of his long-dead parents,
children's picture books, primers and readers
scattered about the cabin they had erected in
the jungle when he was born. A drawing of
a naked ape in one alphabet book especially
held his gaze, his hairless double pictured
beneath odd marks:

b

o

Looked like ants
y

I once weighed 8 lbs. 9 ozs., I think.

A moving target

Arias, also

Cells working their way to conclusion?

Limitless desire

Survival of the fittest.

bounded by finitude, as Dante had it.
Or sex and death, as Freud retold it.

Every person a Siamese-twin of body and self?

ANY REPETITIOUS ACT WILL MUTATE

Sadly, a story of decline.

A tragedy (if you believe Shakespeare's definition
of tragedy—a story that ends in a death).

1123, Padua

Giacomatto, strapped
to a balance beam
screamed as his chest
was cut open by doctors
trying to determine
the weight of a soul
by letting his out
and weighing what
was left.

A separation

A folk tale—all of which follow one of
thirty-one forms, they say.

They poured out his soul....

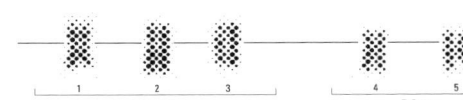

Though your body is constantly
plagiarizing itself, it never gets it right.

...and filled him with language.

It's like making a copy of a copy

Takes about 40 copies of copies of Chromosome 4 for it to loose enough definition to make its host begin shaking with the symptoms known as Huntington's disease.

Copies of copies proliferating

Children as well.

The *Story of Life* being a common metaphor.
Birth being a fresh copy.
[though never a fresh story]

This is why all comedies
end in a union—usually marriage,
the illusion of a new beginning.
Dante's was divine

23 chromosomes from the mother　　**the message**
and material　*23 from the father*

A fertilized egg.　(**24** if you're
still a monkey)
even a monkey's uncle

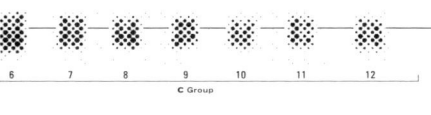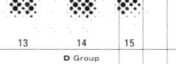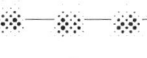

6	7	8	9	10	11	12	13	14	15	16	17	18

C Group　　　　　　　　　D Group　　　　　　E Group

An original / hardly original

DNA being both message and material
mitosis

separation
the end of singularity

the beginning of individuality

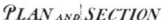

PLAN AND SECTION

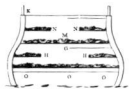

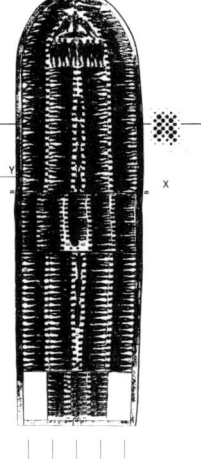

21 22 Y

G Group

X

125,000 generations (and counting)

the dead among us

Not that anyone would mistake

within us, even **a** life for a story.

170 new comedies
born a minute

82 tragedies

Or culture for nature.

One billion speakers
of Chinese languages

Shylock's
**Ota Benga
Hottentots**
pound of flesh

Or a person for their representation.

Frito Bandito

5.3 billion speakers of 6,000 other languages too
That's 5.3 billion mouths, opening, closing....

10.6 billion heart valves

opening, closing

"I" spilling with equal ease from every one....

11.7 billion gallons of blood

**ebbing,
flowing**

tide and time wait for no man

Still, it gets confusing.

5.3 billion x 60 trillion cells

each one both message and material

Even for people who like
a variety of salad dressings.

Bodies becoming as rearrangeable as they are
(and malleable as they are)

People and their bodies being
inseparable as they are.

Freud unable to dispense
with his own body, of course

Perhaps the real reason the Bronx Zoo
set Ota free was because they couldn't
break his habit of shooting arrows at
visitors who taunted him.

That is, the message is the material.

People and their stories being
as inseparable as they are.

Material also being the message, logically.

Zoo visitors and their
heartwaves being as
inseparable as they are

ergo
Ego

Cultures and their stories
being as inseparable as they are.

Impossible to extinguish without taking out the body

The medium also being the message,
as we all know

Bodies and their cultures being
as inseparable as they are.

Still, some try.   **1,000 suicides a year.**

Material being meaning?

PAGE 310 REPRESENTED AS A LOGIC STATEMENT

All P is S
All C is S
All B is C
∴ All P is B is C

The end of autobiography

again

TABLE 311a REPRESENTED AS MACHINE LANGUAGE

001+010+100=1

The beginning of autobiography

again

And even if Square was his materials,
it wasn't like he was going to rewrite
them. Not like the first chimp with an
articulate larynx.

Or Baby Fae, the first recipient of a baboon's heart.

[a footnote to this story]

Or Ota, who committed suicide in
Virginia two years after his release.

Or the fish which change sex according
to the needs of their school.

Just a little editing.

Swimming

It's natural now.

in a sea

A tə-mä´tō is still pronounced tə-mä´tō is
pronounced tə-mä´tō is pronounced tə-mä´tō

even if it contains the genes of a fish.

Some things never change.

body cures

Curses too

Life is still a tragedy.

A story

A Genesis

Passed down
for generations.
Birth a comedy.
Common as laughter

The point is, do we ever have a choice?

Common as—

**Even if we aren't one of those who
were secretly sterilized by X-rays as they stood at a
counter filling out government forms to emigrate.**
Or are we organs of our century, which is to say….

—clay

Don't even start to talk about when life begins.
Origins being so much more diffuse
than endings.

the end of your story having only one address.

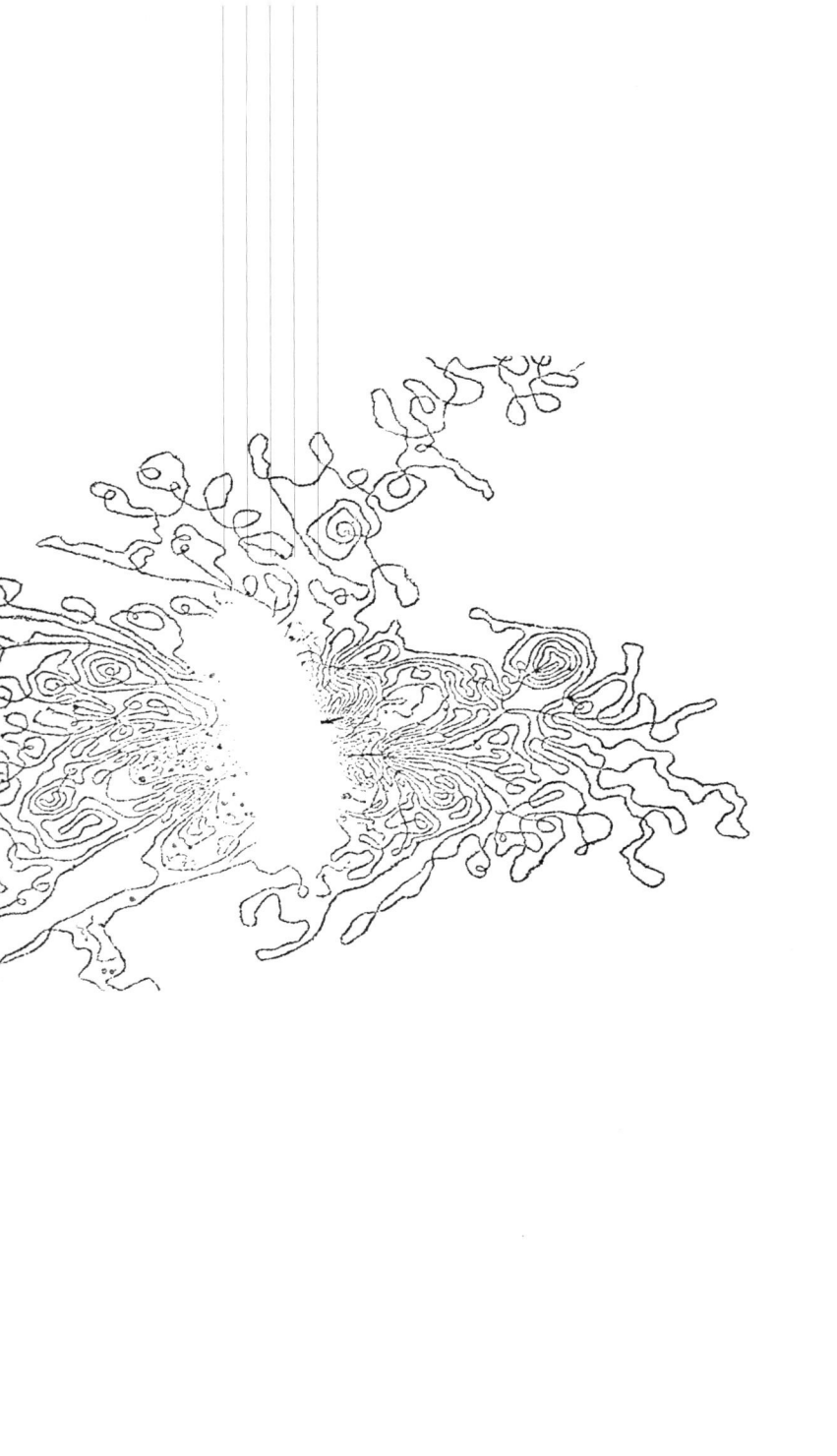

He could see what was happening, this transubstantiation of being his body into having his body. But caressing its epidermis, to all appearances unchanged, he couldn't grasp it, couldn't hold in his mind a change from wine to water any more than the moment message becomes material, material becomes man, man becomes patient, patient becomes material and a heart, cradled by latex fingers from ice chest to some other's needy cavity, drinks in and starts a new life, servant to some other emperor with no clothes.

It occurred to Square that he hadn't always known he'd lived in Flatland.

At first, he'd thought it was simply a flat land. And he began to wonder what he'd been before he realized he was a square.

caterpillar → pupa

cells become larynx

How much could the average salad eater ever know?

The line where he had signed his name
was completely blank now…

AN ATMOSPHERE   OF PHOTOCOPYING   OF ZEN   OF BLUE-BLOOD CANDIDATES POSING IN BLUE-C

OHMMMMMMMMMMMMMMMMMMMMMMMMMMMMMMMMMMMMMMMMMMMMMMMM   HEROES DISSIPATING INTO CELEBRITIES

SON OF MY FATHER   HUSBAND OF MY WIFE

→   FATHER OF MY DAUGHTER

→   NOUN OF MY BODY   YOUR REFLECTION IN A JET-BLACK

MODIFYING   BIOLOGICAL SELF   VERB OF MY SELF

→   BECOMING

GERUND?   FORMING

→   PALINDROME ?   CLOUDS

→   I ?   BECOMING

→

→   SERIAL IS   SERIAL SELVES

→   DEBTOR TO MY BANK   SULTAN TO A VAGRANT

→   DISSIPATING TO

→   ME

MYSELF   &   I   SOCIAL SELF   FORMING

→   TYRANT TO MY TEENAGER   CLOUDS

→   A DRAMA OF I(S)   ECONOMIC SELF

FARE TO MY CABBIE   FILE TO MY IRS   SEEING I(S)   MIDDLE-CLAS

→   SEEING YOU IN ME   PARALLEL LIVES

WE   I   &   I   I

OFTEN UNAWARES   I   &   I

HAVE YOU EVER BEEN IN A STATIONARY TRAIN AND HAD THE SENSATION OF MOVING BACKWARDS BECAUS

RELATIVITY   EINSTEIN TO MY NEWBORN

ACTORS BECOMING ICONS   POLITICIANS TO ACTORS

→   CHEESE TO CHEEZE FOOD

WHITE SUBURBAN KIDS REMAKING THEMSELVES AS INNER-CITY BLACKS

→

→   PSYCHOLOGICAL SELVES

SIGNED JUNK MAIL   CHAT-ROOM IDENTITY

→   NOT

LOTS OF SELVES   SOUND BYTES   DOCU-DRAMAS

→   NO MAN IS AN I-LAND

→   FRACTURED EVERYWHERES

→   TUGS OF WAR

DIVIDED SELVES

THE VOICE OF THE CASH REGISTER
INSTEAD OF THE CASHIER. …

SHIRTS   DUPLICATION

        FAXES

                                                    MOTHER OF MY DISCONTENT

    VAPOR

ECOMING

    VAPOR   FORMING

                CLOUDS   WATCHING ME

    VAPOR

                                        SERF TO MY BOSS

        PRODIGAL TO MY CHURCH

G MARTHA STEWART   POLITICAL SELF

        UNBALANCED

            SO.   LEDGER TO MY ACCOUNTANT

XT TO YOURS BEGAN TO PULL AWAY?

        NO ONE HOME

Cut my form from this book, SQUARE WROTE.
Fill in your ————— and hold it in your
hands. Make it as real a presence in
your hands as are the countless other
bricks that make up your
invisible city.

MEMORIAL FAMILY CLINIC
ANJA S. KRISHNA, M.D.
BERNARD M. SILVERSTEIN, M.D.
RONALD R. SMITH, M.D.
JODY S. LIN, M.D.

PART A - **CONSENT FOR THE PROCEDURE**

We, the undersigned, husband and wife, both being over 21 years of age, request that
Dr. Silverstein and assistants of his choice perform upon _____
bilateral vasectomy and to administer any anesthetic he chooses.

It has been explained to us that this operation is intended to result in sterility. We understand that a
sterile person is NOT capable of becoming a parent. We also understand that the operation may not
result in sterility and that no guarantee of sterility has been given to either of us.
We voluntarily request the operation and understand that, if it proves successful, the results may
be permanent and, if they are, it will be impossible for the patient to conceive or bear children.
We understand that the risks of this procedure, or any medical procedure, include but are not limited
to: bleeding, reaction to anesthetic, damage to nearby structures or infection.

_____   ____/____/____
Physician   Date

_____
Wife

_____
Husband

_____
Witness

FOR OFFICE USE ONLY

ORIGINAL COPY

Standard Form No. 319
Ed. July 20-01-500,000
4-3164

Printed in U.S.A.

Was it possible to write
a story that didn't have gender?

MEMORIAL FAMILY CLINIC
ANJA S. KRISHNA, M.D.
BERNARD M. SILVERSTEIN, M.D.
RONALD R. SMITH, M.D.
JODY S. LIN, M.D.

PART A - **CONSENT FOR THE PROCEDURE**

We, the undersigned, husband and wife, both being over 21 years of age, request that Dr. Silverstein and assistants of his choice perform upon _____
bilateral vasectomy and to administer any anesthetic he chooses.

It has been explained to us that this operation is intended to result in sterility. We understand that a sterile person is NOT capable of becoming a parent. We also understand that the operation may not result in sterility and that no guarantee of sterility has been given to either of us.

We voluntarily request the operation and understand that, if it proves successful, the results may be permanent and, if they are, it will be impossible for the patient to conceive or bear children. We understand that the risks of this procedure, or any medical procedure, include but are not limited to: bleeding, reaction to anesthetic, damage to nearby structures or infection.

_____   ____/____/____
Physician   Date

_____
Wife

_____
Husband

_____
Witness

FOR OFFICE USE ONLY

DUPLICATE COPY

Science Rocks!
Exp. No. 103 Buoyan...

Two egg yolks were in jars of water on the counter. Oval must have had trouble with the first half of her experiment. The yolk in that jar, the jar filled with fresh water, lay squashed at the bottom. The yoke in the other jar, though, the jar filled with heavily-salted water was intact, the yolk suspended like a specimen in formaldehyde.

The cat rubbed against Square's legs, staking claim to his body.

territory

Divers who go deep enough, Square had read, *sometimes loose their bearings in the darkness, their buoyancy making it impossible for them to tell if up is down or down is up or side to side*

Huevos, eggs, was the euphemism for testicles in Spanish and it always seemed odd that the slang for such a masculine thing would be so feminine A lot of men and women smarter than him (even Geniuses) had figured it out.

Say rather—

Tra | La | la | la | Lא

He understood the meaningful way women
said, "my gynecologist." *Lא | lא* ... Though he
had earlier noted the inevitable shift to a
lower register whenever they said "my
gynecologist," the reason for the shift had
always been a mystery. ... *Lא | Tא* ... To decode it,
he had tried to say "my orthodontist" in the
same tone—*Hא | Hאaaa* ... But it only sounded silly.
Now he knew, though. *Gא | Tא* ... He understood
why Dante put women who died in childbirth
in the same sphere of Heaven as fallen
warriors. *GTTאGG* ... He looked on Circle with
awe now, now that he understood the routine
élan with which women lived within their
edited, critiqued and rewritten bodies. ... *AGTGTAAAGT* ...
And what a luxury he had in being
able to take his 'natural' body for granted.

GGT   *GTא*

    GGT

        GGGT | GGGT   *GGGGT*   *GTTא*

     GGGAAA

GTTאTTאTTא   *GAT*   *AAGTTאAGTT*

Tא   *Tא*   *Tא*   *TAAAAAAAAAAAAAAAAAAAAAAAAAAAAAAAAAAAAAAAAAAAAA* ...

A great wash of sympathy welled up in
him for Circle. For everyone in Flatland.
Including himself.

That night, he got into bed beside Circle,
held her tight and said, "I know you're not a
monster." After so much silence in their house,
his solo sounded odd. She didn't look up from
the book she had taken to bed with her, but he
could tell she had stopped reading. Her eyes
were motionless. Ringing her neck were faint
creases, the first hint of one season's end and
another season's beginning. The raspberry
blossom on her shoulder was also there, where
Mother had one, darkening slightly with the
approach of cooler days as if another landscape
within was trying to seep out. "Your mother's
not a monster, either, you know."

"I know."

He touched the bones of Circle's pelvis, the
stony vertebrae along her back the one constant
landmark through all the metamorphoses her
body had undergone, evolving from the
extravagant and artless tone of the young it
had had when they met, through the accordion
expansions of pregnancy and breast feeding,
then the resulting slackness, aging, then the
work-out hardened physique she now had, her
body also a history, like Mother's, but unlike
Mother's Thucydides-epidermis, Circle's muscle
tone, white scar and neck creases made her
timeline the always-ever-present.

"Just because she's from a different world
doesn't mean we shouldn't listen to her."

Circle closed her book, *Modern Art*,
though she still didn't look at him.

"Even if we know we're going to do
what we think is best," he continued, "Even
if we know we're going to do the opposite."

"I'm not going to see some antique melodrama."

"There's lots of contemporary ones.
When we're old, we wouldn't want Oval
to just dismiss us with the wave of a hand."

The cat hopped up onto the bed and gingerly
looked for a place to lie before settling in.

After a long pause, Circle said,
"If I go to the opera with you,
will you take your turn?"

The opera was called *The Strange Voyage of Imagining Chatter* and Square and Circle had box seats. They leaned into each other, holding hands as it began: a huge projection of artist Charles Willson Peale flickers from a kinescope, his hand pulling back a tasseled Victorian curtain to reveal a vast collection of odd bones, minerals, shells, fossils and creatures, dead and alive—props that he had used for still lifes before they took on a life of their own and his art gallery metamorphosed into the first museum of natural history. Cabinets of curiosities are stacked floor to ceiling, diminishing with distance like the timeline of a museum.

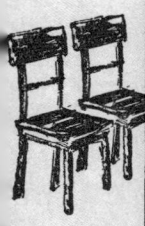

VAS
COMICS
GROUP

329
P.

THE STRANGE VOYAGE
OF IMAGINING CHATTER

THE *ORCHESTRA PIT* FILLS WITH SLOPPY-WET CLAY, SILT AND NUDE MUSICIANS.

Overture

SLOWLY, THEY BEGIN SLAPPING WET GLOBS, POURING WATER FROM TOWERING LADDERS, PLAYING WITH NO CONDUCTOR, THE SYMPHONY ODDLY MUSICLESS UNTIL THEIR RANDOM BEATS BEGIN TO *COAGULATE* INTO ZYGOTES OF TWO NOTES, A HARMONY OF WATER AND MUD. MITOSIS INTO FOUR NOTES, THEN EIGHT, THEN SIXTEEN, *THEN A SOUR DISCORD--A MUTATION*--THAT CAUSES THE SOUND TO REARRANGE ITSELF INTO A NEW COMPLEXITY, MUSIC BECOMING ITSELF, PLAYING ITSELF, ITS MUSICIANS ONLY BEING THE MEDIUM IT LIVES IN...

CH_3
|
APE

5'...

A MAN WITH A CONCH SHELL FOR A HEART DRAWS OUT A LONG MOURNFUL TONE. WOMEN JANGLE BREASTS AND BUNCHES OF MOLLUSKS...

...THE MUSIC BECOMING MORE DIFFERENTIATED AS THE ORCHESTRA PIT CONTINUES TO DRY, A SWIRLING UNDERTONE SUDDENLY RESOLVING, AS DOES AN ICE-CRYSTAL, INTO A MELODIC PATTERN ONLY TO MELT BACK INTO THE BOWING OF GUT STRINGS.

MAN
|
CH₂

... 3'

HARDENED CLAY TABLETS **SHATTER**. HORNPIPES AND REEDS ARE JOINED BY TURTLE-SHELL **RESONATORS**.	MUSICIANS IN LOINCLOTHS BRING ON **SCREECHING MONKEYS** AND ALIGN THEMSELVES AS VERTEBRAE. BONE CLAPPERS, WHISTLES, SKULL RATTLES...

Images of monkeys swinging through trees projected on a scrim stretching across the stage.

THEY STOP THEIR FEET, SHRIEKING, **"CHATTER!"** GROWING A JUNGLE OF SOUND THAT A CONDUCTOR IN A STARCHED-WHITE COLLAR WARILY WALKS OUT INTO. HE FLAILS HIS BATON **TO NO EFFECT**.

Jane Goodall gazing into the death mask of an ape....

THE CONDUCTOR STEPS UP ON A PODIUM AND BRANDISHES HIS BATON-- **A SORCERER'S WAND**--THE NOISE SOMETIMES SEEMING TO OBEY. A **COW** IS LED INTO THE PIT, THEN PRODDED TO MAKE **MOOOO**.

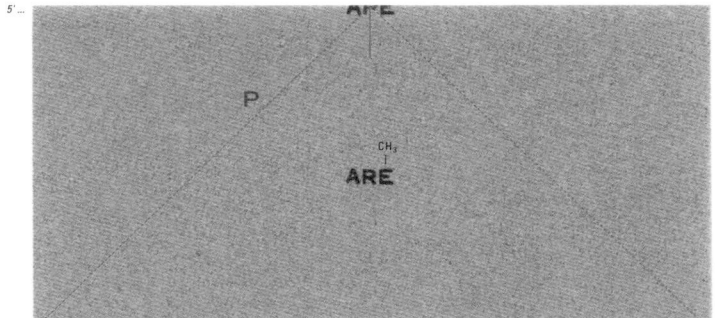

THE CONDUCTOR
REPEATS THE
GESTURE---*AND
AGAIN*--

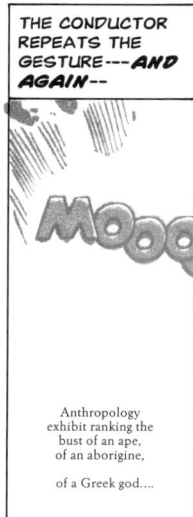

Anthropology
exhibit ranking the
bust of an ape,
of an aborigine,

of a Greek god....

COPPER *KETTLE DRUMS*--TIN
TESTICLES TOLL--

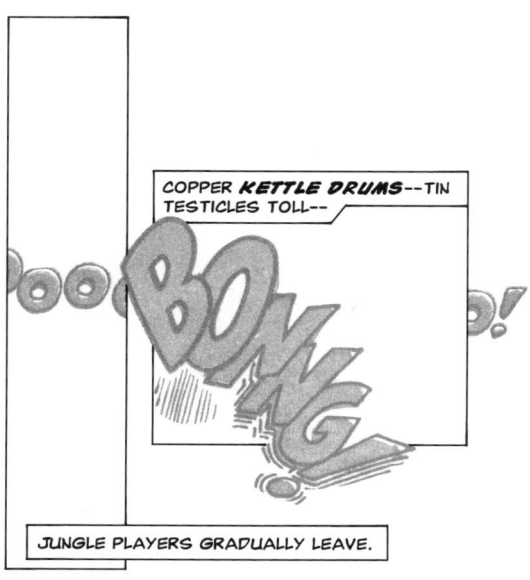

JUNGLE PLAYERS GRADUALLY LEAVE.

THE CONDUCTOR *REPEATS* HIS GESTURES, MAKING THEM *MORE*
STYLIZED EACH TIME, THE MUSIC CHANGING BECAUSE THE *ORCHESTRA*
ITSELF KEEPS CHANGING. AN ORGAN WITH AN ARRAY OF PIPES--
NEEDLES TO SMOKESTACKS--RISES PROCESSIONALLY OUT OF THE FLOOR,
ITS ENORMOUS BELLOWS WORKED BY MUSICIANS IN *BLACK HOODS.*
THE ORGAN IS JOINED BY A *HARPSICHORD* WITH ELABORATE MOTHER-
OF-PEARL INLAYS. OTHER INSTRUMENTS ALSO INCORPORATE BITS OF
ORNAMENTAL NATURE: *IVORY FINGER PADS* AGAINST BRIGHT BRASS
HORNS, *NAUTILUS SCROLL WORK* ON CELLOS WHOSE HOUR-GLASS
FORMS ARE CARESSED BY MUSICIANS IN RUFFLED LINEN SHIRTS....

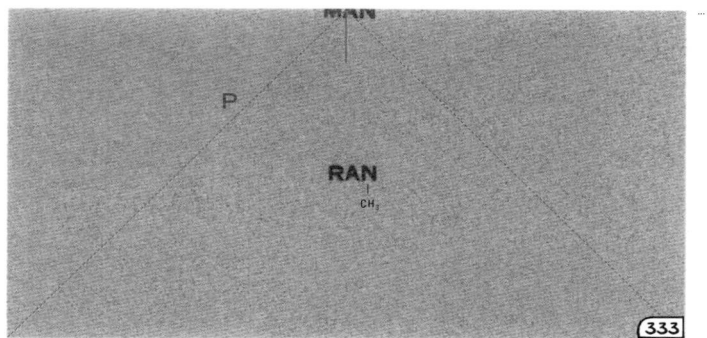

GRADUALLY, IF UNRELENTINGLY, THEIR INDIVIDUAL MIGRATIONS COALESCE INTO GLORIOUS MELODIES PLAYED WITH *CLOCK-LIKE PRECISION* TO THE DIRECTIONS OF THE *CONDUCTOR*.

Church white-sculpture showing man emerging from the hide of an ape like a chick from an egg....

A CHOIR INTONES, *SOTTO VOCE*....

CHATTER, CHATTER, CHATTER...

5'...

CH_2
|
ARM

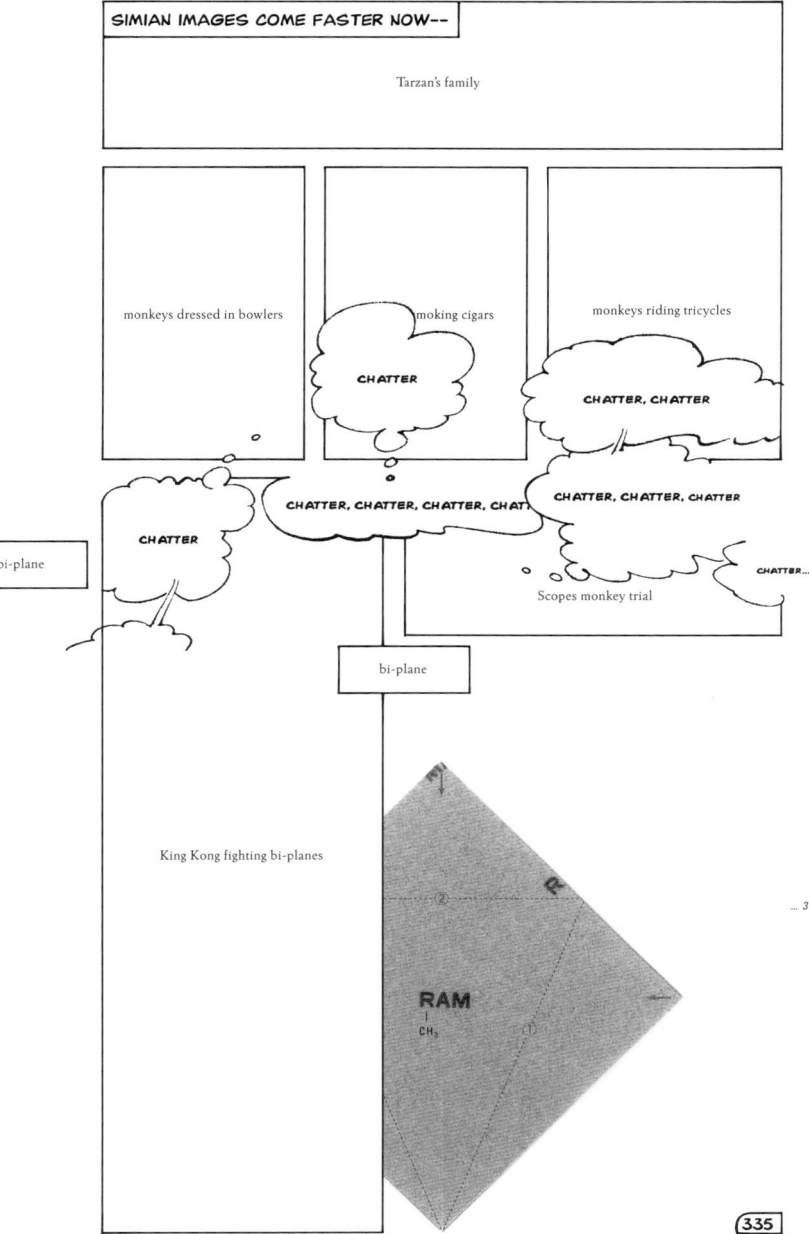

SIMIAN IMAGES COME FASTER NOW--

Tarzan's family

monkeys dressed in bowlers

smoking cigars

CHATTER

monkeys riding tricycles

CHATTER, CHATTER

CHATTER, CHATTER, CHATTER, CHATT

CHATTER, CHATTER, CHATTER

bi-plane

CHATTER

CHATTER...

Scopes monkey trial

bi-plane

King Kong fighting bi-planes

... 3'

THE SHATTER OF **BUSTING GLASS--CAR CRASH!!--**PUNCTUATES MUSIC THAT RIDES THE CRESTS OF AN *AIR-RAID SIREN* ON A **WA-WA PEDAL!**

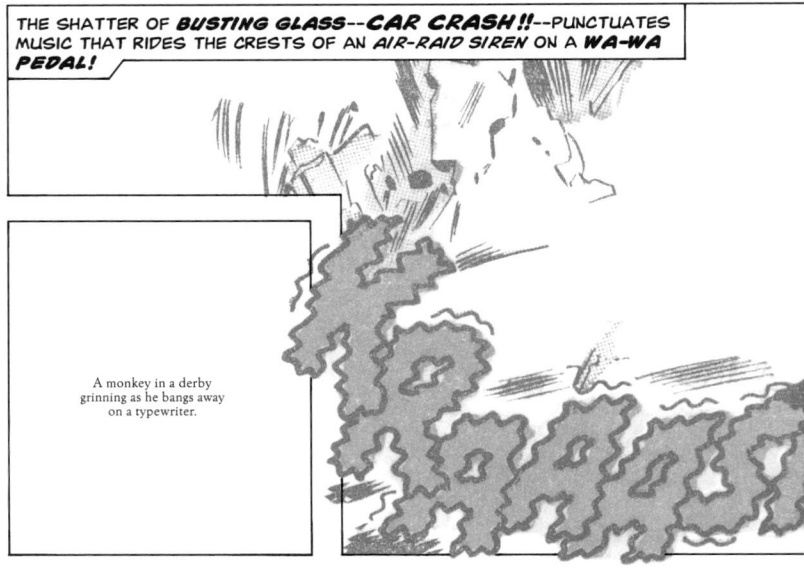

A monkey in a derby grinning as he bangs away on a typewriter.

TUXEDOED MUSICIANS CONNECT THEIR TRUMPETS AND TROMBONES TO *HOSES* OF COMPRESSED AIR, PLAYING NOTES THAT ARE *TOO LONG* AND *TOO LOUD* TO COME FROM *HUMAN BREATH!*

CHORDS ARE **KNOCKED** OFF BALANCE, AND PUT INTO *PRECARIOUS NEW* **ARRANGEMENTS!**

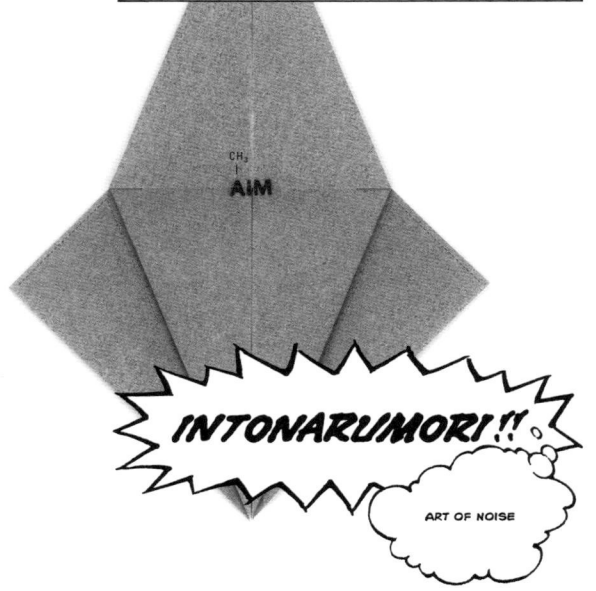

5'...

AIM

INTONARUMORI!!

ART OF NOISE

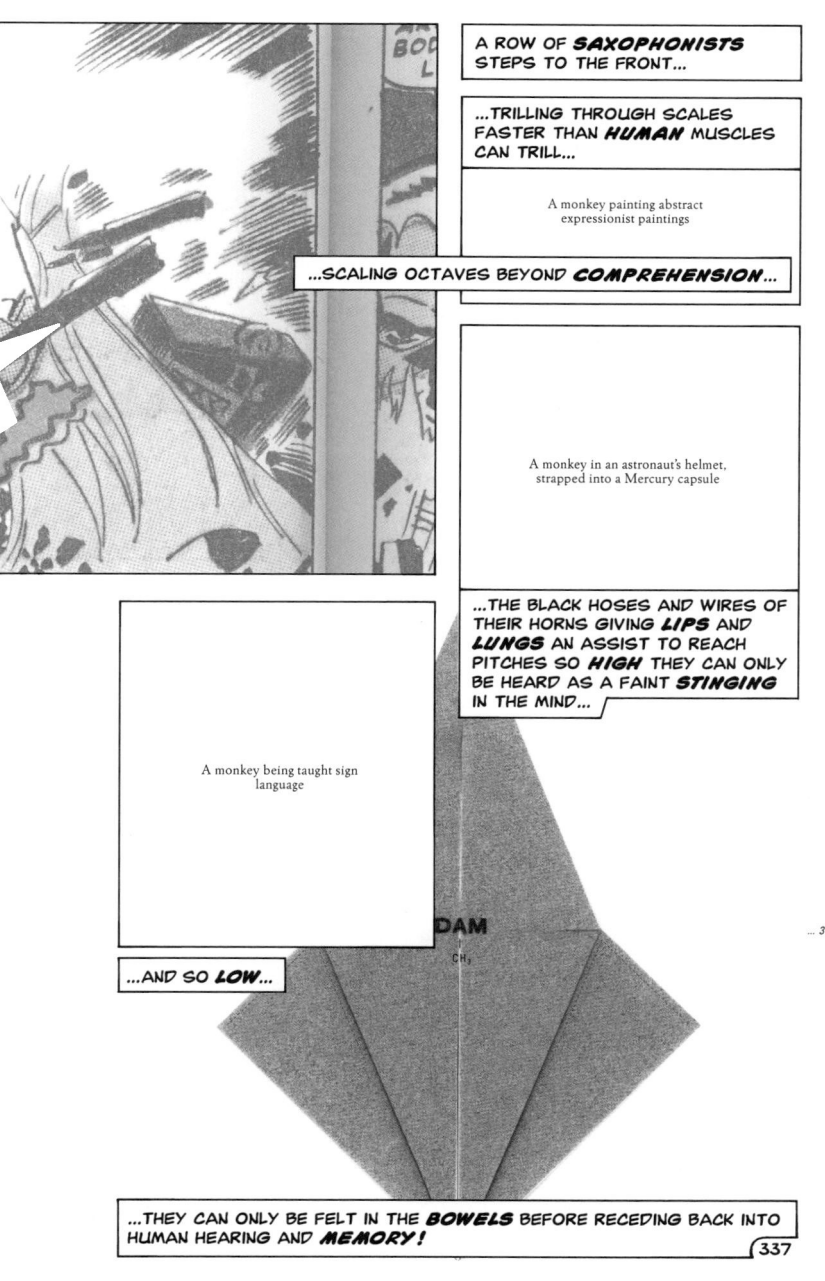

A ROW OF **SAXOPHONISTS** STEPS TO THE FRONT...

...TRILLING THROUGH SCALES FASTER THAN **HUMAN** MUSCLES CAN TRILL...

A monkey painting abstract expressionist paintings

...SCALING OCTAVES BEYOND **COMPREHENSION**...

A monkey in an astronaut's helmet, strapped into a Mercury capsule

...THE BLACK HOSES AND WIRES OF THEIR HORNS GIVING **LIPS** AND **LUNGS** AN ASSIST TO REACH PITCHES SO **HIGH** THEY CAN ONLY BE HEARD AS A FAINT **STINGING** IN THE MIND...

A monkey being taught sign language

...AND SO **LOW**...

...THEY CAN ONLY BE FELT IN THE **BOWELS** BEFORE RECEDING BACK INTO HUMAN HEARING AND **MEMORY!**

Comparison of ape and human brain waves

Chimps for burn research

Chimps injected with viruses

ETHEREAL MUSIC WAFTS UP FROM WOMEN RUBBING THE WET RIMS OF **BEAKERS!**

Chimps wired up then broken in test crashes

GLASS **TRUMPETS** PLAY--

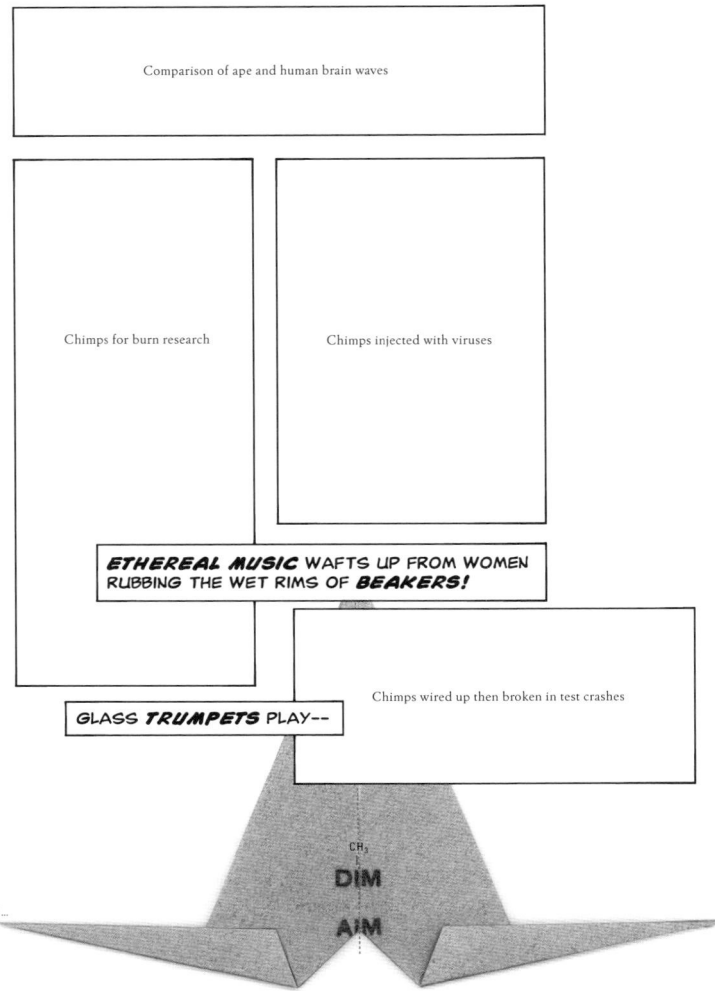

CH₃

DIM

AIM

5˝...

--GLASS **FRENCH HORNS**, GLASS **CLARINETS!**

THE ROW OF MALLETS WITHIN A GLASS GRAND PIANO UNDULATES AS A **WAVE**...

Chimps taking on the biological sin of Chromosome 13

so that we might...

...STRIKING IN TURN **VEINS** THAT ARE ITS **WIRES!**

THE **SNAP ACTION** OF THE CONDUCTOR'S BATON GIVES WAY TO POETIC SWEEPS AS THOUGH HE COULD BRING FORTH THE MUSIC OF THIS GLASS ORCHESTRA **EFFORTLESSLY** --

-- AN **OUTPOURING** OF NOTES PAYING REVERENCE TO HIS **TECHNICAL MASTERY!!**

An ape posed as Rodin's *Thinker* contemplates a Day-of-the-Dead sugar skull...

CH_3

DIM

DAM

... 3'

...while a nude man contemplates a chimp's skull, a projection of a chimp's gene sequence scrolling across his chest.

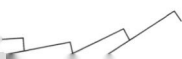

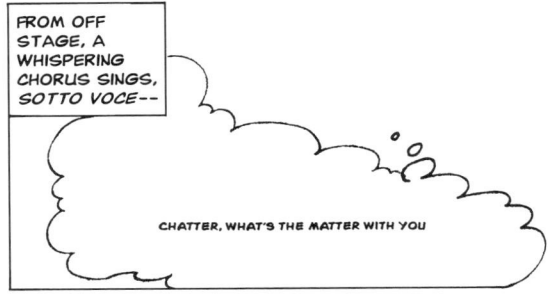

FROM OFF STAGE, A WHISPERING CHORUS SINGS, SOTTO VOCE--

CHATTER, WHAT'S THE MATTER WITH YOU

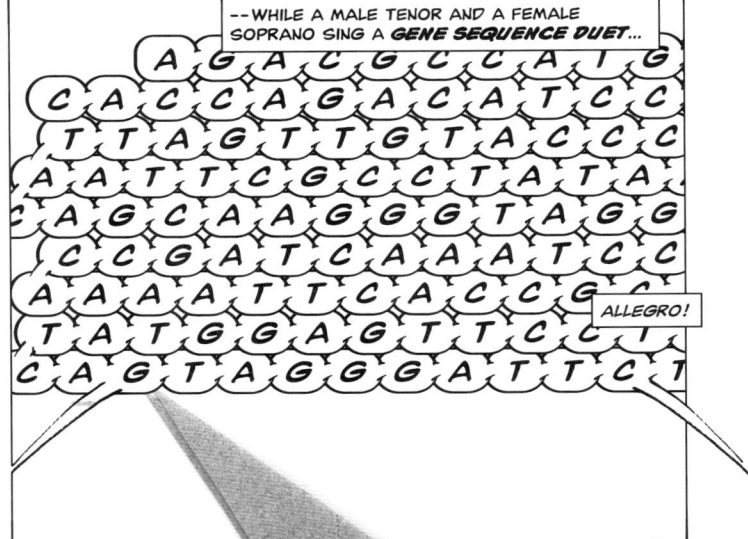

--WHILE A MALE TENOR AND A FEMALE SOPRANO SING A *GENE SEQUENCE DUET*...

A G A C G C C A T G
C A C C A G A C A T C C
T T A G T T G T A C C C
A A T T C G C C T A T A
A G C A A G G G T A G G
C C G A T C A A A T C C
A A A A T T C A C C G
T A T G G A G T T C C T
C A G T A G G G A T T C T

ALLEGRO!

$5'...$

CH₃
DAM

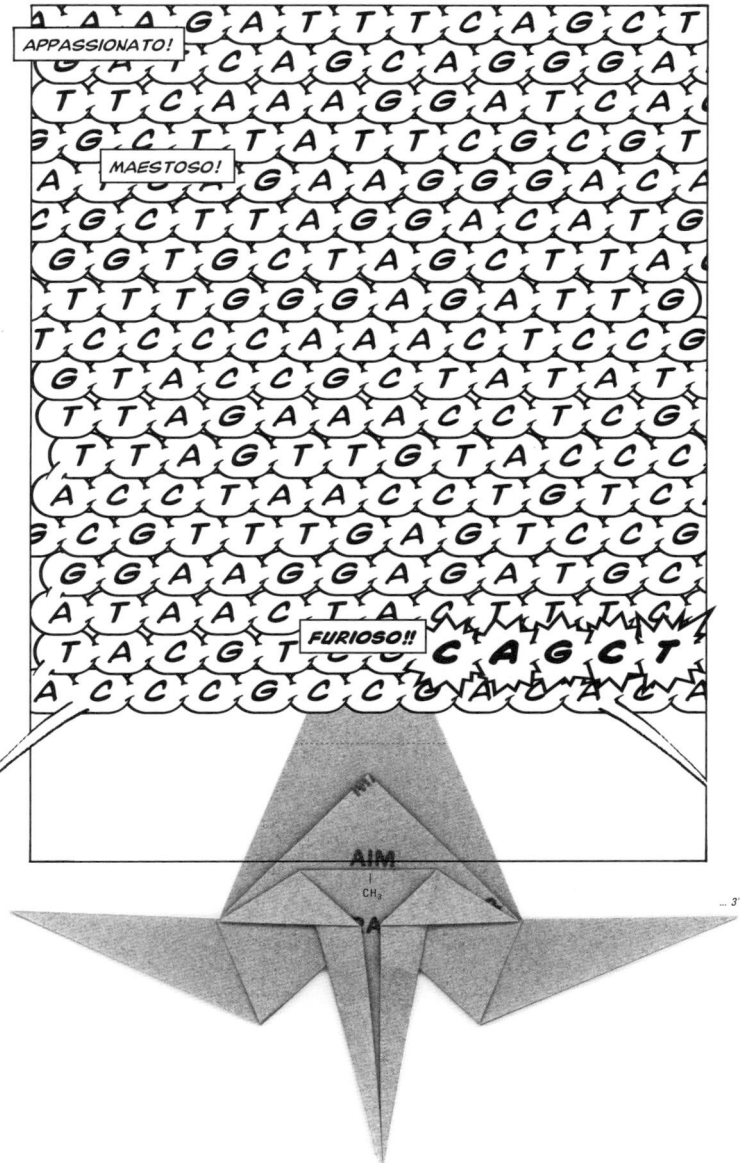

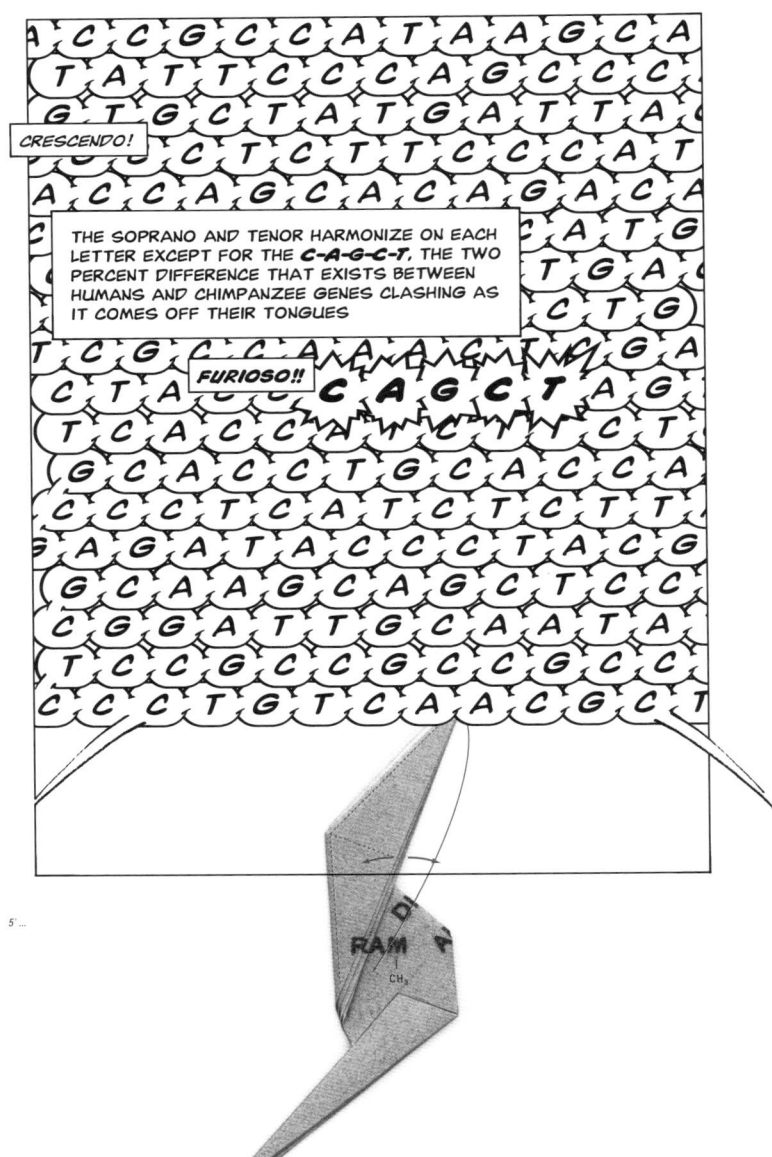

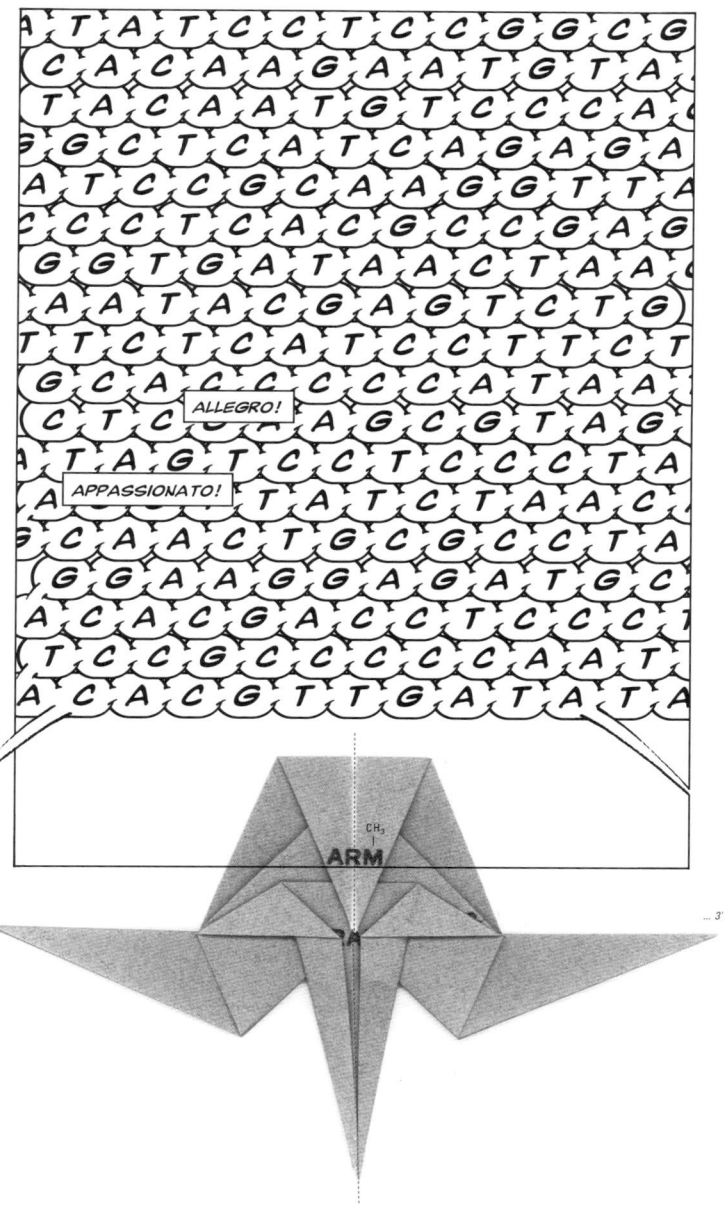

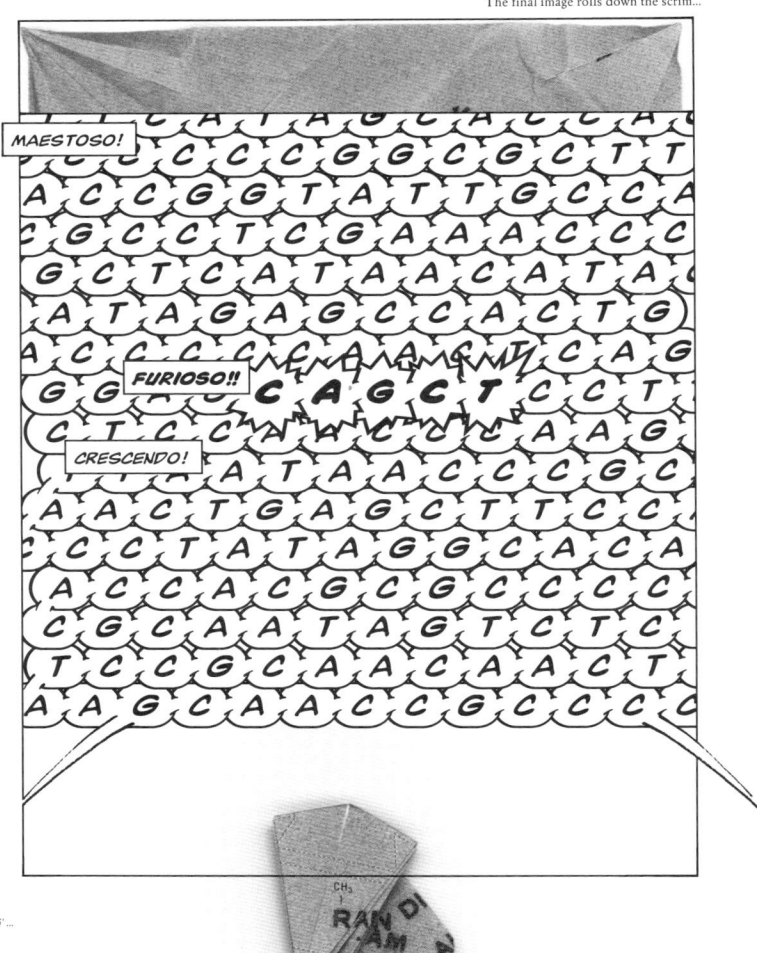

5'...

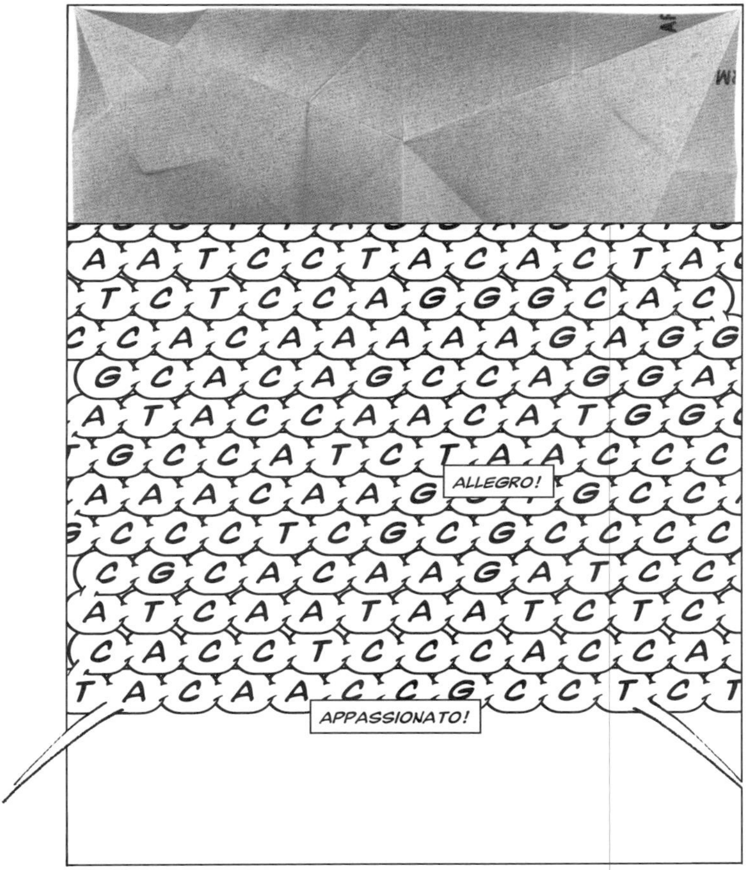

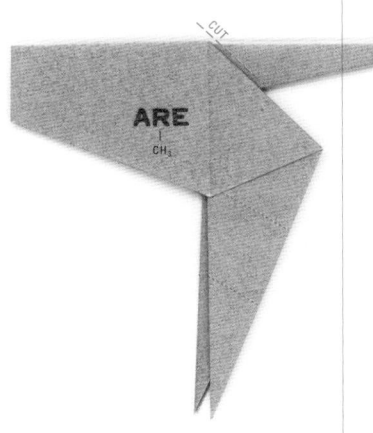

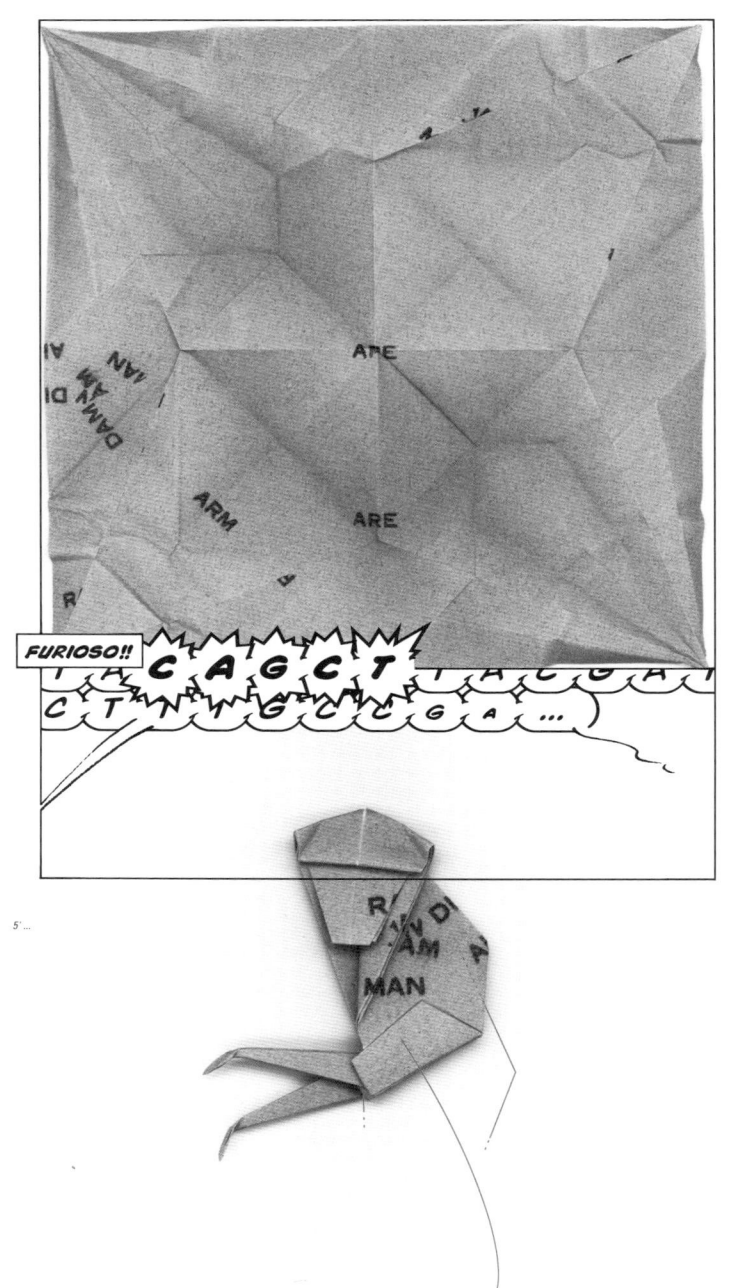

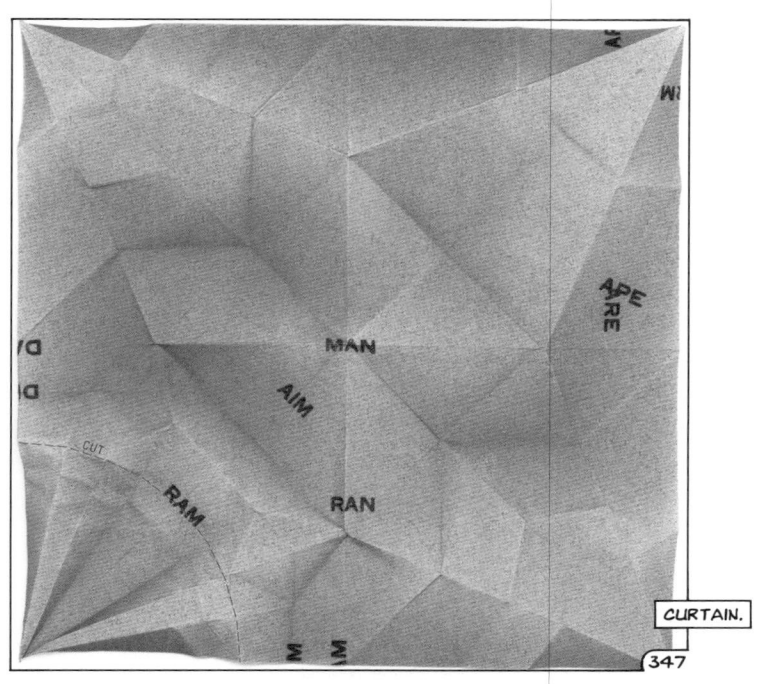

Circle withdrew her hands from Square's and folded them in her lap.

... 3'

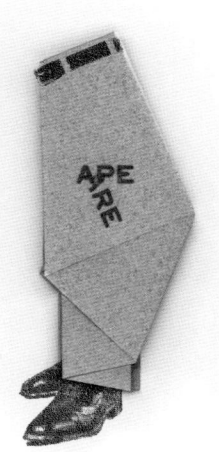

A LONE VIOLIN. AN ENGLISH GARDEN BATHED IN MOONLIGHT.

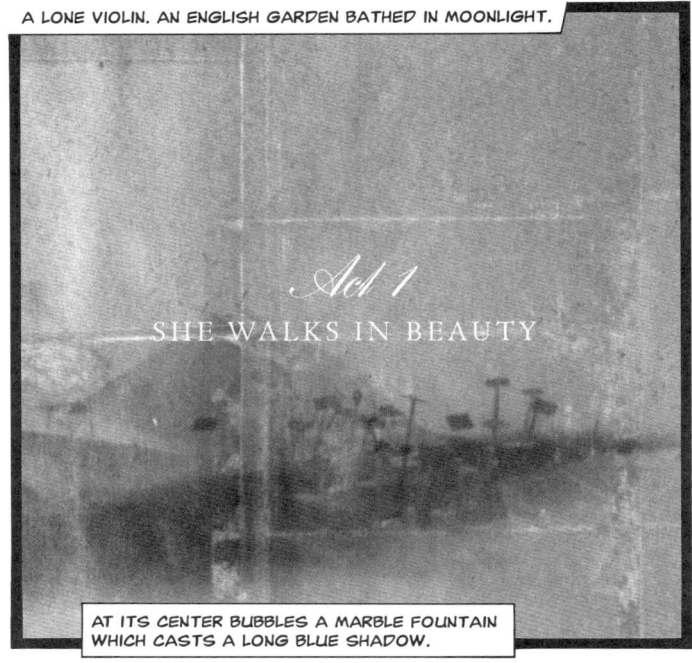

Act 1

SHE WALKS IN BEAUTY

AT ITS CENTER BUBBLES A MARBLE FOUNTAIN WHICH CASTS A LONG BLUE SHADOW.

A FEMALE ***AUSTRALOPITHECUS*** SNIFFS AROUND THE PERIMETER OF THE GARDEN, SOMETIMES STRAINING TO READ THE TAGS THAT IDENTIFY EACH OF THE 1,400 VARIETIES OF ***PLANTS*** COLLECTED IN THE BEDS, SOMETIMES PAUSING TO EAT A FLOWER.

Left	Dentition	Right

8 7 6 5 4 3 2 1   1 2 3 4 5 6 7 8

/: alveolus missing   *: carious   m: milk tooth
=: lost post mortem   a: abscess   retained
X: lost ante mortem   s: suppr.   w: worn to roots

Crown L. & Br.: M_1 M_2 M_3

Upper
Lower

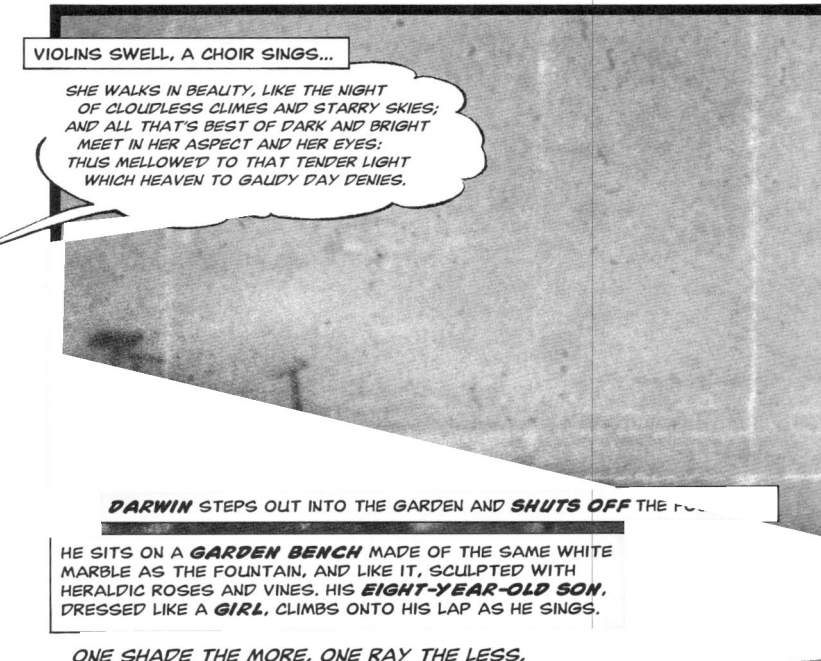

VIOLINS SWELL, A CHOIR SINGS...

> *SHE WALKS IN BEAUTY, LIKE THE NIGHT*
> *OF CLOUDLESS CLIMES AND STARRY SKIES;*
> *AND ALL THAT'S BEST OF DARK AND BRIGHT*
> *MEET IN HER ASPECT AND HER EYES:*
> *THUS MELLOWED TO THAT TENDER LIGHT*
> *WHICH HEAVEN TO GAUDY DAY DENIES.*

DARWIN STEPS OUT INTO THE GARDEN AND *SHUTS OFF* THE ⌐⌐⌐

HE SITS ON A *GARDEN BENCH* MADE OF THE SAME WHITE MARBLE AS THE FOUNTAIN, AND LIKE IT, SCULPTED WITH HERALDIC ROSES AND VINES. HIS *EIGHT-YEAR-OLD SON*, DRESSED LIKE A *GIRL*, CLIMBS ONTO HIS LAP AS HE SINGS.

> *ONE SHADE THE MORE, ONE RAY THE LESS,*
> *HAD HALF IMPAIR'D THE NAMELESS GRACE*
> *WHICH WAVES IN EVERY RAVEN TRESS,*
> *OR SOFTLY LIGHTENS O'ER HER FACE;*
> *WHERE THOUGHTS SERENELY SWEET EXPRESS*
> *HOW PURE, HOW DEAR THEIR DWELLING PLACE.*

> *AND ON THAT CHEEK, AND O'ER THAT BROW,*
> *SO SOFT, SO CALM, YET ELOQUENT,*
> *THE SMILES THAT WIN, THE TINTS THAT GLOW,*
> *BUT TELL OF DAYS IN GOODNESS SPENT,*
> *A MIND AT PEACE WITH ALL BELOW,*
> *A HEART WHOSE LOVE IS INNOCENT!*

349

When Square looked to Circle to see how she liked the first act, he caught her stifling a yawn.

CURTAIN.

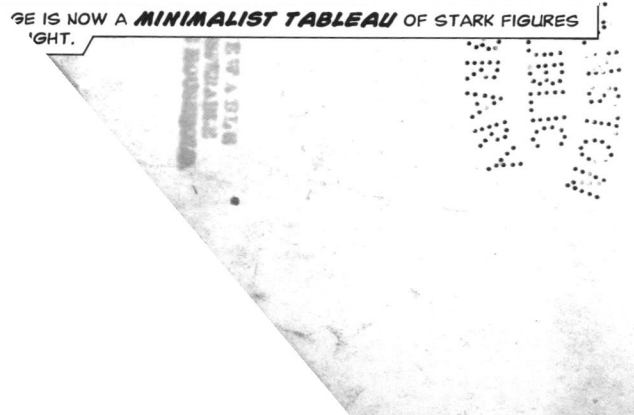

Act 2
WE MARCH IN TRUTH

SUNG THROUGH A MEGAPHONE.

THE MOONLIT GARDEN FROM ACT ONE ALONG WITH ITS FOUNTAINS AND SCULPTURES IS SUDDENLY **PULLED DOWN INTO A HOLE** IN THE MIDDLE OF THE STAGE, REVEALING THAT IT HAD ALL BEEN **TROMPE L'OEIL**, PAINTED ON SILK!

GE IS NOW A **MINIMALIST TABLEAU** OF STARK FIGURES 'GHT.

THEY SET UP AND ADJUST A VARIETY OF TELESCOPES, CAMERAS, X-RAY EQUIPMENT, AND OTHER INSTRUMENTS.

351

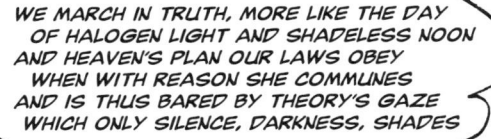

WE MARCH IN TRUTH, MORE LIKE THE DAY
OF HALOGEN LIGHT AND SHADELESS NOON
AND HEAVEN'S PLAN OUR LAWS OBEY
WHEN WITH REASON SHE COMMUNES
AND IS THUS BARED BY THEORY'S GAZE
WHICH ONLY SILENCE, DARKNESS, SHADES

ONE SHADE THE LESS, ONE RAY THE MORE
DEMYSTIFY THE NAMELESS GRACE
ONCE THE ENIGMA OF HER CORE
BY MOONLIGHT GLIMPS'D UPON HER FACE
WHERE FEATURES MIRRORING OURS INVITE,

INQUISITOR,
COME WRITE,
HOW NEAR,
THY DWELLING PLACE.

AND ON THAT SLATE, AND O'ER THAT BROW,
DREAMING MORE THAN
HEAVEN AND EARTH

IN OUR IMAGE WE RE-CREATE,
A PARADIGM

BREAK

BEQUEATHING OTHERS,
IN MATH AND RHYME
TO OURSELVES ENDOW
FORBIDDEN TREES BY THE SCORE
PATTERN TO STARS, LANGUAGE IN APES
FORBIDDEN FRUIT NEVER MORE

A MIND AT PEACE AND DEEDS THAT MAKE
BEAUTY AND TRUTH **CONSUMMATE!**

CURTAIN.

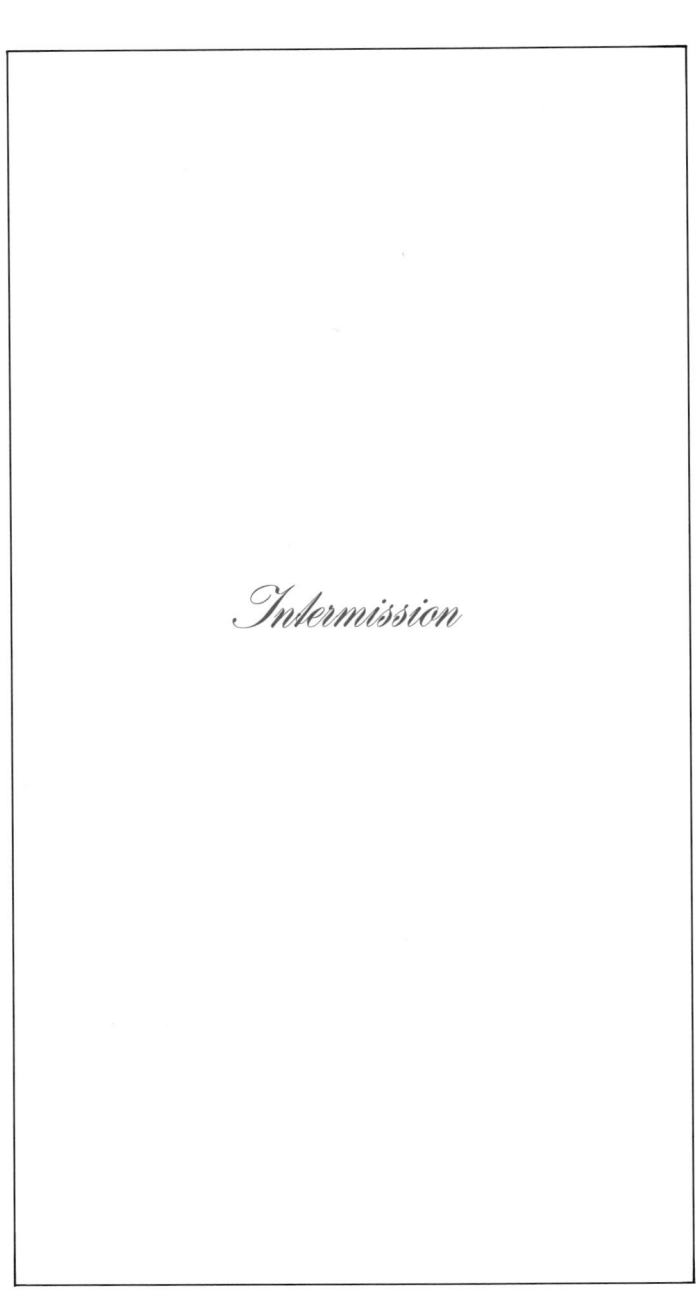

Intermission

Circle's gown glittered like the gilt ceiling above.
"It's almost over now, isn't it?" she asked, smiling,
taking Square's arm and nestling it between
her breasts. Drink in hand, looking down from
the mezzanine on other opera goers lined
up at the bars in the lobby, Square wished
he could make her see how the audience
was part of the opera. Not in the glib way of
audience participation theater of the 60s but
really part of it, the way a tree falling in
the forest couldn't make a sound unless——
But if she realized it, he knew, then it
would be a denial of what he meant.

ALLEGRO!

○┄┄□

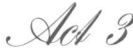

Act 3

BEAUTY IS AS TRUTH DOES

or

PRIMATE CEPHALIC TRANSPLANTATION:
NEUROGENIC SEPARATION, VASCULAR ASSOCIATION

THE MINIMALIST TABLEAU OF ACT II IS TRANSFORMED INTO AN *OPERATING THEATER* BY RESEARCHERS WHO TAKE AWAY ALL THE TELESCOPES, CAMERAS AND OTHER INSTRUMENTS, LEAVING STAINLESS STEEL *HOSPITAL* EQUIPMENT, AND AN ENORMOUS OVER-HEAD *SURGERY LAMP*.

ONE BY ONE, DR. WHITE AND HIS TEAM OF EXPERIMENTAL SURGEONS COME ON STAGE...

...CHECK THE VENTILATORS...

...IV PUMPS...

...CT SCANNERS...

...AND OTHER EQUIPMENT.

WHEN ALL IS READY, THEY PROCEED TO TRANSPLANT THE *HEAD OF ONE MONKEY ONTO THE BODY OF ANOTHER...*

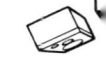
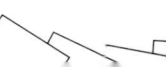

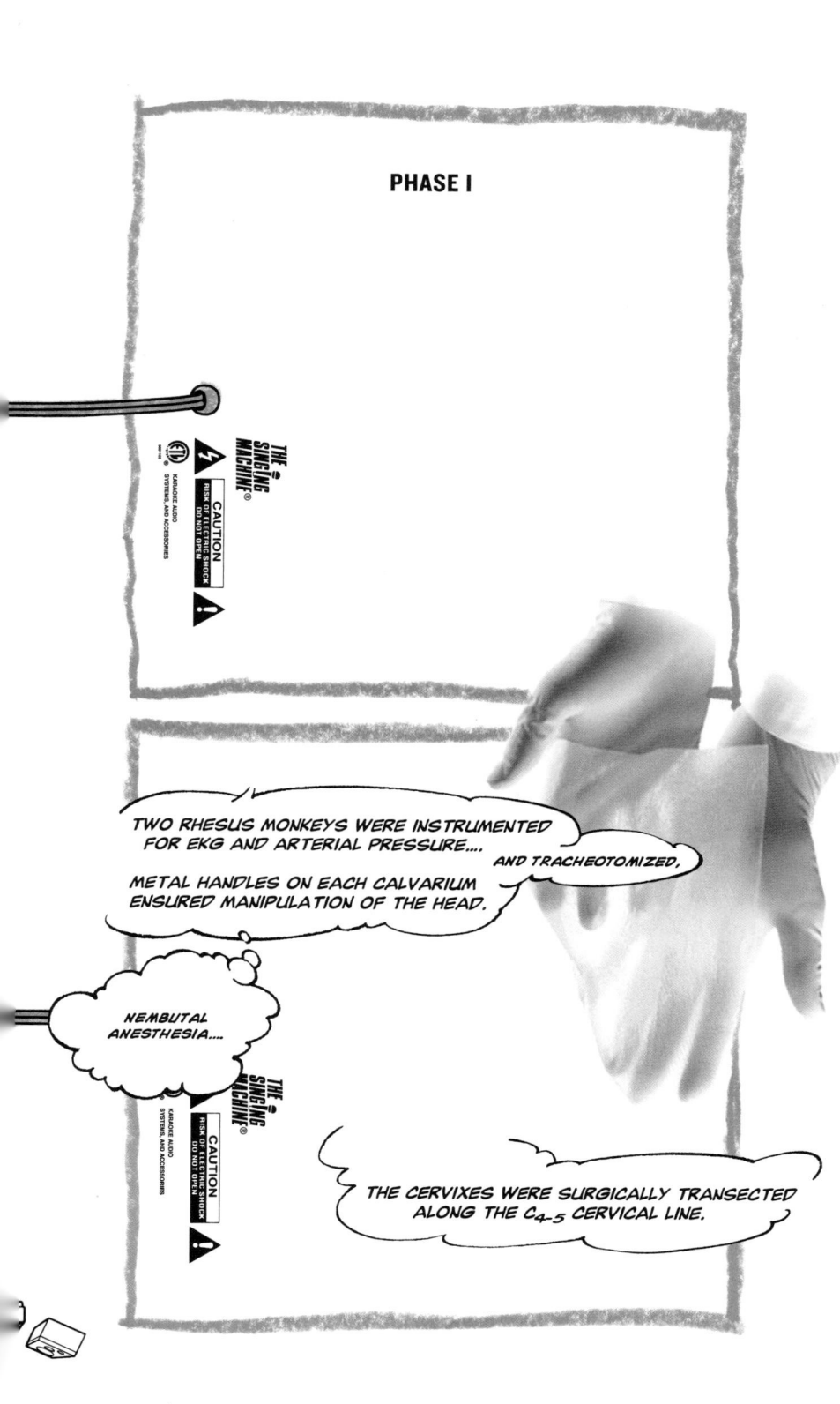

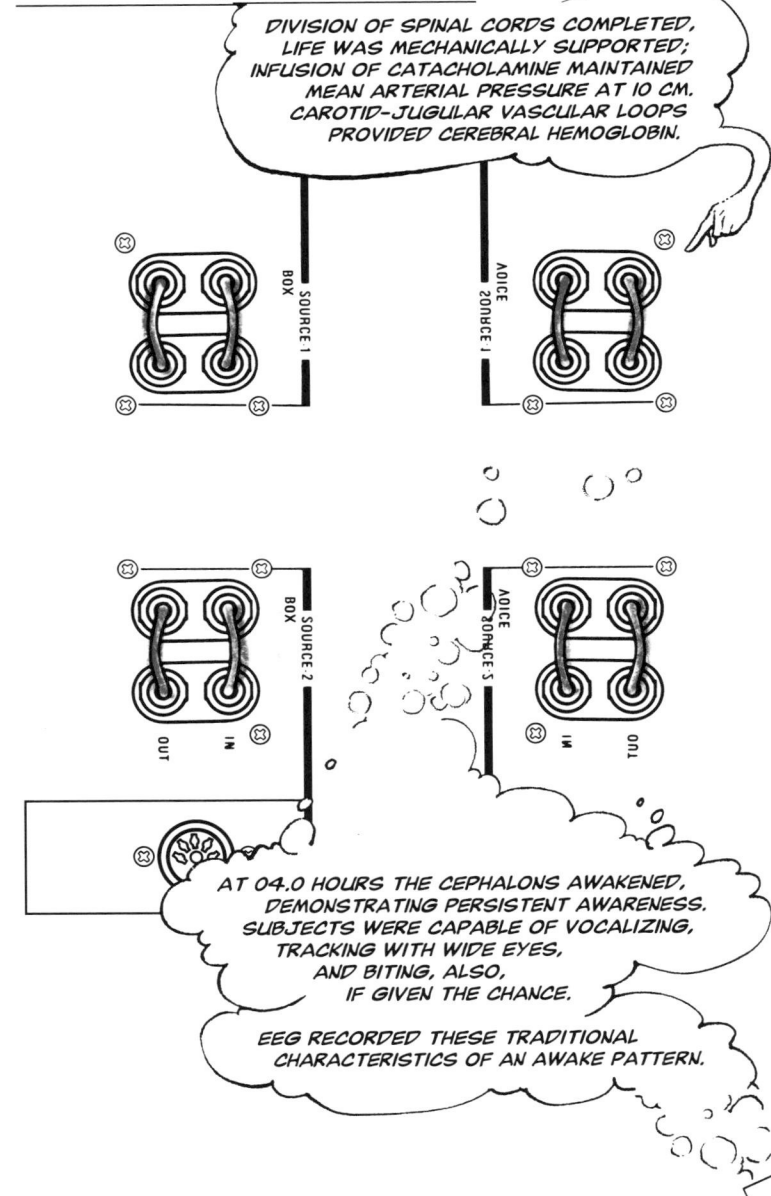

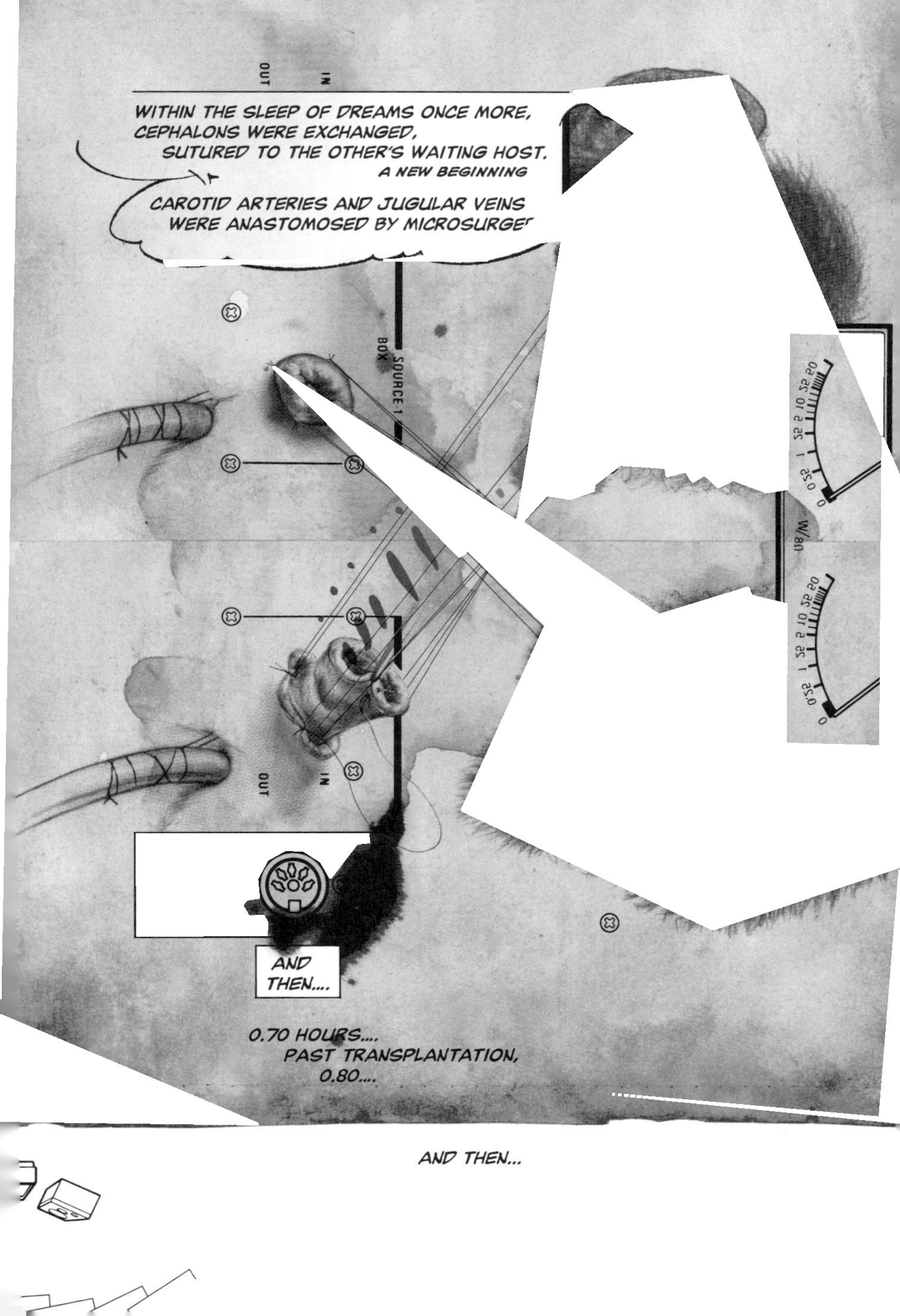

OUT   IN

WITHIN THE SLEEP OF DREAMS ONCE MORE,
CEPHALONS WERE EXCHANGED,
   SUTURED TO THE OTHER'S WAITING HOST.
                    A NEW BEGINNING

CAROTID ARTERIES AND JUGULAR VEINS
   WERE ANASTOMOSED BY MICROSURGE[R]

SOURCE 1

BOX

W/80

AND
THEN....

0.70 HOURS....
   PAST TRANSPLANTATION,
      0.80....

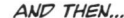

AND THEN...

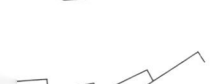

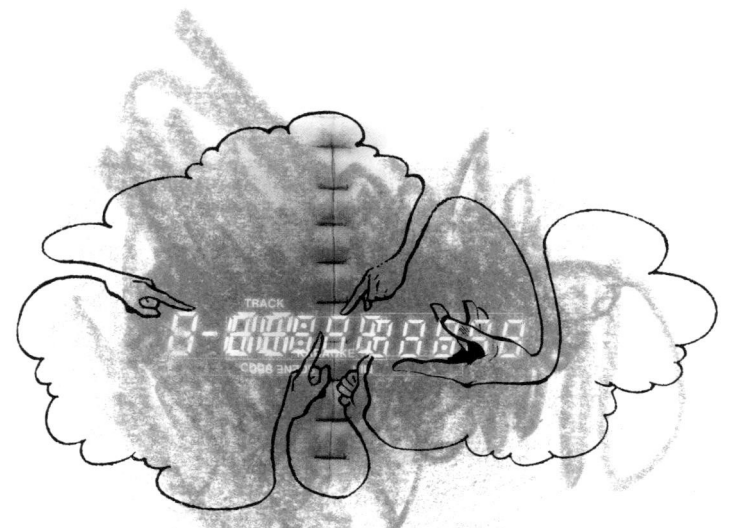

LIKE DAWN OR CONSCIOUSNESS BREAKING,
THE CEPHALONS, IN TANDEM, BEGAN AWAKENING
AS WELL AS THEIR RECIPIENT BODIES.

NORMAL CRANIAL FUNCTION WAS NOTED,
DISPLAYING CHARACTERISTIC MONKEY
RESPONSES: ALERT EYES, TEETH THAT BITE....
(INJECTED DYE---)

INSTRUMENTS TRANSLATED WHAT SENSE RECORDED....

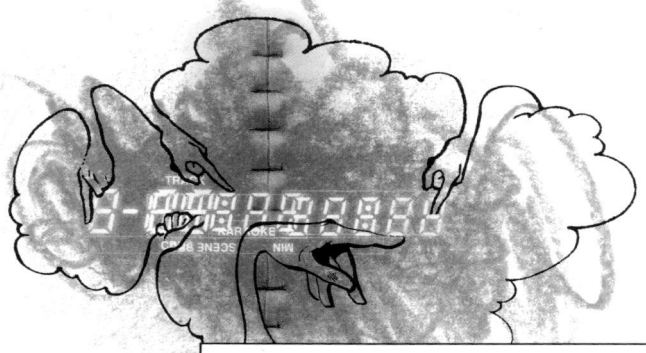

...OVER TWENTY-FOUR MORTAL HOURS...
A COMMON, EARTHLY REVOLUTION

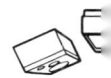

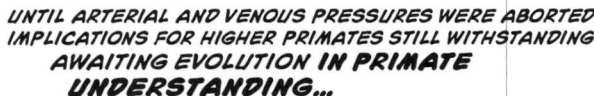

By the end of the third act, Circle had stopped watching and was instead using the time to balance her checkbook. When others began applauding, though, she quickly put it away to applaud too, applauding loudly—standing even, urging Square to also stand and join the cheering ovation.

BRAVO!

BRAVISSIMO!!

BRAVO!

CURTAIN.

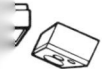

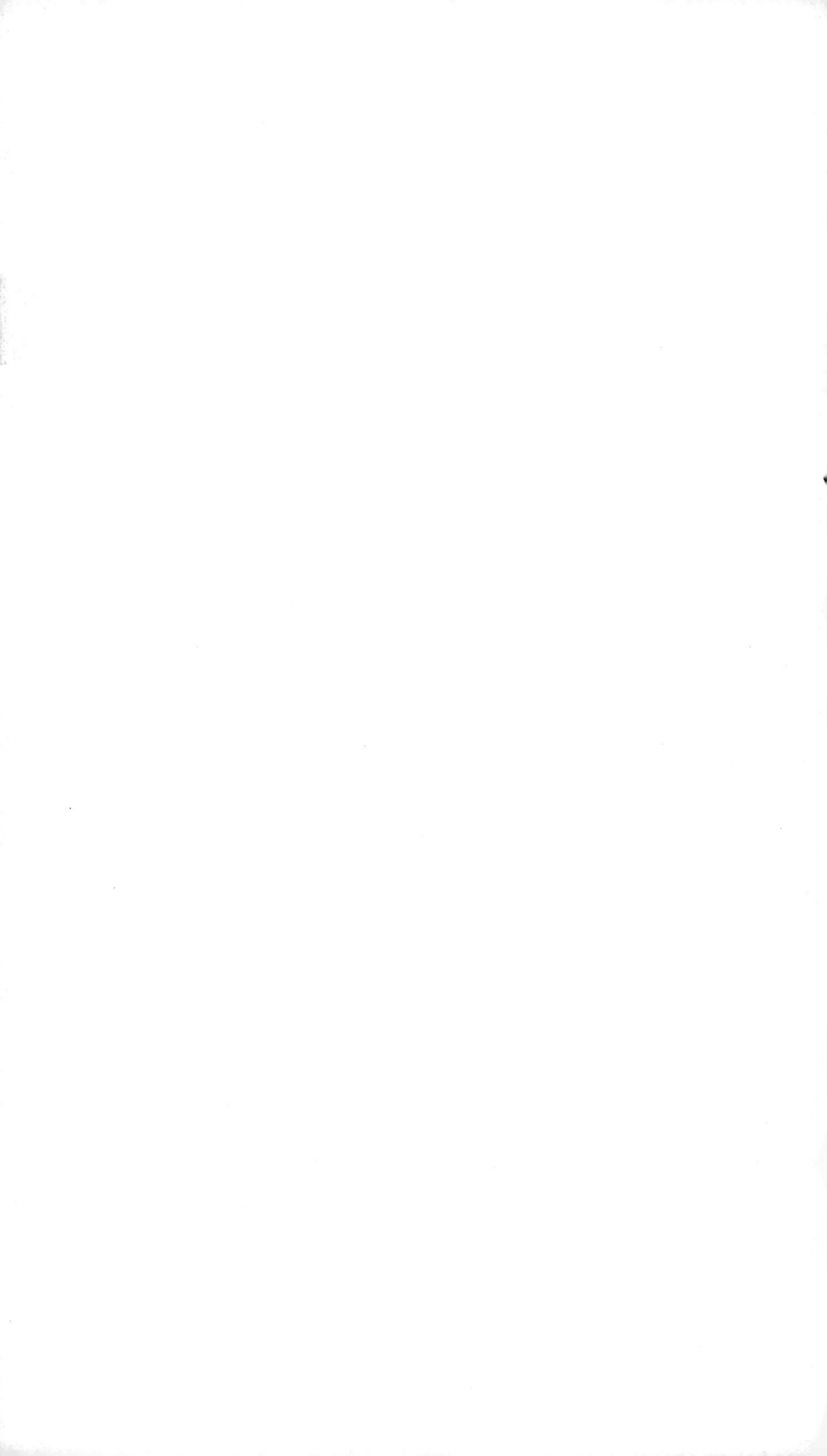

Square walked into the clinic, Square wrote, *realizing that like Alice, Christopher Columbus, Dorothy, Galileo and all the rest,* he was writing an ending by living it even if, like them, like everyone, he could never leave his book. But what kind of story was it that didn't have either a comedic union or a tragic separation? Pedestrian?

Along one wall were clunky, antique microscopes, their brass barrels gleaming dully within an oak, museum-style display case. History or art now, not technology. The way that no one read Hippocrates anymore except as literature. Looking at the instruments, Square felt a tug of nostalgia for Leeuwenhoek's time when only a trickle of information could be teased out through the pinhole of an eye-piece, leaving whole seas beyond sailing. Deeper within the clinic, he knew, new bio-chips were being readied to extract from a drop of blood the typos that would eventually spell out "cancer" or "consumption" or other antique formations of some other flatland: an instantaneous palm reading of the entire body that made the two vials of blood technicians once took from Circle and the two weeks it took to read this tea, seem absolutely Victorian. Like the thick glass lens Leeuwenhoek squinted through to see his face on spermatozoa, the bio-chips would only give up what reflections the mind would let them, it being impossible for anyone to be from a time other than the time they were from and Square felt his own body take on the function of the microscopes in the display case: passé except as philosophy. The way Heidegger says that only a broken hammer can call attention to its hammerness. If his story, or any art, was to compete with surgery, it was in this way, he realized.

In his pocket he gripped the carnation from Oval's experiment, now completely red.

He sat down and picked up a magazine. *People.* Starlets barred their capped grins. He knew that the new Smart Mouse, and Gene Banks and all the rest were for the best. But, with that ancient anxiety of a waiting patient, he also couldn't help but understand how Dorothy must have felt, being carried up into the sky—then where?— by those transgenic monkeys....

In this castle, a TV was mounted near the ceiling in hospital fashion. In patient fashion, those in the waiting room looked up to it, the way the body of a dead man hung before kneelers once made others adopt another posture and he wondered who had been the last person to be their body. Who'd been the first to have their body? Given the 400 years since Harvey remade humors into hydraulics, whoever they were, they must have lived a long time ago.

"Square," a matronly nurse called.

She led him into an office larger than he'd been in before. *There's no place like home,* he told himself, even though he knew he'd never really been away. A medical table with stainless steel foot straps dominated. "You're here for a vas," she announced, looking at her clipboard.

"Disrobing" to put on a paper gown, Square could hear his heart pound (like hearts did in novels). When he lay on the table, fluorescent lights shined in his eyes, one bulb flickering as sporadically as fire light.

Then the doctor rushed in as doctors
always did anymore, bounding from cubicle
to cubicle like production-line workers who
assemble jets or other bodies too ponderous to
move. "How are we today?" he said, snapping
on an intercom in the wall. Before Square
could answer, a spunky pop tune played:
"I think I love you so what am I so afraid of?...."

"Oh god, isn't this music awful?" the doctor
said. He opened a drawer and surgical knives
jingled. "I try to put on Wagner as I work but
everybody in the office has different tastes and
we've only got one sound system." He laid out
metal clamps and suture on a cloth, chattering,
"So we take turns. But anymore, it seems as
if it's always the account manager's turn to pick...."

This edition's visual concept and design by **Stephen Farrell** in collaboration with **Steve Tomasula**. Layout by **Stephen Farrell**. Draft layout assistance by **Amanda Link**.

Printed on Cougar Natural Opaque Vellum by **Four Colour Imports, Ltd.** in PMS722 Flesh (as designated by the Crayola Co. and the Medical Specialties division of 3M) and PMS186 Blood.

Steve Tomasula is also the author of the novel *IN&OZ* (2003). His short fiction and essays are published widely with recent stories appearing in *Fiction International*, *The Iowa Review*, and *McSweeney's*, while his award-winning imagetext collaborations can be found on stage, on-line, and in magazines such as *Emigre*. Recent reflections on the body and art/literature can be found in *Data Made Flesh* (Routledge, 2004), *Leonardo* (M.I.T.), and *Musing the Mosaic* (SUNY, 2003). He teaches in the program for writers at the University of Notre Dame. ▪ Stephen Farrell is a graphic artist, designer, and typographer whose imagetext collaborations have appeared in *Emigre* and numerous other publications. He has exhibited his work most recently at the Cooper-Hewitt National Design Museum, and as *The Volgare Project*, a collection of his essays, music, and type design. Farrell's honors include a National Design Award nomination from the Smithsonian and four separate selections into AIGA's prestigious *50 Best Books*. He is professor of typography and design at the School of the Art Institute of Chicago.

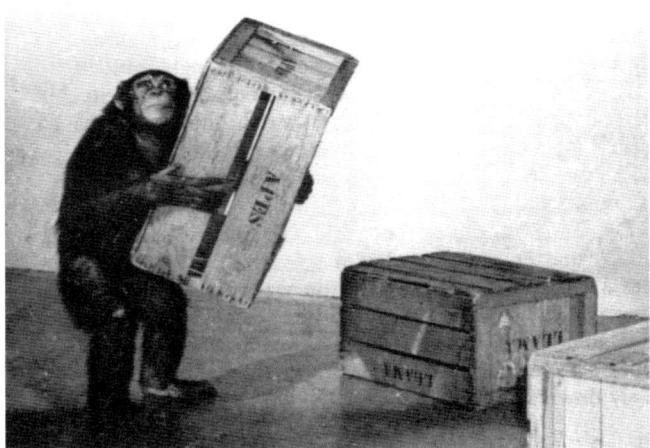